THE APPEAL

JANICE HALLETT

First published in Great Britain in 2021 by
VIPER, part of Serpent's Tail,
an imprint of Profile Books Ltd
29 Cloth Fair
London
EC1A 7JQ
www.serpentstail.com

Text design by Crow Books

1 3 5 7 9 10 8 6 4 2

Printed and bound in Great Britain by
CPI Group (UK) Ltd, Croydon, CR0 4YY

A CIP catalogue record for this book is available from the British Library.

ISBN 978 1 78816 5280
Export ISBN 978 1 78816 5297
eISBN 978 1 78283 7053

For the Raglan Players

Sandra, please deliver to Femi
and Charlotte

Olufemi Hassan
Charlotte Holroyd

Dear both,

As discussed, it is best you know nothing before you read the enclosed. Please bear in mind:

1. Only a limited number of emails, texts and messages could be recovered, so the correspondence is not complete.
2. It is, however, broadly chronological.
3. I've included various extras – i.e. newspaper clippings, social-media activity and other sundries – in the pursuit of context.
4. If I come across anything else of interest I will forward it to you.

See what you think.

RT

Roderick Tanner, QC
Senior Partner
Tanner & Dewey LLP

Femi
Got it?

Charlotte
Literally just got it. Flicking through. There's a *lot* here. Gulp.

Femi
We just need to focus, immerse ourselves, get a clear perspective

Charlotte
But have you seen it? It's all emails and messages. Wonder why Tanner won't tell us the background? Intrigued already.

Femi
Perhaps he's showing us something about the job. We won't always know what's happened. All we'll have is a spectrum of interpretation to examine, analyse and frame into something solid.

Charlotte
Need to log off. Concentrate. Speak end of play today?

Femi
Good plan. Here goes.

Charlotte
Happy reading.

Dr Sonja Ajanlekoko, MBBS (Nigeria) 2008, DRCOG
c/o Médecins Sans Frontières
Orion Building, 3rd Floor
49 Jorissen Street
Braamfontein 2017
Johannesburg
South Africa

27 February 2018

To whom it may concern:

This letter is one of recommendation. Samantha Greenwood worked as a volunteer nurse for Médecins Sans Frontières from September 2010 through January 2018. She was a valuable and popular member of the Women's Health team, assisted with antenatal and post-partum care, fistula repair and sexual-health education projects in rural communities. She is an honest and hard-working lady of principle, who is not afraid to speak.

Samantha Greenwood also undertook emergency medical-aid work in Chad, South Sudan and the Central African Republic, assisting at operations resulting from armed conflict: shot extraction, limb amputation, eye removal and urgent wound repair, much of it undertaken in situations of challenging circumstance. I have heard nothing but good reports of her medical training and personal conduct.

I do not hesitate to recommend Samantha Greenwood for nursing and medical-assistance positions.

Yours sincerely,

Dr Sonja Ajanlekoko, MBBS (Nigeria) 2008, DRCOG
Project Coordinator, Médecins Sans Frontières

Médecins Sans Frontières is an international, independent, medical humanitarian organisation. We offer assistance to people based on need, irrespective of race, religion, gender or political affiliation. Our actions are guided by medical ethics and the principles of neutrality and impartiality.

English charity reg. no. 1026588

FROM: Isabel Beck
SUBJECT: Sorry!
DATE: 26 March 2018 at 06:39
TO: Martin Hayward

Dear Martin,
Sorry to bother you. I couldn't speak to Helen at last night's rehearsal. Could you pass a message on, please? A new girl at work, Sam, is coming to see the play on Saturday night. I'd love her to join Fairways. She hasn't done any drama before, and spent the last few years in Africa of all places, but she's got a husband and we should grab them both while they're still new to the area and friendless! She's very nice – a staff nurse in Geriatrics, so a shift-worker, boo – but her husband is probably the same age (30s) and Helen has said how badly we need men, especially if we do *All My Sons* next. This is just in case Helen speaks to them after the play, so she knows to be in full promotional mode. Thanks, Martin. Love Issy

---

FROM: Martin Hayward
SUBJECT: Re: Sorry!
DATE: 26 March 2018 at 18:16
TO: Isabel Beck

Will do. Regards.

FROM: Isabel Beck
SUBJECT: The morning after!
DATE: 1 April 2018 at 10:45
TO: Martin Hayward

Dear Martin,
Phew! Thank goodness that's over. Not that I didn't love being Edith the Maid (I did), but fitting rehearsals and line-learning around shifts is like trying to live two lives at the same time. Anyway, Sam LOVED the play! I don't think they are regular theatregoers because she asked if we'd written it. I explained it was by Noel Coward. Helen spoke to Sam and her husband (Kel? Kelly?), and if anyone can convince them to join, she can. Wasn't Helen an absolute shining star? All my friends remarked on how

brilliant she was. No one knows how she manages to chair The Fairway Players, run The Grange and still learn all those lines. She must have a lot of support from you, Martin! Do send my best wishes to Paige and James. You were all so busy last night I didn't get a chance to speak to you. What a lovely family! Thanks again, and let's hope Sam and Kel become Fairway Players for the next production. Love Issy

---

FROM: Martin Hayward
SUBJECT: Re: The morning after
DATE: 1 April 2018 at 19:32
TO: Isabel Beck

Thanks. Regards.

FROM: The Fairway Players Admin
SUBJECT: All My Sons
DATE: 2 April 2018 at 11:08
TO: Current Members

Dear all,
So, as we put *Blithe Spirit* quietly to bed, our thoughts turn to our next production. The Committee has decided on Arthur Miller's *All My Sons*. Martin will direct, assisted by James. Please bear in mind you will need to perfect your American accents for this one. We love a challenge.

Auditions will be held on Sunday 8 and Monday 9 April in the church hall. If you have any potential new members you'd like to bring, do. Helen will organise wine, crisps, etc. for *après* audition on Sunday. Please make newbies feel welcome. Also, can I ask that parents keep very young children at home for the auditions? Martin and James need to concentrate, and we can't expect little ones to sit still and quiet for two hours. If you need to alternate your audition nights – mum one night, dad the next – it can be arranged.

Thanks again, everyone, for a successful *Blithe Spirit*. We look forward to seeing you all – and more – on the 8th.

The Fairway Players Committee

FROM: Isabel Beck
SUBJECT: Audition tonight!
DATE: 8 April 2018 at 07:44
TO: Samantha Greenwood

Hiya Sam,

Thanks for helping out yesterday. The ward's a nightmare with so many off. I don't know what I'd have done without you. There may not be as many lions and tigers as in Africa, but it can get pretty wild in Geriatrics! Hope you caught up on sleep over the weekend.

Can't wait to introduce you and Kel to the drama group. Don't be put off by the auditiony atmosphere. You don't have to act – the long-standing members always get the best parts anyway – there are lots of other things to do. You met Helen on play night – she's brilliant and always the leading lady – but everyone's really friendly and putting a play on is so exciting. There's a lovely community feel; you'll both enjoy it, I promise. Joining The Fairways saved my life. Really. I can't recommend it enough. Love Issy

---

FROM: Isabel Beck
SUBJECT: All My Sons!
DATE: 9 April 2018 at 23:02
TO: Martin Hayward
CC: James Hayward

Hi guys,

Great auditions! What an interesting play. Quite serious, but you can still understand it. Helen read the part of the mother so well. It was lovely to see little Poppy running around. I can't believe she's two already. Paige looks a picture. You'd not know she'd had a baby at all. Then again, who'd have thought Helen was a grandma?

My friends Sam and Kel would be great assets to the group. I'm no expert, but for someone who has never acted before, he read the part of the son very well. I know they're both at a loose end as they've been volunteering in Africa for years. She's hinted they didn't really want to leave, and I think adjusting to life back here is tough. That's between you and me. I'm sure if they were made to feel extra-welcome, by getting parts in the play, then it would really make a difference to them. Anyway, hope you and Helen are well and I look forward to hearing the cast announcement in due course. Love Issy

---

FROM: Isabel Beck
SUBJECT: Any news?
DATE: 16 April 2018 at 13:09
TO: Sarah-Jane MacDonald

Hey SJ,
Have you heard about the play? I emailed Martin and James after the auditions but didn't get a reply and don't want to bother them again. I assume Helen will play the mother, but I'm dying to know if my friends Sam and Kel have been cast. Love Issy

---

FROM: Sarah-Jane MacDonald
SUBJECT: Re: Any news?
DATE: 16 April 2018 at 13:22
TO: Isabel Beck

Helen would be a perfect Kate Keller. She has the best accent and is the right age, not to mention the most charismatic actress we have.
Sarah-Jane MacDonald

FROM: Isabel Beck
SUBJECT: Re: Any news?
DATE: 16 April 2018 at 13:34
TO: Sarah-Jane MacDonald

Hi SJ,
Absolutely! Helen is the natural choice for the mother. I didn't mean for one moment she wasn't. I just wonder if the other roles have been cast yet? Only I've been encouraging Sam and Kel to join the group and, now they're enthusiastic, I don't want them to go cold. It would be lovely if they both have roles. You know what it's like when you're new and don't know anyone. That was me not so long ago, so I've taken them under my wing,

that's all. Hope everything's well with you and Harley. He's growing up so fast: what a lovely young man. If you hear anything, do let me know! Love Issy

---

FROM: The Fairway Players Admin
SUBJECT: Cast List – All My Sons
DATE: 17 April 2018 at 17:38
TO: Current Members

Sorry, a few things going on *chez* Hayward, but without further ado: cast list is attached. Can't confirm rehearsal dates just yet. Bear with me. Regards.

The Fairway Players

All My Sons by Arthur Miller

Cast List

Kate Keller *Helen Grace-Hayward*
Joe Keller *John O'Dea*
Dr Jim Bayliss *Kevin MacDonald*
Frank Lubey *Kel Greenwood*
Sue Bayliss *Sam Greenwood*
Lydia Lubey *Paige Reswick*
Chris Keller *Barry Walford*
Bert *Harley MacDonald*
Ann Deever *Sarah-Jane MacDonald*
George Deever *Nick Walford*

THE HAYWARDS
Martin is married to Helen

their son James is married to Olivia
*expecting twins

THE MACDONALDS
Sarah-Jane MacDonald née Dearing is married to

Kevin MacDonald, their son is Harley (about 10?)

THE RESWICKS

their daughter Paige is married to Glen Reswick

they have Poppy Reswick, age two

THE DEARINGS
Carol Dearing = Sarah-Jane's mum, Margaret Dearing her grandmother

FROM: Lauren Malden
SUBJECT: Sorry, my lovely!
DATE: 17 April 2018 at 18:23
TO: Isabel Beck

Hello lovely,
Aw, you must be so gutted. Sorry you didn't get a part. You were so good as the maid too, what is Martin thinking? Josh and I had our first anniversary yesterday. I'd never have believed a year could go so quickly. We're so in love it's embarrassing. Sorry I haven't been around. I've turned into that friend who gets a boyfriend and you don't see her for dust. Trouble is these retro club-nights are such hard work (all-nighters at my age, boo), but fun. You should come along, bring some friends. See if I can do a mates-rates thing. Now you're not in the next play you can let your hair down. Kiss kiss, L xx

---

FROM: Isabel Beck
SUBJECT: Re: Sorry, my lovely!
DATE: 17 April 2018 at 18:33
TO: Lauren Malden

I'm fine about not having a part. I can help other people learn their lines and maybe do something backstage. Glad you're having a good time. Issy

---

FROM: Isabel Beck
SUBJECT: Yipppeeee!
DATE: 17 April 2018 at 18:39
TO: Samantha Greenwood

Yaaay! Congratulations! I'm sooo pleased for you both. Don't worry about fitting rehearsals around shifts – we'll sort something out. I had no idea Kel worked at St Ann's too – then again, I never go down to Psychiatric. We can all get together and I'll help you learn lines over lunch or after work. Once the rehearsal schedule arrives, you can swap shifts with Gaynor and Riley (she's in debt, so always looking for extra hours; his boyfriend hates him working nights, so he'll swap for your days). You're going to have a wonderful time! Love Issy

---

FROM: Sarah-Jane MacDonald
SUBJECT: Rehearsal schedule
DATE: 20 April 2018 at 09:19
TO: Martin Hayward

I haven't received a rehearsal schedule yet, Martin. If you've sent it out, please send again as I need to organise childcare etc. Also scripts. I know you want us all to have the Drake Classics version, but it's the most expensive one and I don't see why we should have to pay for them ourselves, especially as Harley is a child.
Sarah-Jane MacDonald

FROM: Nick Walford
SUBJECT: Rehearsal schedule
DATE: 20 April 2018 at 11:50
TO: Martin Hayward

Hey, when's the first rehearsal? Can't wait to nail this one.

PS Five–nil disaster.

FROM: Isabel Beck
SUBJECT: Sorry!
DATE: 21 April 2018 at 08:29
TO: Martin Hayward

Dear Martin,
Sorry to bother you, but Sam, Kel and I are wondering when rehearsals start for *All My Sons*? It's been two weeks since the cast was announced. I popped into The Grange to see if Helen was there, but the Polish lady on reception said she'd been off. Hope everything's ok. Meanwhile we've bought our scripts (I got one myself, so I can help out) and they are busy learning lines. It's funny how easily the accent comes when you're speaking words written in that accent. Can't wait to start. Send my love to Helen, Paige, James and Poppy. Love Issy

---

FROM: Sarah-Jane MacDonald
SUBJECT: Rehearsal schedule
DATE: 21 April 2018 at 09:11
TO: Joyce Walford

What's going on, Joyce? Have Martin and Helen said anything at work about rehearsals?

FROM: Sarah-Jane MacDonald
SUBJECT: Rehearsal schedule
DATE: 21 April 2018 at 09:14
TO: Isabel Beck

Have you been sent a rehearsal schedule? I need to get organised and can't without dates. I emailed Joyce, who sees Helen and Martin every day. No reply.
Sarah-Jane MacDonald

FROM: Isabel Beck
SUBJECT: Re: Rehearsal schedule
DATE: 21 April 2018 at 09:18
TO: Sarah-Jane MacDonald

Hi SJ,
Lovely to hear from you. I've not had a rehearsal schedule, either. Sam, Kel and I have cracked on anyway and are learning lines. The accent is so much easier than you'd think, so don't worry about getting it right. Sam is really enjoying reading through her lines with me. She's never acted before, but she's a natural. It's funny about the rehearsal schedule. Helen and Martin are so busy I don't like to bother them. Is Harley looking forward to his first grown-up role? How lovely that you, Kevin and Harley are all in the play. Let me know if you want to meet up for line-learning. Love Issy

---

FROM: Sarah-Jane MacDonald
SUBJECT: Re: Rehearsal schedule
DATE: 21 April 2018 at 09:20
TO: Isabel Beck

I'm not worried about the accent, just dates for rehearsals.
Sarah-Jane MacDonald

FROM: Barry Walford
SUBJECT: Dates
DATE: 21 April 2018 at 10:10
TO: Martin Hayward

Will there be rehearsals on the 6th, 14th, 27th or 31st? The first two are my Krav Maga exams and the others are football. Cheers, Barry

Olufemi Hassan
Charlotte Holroyd

Dear both,

I have asked Sandra to draw up a full list of individuals involved in this case, along with brief notes as to their relationships and connections. You may find this a useful reference to keep your thumb in as you work through the documentation. As it seems to be taking her some time, I am sending you her preliminary document (see below), detailing all the members of The Fairway Players. More anon.

RT

Roderick Tanner, QC
Senior Partner
Tanner & Dewey LLP

The Fairway Players

Martin Hayward, 59, chairperson of The Fairway Players and joint owner of The Grange

Helen Grace-Hayward, 62, secretary of The Fairway Players and joint owner of The Grange

James Hayward, 36, their son

Olivia Hayward, 33, his wife

Paige Reswick, 33 (née Hayward), their daughter

Glen Reswick, 31, her husband

Poppy Reswick, 2, their daughter

Woof, 3, their dog

Sarah-Jane MacDonald, 34 (née Dearing)

Kevin MacDonald, 37, her husband

Harley MacDonald, 10, their son

Carol Dearing, 61, Sarah-Jane's mother

Margaret Dearing, 88, mother of Carol and Shelley, grandmother of Sarah-Jane

Shelley Dearing, 63, Carol's sister, Sarah-Jane's aunt

Isabel Beck, 29, staff nurse, Elderly Care at St Ann's hospital

Lauren Malden, 29, former staff nurse, Elderly Care at St Ann's Hospital

Josh, 30, her boyfriend

Lauren's mother, *c.* 57

Kel Greenwood, 34, staff nurse, Mental Health, St Ann's Hospital

Samantha Greenwood, 34, staff nurse, Elderly Care, St Ann's Hospital

Joyce Walford, 63, tea lady at The Fairway Players and retired receptionist at The Grange
Nick Walford, 33, her son
Barry Walford, 28, her son
Harry, 62, Joyce's partner

John O'Dea, 56, treasurer

Denise Malcolm, 59, wardrobe and make-up
Steve Malcolm, 60, her husband
Marianne Payne, 48, wardrobe and make-up
Mick Payne, 51, her husband
Karen Payne, 26, their daughter

Jackie Marsh, 23, currently travelling

Joel Halliday, 54, set designer
Celia Halliday, 55, his wife
Beth Halliday, 16, their daughter

Charlotte
I'm up to Barry Walford's martial-arts exam and literally nothing has happened except auditions for a play. Where are you in all this?

Femi
Further than that. Keep going.

Charlotte
Do we need to read *All My Sons*? The script is online.

Femi
No. Whatever this is, it's not about a play.

FROM: Martin Hayward
SUBJECT: Poppy
DATE: 21 April 2018 at 14:47
TO: Current Members

Dear all,
I apologise for the unanswered calls, texts, messages and emails. As you know, Helen refuses to embrace electronic means of communication, so it falls to me to send this email. There is no easy way to say this, but here it is: our darling granddaughter Poppy has been diagnosed with a rare type of brain cancer. We are reeling, devastated, not least because it came completely out of the blue after a routine check-up.

For new members who don't know us: Paige is our daughter, she and her husband Glen have Poppy, who is just two; and James is our son. His wife Olivia is pregnant with twins, which hasn't been straightforward, either.

The last few weeks have been a whirl of tests, scans, meetings, decisions and lots of tears. But tears don't cure cancer. If only. The doctors are in the process of drawing up a treatment plan, while Paige and Helen are sourcing options and opinions from around the world. The Hayward women are made of stern stuff without a doubt.

We have seriously considered cancelling The Fairway Players' production of *All My Sons*, and for a while assumed we would. But now we've had some time to get used to this – our new status as a family living with cancer – we've taken the decision to continue with the play. The doctors have impressed upon us how important it is for the family to maintain a sense of normality and not let this diagnosis take over all our lives, so . . . the show must go on.

I will, however, step down as director. James will direct and I'll assist when I can. Of course Paige will no longer be involved, but – for the moment at least – Helen will continue as Kate Keller. It's a large role, but Helen is blessed with unflagging energy and is keener than ever to stay occupied. She'll need to support Paige and Glen whenever required, so please take the Rehearsal Schedule attached as a work in progress.

Thanks, everyone, for your understanding. Regards, Martin

FROM: John O'Dea
SUBJECT: Re: Poppy
DATE: 21 April 2018 at 14:59
TO: Martin Hayward

Sorry to hear this sad news. Our thoughts are with you all at this difficult time.

FROM: Sarah-Jane MacDonald
SUBJECT: Re: Poppy
DATE: 21 April 2018 at 15:08
TO: Martin Hayward

Dearest Helen, Martin and family, I am in shock. Poor Poppy. My heart goes out to you all. Send my love to Helen and Paige. Assure them that if they need anything, however small, you know where we are. I remember when Harley fell off his bike and had a severe concussion. It was the worst few hours of my life, so I know how you must be feeling.
Sarah-Jane MacDonald

FROM: Denise Malcolm
SUBJECT: Re: Poppy
DATE: 21 April 2018 at 15:15
TO: Martin Hayward

My second cousin had a brain tumour many years ago. They gave him an operation where they sawed off his skull and scraped the tumour out while he was awake. He's been fine ever since and turns sixty next year. Poppy is so young and the doctors are so clever, they can do anything. She will be fine, don't you worry. God bless, Denise

---

FROM: Marianne Payne
SUBJECT: Re: Poppy
DATE: 21 April 2018 at 15:20
TO: Martin Hayward

Oh Martin, I'm so sorry to hear this. Please send my love to Helen and Paige. I've known you all so long, it's like a member of my own family is ill. My thoughts and prayers go out to you, and if you need anything, just ask. At times like these you feel so helpless, don't you? But there's nothing you can do. Just trust the doctors, know she's in the best place and pray she can fight it. Well, if little Poppy is anything like her mum and grandma, she will beat this. I will light a candle in church on Sunday. All my love, Marianne

---

FROM: Joyce Walford
SUBJECT: Re: Poppy
DATE: 21 April 2018 at 15:22
TO: Martin Hayward

Dear Martin and Helen,
It's been nothing but bad news this week. My friend from school died suddenly on Sunday: heart attack at sixty-three. On Tuesday Harry had a call back from his annual scan, so we don't know how that's going to end. Yesterday my lovely neighbour called round to say she had cancer of the pancreas. Now little Poppy is poorly. Life can be so cruel. Our thoughts and prayers are with you all. Joyce, Harry and the boys

---

FROM: Jackie Marsh
SUBJECT: Re: Poppy
DATE: 21 April 2018 at 17:41
TO: Martin Hayward

I;'m on hoiday in Marrakesh but want to say how shocked I to hear about poppy that am praying for her to make a quick recovery. Chin up all she will get better I know.x

Sent from my Samsung Galaxy S9

POW! Still on contract when you can switch to SIM-only and save up to £30** per month? Visit www.vistadeals.com code POW **amount varies terms and conditions apply

---

FROM: Isabel Beck
SUBJECT: Re: Poppy
DATE: 21 April 2018 at 17:50
TO: Martin Hayward

Dear Martin and Helen,
Thank you for taking the time to let us all know. I am so sorry you are going through this. Cancer is a long road, but treatment has improved in recent years, so there's no reason to think Poppy can't beat it. Which tumour does she have? Is she under St Ann's? You know I work in Geriatrics there, so does the new girl Sam (Kel is in Psychiatrics), so we'll do all we can to help out. Love Issy

---

FROM: Isabel Beck
SUBJECT: A quick suggestion
DATE: 21 April 2018 at 17:56
TO: James Hayward

Dear James,
I'm so sorry to hear the news about Poppy. A diagnosis like that is tough on the whole family. Hope you and Olivia (and the bumps) are doing ok. This is just a quick suggestion. As Paige has had to pull out of *All My Sons*, you'll be re-casting the role of Lydia. This is just to let you know I've been helping Sam and Kel with their lines and have already bought the script. I'm exactly the right age for Lydia and am happy to do it. Love Issy

---

FROM: Isabel Beck
SUBJECT: Hiya!
DATE: 21 April 2018 at 18:54
TO: Samantha Greenwood

Hi Sam,
Gutting news about little Poppy. Hope it's one of the more responsive tumours (I've asked). Nice of James to step up and direct, when he's got a lot going on too. They are a lovely family. James hasn't got back to me about the role of Lydia. I'm dying to ask if he's made a decision, but he's got so

many more serious things to think about. One moment I'm excited about possibly doing it – and the next my heart sinks, because it's so unlikely. I don't fancy my chances against Beth or Emma (the Haywards are very close to Beth's parents, and Emma is Paige's best friend), so my hope is they have other plans. Sorry we won't see each other today – staggered breaks, boo – Love Issy

---

FROM: Isabel Beck
SUBJECT: Sorry!
DATE: 21 April 2018 at 18:59
TO: Samantha Greenwood

Sorry, sorry, totally forgot what I started to email you about. I've been thinking over what you said – about the attitude of the A-team at work. You're right, they are inexperienced and she isn't the best people-manager in the world (understatement alert), but I've always found Geriatrics like that. It's where staff 'end up' rather than where they choose to be. Speak to anyone on that ward and they'll tell you what they'd rather be doing. You can't change it. I avoid the difficult ones, ignore all the bitching and focus on the patients. Try to do the same – you'll be fine. Love Issy

---

FROM: Beth Halliday
SUBJECT: Re: All My Sons
DATE: 22 April 2018 at 13:09
TO: James Hayward
CC: Martin Hayward

Hi James, thanks for the offer to be Lydia in the play. Sorry, but I've got my GCSEs. Thank you, though, Beth

---

FROM: Emma Crooks
SUBJECT: Re: All My Sons
DATE: 22 April 2018 at 13:49
TO: James Hayward
CC: Martin Hayward

So sorry, but I can't take on Paige's part in the play. I'm already covering her classes at The Grange and dog-sitting Woof – they can't have him in the house because he's a risk of infection and, as you know, he's a little shit, only not so little. Anyway, my heart wouldn't be in it, not now. So sorry, hope you find someone. What about the mousy girl who played the maid last time? Emma

---

FROM: James Hayward
SUBJECT: All My Sons
DATE: 22 April 2018 at 14:19
TO: Isabel Beck
CC: Martin Hayward

Dearest Issy, I thought to myself 'Who can possibly play Lydia?' and you were the first in mind. The part is yours. Here's the revised rehearsal schedule. Look forward to working with you, James

---

FROM: Isabel Beck
SUBJECT: Yaaaaaay!
DATE: 22 April 2018 at 14:22
TO: Samantha Greenwood

Yippee! I've got the part! James said I'd read it so well in the initial auditions I was the first he thought of. Hope you're feeling better about work, now you've had a bit longer to get used to it. It's so lovely to have a friend on the ward again. Lauren and I trained together and both ended up here for a while, but she left a year ago. Hope nights are calm and uneventful for you this week. Can't wait to catch up again – love to Kel – tell him he'd better watch out, now we are married (in the play, I mean)! Love Issy

---

FROM: Claudia D'Souza
SUBJECT: Thank you
DATE: 23 April 2018 at 10:03
TO: Samantha Greenwood

Dear Sam,

It was lovely chatting with you yesterday about your first month at St Ann's and all things Africa. Sadly, my window for humanitarian volunteering closed about ten years ago, but I can still dream . . .

I know you want to keep it informal, but the issues you raise are very serious and I want to address them here. I will precis as follows:

1. Poor standards of engagement among staff.
2. Lack of perception among staff that family members of the elderly can be as needful of care and understanding as the patient. You cite best practice in Paediatrics as the ideal.
3. A culture of intimidation that precludes staff from addressing the issues above.
4. Incidents of 'bullying' involving one member of staff in particular.

We welcome feedback and guarantee anonymity for anyone who reports unacceptable behaviour by colleagues. If you wish to make a formal complaint re points 1–3 above, I can open the official channels for you.

I have worked at St Ann's for twelve years and will say that Elderly Care has always been subject to a high turnover of staff. It is an unpopular discipline and we find it difficult attracting and keeping experienced colleagues. You are quite right to say patients and their families deserve more engaged care, and Paediatrics is holistic in this respect. Perhaps colleagues more readily engage with the worried parents of vulnerable young children than they do with difficult elderly patients and their stressed middle-aged relatives?

We are working to improve our staff engagement all the time. You'll have seen the CPD notices in the staffroom, plus some minor restructuring in the next six months will place care teams in smaller groups than at present. Hopefully you will see the situation improve.

Re point 4 above. St Ann's has a zero-tolerance approach to bullying and I would say to impress upon this colleague that she can contact her line manager – or my department – at any time. I appreciate that she is non-confrontational, but victims must come forward in person for the correct procedures to be initiated.

Again Sam, thank you for our chat and I look forward to seeing you again next month for your eight-week appraisal.

Yours, Claudia D'Souza
Human Resources Manager
St Ann's Hospital

FROM: Isabel Beck
SUBJECT: Morning!
DATE: 24 April 2018 at 05:19
TO: Samantha Greenwood

Hiya Sam,
Hope everything was ok on the ward last night. I'm just about to leave for another uplifting day in Jelly Antics myself. Sorry you and Kel missed the rehearsal. We had a technical walk-through for Act Two, so it was a bit chaotic. Between you and me, James isn't as decisive as his dad, so it felt as if everyone was trying to direct. At least I got to be Lydia for the first time! It's so good to forget everything for a couple of hours. The Haywards never cease to amaze me. Helen is such a trouper. She's already got the accent and you can see she'll blow people away with her portrayal of the mother. Who'd have thought her granddaughter was seriously ill and her daughter so worried? You never know what people are going through inside. I wanted to find out more about Poppy's diagnosis but didn't get a chance. They haven't asked me any medical questions, have they you? They must have people on all sides offering opinions and advice. I suppose it makes a change from friends who are forever telling you their symptoms. See you soon. Love Issy

---

Message exchange between Sarah-Jane MacDonald and James Hayward on 24 April 2018:

09:41 Sarah-Jane wrote:
I know I was outspoken last night, but are you sure that drippy girl is the best choice to play Lydia? Give me a few days and I'll talk Emma round.

09:48 James Hayward wrote:
It's not always about who is best for a role. Sometimes it's who would benefit most from the experience. This is amateur dramatics, not the RSC. Do not speak to Emma. Isabel is doing well and deserves a chance.

Message exchange between James Hayward and Isabel Beck on 24 April 2018:

09:50 James Hayward wrote:
Don't let what other people say get you down. I think you're doing a sterling job in the role of Lydia, and my opinion is the only one that counts.

09:51 Isabel Beck wrote:
Aw, thanks. That means such a lot. I missed Sam last night. No one says anything bad to me when she's there. I love being in the play – and won't let you down by not giving it my best shot! xx

---

FROM: Lauren Malden
SUBJECT: Oh no!
DATE: 24 April 2018 at 19:43
TO: Isabel Beck

Hello lovely! Josh and I popped into The Grange to talk about maybe hiring it, and Helen told us about Poppy. Did you know she has a brain tumour? What do you say? I wish I didn't have any medical training, so I could feel as positive and hopeful as they do. Managed to fake it eventually, but my face dropped a mile when I first heard. They seem to have a glittering life on the surface, but they are just as helpless as the next family in the face of something like this. Paige brought Poppy in while we were there. They'd just been to Mount More to have her Hickman line fitted. She was groggy, but still sang us a song. Gutting. Anyway, how are you, my lovely? Josh's old friend from uni just got divorced. Come to 90s Night this Saturday – I can introduce you . . . kiss kiss, L xxx

---

FROM: Isabel Beck
SUBJECT: Re: Oh no!
DATE: 24 April 2018 at 19:58
TO: Lauren Malden

We've known for a while. Martin sent an email to The Fairways – maybe you've been taken off the list because you haven't been to rehearsals for so long. James is directing the play now. Paige had to drop out, so he asked me to take over her role. Sorry about Saturday, I'm on nights. Issy

---

FROM: Martin Hayward
SUBJECT: Poppy news
DATE: 26 April 2018 at 12:45
TO: Current Members

Dear all,
Again, apologies for unanswered messages and emails. Helen and I are truly humbled by the thoughts, prayers and numerous offers of help we have received. We read and appreciate every message, but it's not possible to reply to them all and give Poppy, Paige and Glen the support they need. We hope you understand.

In the weeks since Poppy's diagnosis, Helen and Paige have been sourcing global research into Medulloblastoma. Last year a pioneering drug therapy was tested at a leading cancer hospital in Massachusetts, USA. In these comprehensive tests one particular drug combination showed significant positive results in the treatment of Poppy's rare type of cancer. These exciting results indicate that its success rate as a cure will far exceed that of the drugs currently used to treat brain cancer in the UK. The trouble is, that experimental phase is over and the drug won't be available here for many years, thanks to the process involved in introducing a new drug therapy to the NHS. We fear this delay will be too late for Poppy. So, we propose to buy a course of treatment from the research-and-development laboratory.

We have the support of Poppy's doctors at Mount More, in particular the incomparable Consultant Oncologist Dr Tish Bhatoa, who will give Poppy an initial course of conventional chemotherapy from Monday, to arrest and stabilise her tumour while we raise the necessary funds. Here's where I take a deep breath . . .

The American drug combination costs a staggering £250,000. This is a huge amount, but Poppy is facing her illness with such bravery and good humour, it is unthinkable we could let that stand in the way of her being cured. Her little smile lights up our world. She laughs all the time and jokes with the nurses and doctors, even when she's feeling poorly. She doesn't let the bad days stop her from enjoying every moment of every good day, and we can all learn a lesson from that.

This is where we can all do something positive and productive. We have set up a crowdfunding page and would like to ask that you share the link with friends, family, colleagues and acquaintances. Every little helps. A flyer is attached for those who would prefer to print something out or forward it. We are not people who readily ask for help, but we owe it to Poppy to pursue every avenue and take every opportunity if it means she can be well again. We would be eternally grateful for your support. Together we can cure Poppy.

With much love, thanks and gratitude, Martin, Paige, Glen, Helen and Poppy

Support A Cure for Poppy Campaign at www.wefund.com/acureforpoppy, thank you!

FROM: Sarah-Jane MacDonald
SUBJECT: Re: Poppy news
DATE: 26 April 2018 at 13:15
TO: Martin Hayward

You know I worked in fundraising before Harley. I propose the following:

1. A large event to launch the appeal. Black tie, food, wine, music, dancing, raffle, auction.
2. Sponsorship. Marathons, cycle rides, extreme sports, muddy runs, swims, walks. If someone signs up for something, Poppy must be front-of-mind.

3. Targeting of high-net-worth individuals and corporate donations. Let's brainstorm.
4. Social media. Share, share, share.
5. Small events. Keep the momentum going between larger initiatives.

I can start on the launch event today, pull in a few favours, get some local press and fix a date asap. It will free you all to concentrate on Poppy.
Sarah-Jane MacDonald

FROM: Beth Halliday
SUBJECT: Re: Poppy news
DATE: 26 April 2018 at 13:40
TO: Martin Hayward

Hi Martin, we're having a Charity Bake Off after our exams and will do it for Poppy's appeal. Good luck, Beth

---

FROM: Joyce Walford
SUBJECT: Re: Poppy news
DATE: 26 April 2018 at 14:00
TO: Martin Hayward

I'm not clicking on anything. Last time I got a virus. But I've withdrawn a donation for Poppy at the building society and will give it to Helen at the next rehearsal. Bless Poppy's little heart and pray God this is her cure.
Joyce

FROM: John O'Dea
SUBJECT: Re: Poppy news
DATE: 26 April 2018 at 14:14
TO: Martin Hayward

We donated to the appeal. John and family

FROM: Marianne Payne
SUBJECT: Re: Poppy news
DATE: 26 April 2018 at 14:20
TO: Martin Hayward

Dear Martin and Helen, I've just donated on your charity page, as will the rest of the family after payday. I'll send your email round at work, then to the football club and the gym. Mick will print off the flyers and take them to the pub, and Karen's already asked if she can put some up at work. They are usually very good with things like that and have even fund-matched for charity events in the past, so we'll get a form for you. We'll raise that £250,000 in no time, just you watch. Love to you all, Marianne

---

FROM: Isabel Beck
SUBJECT: Hiya!
DATE: 26 April 2018 at 20:06
TO: Samantha Greenwood

Hiya Sam,
Medulloblastoma – that's not good news. I've started an email to Martin a couple of times and deleted it. Gearing myself up to be positive. I hope they've found a cure, but really, what are the chances? Still, if they all focus on the fundraising, they'll feel like they're doing something, won't they? It's a good thing. And who knows, maybe this really is a breakthrough in treatment. Wow, £250,000 makes you realise how lucky we are. It's easy to forget everything has a price. A whole box of Rivaroxaban went out of date yesterday and the B-team binned the lot. What a waste. Are you around at lunch for line-learning? I'm free, so message me at break. Love Issy

---

FROM: Dr Alicja Szkatulska
SUBJECT: Re: a friend with cancer
DATE: 27 April 2018 at 08:10
TO: Samantha Greenwood

Dear Ms Greenwood,
I think I remember you from the medical centre in Mobaye, although it was six years ago. Thank you for your email. I am truly sorry to hear about

your friend's granddaughter. Medulloblastoma is usually aggressive and difficult to treat. Hopefully the American drug you mention will prove a positive step. Unfortunately, I have no means of finding out more about it. US R&D is generally funded by commercial operations, so is kept under wraps to protect the company's financial interests. Once it is released on to the US market, they will no doubt approach us about taking it, but I've known drugs take ten years to be approved for NHS use. I have no way of knowing whether the new combination will be effective and haven't heard of any other new treatments aimed specifically at Medulloblastoma in recent years. Mount More is certain to have the latest available. I am sorry I can't be of any further help, but wish your friends well with their fundraising and you with your half-marathon.

Yours sincerely,
Dr Alicja Szkatulska
SAS Doctor, Department of Oncology
Edinburgh University Hospital

FROM: A Cure for Poppy
SUBJECT: Poppy's Ball
DATE: 30 April 2018 at 09:35
TO: Current Members

You are cordially invited to Poppy's Ball on
Saturday 19 May 2018 at 7 p.m.
all proceeds to A Cure for Poppy

A Cure for Poppy is an appeal to raise £250,000 so that two-year-old Poppy Reswick can receive groundbreaking drug treatment from America for her rare brain cancer. To launch this crowdfunding appeal we are holding a black-tie ball on 19 May. This fun and glamorous event is not to be missed!

In the Horizon Room at The Grange Country Club guests can enjoy a three-course meal with specially selected Casillero del Diablo wines, treat themselves to a rainbow of delectable sweets in the Candy Grotto and create lifelong memories of the evening in our free photo-booths. Tony

Zucchero and his big swing band will provide the music, while Cameron Hilford, star of Radio 4's late-night panel show *Blindfold*, will host a luxury raffle and celebrity auction.

Tickets are £80 each. For further details please click on the link below, or contact Campaign Coordinator Sarah-Jane MacDonald.

Support A Cure for Poppy Campaign at www.wefund.com/acureforpoppy, thank you!

FROM: John O'Dea
SUBJECT: Re: Poppy's Ball
DATE: 30 April 2018 at 09:37
TO: A Cure for Poppy

We will be away. John and family

FROM: Denise Malcolm
SUBJECT: Re: Poppy's Ball
DATE: 30 April 2018 at 10:26
TO: A Cure for Poppy

Steve can't drink Chilean wine and none of us will eat the sweets. How much are reduced tickets?

FROM: Martin Hayward
SUBJECT: Re: A suggestion
DATE: 30 April 2018 at 19:15
TO: Samantha Greenwood

Thank you for your thoughts and suggestions. Actually we did consider campaigning to fast-track the drug's approval process, but on balance decided that time is not on our side and that raising money to buy the drug would be the fastest, most effective course of action for Poppy. We have been overwhelmed by the response to our campaign and simply cannot thank everyone enough. Best wishes training for your run. Regards, Martin

---

FROM: Isabel Beck
SUBJECT: Hiya!
DATE: 1 May 2018 at 07:32
TO: Samantha Greenwood

Hi Sam, really enjoyed last night's rehearsal. It's so much better to have a friend there. Barry and Nick have terrible American accents, don't you think? I know mine comes and goes, but I'm working on it. Only Helen has nailed it completely, but then she's brilliant at accents. You and Kel are very close, too. I saw you speaking to Helen at tea break. Was it about the play? If there's anything you need to know, ask me and I'll find out – to save bothering her. Have you and Kel bought your tickets to the ball yet? I thought it was a typing error when I read they cost £80. Might catch you as we change shifts this afternoon. Love Issy

---

FROM: Isabel Beck
SUBJECT: Sorry!
DATE: 1 May 2018 at 07:35
TO: Samantha Greenwood

Sorry, forgot to mention in my last email – I'm thinking of taking up running. Can I come out with you when you go training? I won't be able to tackle a half-marathon yet, but perhaps I could work my way up to a 5k? Anyway, it will be nice to go jogging together and better for me than sitting in the staffroom on my own. Love Issy

---

FROM: Joyce Walford
SUBJECT: Little Poppy
DATE: 2 May 2018 at 09:24
TO: Sarah-Jane MacDonald

Wonderful news, Sarah-Jane! Marianne's given me a form from Sainsbury's. All you have to do is fill in how much you raise and they pay the same amount. They really do pay up – her Karen did a Race for Life last year. So now you only have to get £125,000 and they pay the rest. Poppy is going to be over this and back to full health in no time!

FROM: Sarah-Jane MacDonald
SUBJECT: Re: Little Poppy
DATE: 2 May 2018 at 09:28
TO: Joyce Walford

No they won't, Joyce. They only do that for registered charities, and only if one of their employees completes a sponsored event. Poppy's appeal is different. It's a crowdfunding campaign. I also believe the amount is capped, so they wouldn't pay £125,000 even if it were a registered charity.
Sarah-Jane MacDonald

FROM: Martin Hayward
SUBJECT: Thank you, but . . .
DATE: 2 May 2018 at 23:19
TO: Samantha Greenwood

Helen tells me you would like to know more about the American drug manufacturer, so you can apply some pressure on the approval system. Do be assured we have the support of our oncologist at Mount More, who is liaising with the US on our behalf. We want to concentrate on fundraising and not risk them becoming reluctant to sell to us – even if that's a remote chance. But thank you so much, Sam, we really appreciate you looking at the bigger picture. Regards, Martin

---

FROM: Dr Tish Bhatoa
SUBJECT: Re:
DATE: 3 May 2018 at 16:40
TO: Samantha Greenwood

I cannot discuss any of the subjects you raise. The treatment of patients is highly confidential. This is something I am sure you, with your medical background, will understand.

Dr Tish Bhatoa, MA, PhD, MRCP
CONSULTANT CLINICAL ONCOLOGIST
MOUNT MORE HOSPITAL

FROM: Joyce Walford
SUBJECT: Re: Little Poppy
DATE: 3 May 2018 at 17:00
TO: Sarah-Jane MacDonald

If a charity to save the life of a little two-year-old girl isn't registered, then I don't know what is. I'll give the form to Helen when I see her.

FROM: Tanya Strickland
SUBJECT: Re: hello, old friend
DATE: 3 May 2018 at 18:09
TO: Kel Greenwood

Hey Kel! Good to hear from you. So you're back in the UK? I didn't think you would ever come home. We must get together and reminisce about MSF. Is Sam all right now? Yes, I'm in R&D at Koyami Corp, or put another way: a doctor without patients. It's different.

Sorry to hear about your friend's child. But I can't officially recommend they use an unapproved drug. There's a reason it takes so long for a new combination to make it to the front line: remember Thalidomide . . . But even if you put those concerns aside, theoretically anyone can come up with a new wonder-drug and offer it to the NHS – promising the earth, like salespeople do. If we don't put it through our own trials, how would we know whether it was more, less or equally as effective as a drug we already use? We'd waste millions. The money that changes hands at this level you wouldn't believe.

Having said all that, if my child had Medulloblastoma and there was a drug available anywhere else on earth, with a remote chance it could cure them, I'd do exactly the same as your friends. I'll sponsor Sam for her run – send the link to my personal email above – and let's get together soon. All the best, Tanya

---

* UB

FROM: Dr Tish Bhatoa
SUBJECT: Re:
DATE: 3 May 2018 at 21:57
TO: Samantha Greenwood

I appreciate your questions were not specific to the treatment of an individual patient, and that you only wish to help a friend. But I consider them inappropriate and will not enter into any further correspondence – unless it is to inform St Ann's of the real reason you left Bangui.

Dr Tish Bhatoa, MA, PhD, MRCP
CONSULTANT CLINICAL ONCOLOGIST
MOUNT MORE HOSPITAL

FROM: Isabel Beck
SUBJECT: Sob!
DATE: 4 May 2018 at 11:44
TO: Samantha Greenwood

Hiya Sam, Gaynor said you called in sick today. I brought my jogging bottoms and trainers in too . . . Oh well, we can go out for our run when you're back. Hope you're not too poorly. At least you get to learn lines all day . . . It's my worst nightmare here: you-know-who on the desk, the A-team on ward and Gaynor in one of her moods. Triple-whammy. Marianne is coming to the next rehearsal to measure us up for costumes. I can't wait! Once you're dressed as your character you really feel the part. I loved my maid's outfit for *Blithe Spirit*. Hope you feel better soon. Love Issy

---

FROM: Sarah-Jane MacDonald
SUBJECT: A Cure for Poppy – Fundraising Update
DATE: 5 May 2018 at 08:30
TO: Martin Hayward

Amount raised to date: £74,000 – that's just from the crowdfunding page. Let me know how much you've received offline, so I can quote an accurate figure. Ball update: Ticket sales are up to 65%. Kevin has asked permission at his

Lodge to promote the event there, which could make all the difference – why he needs to ask permission, I know not, but then I'm just a woman. For a breakdown of costs, sales and profit forecast, see the spreadsheet attached.

Social media: There was a steep spike in donations when we uploaded the photographs of Poppy at last year's picnic, alongside the shot of her with Paige and Helen at the entrance to the children's chemo suite. If you have any more pics we could use in this way, send them to me. This is a visual world and images speak louder than words.

Smaller/other events/activities I've been made aware of:
Lion's Club monthly quiz night and raffle
Lockwood Rovers charity football match
St Richard's Church afternoon tea and cake sale
Beth Halliday's Bake Off
Harley MacDonald's sponsored swim to Pirate's Island
Sam Greenwood's sponsored half-marathon
Barry Walford's Elvis Cookathon (?)
Dearing family sponsored cycle across the South Downs

Unfortunately, the revenue from these is small, and the amount to be raised is large, so we must target high-net-worth individuals and corporations we don't know personally. You saw how effective this was with your own friends and associates. Believe me, there are some very wealthy people out there looking to ease their guilt, we just need to reach them.
Sarah-Jane MacDonald

FROM: Lauren Malden
SUBJECT: See you tomorrow?
DATE: 18 May 2018 at 07:06
TO: Isabel Beck

Hello lovely!
Are you going to Poppy's Ball? They're auctioning a signed Lockwood Rovers shirt in a frame and Dad's birthday is coming up. I bumped into Gaynor in TK Maxx. Why don't you apply to move wards, Issy? That place is toxic. People come and people go, but they're the same sort of people:

nasty, controlling, manipulative. I've never been happier than since I left. See you Saturday. Kiss kiss, L xx

---

FROM: Hilary Mulvey
SUBJECT: Transfer application 09/7345620/HM
DATE: 18 May 2018 at 09:06
TO: Isabel Beck

Dear Ms Beck,
Re: your application to move from Elderly Care. As your disciplinary probation has nine months left to run, it is not possible to action a transfer on your behalf. You can approach your usual Human Resources manager when your restrictions are lifted.

Yours sincerely,
Hilary Mulvey
Human Resources Manager (maternity cover)
St Ann's Hospital

FROM: Isabel Beck
SUBJECT: Re: See you tomorrow?
DATE: 18 May 2018 at 10:11
TO: Lauren Malden

Thanks but I've got a friend here now. She's joined The Fairways too and we're really close. It's made all the difference. Issy

---

FROM: Claudia D'Souza
SUBJECT: Thank you
DATE: 18 May 2018 at 10:33
TO: Samantha Greenwood

Dear Sam,
It was a pleasure to meet with you again today. I'm glad you feel more settled and yes, I too hope the forthcoming restructure will lead to improved patient care. A nurse of your calibre will help Elderly Care rise

above its reputation as a dumping ground for underperforming staff. I would hate to lose you.

I'm sorry to hear about your friends' granddaughter. As I said, I don't know Dr Bhatoa, but a quick search of our database and I see that not only is she a consultant at Mount More, but also runs her own private practice. She sits on a variety of committees and chairs the advisory board for overseas volunteering at the Department for International Development. Where does she find the time to see patients?

Seriously, it sounds as if the little girl is in the best hands possible. What a lovely friend you are, to want to check up on her consultant. It's lucky for patients they don't realise how widely medical professionals can vary.

I'm sorry to hear your other friend is reluctant to report problems with colleagues. Is it possible she doesn't recognise their behaviour as bullying? It sounds as if she compensates for their rejection by clinging that much harder to you. Can you get her out and about? Introduce her to some new people. We talk a lot about the elderly being isolated, but loneliness can happen at any age and for all sorts of reasons.

I would love to see the new Meryl Streep film. Let's get in quickly before it goes. Message me at this (my personal) email Thursday and we'll pick a screening over the weekend. Thanks, Claudia x

---

FROM: Nigel Crowley
SUBJECT: Booking 19/05/18
DATE: 18 May 2018 at 11:34
TO: Sarah-Jane MacDonald

Re: Tomorrow. We'll be there at 3 p.m. for sound check at 5 p.m. We have two roadies and a runner, on top of the six band members and myself. I've told them food is provided (eight will eat anything, one doesn't eat pork, one is vegetarian). They are happy to eat in the green room.

Friendly reminder, we also require:

- A case of 300ml bottles of Evian mineral water (48 bottles minimum)
- An iron and ironing board (ideally two of each)
- Nibbles – jelly babies and other gummy sweets. No crisps or dry snacks.

Invoice attached. To be paid in full by 5 p.m. today.

Best, Nigel

FROM: Sarah-Jane MacDonald
SUBJECT: Re: Booking 19/05/18
DATE: 18 May 2018 at 11:37
TO: Nigel Crowley

Dear Nigel,
When I initially contacted you I made it clear this was a charity event and am therefore surprised to receive an invoice for your full fee.

A Cure for Poppy is a crowdfunding campaign to buy life-saving drugs for a beautiful little two-year-old girl who was recently diagnosed with a rare type of brain cancer. Her heartbroken parents asked me to book you especially because little Poppy loves your music so much. I understand her mother, Paige, has been playing your CD during her chemotherapy sessions because it's the only thing that helps her forget what she's going through. The *Gazette* will be there to take photographs of Poppy just before the event starts, and I know they will want one of her with Tony Zucchero for their website and print editions. This will be excellent publicity for you. Her parents must raise a staggering £250,000, so we are conducting a widespread national campaign. Every penny counts in this exceptional situation, so I implore you to rethink your fee and reduce it to expenses only, which is what I understood this booking to be when we first spoke. I look forward to hearing from you.

Sarah-Jane MacDonald

PS Attached is a photograph of poor little Poppy about to endure her first bout of chemotherapy.

FROM: Nigel Crowley
SUBJECT: Re: Booking 19/05/18
DATE: 18 May 2018 at 11:46
TO: Sarah-Jane MacDonald

Sorry about the kid, but I can't ask the guys to work for nothing. These are professional musicians with families themselves to support. I'd never agree to an expenses-only gig – Tony Zucchero hasn't done those for years. But look, I'm not a monster. If you've changed your mind, I'll waive the cancellation fee with no hard feelings. Best, Nigel

---

FROM: Sarah-Jane MacDonald
SUBJECT: Re: Booking 19/05/18
DATE: 18 May 2018 at 11:48
TO: Nigel Crowley

Nigel, this is no ordinary booking. Little Poppy is fast losing her eyesight and they want her to enjoy this spectacular evening's entertainment before she goes blind. Little Poppy has fallen in love with the picture of Tony in his sparkly pink suit on the cover of the CD, and we are all desperate for her to see him in the flesh before she sinks into darkness. The fund simply can't afford to pay you the full fee – it just can't. Please, Nigel, please can you make an exception this one time. Just this once. For little Poppy.
Sarah-Jane MacDonald

FROM: Sarah-Jane MacDonald
SUBJECT: Re: Booking 19/05/18
DATE: 18 May 2018 at 12:20
TO: Nigel Crowley

Did you receive my last email, only I've had no reply? If we lose our band, the whole event is in jeopardy. Please let me know. Please. I'm waiting for your response.
Sarah-Jane MacDonald

FROM: Joyce Walford
SUBJECT: Re: Little Poppy
DATE: 18 May 2018 at 12:21
TO: Sarah-Jane MacDonald

I gave the Sainsbury's form to Helen and she said she's sure they'll pay the £125,000. I told her you said they wouldn't. She said it's worth a try. I said I thought so too. What do you think?

FROM: Sarah-Jane MacDonald
SUBJECT: Re: Little Poppy
DATE: 18 May 2018 at 12:22
TO: Joyce Walford

For goodness' sake, Joyce, do what you like with the form – Sainsbury's will NOT pay £125,000 to Poppy's appeal.
Sarah-Jane MacDonald

FROM: Nigel Crowley
SUBJECT: Re: Booking 19/05/18
DATE: 18 May 2018 at 12:25
TO: Sarah-Jane MacDonald

Look, this isn't what I'd normally agree to, and my life will be made hell because of it, but ok, just this once, and just because the girl is losing her sight. Both my boys have sight impairment and I know how important music is to them. We'll see you tomorrow at 3 p.m.
Best, Nigel

FROM: Sarah-Jane MacDonald
SUBJECT: Re: Booking 19/05/18
DATE: 18 May 2018 at 12:26
TO: Nigel Crowley

Thank you, thank you, thank you, Nigel. You don't know what this means. Little Poppy will be over the moon to finally meet her hero. If Tony still has his sparkly pink suit, I know she'd love to see it. Thank

you again, and please thank the entire band on behalf of little Poppy and her family.
Sarah-Jane MacDonald

FROM: Sarah-Jane MacDonald
SUBJECT: Tony Zucchero
DATE: 18 May 2018 at 12:32
TO: Martin Hayward
CC: Paige Hayward

Oh my God, what have I done? I've had to tell an enormous whopper to keep Tony Zucchero sweet. He wanted his full fee (five figures), despite agreeing weeks ago to expenses-only over the phone. Well, what could I do? I panicked. The publicity has gone out, everyone's expecting him and there's no way I could get another big band at 24 hours' notice – not for expenses only, anyway. Sorry, Martin, sorry, Paige, but I've had to tell him Poppy is a huge fan of his music and listens to it during her chemo sessions. I've even said she's fallen in love with his sparkly pink suit, so he's going to wear it specially.
Sarah-Jane MacDonald

FROM: Paige Reswick
SUBJECT: Re: Tony Zucchero
DATE: 18 May 2018 at 12:43
TO: Sarah-Jane MacDonald
CC: Martin Hayward

Oh Sarah-Jane! I am literally crying with laughter at your email. I read it to Mum and it must be hysteria or something, because we've both been completely helpless for about ten minutes. (Poppy had chemo again yesterday, so we've been up all night and are exhausted.) Honestly, I thought I'd wet myself! You poor thing, being put on the spot like that! I'm sure Poppy will love Tony Zucchero, and especially his sparkly pink suit. If you can pop his CD round, we'll play it to her so she knows a few songs. Thank you for making us laugh! Paige x

---

FROM: Sarah-Jane MacDonald
SUBJECT: Re: Tony Zucchero
DATE: 18 May 2018 at 12:51
TO: Martin Hayward
CC: Paige Reswick

I'm afraid that's not all I've had to lie about. He wasn't backing down and I had visions of an empty stage and silent ballroom . . . so I told him Poppy is losing her eyesight and the evening is partly to show her a spectacular night before she goes blind. It turns out this is what convinced him to waive his fee, but what was I thinking? Oh my God, I am so sorry. Where do we go from here?
Sarah-Jane MacDonald

FROM: Martin Hayward
SUBJECT: Re: Tony Zucchero
DATE: 18 May 2018 at 13:28
TO: Sarah-Jane MacDonald
CC: Paige Reswick

Sarah-Jane, you've just annihilated my wife and daughter. They are howling with laughter. Helen had to dig out her Ventolin inhaler and I haven't seen that for years. I'm not sure why the thought of poor Poppy going blind is so hilarious, although given the possible side-effects of the chemo, it's more likely than a two-year-old being the number-one fan of a swing band. Seriously, the situation is bad enough without telling porkies to convince people to commit. But we appreciate the situation you were in, and that needs must. When Poppy has the new treatment and is making progress, it will all have been worth it. Regards, Martin

---

FROM: Sarah-Jane MacDonald
SUBJECT: Re: Tony Zucchero
DATE: 18 May 2018 at 13:38
TO: Martin Hayward
CC: Paige Reswick

I have a plan. I'll tell him not to mention the sight loss at the event, as the family wants to keep it private. It's not as if he's a paragon of honesty

himself. His name's not Tony Zucchero, it's Nigel Crowley. He's not even Italian.
Sarah-Jane MacDonald

FROM: Shelley Dearing
SUBJECT: Poppy's Ball
DATE: 18 May 2018 at 14:02
TO: Martin Hayward
CC: Sarah-Jane MacDonald

Dear Martin, I know you are all frantically busy with Poppy's treatment and arrangements for the ball – so I wouldn't bother you if it weren't *very* important. We've booked six tickets for the family, but we're extremely worried about the other four seats at our table. We don't want to be *anywhere* near the Walford boys (too loud) or the Paynes (she drives us mad and he's boring when drunk). Ideally we'd love to be on yours and Helen's table, plus Sarah-Jane and Kevin. Please confirm and put our minds at rest. Thank you, Shelley

---

Message from Sarah-Jane MacDonald to Carol Dearing on 18 May 2018:

14:05 Sarah-Jane wrote:
Mum, have a word with Aunty Shelley. She's trying to get on the top table and it just isn't possible.

FROM: Isabel Beck
SUBJECT: Quick question
DATE: 18 May 2018 at 15:43
TO: Sarah-Jane MacDonald

Hi SJ, sorry to bother you, but Sam and I are talking about seating arrangements for Poppy's Ball. Please, please, please, can we be seated together? I'm hoping to run a 5k race in the next few months and will try to get sponsorship for Poppy's fund. Sam is doing her half-marathon too. Also, I overheard Sam on the phone to Kel earlier – they were discussing whether Poppy's oncologist is going to be at the ball. Can you tell me whether she is or not, just to save Sam asking you? I'll pass the message on for you, as I'll see her before anyone else. Love Issy

---

FROM: Sarah-Jane MacDonald
SUBJECT: Re: Quick question
DATE: 18 May 2018 at 15:50
TO: Isabel Beck

Yes to both.

FROM: Isabel Beck
SUBJECT: Yay!
DATE: 18 May 2018 at 15:59
TO: Samantha Greenwood

Yay! We are sitting next to each other at the dinner. Phew! Thought I might get stuck with the Dearing grandma. I asked about the doctor for you and yes, she's going to be there. You're not thinking of leaving St Ann's for Mount More are you? I did a placement in Oncology there when I was training. Found it very upsetting, to be honest. The good thing about Geriatrics is at least everyone's had a long life and most are there for the simple reason they haven't died of anything else.

Before I forget, I want to warn you about my old friend Lauren, who you might see at the ball. I'll try to keep her away from you, but just in case I can't . . . She seems nice on the surface, but I would advise against getting too close to her. She's the one who left nursing to organise parties with her boyfriend – that says it all. See you tomorrow night. Love Issy

---

FROM: Alasdair Hynes
SUBJECT: Heads up
DATE: 18 May 2018 at 16:09
TO: Tish Bhatoa

Hi Tish,
Hope you're well and busy as ever. You'll want to know this: someone has

submitted a 'conflict of interest' form to my office at the BMA – don't ask me who, it's anonymous – regarding your link with a charity to raise money for private treatment with unapproved drugs. It will take us a week, no more, to process the claim, so this is a friendly, unofficial nudge to drop any links to them and clean up your affiliations generally, before we get there. You didn't hear it from me . . . Alex

PS Us CAFOD alumni stick together, right?

FROM: Tish Bhatoa
SUBJECT: Urgent
DATE: 18 May 2018 at 16:19
TO: Martin Hayward

Dear Martin,
Sorry, but I will have to step back from my role as medical advisor to A Cure for Poppy. Please be assured that I remain as personally committed as ever to obtaining Poppy's life-saving drugs, but due to a plethora of other roles and positions on medical councils and committees, it has been brought to my attention that appearing to be involved with such a charity could be deemed a conflict of interest. It isn't, of course, but rules are rules to these people. I am sorry to let you down, as I was looking forward to speaking at your fundraising event tomorrow. Please be assured my commitment to Poppy's appeal is not affected and I will continue to liaise closely with my Boston contacts. I see you have already raised nearly £80,000 – keep up the good work. Once we reach halfway, I can start making arrangements for the phials to be sent over. Best wishes, Tish

---

FROM: Dr Tish Bhatoa
SUBJECT: Urgent
DATE: 18 May 2018 at 16:25
TO: A Cure for Poppy

Without prejudice:

I request that you remove my name from all publicity material and correspondence regarding A Cure for Poppy. I am not affiliated to this campaign in any way and never have been. I am not able to speak at your fundraising event as requested.

Dr Tish Bhatoa, MA, PhD, MRCP
CONSULTANT CLINICAL ONCOLOGIST
MOUNT MORE HOSPITAL

Message exchange between Sarah-Jane MacDonald and Martin Hayward on 18 May 2018:

16:29 Sarah-Jane wrote:
Your doctor has pulled out. It's not quite the crisis we had when Tony Zucchero threatened to walk, but the schedule and timings are already signed off. Could Helen speak instead?

16:46 Martin Hayward wrote:
Of course, Helen will be delighted to speak.

FROM: James Hayward
SUBJECT: All My Sons
DATE: 19 May 2018 at 00:04
TO: Isabel Beck

Dearest Issy, sorry we haven't caught up at rehearsals. Are you enjoying it still? You're always so quiet I feel I need to check there's nothing wrong. I have to hold the play together while there's so much going on, so I apologise if I'm neglecting you or the other newbies. I never wanted to be a part of this. I tried to talk them out of doing it in the first place. But Mum lives for The Fairways, and it's worth it just to see her back to her old self again onstage a couple of times a week. I wish Paige had a way to forget what's going on, but she won't let go. Dad is like a rock in a storm. The happiest of us all at the moment is Poppy, who sings her way through her chemo sessions and bounces back with a big smile on her face. The innocence of childhood. James

FROM: Isabel Beck
SUBJECT: Re: All My Sons
DATE: 19 May 2018 at 07:17
TO: James Hayward

Dear James, aw, how lovely of you to think about me. I love being in the play. It's a bigger part than I had in *Blithe Spirit*, but I'm getting there. Sorry you're having such a tough time. My bus passed The Grange today and I saw the banner for Poppy's Ball tonight. Sarah-Jane has done so well to organise it in such a short time. And to raise all that money so quickly – everyone is on your side. You'll soon have enough for Poppy's treatment and all this will be behind you. Look forward to catching up with you later at the ball. Love Issy

---

FROM: James Hayward
SUBJECT: Re: All My Sons
DATE: 19 May 2018 at 17:26
TO: Isabel Beck

Olivia and I are not going. James

Messages sent from Isabel Beck to Samantha Greenwood and Kel Greenwood on 19 May 2018:

18:04 Isabel Beck wrote:
I'm at The Grange super-early to make sure we're sitting together. They're still setting up, so asked me to wait outside. You won't believe this, but they've got an alcove the size of the sluice room at work full of pick-and-mix. Cola bottles, jelly snakes, fruit chews, fizzy strawberries, lollies . . . all FREE. This is so you know to bring a big bag. I've only got my clutch and that's already full. I don't suppose you've got a bigger handbag you could bring for me to borrow? I would be so grateful. See you soon xxx

18:16 Isabel Beck wrote:
Tony Zucchero just walked right past! Shiny pink suit, white fur trim and two-

tone brogues – but smoking a roll-up, and I'm sure he dyes his hair, but still . . . The Haywards are inside having photos taken for the local news website. I saw Poppy with Paige and Glen. She's such a little trouper you'd not think she was ill, if you didn't know. She hasn't lost her hair yet and that makes all the difference. Have you set off? Looking forward to showing you around the pick-and-mix. Joyce was here just now. She must be party to inside information, because she has two handbags. See you soon xxx

18:20 Isabel Beck wrote:
No. I'm looking at the entire table plan now and can't see the doctor's name anywhere. We are all sitting together, though, hurrah! See you very soon xxx

Poppy's Ball

The official launch of

A Cure for Poppy

Welcome to a fun-filled evening of entertainment. Sit back and enjoy a glittering night of food, wine, music and dancing, while we fund life-saving treatment for two-year-old Poppy Reswick.

7 p.m.	BBC Radio 4's Cameron Hilford welcomes us to The Grange
7.10 p.m.	First course – Goat's cheese and fig salad
7.45 p.m.	Main course – Chicken Maryland
8.30 p.m.	Dr Tish Bhatoa, Consultant Clinical Oncologist at Mount More Hospital
8.45 p.m.	Dessert – Sticky toffee pudding
9.15 p.m.	Charity auction hosted by Cameron Hilford, followed by raffle draw
10 p.m.	Tony Zucchero's Big Swing Band is onstage in the Horizon Room
1 a.m.	Carriages

Stella Cornwall's String Quartet will play throughout dinner.

Message exchange between Sarah-Jane MacDonald and Kevin MacDonald on 19 May 2018:

21:50 Sarah-Jane wrote:
In the kitchen with Emma and a toffee-sauce crisis. We're slightly behind with dessert. Please visit the little man by the bar who seems to be hawking wares from a suitcase, and let me know WTF he is doing.

22:16 Kevin wrote:
He's with the band and is selling CDs.

22:17 Sarah-Jane wrote:
That's not part of the agreement. This is a black-tie ball, not a pub gig. What did you do?

22:18 Kevin wrote:
Bought one for the car.

Item published in the *Lockwood Gazette* online 20 May and in print 25 May 2018:

£250,000 APPEAL FOR CANCER DRUG

A family has launched a £250,000 appeal to fund potentially life-saving treatment for their two-year-old daughter. Poppy Reswick was diagnosed with stage-two Medulloblastoma last month. This rare form of brain cancer usually has a low chance of survival, yet clinical trials in America have reportedly shown that a new drug can shrink its aggressive tumours. The appeal was launched on Saturday night with a gala dinner at The Grange Country Club in Upper Lockwood, where bandleader and local celebrity Tony Zucchero (pictured here with Poppy and Paige Reswick, alongside family friend Emma Crooks) helped promote the appeal. Poppy's mother Paige said, 'The drugs won't be available here for many years, yet Poppy needs this life-saving treatment now. It's a huge amount of money, but we will do anything to give her this chance. Anything.' Donations can be made at: www.wefund.com/acureforpoppy

Message exchange between Sarah-Jane MacDonald and Barry Walford on 20 May 2018:

09:02 Barry wrote:
Can you remember who I hit?

09:05 Sarah-Jane wrote:
Your brother Nick.

09:08 Barry wrote:
Thank God.

FROM: Marianne Payne
SUBJECT: Thank you
DATE: 20 May 2018 at 12:09
TO: Martin Hayward

What a lovely evening, Martin. You did so well to organise it along with everything else you do, but it was Helen's speech that moved us all to tears. My Karen was in floods and – he won't admit it – even Mick shed a tear when she talked about the children's cancer ward. Everyone was humbled. It was lovely to have a nice dinner and a few drinks, but Helen reminded us why we were really there. We hope and pray this has raised the money Poppy needs. All our love, Marianne and family

---

FROM: Isabel Beck
SUBJECT: Best night ever!
DATE: 20 May 2018 at 12:18
TO: Samantha Greenwood

My head! I know not to mix red wine with white, but didn't realise mixing it with jelly snakes would give me such a terrible hangover. Thank you so much for bringing me a bag, and such a lovely one too. It's beautifully decorated. Is it African? Are you sure you don't mind if I keep it? I'll make it my rehearsal bag. It fits my script, purse and water bottle perfectly – or it will, once I take the pick-and-mix out. Can't face unpacking it yet . . . just thinking about the smell makes me heave. How are you two? I may feel like death warmed up now, but my goodness I loved every moment! It was one of the best nights of my life. Not even exaggerating. I've never danced like that. Tony Zucchero was amazing. What was he like to speak to? I'd have got his signed CD myself, but blew all my money on the ticket. Thanks for the lift home too. It looked as if the Walford boys were heading for another punch-up in the foyer, so I'd have waited ages for a cab.

Did Sarah-Jane say why the doctor wasn't there? She may have been on call, like they said, but I wonder if she only agreed to attend out of sympathy and then cancelled at the last moment, never really intending to come. In any case, Helen's speech was way more moving than anything a doctor could ever say (meow).

Let's hope they've raised the money. There were so many drunk business-type men there, it's a distinct possibility. Who'd have thought a signed Lockwood Rovers football shirt would sell for over £800! My ex-friend Lauren – the one I warned you about – wanted it for her dad, but she was outbid. Luckily I managed to keep her away from you all night, phew! I'll sort out the photo-booth pictures later and save some for you. That way we'll all have some memories of the evening. Well, between the pick-and-mix, the free photographs and the bottles of wine Kel smuggled out under his coat, I think we can safely say we each got our £80 back. It was so good to see you outside work and get to know Kel a bit better. We should all go out together more often. I'm planning to spend today in bed, but will see you at work tomorrow. Lots of love, Issy xxx

---

Message exchange between Joyce Walford and Sarah-Jane MacDonald on 20 May 2018:

12:20 Joyce wrote:
I left a lilac cardigan on the back of my chair last night. Just pop it round as soon as you can.

12:24 Sarah-Jane wrote:
If it's there, it'll still be there Monday.

12:29 Joyce wrote:

But I don't work at The Grange any more. I've retired, SJ. They were going to get rid of Magda, but she's a single mum with two boys and I thought, well, I'm sixty-three and it's time I had a rest – let *my* boys look after me for a change. Just bring the cardigan back whenever you can today.

FROM: Sarah-Jane MacDonald
SUBJECT: Re: Booking 19/05/18
DATE: 20 May 2018 at 13:00
TO: Nigel Crowley

Nigel, I didn't speak to you last night, but understand one of your people was selling CDs. I have looked through our entire email correspondence and at no point was merchandising discussed, so I think we can safely say it was not part of our agreement. My objection is twofold. One: hawking goods from a suitcase made a stylish black-tie ball look cheap and amateurish. Two: people buying merchandise at such an event will assume their money is going towards the charity of the night, when it is not. This could be seen as fraud. Of course if I have totally misunderstood the situation, and you were indeed selling the items in aid of A Cure for Poppy, then it is different. If this is the case, then let me know how much was raised and when we can expect the donation.
Sarah-Jane MacDonald

FROM: Nigel Crowley
SUBJECT: Re: Booking 19/05/18
DATE: 20 May 2018 at 14:56
TO: Sarah-Jane MacDonald

That was my dad. I sign the CDs – he sells them. We always sell merchandise at our gigs, no matter what the event. It's an important part of the guys' income – even more important when they aren't getting their usual fee. I don't see the problem myself, but if you're not happy, then don't book us again. Best, Nigel

---

FROM: Martin Hayward
SUBJECT: Thank You
DATE: 20 May 2018 at 15:44
TO: Sarah-Jane MacDonald

Dear Sarah-Jane,
What can I say? On behalf of the Haywards and the Reswicks, thank you for doing an incredible job last night. We could never have organised such an event ourselves, and to know there are so many people out there supporting us makes the whole family feel less, well, isolated – for want of a better word. Surprising though it sounds, especially for a close family like ours, a cancer diagnosis does not necessarily bring people together. For each person who pledges support, there's someone who will avoid you. We have learned who our friends are – and who they aren't. Last night was humbling for us all.

We are so proud of Helen. I know I could never speak so eloquently about Poppy's situation. Yet she didn't even make notes. It was all from the heart. She really is our leading lady onstage and off. Thank you again, Sarah-Jane. We'll catch up about the funds raised in due course, but I hope you can spend today resting and reflecting on what an extraordinary feat you achieved. Regards, Martin

---

FROM: Sarah-Jane MacDonald
SUBJECT: Re: Thank You
DATE: 20 May 2018 at 16:18
TO: Martin Hayward

Dear Martin,
I'm just pleased I can help and that I have the skills, experience and contacts. That's not to say A Cure for Poppy wouldn't benefit from a fundraising committee, but we'll discuss that in the week, when my head is clearer and my eyeballs do not feel like sandpaper.

You will want to know the excellent news that Poppy's Ball generated a heart-warming profit of £89,750 last night. One huge positive is that you own The Grange and everyone there respects you so much. I'll admit it was touch-and-go in the kitchen at times, but both chefs and all the waiting staff were fully committed to the task and were so generous in giving their time and expertise. The major cost in any event like this is venue hire and catering, so it's thanks to them that we really kicked our funds into the ballpark.

Most suppliers either waived their cost or worked on expenses only. The Candy Grotto and Photo-booth were provided free of charge by a very old friend and colleague of mine. The wine was also free, as the supplier is bidding for a big contract with Kevin's company.

I'm furious that Tony Zucchero was selling CDs for his own profit. When I suggested he donate the money to the appeal, he basically told me where I should stick it. We could press the point that our guests assumed the money they paid him was for the appeal, and that what he did was technically fraud – let me know what you think. The only good thing that came of it was the idea to create a range of merchandise for Poppy's appeal. We will need to get more creative as the campaign goes on. Again, let's discuss.

I expect more donations to roll in over the next few days and will keep you posted. There's an automatic reply set up on the email address, so we don't become bogged down answering basic questions time and again. Please let me know how much you've received offline, so I can update the spreadsheet.
Sarah-Jane MacDonald

Message exchange between Sarah-Jane MacDonald and Emma Crooks on 20 May 2018:

16:47 Sarah-Jane wrote:
Thank you, thank you, thank you for your help last night. Can't blame anyone, just sheer number of dishes. Adrenalin overload. Didn't sleep all night and feel lousy now, but huge profit for the appeal, so worth it. Again, thank you.

16:59 Emma wrote:
Happy to help. When I got home, Woof had only disembowelled one cushion. Karmic payback.

FROM: Isabel Beck
SUBJECT: Re: All My Sons
DATE: 20 May 2018 at 17:14
TO: James Hayward

Hiya James,
Sorry, didn't see your message before I left last night and I'm only just catching up on emails after being in bed for most of the day! You missed a classic night at Poppy's Ball. What a shame you couldn't make it. But of course Olivia would find it tough, and someone had to babysit Poppy after her photoshoot. My friends Sam and Kel had a wonderful time. They loved the free pick-and-mix. I hope someone remembered to get a bag for you. I'm spending today in bed, learning lines ready for rehearsals next week. See you then. Love Issy xxx

---

FROM: Paige Reswick
SUBJECT: thank you
DATE: 20 May 2018 at 17:29
TO: Beth Halliday

Dear Beth, thank you for babysitting Poppy last night. Right up to the last minute I was in two minds whether to stay home myself, but the ball was beautiful and I'm so glad I was there to see everyone come together to help Poppy. I hope your mum and dad aren't too hungover today. Love Paige x

---

FROM: Beth Halliday
SUBJECT: Re: thank you
DATE: 20 May 2018 at 17:49
TO: Paige Reswick

Poppy was no trouble. She went down about nine-thirty and I revised until Glen dropped me home at one-thirty. Mum and Dad aren't up yet, so they must have enjoyed it. Beth

---

FROM: Martin Hayward
SUBJECT: Re: Thank You
DATE: 20 May 2018 at 17:58
TO: Sarah-Jane MacDonald

Dear Sarah-Jane,
I suggest we forget the Tony Zucchero issue, frustrating as it is. Let's not create bad feeling among those who've given their time and energy to help Poppy. Can I make you aware that The Grange will have to invoice A Cure for Poppy for venue hire and catering. Our stringent tax accountants will red-flag anything that has a negative cost. Regards, Martin

---

Message exchange between Sarah-Jane MacDonald and Martin Hayward on 20 May 2018:

18:05 Sarah-Jane wrote:
Of course. Invoice the appeal for £1. I find that wards off red flags.

18:12 Martin wrote:
The invoice will be for £20,000.

£74,000 +
£89,750
= £163,750
– £20,000
= £143,750

FROM: Lauren Malden
SUBJECT: So lovely to see you!
DATE: 20 May 2018 at 18:30
TO: Isabel Beck

Hello lovely! What a fantastic evening and sooo nice to see you again after so long. You looked gorgeous in your dress. You've lost weight too, well done. And who was that you were dancing with, madam? Got any news? I'm sorry I didn't get to meet your new friend Sam – was that her in the blue? She looks nice. Gutted about the football shirt, but £850! There must have been some rich people there for sure. Helen's speech . . . she was so heartfelt and articulate, but you could see Paige crying and poor Martin just holding it together. Let's hope they've raised the money now. We must get together soon for a coffee and chat. Kiss kiss, L xx

FROM: Isabel Beck
SUBJECT: Re: So lovely to see you!
DATE: 20 May 2018 at 18:37
TO: Lauren Malden

Thanks. I was dancing with Kel, Sam's husband, and only because she has plantar fasciitis from half-marathon training, so no news there. I think everyone enjoyed it and they must have raised quite a lot of money. Work is really busy at the moment, and then there's the play, but maybe in a while.

FROM: Jackie Marsh
SUBJECT: Re: Poppy
DATE: 20 May 2018 at 20:19
TO: A Cure for Poppy

□□□□□□□□□□□□e donated to poppys appeal on the website but lost thepage beforeit ended >shouldbe €5 if theyve taken €50 let me know boom-boom lets kick cancers butt Jackie

Sent from my Samsung Galaxy S9
ةأرماو لجر www.f*ckbuddy.com ةرايز مث كلذكرمألا ناك اذإ قيشع يف بغرت له
كلذ ىلع مدنت نل www.f*ckbuddy.com ةرايز طقف امهيلك وأ

FROM: Chris Wilkinson
SUBJECT: Donation
DATE: 20 May 2018 at 21:13
TO: A Cure for Poppy

Dear A Cure for Poppy,
My wife and I were greatly moved by Helen Grace-Hayward's speech last night. We would like to donate £500 to the 'Poppy Appeal' in memory of our daughter.

Belinda was born in 1973, a very happy, energetic and artistic little girl. She was the only one, so she had all our attention, and we had all hers. Unfortunately the wonderful life we thought we had, and barely appreciated at the time, was not to last. Just after her fifth birthday we noticed Belinda's speech becoming slower and her hand movements uncoordinated. She was eventually diagnosed with inoperable Fibrillary Diffuse Astrocytoma, a slow-growing brain cancer. That term was to haunt us. 'Slow-growing' seems preferable to 'aggressive', and yet it only meant she died more slowly. Appalling to experience and to watch. She would endure various treatments over the years. We tried conventional and alternative therapies, but sadly in 1989 at the age of 16, Belinda died.

It seems so cruel to allow someone to live just long enough to appreciate the life they will never experience. She has been dead now for many years longer than she was ever alive. Yet for us time stopped then. Nothing since has had as much meaning as her death. She was robbed of her future and we were robbed of ours. The pain and sadness have scarred us forever. Even our nieces and nephews born since Belinda died consider her death to be something that happened to them. The shockwaves have been felt throughout our family for a generation and more. That is the legacy of tragedy.

The question 'Do you have children?' haunted us from that moment. There is no comfortable answer. If we say 'no' we deny her any existence at all, and in no time we are in a conversation about childlessness that we know nothing about. If we reply 'yes, but our daughter died', it creates a mortifying moment for whoever asked. It is human nature to seek out even a shred of positive in any overwhelming disaster. Over the years, so many people have assured us we are 'lucky' to have had the 'privilege of knowing her', and that is 'better than never having known her at all'. I just nod in response. It wasn't a question, and that isn't my answer.

Just after Belinda died, her school planted a sapling in her memory, alongside a beautiful commemorative plaque. But recently we discovered both were removed years ago to make way for a new classroom block. They hadn't thought to tell us at the time and no one at the school knew what, if anything, had become of the tree or the plaque. We were also struck by the realisation that no one at the school today remembers our daughter at all. We considered dedicating a bench on the hill, in a final effort to keep her memory alive after we are gone, but at Saturday's event we realised the best way to remember Belinda is to help give another young girl the chance of life she never had.

Please let me know the address I should send our cheque to. With it we will enclose love, light and a lifetime of good wishes to Poppy, her family and the doctors treating her – all in the hope they will not endure what we have.

Chris and Marion Wilkinson

FROM: A Cure for Poppy
SUBJECT: [Automatic reply] Re: Donation
DATE: 20 May 2018 at 21:13
TO: Chris Wilkinson

Dear Donor,
Please make cheques payable to Martin Hayward and send to the address below, or hand to Reception at The Grange Country Club. Your contribution is very much appreciated.

A Cure for Poppy

FROM: Sarah-Jane MacDonald
SUBJECT: Email
DATE: 20 May 2018 at 21:31
TO: Martin Hayward

Please see the email forwarded below. You might want to sit down before you read . . .

> *On 20 May 2018 at 21:27 Clive Handler wrote:*
>
> Dear Ms MacDonald,
> I attended last night's fundraising ball in aid of A Cure for Poppy and want to say how moved I am by Poppy's story and her friends' and family's obvious devotion to finding a cure for her. When we can launch hardware into space and create entire virtual worlds, I find it unthinkable that the drugs Poppy needs are available but unattainable. In the face of a situation like this, all other progress is pointless.
>
> Whatever the appeal raises, I want to donate the remainder of the required £250,000, but only on the basis that I can do so anonymously.

> This email account is a pseudonym.
>
> However, I have not made this type of donation before and must seek financial advice to ensure I do not make the family (or my company) the unwitting recipients of a large tax bill or other unforeseen legal penalty. Please bear with me and I will be in touch regarding protocol for the payment.
>
> Yours sincerely, Clive Handler

FROM: Martin Hayward
SUBJECT: Re: Email
DATE: 20 May 2018 at 21:49
TO: Sarah-Jane MacDonald

I'm lost for words. How remarkably generous. Do you know who it could be? If you don't mind, can we keep this to ourselves – at least until the money arrives? Just in case it doesn't happen. I don't want to raise hopes only to dash them again. We've had enough of that these last few weeks.
Regards.

FROM: Sarah-Jane MacDonald
SUBJECT: Re: Email
DATE: 20 May 2018 at 22:06
TO: Martin Hayward

Good idea. There's many a slip 'twixt cup and lip. I asked Kevin who it could be (don't worry, he won't say a word). The fact that he mentions space travel and virtual reality, plus not having made a corporate donation before, might suggest a young entrepreneur. I want to stay calm and realistic. But if this is a genuine offer, then A Cure for Poppy's work is done. We can secure the treatment and get Poppy on the road to recovery. I'm not a believer in luck, but this could convert me.
Sarah-Jane MacDonald

PS The website and ball proceeds take us to almost £170,000 – please let me know how much you've received offline, so I can quote an accurate figure. Well over halfway.

FROM: Martin Hayward
SUBJECT: Important
DATE: 20 May 2018 at 22:15
TO: Tish Bhatoa

Dear Dr Bhatoa,
We are sorry you had to miss Poppy's Ball yesterday. It was a huge success and we now have £125,000 available to send as our first payment. I anticipate raising the remainder very soon. Please can you let me know where we go from here? Regards, Martin

---

FROM: Tish Bhatoa
SUBJECT: Re: Important
DATE: 20 May 2018 at 22:22
TO: Martin Hayward

Dear Martin, that is excellent news. I will place the order via my private practice as soon as I receive the funds. Please transfer £125,000 to my business account, details below. Again, I was sorry to miss the event. Tish

---

FROM: Isabel Beck
SUBJECT: Bits and bobs!
DATE: 21 May 2018 at 13:02
TO: Samantha Greenwood

I'm in the roof garden. Still haven't recovered from Saturday night, and enjoying the peace and quiet up here. It's a lovely view. I don't know why more people don't come here for lunch. I'm focusing on tomorrow's first rehearsal without scripts. I've been thinking about what you said, and I'm sure Tony Zucchero must have been mistaken about Poppy going blind. You know how civvies get the wrong end of the stick. I suppose she may have metastatic tumours on her optic nerve or a separate condition, but I'm not aware of any paedy-chemo that causes blindness. Are you? Anyway, why would the Haywards keep it secret when they've been so open about everything else? See you after work for our jog. Never thought I'd say this about exercise but I can't bloody wait. Love Issy xxx

---

FROM: Paige Reswick
SUBJECT: Wig
DATE: 21 May 2018 at 14:30
TO: The Little Princess Trust

Dear Wendy, thank you for our chat on the phone. Just to confirm: the wig is for my daughter Poppy, who is 29 months old. She is having chemo for eight weeks and her hair seems thinner already. I want her to get used to wearing a wig as soon as possible. I look forward to receiving your list of participating salons. I'm afraid I am unable to pay anything towards the cost. Thanks again.

FROM: Claudia D'Souza
SUBJECT: Hello
DATE: 21 May 2018 at 14:50
TO: Samantha Greenwood

Dear Sam,
I hope you had a lovely weekend and enjoyed your big charity event. I thought of you on Saturday night and wondered if it was going well. Must be very motivating to have a target to aim for. Like the old scanner appeals – when every hospital had a big thermometer outside the main entrance . . . money is quantifiable in a way so many other things are not. A good friend of mine is in Patient Liaison over at Mount More, so I can ask her about the chemo your friends' little girl may be on. She won't comment on individual cases, but she knows about the drugs. How terrible if she's going blind as well. Life is not fair. Shall we meet up for lunch one day this week? Let me know when your clingy friend isn't around – don't want to cause more trouble in the ward-zone. C x

---

FROM: James Hayward
SUBJECT: Tonight's rehearsal
DATE: 21 May 2018 at 15:00
TO: All My Sons cast and crew

Dear all,
This is a gentle reminder that tonight's rehearsal is strictly books-down. No hiding your script in a newspaper (Barry) and no writing lines on the scenery (Nick). It will feel as if we're going backwards when the play was

starting to take shape, but anyone who has acted before will know this is a necessary step to move the production on to the next level. My father has sneaked in a cheeky bet that at least one cast member will have to pick up their book at some point during the rehearsal. I have a counter-bet that you won't. DON'T LET HIM WIN. See you tonight. James

---

Message from Martin Hayward to James Hayward on 21 May 2018:

15:10 Martin wrote:
What are you talking about? I haven't bet on anything. Why do you say such stupid things?

FROM: Carol Dearing
SUBJECT: You!
DATE: 21 May 2018 at 13:20
TO: Sarah-Jane MacDonald

Did the dinner dance raise all Poppy's money? It looked like they made a fortune. There was some cash in that room all right. You were practically running that event single-handed, Sarah-Jane. I hope the Haywards are paying you for all your work. I know it's a good cause, but you've got a home and family of your own. I love Helen and Martin as much as anyone, but would they do the same for you if Harley were ill? Perhaps you can have a rest now and they can take over the appeal. Mum

---

FROM: Sarah-Jane MacDonald
SUBJECT: Re: You!
DATE: 21 May 2018 at 13:32
TO: Carol Dearing

Of course I'm not being paid, Mum. It's a crowdfunding campaign. The Haywards are beside themselves looking after Poppy. James and Olivia are about to have twins. Anyway, without tempting fate, the appeal may have done its job.
Sarah-Jane MacDonald

FROM: Martin Hayward
SUBJECT: News update
DATE: 21 May 2018 at 18:23
TO: Current Members

Dear all,
I seem to start every letter with an apology, and on this occasion it's for the sheer length of time between our last update and this one – as well as for the customary unanswered emails, messages and texts. I know Helen keeps some of you updated at rehearsals, but for those not directly involved in the play . . .

First things first. Poppy has just undergone her third bout of chemotherapy at Mount More. While after her first two treatments she would bounce back with little more than a day in bed, this time round she's been knocked for six. As if to make things worse, her hair is falling out. Of course this is to be expected and is a sign the drugs are taking effect. However, as you either know or can imagine, it is also devastating evidence that something is very wrong with her. We are therefore entering a difficult stage for the family and (another apology) I'm sorry if we do not seem our usual selves over the next few weeks.

Through it all, one thing that keeps us going – apart from little Poppy herself – is the support of our friends. On behalf of the Haywards and the Reswicks, we would like to thank everyone who helped organise and/or attended the recent charity ball. I am delighted and humbled to report that, as a result, we have raised enough money to place an initial order with the US manufacturer. While this is more than we could possibly have hoped for, it is still not enough. Now the order is placed, we are committed to raising a further £200,000 in the next twelve weeks. Therefore our fundraising continues apace.

Sarah-Jane has done a sterling job launching the appeal, but going forward we believe the most productive course of action will be to establish a fundraising committee to spread the word and the work more evenly. So if you have a few hours a week to spare for fundraising activities, let us know. Sarah-Jane will remain as Campaign Coordinator and is brimming with ideas for the next stage.

The Fairway Players committee has already agreed to donate the proceeds of our forthcoming play *All My Sons*, and various other members have events coming up, including Sam's half-marathon and Beth's charity Bake Off. Words do not do justice to the gratitude we feel for the kind and generous people who surround us. Regards, Martin

---

FROM: Sarah-Jane MacDonald
SUBJECT: Money raised?
DATE: 21 May 2018 at 18:26
TO: Martin Hayward

I make the amount raised so far, less expenses, £143,750. Surely the figure required now is £106,250, less the amount raised offline (let me know this, so I can add it to the final figure) . . . Your email says we need £200,000 – are there expenses I'm not aware of? I haven't heard from Mr Handler, but if he emails again we'll need an accurate figure for him.
Sarah-Jane MacDonald

FROM: Martin Hayward
SUBJECT: Re: Money raised?
DATE: 21 May 2018 at 18:33
TO: Sarah-Jane MacDonald

I'll speak to you tonight before the rehearsal. Regards.

FROM: Marianne Payne
SUBJECT: Re: News update
DATE: 21 May 2018 at 18:44
TO: Martin Hayward

Count us in on the committee, Martin. In the meantime we're all saying double prayers for Poppy. Karen went on a hen night to Liverpool and lit a candle at the cathedral. Mick asked St Peregrine for his intercession, so we're doing everything we can.

I'd like to speak privately to you about another matter. Mick says I shouldn't, and that it's all about personal choice, but I'm going to anyway. I know a lady who organised a trip to Lourdes for her son. She brought back some little bottles of holy water and has some left. I know you are not Catholics, but the healing power of Lourdes is unconditional. You can slip the water into Poppy's juice. No one need know. If this is something you are open to, just ask. If not, then at least I've mentioned it. With all our love, Marianne and Mick

---

FROM: Isabel Beck
SUBJECT: Hugs!
DATE: 21 May 2018 at 19:28
TO: Samantha Greenwood

Hiya Sam,
Thanks for your help today. I'd forgotten how much fun work could be! We should ask to be placed together more often. Yay! Books down tonight ... I'm a bit nervous, but a bit tingly as well. I know we'll see each other in half an hour, but I just want you and Kel to enjoy tonight and not worry too much. At this stage in *Blithe Spirit* I had a massive confidence crisis. I felt I was letting the whole group down and no one else seemed to understand, even though they knew it was my first play. It was James who took me aside and said everyone feels like that, they just don't let on. Perhaps that's why they hate it when someone voices those fears – if it's all left unsaid, they can pretend everything's fine.

Will you be volunteering for the fundraising committee? I'm not sure I'd be much help on my own, but I'll do it if you do. So, not long now until we find out if all our word rehearsals were worthwhile ... If you're feeling wobbly, just send me a text. I'm only sitting outside waiting for Martin to unlock the hall, so you won't disturb me. See you later. Love Issy xxx

---

FROM: Ben Taylor
SUBJECT: Sorry
DATE: 22 May 2018 at 08:29
TO: Glen Reswick

Dear Glen,
I'm sorry to hear about your daughter and wish her a full and speedy

recovery. I understand you are busy with family matters, so won't beat about the bush. Unfortunately, under the circumstances discussed at our meeting last week, we cannot justify renewing your contract with Robinson EcoField. Apologies if this comes at a bad time, but I'm sure you understand that our priorities must remain with our permanent workforce and the best interests of the company as a whole. However, if anything changes in the future we will be in touch.

Yours sincerely,
Ben Taylor
Chief Executive Officer, Robinson EcoField Ltd

FROM: Lydia Drake
SUBJECT: Fundraising
DATE: 22 May 2018 at 08:41
TO: Martin Hayward

Dear Mr Hayward,
Emma Crooks, a very good friend of mine, gave me your email address. I believe I can help you raise the money for your granddaughter's treatment. I recently helped a family in Bradford raise £60,000 in nine days for proton-beam therapy in Sapporo. My highly effective strategy combines conventional fundraising with trading in stocks, shares and other capital investments. I will explain in detail when we meet. I am available at a time convenient to you.

Regards,
Lydia Drake

Message from Sarah-Jane MacDonald to Martin Hayward on 22 May 2018:

09:01 Sarah-Jane wrote:

I've just spoken to Emma. She's never heard of a Lydia Drake. Ignore and delete.

FROM: Isabel Beck
SUBJECT: Don't worry
DATE: 22 May 2018 at 13:00
TO: Sarah-Jane MacDonald

Hey SJ,
I didn't get to speak to you at last night's rehearsal, but just want to reassure you that everyone understands you haven't had a chance to learn lines yet. You've been super-busy and I'm sure sitting down with Kevin and Harley to trawl through your words was simply not on the agenda. Now the ball's over and, with the support of a fundraising committee, you'll be much freer to concentrate on the play. If you'd like help learning your lines I'm happy to go through them with you. I've got a process that works for me. Speaking of the committee, I think I've talked my friends Sam and Kel into volunteering for it. As you know, all three of us work shifts at St Ann's, but it means we could commit time to the appeal when other people are doing their regular jobs. We work so well together, perhaps you could think of us as a little team within the committee. A task force! Harley was brilliant as Bert. He is word-perfect already and you can see he has natural talent. A chip off the old block! I hope you don't mind me emailing like this, but I don't want you to feel down about the rehearsal. Love Issy

---

FROM: Sarah-Jane MacDonald
SUBJECT: Re: Don't worry
DATE: 22 May 2018 at 13:07
TO: Isabel Beck

There's plenty of time to learn lines. It's quality of performance that counts.
Sarah-Jane MacDonald

FROM: Sarah-Jane MacDonald
SUBJECT: Sorry
DATE: 22 May 2018 at 13:34
TO: James Hayward

Safe to say I was bottom of the class last night. I literally haven't had a chance to pick up my script for the last month. Then before rehearsal began, I had a quick meeting with your dad, which threw me further off... Needless to say, I'm learning lines all this week, so it won't happen again. Sarah-Jane MacDonald

---

FROM: James Hayward
SUBJECT: Re: Sorry
DATE: 22 May 2018 at 13:50
TO: Sarah-Jane MacDonald

Dear Sarah-Jane,
It's hardly surprising you didn't know your lines when you've pulled together an event that was more spectacular than anyone imagined. I haven't stopped hearing about the night – from the pick-and-mix to the money raised – so I'll happily let you off the hook about your words. Hope Dad was ok with you. He's under a lot of pressure and is not himself, as you can imagine. If you want someone to help you with lines, I know Issy has a good strategy she used in *Blithe Spirit*. James

---

FROM: Sarah-Jane MacDonald
SUBJECT: Re: Sorry
DATE: 22 May 2018 at 13:55
TO: James Hayward

Heavens, no. I can learn lines easily, when I put my mind to it. Your dad is struggling to stay on top of the numbers involved in Poppy's appeal – although understandably he's keen to be closely involved. Not a huge problem because I can do the sums, but perhaps he could leave financial updates to me in future. Thank you for your comments. The ball snowballed (!) as time went on. I've been out of the game since Harley was born and forgot how that happens when you're planning a big event. I'm sorry you and Olivia couldn't make it, but everyone understands your situation. It was good of you both to babysit Poppy. I wouldn't feel able to look after a seriously ill child. Olivia is clearly cut out to be a mother.
Sarah-Jane MacDonald

FROM: James Hayward
SUBJECT: Re: Sorry
DATE: 22 May 2018 at 13:59
TO: Sarah-Jane MacDonald

Sorry about Dad. Stress brings out a petulant vagueness in him. Meanwhile, Olivia is a star and Poppy was absolutely fine. James

---

FROM: Isabel Beck
SUBJECT: Hiya!
DATE: 22 May 2018 at 14:00
TO: Samantha Greenwood

Hiya Sam!
Congratulations to all three of us for getting through last night's rehearsal with so few prompts (we had just two each and Kel had three). I can't believe how much better life is now, compared to this time last year. I felt so sorry for Sarah-Jane as she didn't know a single word, yet obviously hated having to pick up her book again. She was worse than Barry and Nick (who are always last to know their lines). I sent her a little email to reassure her, and I could tell how grateful she was. Just to make her feel better, I mentioned we were all volunteering for the committee. She suggested we form our own task force to fundraise around our shift patterns. It's a good idea: what do you think? I can hear you-know-who in the staffroom, so better go. See you at 1.30 p.m. in our running gear. Love Issy xxx

---

FROM: Sarah-Jane MacDonald
SUBJECT: Clive Handler
DATE: 30 May 2018 at 09:29
TO: Martin Hayward

Dear Martin, good news below!

On 29 May 2018 at 23:11 Clive Handler wrote:

> Dear Ms MacDonald,
> Further to my previous email, I have been looking into how I can donate the remaining money legally, but with minimal tax impact. After

seeking information from various sources I understand the best course of action is for my company to transfer the money directly to the US drug manufacturer. I can process this payment through a holding company in the Cayman Islands. Please can you let me know the following details:

1. The exact amount of money you require.
2. The drug manufacturer: head-office address and contact personnel.
3. Reference details for the order of Poppy's drugs.

Once I have this information it will take approximately one week to clear these funds into the US payment system. I hope this timescale is workable, given Poppy's health.

Yours sincerely, Clive Handler

FROM: Martin Hayward
SUBJECT: Re: Clive Handler
DATE: 30 May 2018 at 09:50
TO: Sarah-Jane MacDonald

Good news indeed . . . for now. Still, let's not say anything until the money has firmly arrived and the drugs are in our hands. I'll let you know if and when the funds have landed. Regards.

FROM: Tish Bhatoa
SUBJECT: Re: Clive Handler
DATE: 30 May 2018 at 10:05
TO: Martin Hayward

Dear Martin,
Re the information Mr Handler requires, please send me his details and I will liaise with him directly. You are wise to take his offer with a pinch of salt until the money has changed hands. These campaigns attract fantasists, dreamers and attention-seekers, not to mention fraudsters. Meanwhile, keep up the fundraising. Tish

---

FROM: Dr Tish Bhatoa
SUBJECT: Poppy Reswick
DATE: 30 May 2018 at 10:43
TO: Clive Handler

Dear Mr Handler,
I understand you have offered to pay the remaining funds for Poppy Reswick's life-saving brain-tumour treatment. This is excellent news. My company is liaising with the US drug manufacturer on the family's behalf and can confirm the following details for the payment of £200,000 or $280,000. Please deposit this amount via my IBAN and BIC numbers below by wire transfer. This will complete the payment for the drugs and Poppy can start her treatment as soon as they arrive. If you require any further details, please do not hesitate to contact me.

Yours sincerely,
Dr Tish Bhatoa
Managing Director
CloudRegal SA

FROM: Clive Handler
SUBJECT: Re: Poppy Reswick
DATE: 30 May 2018 at 13:19
TO: Dr Tish Bhatoa

Dear Dr Bhatoa,
There seems to be a misunderstanding. I must send the money directly to the US manufacturer in order to transfer the funds with minimal tax implications for my company and for the family of the girl. The details you've sent are for a privately owned offshore investment account in your name. As soon as I have the correct details, I will instruct my accountant to action this payment.

Yours sincerely, Clive Handler

FROM: Dr Tish Bhatoa
SUBJECT: Re: Poppy Reswick
DATE: 30 May 2018 at 13:30
TO: Clive Handler

This is the account through which I will order the drugs on behalf of Poppy. It is my usual route for financial payments to the US, via my private practice here in the UK. It is quite legitimate and HMRC will not penalise you. I've conducted this type of transaction many times before. I'm sure you understand that disclosing any further information would be inappropriate, especially as I do not know your real name or company details.

FROM: Clive Handler
SUBJECT: Re: Poppy Reswick
DATE: 30 May 2018 at 13:34
TO: Dr Tish Bhatoa

In common with many charity donors, it is important to me that I remain anonymous. This has nothing to do with HMRC. I simply prefer to donate to charity as and when I see fit, and do not wish to become a target for desperate people or those with nefarious intentions. As we both know very well, this transaction is not 'quite legitimate', it is a loophole, but one I am prepared to jump through for the greater good. Now, I am offering to donate the not-insubstantial amount of £200,000 to complete the payment for a young child's life-saving drugs. I would like to know the name and address of the company that manufactures those drugs in order that I can pay them directly. It is a simple request for basic information.

FROM: Dr Tish Bhatoa
SUBJECT: Re: Poppy Reswick
DATE: 30 May 2018 at 13:40
TO: Clive Handler

On behalf of the Haywards, I very much appreciate the generous donation you say you are willing to make. I may be in a better position to discuss the company details with you when you tell me who you are. You have my full assurance that I will not disclose your identity to anyone. This, too, is a simple request for basic information. If you insist on withholding it, I will assume you are not serious about making this donation, and more: that you have given false hope to the family of a seriously ill child.

FROM: Clive Handler
SUBJECT: Re: Poppy Reswick
DATE: 30 May 2018 at 13:42
TO: Dr Tish Bhatoa

If you insist on withholding the details I have requested, I will assume the following: there is no American manufacturer, no life-saving drug treatment, and no truth in anything you've told the Haywards.

Femi
Where are you up to now?

Charlotte
Poppy's Ball. You?

Femi
Handler accuses Bhatoa of lying to the Haywards

Charlotte
This is real, isn't it?

Femi
Yes. And I suspect it's an ongoing case.

Charlotte
Arrrgh! Breathe. Breathe.

Femi
Hey, real is good. We can make a difference.

Charlotte
So many questions.

Femi
We just need to ask the right ones.

Charlotte
Here's one for you: spotted any baddies yet?

Femi
There's something fishy about Bhatoa.

Charlotte
The Haywards are intelligent business people and they trust her.

Femi
They have to – Poppy's life is in her hands.

Charlotte
Handler has dug up something about her. But is he right? Issy is SO annoying. Obsessed with Sam?

Femi
She tries hard to be friendly, but she's at the bottom of the social ladder. Ignored or dismissed.

Charlotte
I'd like to know what Sam really thinks of Issy. We've only got Issy's word for it they're friends at all.

Femi
It's like we're looking through other people's eyes.

Charlotte
Sam and Kel. After eight years working in conflict zones, it must be a culture shock to return. Potential context for disaster?

Femi
Maybe. If we knew what the disaster was.

Charlotte
Love how the community comes together to fundraise.

Femi
Yet they're an insular bunch. Repressed, judgemental – and they don't like strangers.

Charlotte
I sense Sam and Kel are keen to fit in. Throw themselves into work, join the drama group, take an active part in the appeal, etc.

Femi
There's one thing we don't know yet and that's why they left their volunteer posts in Africa. Why are they home now?

FROM: Tish Bhatoa
SUBJECT: Re: Clive Handler
DATE: 30 May 2018 at 17:10
TO: Martin Hayward

Dear Martin,
I'm very sorry to have to tell you this, but Mr Handler's offer was indeed too good to be true. He wanted increasingly sensitive information – remember, we don't even know who he is – and when I refused to disclose more details than I am comfortable revealing to a complete stranger, he used that as an excuse to withdraw his 'kind' offer and make a stream of unfounded accusations into the bargain. It's not the first time I've had this sort of time-waster and I've no idea what they get out of playing games with people whose lives are already in turmoil. But you are intelligent and sensible enough to have doubted him from the off. I suggest you either block him completely or at least ignore him if he contacts you again. I'm sorry not to have better news. Tish

---

Message exchange between Martin Hayward and James Hayward on 30 May 2018:

17:15 Martin Hayward wrote:
Urgent family meeting: 6.30 p.m. at the house.

17:16 James Hayward wrote:
I'm at a word rehearsal for the Walfords tonight. You wanted me to take over the play for Mum, and despite everything on my own plate, I am doing so. Speak tomorrow.

17:17 Martin Hayward wrote:
James, we are all in this together. Paige has been at the hospital all day, with Poppy running a temperature, possibly rejecting her chemo. If she's coming, then so can you.

17:18 James Hayward wrote:
Unbelievable.

17:19 Martin Hayward wrote:
Have you no idea what we're going through? Just being grateful all the time is so bloody exhausting.

FROM: Isabel Beck
SUBJECT: Hiya!
DATE: 31 May 2018 at 07:07
TO: Samantha Greenwood

Hiya Sam,
Great word rehearsal last night. They really help, don't you think? I know James was thinking of Nick, Barry and Sarah-Jane when he suggested it, but it's good for the entire cast to focus on words between regular rehearsals. Shame not everyone was there, especially Kel – shift-work, boo. But at least without Helen we could all concentrate on us, if you know what I mean. She's so larger than life that if she's in a scene, no one else is. I'm probably not making sense. Surprising that James was so late. He seemed a bit off. I wonder if Olivia is having problems again (she had a pre-eclampsia scare in the first trimester, then up and down with protein fluctuations ever since. They had IVF at a private clinic in London.) Still, Martin said the family weren't themselves. I can't wait to cheer you on in the half-marathon on Sunday. I only wish I could run as far. Speaking of which, I'll see you by Costa for our jog at lunch. Until then, it's another jolly morning in Jelly Antics! Love Issy xxx

---

FROM: Isabel Beck
SUBJECT: Where were you?
DATE: 31 May 2018 at 13:26
TO: Samantha Greenwood

Hi Sam, just wondering where you are. I waited by Costa as usual but you didn't turn up, so I got changed and sat in the staffroom on my own. I hope you're ok. Love Issy xxx

---

FROM: Claudia D'Souza
SUBJECT: Thanks
DATE: 31 May 2018 at 14:04
TO: Samantha Greenwood

Dear Sam,
What a lovely lunch! How wonderful the sunshine came too. You're right, the Orangery is too expensive to eat there all the time, but it doesn't hurt every once in a while. I chased Una again for you, and she says chemo has a high ocular toxicity that can affect vision in the long-term. Whether that can be described as technically 'going blind' is less certain. If your friend's granddaughter has only just started her chemo, Una said the family is more than likely fixated on the possible long-term side-effect it fears the most. Who'd be a parent? If I hadn't had my two after getting pissed and forgetting contraception, I'd never have taken the plunge – not after seeing how wrong it can go. On that cheerful note, thank you again for a lovely time and I'll see you on Sunday. C x

---

FROM: Lauren Malden
SUBJECT: Hiya!
DATE: 31 May 2018 at 18:45
TO: Isabel Beck

Hello lovely! Josh is speaking at a seminar in Brecon this week so we can meet up whenever you're free. What lunch are you on? I can meet you in Costa or the Orangery. I'm sure walking into St Ann's will give me the shivers, but it'll be worth it for the catch-up. I can't believe you're still in Geriatrics. You are much too good for that place, and all the people there. What's the Fairways gossip? Mum visited a friend at Mount More (stage-four liver, not good) and bumped into Helen and Paige in the chemo suite. Helen said her fingers were crossed for some news. What did she mean? Hope it means they've raised all the money. Did you know they are building a swimming pool at The Grange? Helen said they booked the builders before Poppy was ill and can't cancel them. Look forward to catching up. L x

---

FROM: Isabel Beck
SUBJECT: Re: Hiya!
DATE: 31 May 2018 at 18:53
TO: Lauren Malden

I know the news about Poppy, but it's sensitive, so I can't say. I'm busy all this week: jogging, rehearsing and being on Poppy's fundraising committee. Maybe meet up in a few months. Issy

---

FROM: Lauren Malden
SUBJECT: Re: Hiya!
DATE: 31 May 2018 at 18:59
TO: Isabel Beck

Is it good news? Please don't say it's bad. Oh my God, has the cancer spread? Please tell me, Issy. If you don't, I'll end up putting my foot in it with someone. I won't whisper a word to anyone. Go on, you know you can trust me. I've never told anyone about our accident with the IV that time, have I? Pretty please . . . L x

---

FROM: Isabel Beck
SUBJECT: Re: Hiya!
DATE: 31 May 2018 at 19:04
TO: Lauren Malden

Poppy is going blind. Caused by the chemo she's on at Mount More. It's another reason we need to raise the money for her American drugs as soon as possible. The family is keeping it quiet, so no one treats Poppy any differently. I think it's just me and Sam who know at the moment, so don't say anything. Not to anyone. Issy

---

FROM: Martin Hayward
SUBJECT: Re: Half-Marathon
DATE: 31 May 2018 at 19:33
TO: Samantha Greenwood

That's excellent news about your half-marathon sponsorship. Thank you, Sam. The whole family is very grateful. Good luck with your final preparations. Unfortunately we won't be able to come and cheer you on, but we'll be with you in thought every step of the way. Please don't come all the way over here. Have a chat with James at the next rehearsal. Regards, Martin

---

Message exchange between Martin Hayward and James Hayward on 31 May 2018:

19:34 Martin Hayward wrote:
Had an email from the new girl, Sam. Wants to see me 'about something, in private' and suggested she comes to the house. Any idea? I don't want her here. Told her to see you tonight.

19:36 James Hayward wrote:
She's a nurse, so chances are it's a medical thing about Poppy. Thanks, Dad, I don't have enough plates to spin at rehearsals as is.

FROM: Isabel Beck
SUBJECT: Hiya!
DATE: 1 June 2018 at 14:20
TO: Samantha Greenwood

Hi Sam, are you coming to rehearsal? Riley said you went home sick after lunch. I told him it was before lunch, because you missed our jogging session and didn't even text, so I knew it had to be bad. Really worried and hope you're ok. Rehearsals aren't the same without you, so wishing hard for your recovery. Really looking forward to the half-marathon on Sunday. I'm planning a surprise for you. Hope that hasn't spoiled the surprise. Is it ok if I stand with Kel? I won't know anyone else there and if he's watched a half-marathon before, he'll know where to stand. Well, off to read through my lines before tonight – mustn't get complacent! Lots of love, Issy xxx

---

FROM: Martin Hayward
SUBJECT:
DATE: 1 June 2018 at 16:18
TO: James Hayward

For goodness' sake! Sam turned up here unannounced. I've only just got rid of her. Can you believe it? There was I, frantically trying to close doors and keep her in the hall (Mum was on the phone in the extension), when she asked me outright how much we've paid Tish Bhatoa. I told her £125,000 – half the fee as a deposit on the order. She turns marble-white, then says she thinks Tish is lying about the drugs, stealing the money and will probably administer conventional chemo and tell us it's the experimental combination. I knew this Sam was one of those who instinctively distrust authority, from an email she sent about lobbying Parliament to fast-track the drugs, but this is pure paranoia. I only hope she hasn't told anyone. It could scupper the appeal, precisely when we need to ramp it up. Oh, and she assured me it's very unlikely Poppy will go blind, and that it's probably something Tish is telling us to keep us raising money. Well, Tish hasn't said anything about Poppy going blind. What do you think of that? What should I do?

FROM: James Hayward
SUBJECT: Re:
DATE: 1 June 2018 at 16:20
TO: Martin Hayward

She 'thinks' Tish is lying? Well, does she have proof? She's just a nurse, remember. What did you say to her? Have you told Mum?

FROM: Martin Hayward
SUBJECT: Re:
DATE: 1 June 2018 at 16:23
TO: James Hayward

That was my first question. She didn't offer any proof, just said she 'has a gut feeling'. We can't have her going round saying these things. But what if she does? The big donor falls through, and now all this. I don't know what to do or which way to turn. I'm sorry about everything else. I know how you feel, but we need you on our side. Can you come over? Don't mention it to Mum; she still thinks the money is being paid by Clive Handler.

FROM: James Hayward
SUBJECT: Re:
DATE: 1 June 2018 at 16:31
TO: Martin Hayward

Dad, don't panic. I'm sure everything's fine. I'll speak to Sam at rehearsal and tell her to keep any conspiracy theories to herself while we look into it. You trust Tish, don't you? If Sam has no proof, then it's just her putting two and two together and making five. As for the blindness thing, well, we know where that comes from – the singer in the band Sarah-Jane booked. That's neither here nor there. Ask Tish for documents to clarify the order. Probably a good idea anyway, in case anyone else questions the appeal. Just to be on the safe side, we won't pay her any more until we can prove the money's going where we intend it to go. I'll pop in before rehearsal but can't stay for long. DON'T WORRY.

FROM: James Hayward
SUBJECT: Hello there
DATE: 1 June 2018 at 16:35
TO: Isabel Beck

Dearest Issy! How is my star line-learner? Quick question: you work with Sam, don't you – what's she like? She's only just arrived here, but she's generous enough to run a half-marathon for us … we're putting this fundraising committee together and want it to be a cohesive team. I wouldn't want to approach her about more volunteering without knowing, for example, whether she's very busy at work or even planning to stay in the area long-term, given their history of working abroad. Don't mention that I asked . . . I don't want to make a big thing of it. See you tonight, James

---

FROM: Isabel Beck
SUBJECT: Re: Hello there
DATE: 1 June 2018 at 16:59
TO: James Hayward

Hi James! You must be psychic, I'm reading through my lines now. No problem, I know you want the most productive people on the committee and, as Sam and I are best friends, I'm the one to ask! Well, she's lovely, kind, funny and so good with the patients. In Geriatrics, all our patients are at the ends of their lives, so we have to be careful not to get attached. Some of our colleagues go too far the other way and don't care enough. Sam gets the balance exactly right. She even gets along with all the staff, and if you worked there you'd know what a statement that is! One thing I've noticed is that people care about what she says. At work, when I've mentioned that such-and-such a thing could be done better, I've been either ignored or contradicted. 'Oh, Issy's whining again.' But if Sam says it, they listen and it gets sorted. She doesn't talk much about Africa, but they must have loved it, to stay so long. Life here probably seems very dull in comparison. Sam's the sort of person who can do anything if she sets her mind to it. She's the opposite of me. I can mess up the easiest task. I know she would be an excellent member of the fundraising committee. Perhaps Sam could lead a sub-committee of Kel and me – we could form our own little gang! Sarah-Jane seemed keen on that idea. If you need to know anything else, just ask. Now, back to learning Act Two for tonight! Love Issy xxx

---

FROM: Martin Hayward
SUBJECT: Committee thoughts
DATE: 1 June 2018 at 17:36
TO: Sarah-Jane MacDonald
CC: James Hayward

Re the fundraising committee, can we keep it to people we know well, please? After Clive Handler, it's occurred to me that maybe we've been too open. Especially where money is concerned. We should be able to vouch for anyone who works for the appeal. We can't be too careful. Regards.

FROM: Sarah-Jane MacDonald
SUBJECT: Re: Committee thoughts
DATE: 1 June 2018 at 17:43
TO: Martin Hayward
CC: James Hayward

Most people are honest and true to their word, but those who aren't make a more lasting impression. Once the next stage of fundraising is under way, we'll soon forget Mr H. For my part, I'm keen the committee isn't populated by friends who are sympathetic and well meaning but hopeless at getting things done. We need doers. People who will throw themselves into every task and get behind whatever fundraising event we're planning. I've drawn up a shortlist as follows:

Emma Crooks, Kevin MacDonald, Celia and Joel Halliday, Karen Payne, Sam and Kel Greenwood. Of course others are still keen to help and that's fine, but as a core team I think these seven will seriously get things done.
Sarah-Jane MacDonald

FROM: Martin Hayward
SUBJECT: Re: Committee thoughts
DATE: 1 June 2018 at 17:45
TO: Sarah-Jane MacDonald
CC: James Hayward

Not Sam or Kel.

FROM: James Hayward
SUBJECT: Re: Committee thoughts
DATE: 1 June 2018 at 17:50
TO: Sarah-Jane MacDonald
CC: Martin Hayward

That shortlist is fine, Sarah-Jane, just not Sam or Kel.

FROM: Sarah-Jane MacDonald
SUBJECT: Re: Committee thoughts
DATE: 1 June 2018 at 17:54
TO: Martin Hayward
CC: James Hayward

Why on earth not? I know they're new, but they seem very honest and competent. Both nurses – so practical, hands-on people-people. The worst thing I can say about them is they seem unable to shake off that drippy girl who has latched on with a vengeance.

FROM: James Hayward
SUBJECT: Re: Committee thoughts
DATE: 1 June 2018 at 17:55
TO: Martin Hayward

Don't reply, Dad, leave it to me.

FROM: James Hayward
SUBJECT: Re: Committee thoughts
DATE: 1 June 2018 at 18:01
TO: Sarah-Jane MacDonald

Between you and me, Dad's been badly shaken by the Clive Handler thing. I know we said from the start it could be dodgy, but you can't help your mind racing ahead. He's taken it personally and I think he suspects Mr H is someone we know – jealous, messing with us just because they can. That's why he wants to limit our exposure to those on the periphery of our social circle. Poppy's illness – even the appeal itself – puts us in a very vulnerable situation. We're not in control, and suddenly everything we have and everything we've done means nothing. There are people who instinctively take advantage of vulnerability. I feel we've had a brush with that. I don't know. It's tricky to explain. I like Sam and Kel and would be happy for them to be included, but it will put Dad on edge, and at the moment he's the family rock. James

---

FROM: Sarah-Jane MacDonald
SUBJECT: Re: Committee thoughts
DATE: 1 June 2018 at 18:06
TO: James Hayward

Ok. Fine with me. Let's draw a line under Mr Handler and move on. We've got work to do and money to raise. I propose announcing the committee tonight and holding our first meeting later in the week.
Sarah-Jane MacDonald

FROM: Isabel Beck
SUBJECT: Ok?
DATE: 2 June 2018 at 01:09
TO: Samantha Greenwood

Sorry to message you in the middle of the night, but on the off-chance you're still awake too, I just wondered if you're ok? I was so relieved when you turned up to rehearsal last night. The Fairways is just like work: everyone is so much nicer to me when you're there. It was good of James to take you aside like that and let you know about the committee decision. You seemed really disappointed, but please don't be. I wasn't really expecting us to be selected and hoped you hadn't pinned any hopes on it. The Haywards have known all those people for years, so it's like getting a part in the play: it's who you know. I'm going to miss you for the rest of this week – earlies, boo – but really looking forward to the race on Sunday! Lovely of Kel to let me stand with him; and don't forget I've got a surprise for you . . . There I go, I've spoiled the surprise again! Night-night . . . Love Issy xxx

FROM: James Hayward
SUBJECT: Sam
DATE: 2 June 2018 at 05:22
TO: Martin Hayward

Spoke to Sam last night and she's simmered down. I assured her I've double-checked everything and there's no possibility the new drug combination is not what Tish says it is. She seemed satisfied with that. I pressed her for who she'd shared her unfounded suspicions with, and luckily it's just Kel. I was emphatic they shouldn't say such things to anyone, as we desperately need to raise the remaining money. She agreed, albeit a little crestfallen. So, Dad, that panic is over. Sarah-Jane is fired up about the campaign, but I warned her things are starting to get worse for Poppy and therefore we are all going to be walking wrecks before long. She's happy to chair the committee – I'll ask her to forward the minutes of each meeting, so we keep up with it, but the whole point of this exercise is that we sit back and leave the fundraising to them. Let's all pull together and support each other. We must enjoy the good days, so we have those memories for the future. James

---

FROM: Martin Hayward
SUBJECT: Re: Sam
DATE: 2 June 2018 at 06:59
TO: James Hayward

I know what you mean. Thank you.

FROM: Martin Hayward
SUBJECT: My granddaughter
DATE: 2 June 2018 at 07:37
TO: Clive Handler

Dear Mr Handler,
You have lately been corresponding with our Campaign Coordinator Sarah-Jane MacDonald, and more recently with Dr Tish Bhatoa, regarding our campaign to raise £250,000 for my granddaughter Poppy's life-saving

drug treatment. I understand those negotiations have broken down.

Firstly, may I apologise without reservation for any offence Dr Bhatoa may have caused. Like so many doctors, she is extremely knowledgeable and clever, at the expense of her people-skills. She may be abrupt and uncompromising, but she is very well respected and I know she has Poppy's best interests at heart. Our family has placed all our trust in her, and we do not do that lightly. Secondly, and this is something I have not even told my closest family members, if Poppy is to receive her life-saving drug treatment, it will cost a lot more than £250,000. That figure, huge as it may be, is for just *one* course of the new drug combination. If it proves effective, we will need at least four. But time is running out.

This email is to implore you to rethink your decision to withdraw your kind offer. I don't know whether you are a father or grandfather yourself, but if so, you may have some understanding of how it must feel to watch helplessly as those you love suffer. If Poppy does not recover, she will be robbed of her future, and we will be robbed of ours. That pain and sadness will scar us forever. The shockwaves will be felt throughout our family for a generation or more. That is the legacy of tragedy.

If there is anything I can do to change your mind, please, please let me know what it is. I am happy to provide any information you require and to deal with you directly myself – anonymously, if that is what you prefer. Many, many thanks again for the interest you have shown in my family and for the boundless generosity and kindness behind your offer.

Yours sincerely, Martin Hayward

FROM: MAILER-DAEMON Clive Handler
SUBJECT: Re: My granddaughter
DATE: 2 June 2018 at 07:38
TO: Martin Hayward

[Failure notice] Sorry we were unable to deliver your message. Address unknown.

FROM: James Hayward
SUBJECT: Committee meeting
DATE: 2 June 2018 at 11:28
TO: Isabel Beck

Dearest Issy, what can I say but a huge well done on your line-learning. Now your book is down, you are also finding Lydia's character and making it your own. You can be very proud of the work you've done for *All My Sons*, not least in helping Sam and Kel settle in. On another matter, due to Olivia's pregnancy, and of course Mum and Dad's commitment to supporting Poppy, Paige and Glen, the Haywards and Reswicks will be unable to attend the committee meetings Sarah-Jane is organising. I've therefore asked her if you can take the minutes. Is that ok? The first meeting is this Tuesday at 7 p.m. I believe it's at Sarah-Jane's, but I'll ask her to confirm all the details with you. James

---

FROM: Isabel Beck
SUBJECT: Re: Committee meeting
DATE: 2 June 2018 at 11:35
TO: James Hayward

Gasp! I would LOVE to take the minutes for the committee meetings! Thank you so much, James. I've worked very hard to make Sam and Kel feel at home and it's worth it to see them blossom in their roles. I think they were a little disappointed to be left out of the fundraising committee, but I assured them it's nothing personal. Sam's half-marathon is this Sunday. I'm in the middle of making an enormous banner to cheer her on (don't mention it – it's a surprise). Again, thank you soooo much! Love to Olivia and the bumps! Issy xxx

---

FROM: Isabel Beck
SUBJECT: Yippee!
DATE: 2 June 2018 at 11:37
TO: Samantha Greenwood

Yay! James just emailed to say how well I'm doing in the play and could I take the minutes for the committee meetings! And I've only been a member of The Fairways for just over a year! I'm so sorry you can't be there, but if I spot a chance to bring you on board, I will. As I said, it's who you know! Yay! I'm doing a little dance of excitement! Just one thing: I didn't want to ask James, in case he thought I was a bit dim, but do you know what 'take the minutes' means? Presumably I'll have to time the meeting, so I'll wear my good watch. Yay again! Love Issy xxx

---

FROM: Sarah-Jane MacDonald
SUBJECT: Committee meeting
DATE: 2 June 2018 at 13:55
TO: Isabel Beck

My house, 7 p.m., Tuesday. Bring notebook and pen.

FROM: Marianne Payne
SUBJECT: Poppy
DATE: 3 June 2018 at 14:56
TO: Martin Hayward

Dear Martin, I've just heard the terribly sad news and want to reassure you that, despite all you're going through now, being blind is no barrier to living a full and happy life. I had an aunt on my mother's side completely blind from birth. She went to college, worked for an equine insurer, married a Scot and died at sixty-nine of a brain bleed. Being so young means Poppy won't remember being sighted at all, and her other senses will compensate. The body is a wonderful gift. We are all praying for you, Martin, and if you change your mind about the Lourdes water, just let me know. All my love, Marianne

---

FROM: Denise Malcolm
SUBJECT: Poor little Poppy
DATE: 3 June 2018 at 15:30
TO: Martin Hayward

Dear Martin and Helen, as if you haven't suffered enough. Poor, poor Poppy. I used to see a blind man every day on the Tube when I worked in

London. I'd watch him read things in Braille and carry his guide dog on the escalator. I don't know what he did, but it must've been a job. Martin, make sure you apply for a blue badge. The application takes ages and they make you jump through hoops, but it's a godsend in town on Saturdays.
God bless, Denise

FROM: John O'Dea
SUBJECT:
DATE: 3 June 2018 at 18:05
TO: Martin Hayward . . .

Clearing out Mum's things, we found a box of audio books. We can discuss price.

FROM: Sarah-Jane MacDonald
SUBJECT: Bloody Tony Zucchero!
DATE: 3 June 2018 at 18:36
TO: Martin Hayward

Bloody Tony Zucchero! I don't know who he told, and it doesn't really matter, because the grapevine has decreed that Poppy is now blind. Please don't worry about this, or take up valuable time trying to set the record straight. I'll put something definitive in my first committee update at the end of the week. I can only apologise for cooking up such a story in the first place. On a positive note, the committee meeting is full steam ahead for Tuesday. Everyone I hoped for is on board – and more. James enlisted that mousy girl to take minutes, so if by a miracle she manages to do so, I'll forward them on. I'll take my own notes, just in case. Meanwhile, Kevin is sourcing suppliers for T-shirts, badges and keyrings, so he'll let you know how much we need from the account in due course.
Sarah-Jane MacDonald

FROM: Glen Reswick
SUBJECT: Money
DATE: 3 June 2018 at 19:00
TO: Martin Hayward

Have you seen the fundraising page? It's jumped by more than £4k overnight, thanks to donations from people who think Poppy is going blind. Will they be suspicious when they see us out and about? We don't want anyone feeling they've been conned, when they've been kind enough to support us.

FROM: Martin Hayward
SUBJECT: Re: Bloody Tony Zucchero!
DATE: 3 June 2018 at 20:09
TO: Sarah-Jane MacDonald

Yes, we have had a significant response to the Zucchero rumour. It seems all our friends know a blind person who lives a happy and fulfilling life. While Poppy is not sight-impaired at the moment, vision problems are a long-term side-effect of the conventional chemo she is on, so while the rumour is overblown, it is not without foundation. The sooner she can be taken off these horrible drugs and put on the new combination, the sooner the risk of that side-effect will abate. Perhaps you could include that explanation in your committee update? Regards.

FROM: Martin Hayward
SUBJECT: Re: Fundraising
DATE: 3 June 2018 at 20:34
TO: Lydia Drake

Dear Ms Drake,
Many thanks for your email. I would be very interested to hear about your strategy. I see you are based in London – I can meet you there. Are you available next Monday, 11 June?

Regards, Martin Hayward

FROM: Isabel Beck
SUBJECT: Tonight!
DATE: 5 June 2018 at 09:51
TO: Sarah-Jane MacDonald

Hiya SJ, sorry to bother you, but this is just to let you know I am fully prepared for the committee meeting tonight. Sam has explained what taking the minutes entails, so I've bought everything I need: a matching notebook and pen, a mini pencil case and a plastic folder to put everything in. If there's anything else you need me to bring, just say, as I'll pass Paperchase again on the way home. Thank you so much for giving me this opportunity to help Poppy. Feeling useful makes all the difference. Love Issy xxx

PS If you need someone to make the tea or help me take the minutes, I know Sam is still keen to be involved. Just say the word!

FROM: Alasdair Hynes
SUBJECT:
DATE: 5 June 2018 at 11:40
TO: Tish Bhatoa

Hi Tish, look, we have to run a full audit on this. We've been sent a professionally printed order of service for an event called Poppy's Ball in aid of this charity, and it very clearly names you as a speaker. I've had to declare myself an acquaintance of yours and have passed the case on to a colleague. I'm sorry, but there's nothing more I can do. Alex

---

FROM: Tish Bhatoa
SUBJECT: Re:
DATE: 5 June 2018 at 13:14
TO: Alasdair Hynes

Dear Alex, I'm sorry you've been put in this position. They named me as a speaker at the event, without asking me first. As soon as I heard about it, I told them it was never going to happen and didn't even attend. These are the people you have to see in private practice: the epitome of white entitlement. They think the earth should stop turning for their child to be cured. It doesn't occur to them no one else is as committed to their family as they are. If they'd seen what we have, they'd be grateful for the many privileges they not only take for granted, but demand, with no sense of their own insignificance in the world. They could afford these drugs if they sold their assets, but they are affronted by the very idea of paying for healthcare and prefer others to foot the bill. These are the people I must deal with to save children. On another matter, I know who sent you the document: someone with a grudge and their own agenda. Thank you for your support, Alex, and again, I'm sorry. Tish

---

FROM: Tish Bhatoa
SUBJECT: Question
DATE: 5 June 2018 at 13:33
TO: Martin Hayward

A quick confidential question, Martin. You know a Samantha Greenwood who works as a nurse at St Ann's. Has she, by any chance, ever mentioned me?

FROM: Martin Hayward
SUBJECT: Re: Question
DATE: 5 June 2018 at 14:46
TO: Tish Bhatoa

Yes. She recently joined our drama group. I didn't want to bother you with it. In short, she questioned your involvement in Poppy's appeal. Implied you were bamboozling us. She's running a half-marathon for the appeal, so she means well, but she's one of those who has a problem with authority and will more readily believe a fanciful conspiracy theory than the mundane truth. We are already distancing ourselves from her. She's nothing for you to worry about. Regards.

FROM: Tish Bhatoa
SUBJECT: Re: Question
DATE: 5 June 2018 at 14:51
TO: Martin Hayward

I suspected as much. She's a troublemaker and has tried to report me to the BMA. All nonsense, but they have to investigate. They won't find anything. It's just irritating. Tish

---

FROM: Tish Bhatoa
SUBJECT:
DATE: 5 June 2018 at 15:00
TO: Samantha Greenwood

Your attempts to get back at me are childish and futile. When they know what you tried to do, they will simply dismiss every word you say. That's what happens when you make false accusations.

FROM: Isabel Beck
SUBJECT: OMG!
DATE: 5 June 2018 at 23:18
TO: Samantha Greenwood

Hiya Sam! Sorry if this email wakes you up, but I'm just back from the committee meeting and literally buzzing with excitement. People speak so quickly – much quicker than I can write – so I hope I can remember some of the things I didn't have time to scribble down. I took so many notes I've half-filled my new notebook. I've downloaded a template, now I have to type up everything and number each point. Did you realise taking the minutes was such a responsibility? I feel quite moved that James and Sarah-Jane trust me with it. Hope I don't mess up. Would you mind looking over the minutes before I send them in, just to check I'm doing the right thing? I would be so grateful. Now I have to kick-start my old laptop – wait ages for it to update and crash a few times – so I can begin. Have to be up at five, so should really go to bed, but know I won't sleep a wink. So sorry you couldn't be there. I didn't get a chance to say anything, but luckily taking minutes is more listening than talking, so it suits me down to the ground. I've already mentioned to Sarah-Jane that you could pop along and help me in future; so that seed is sown, it just needs to germinate. I must wind down. Thanks, Sam, for all your help, you are such a lovely friend to me. Love Issy xxx

---

FROM: Arnie Ballancore
SUBJECT: How's it going?
DATE: 5 June 2018 at 23:22
TO: Kel Greenwood

How's it going? Heard you were back and got your new email address from Tanya. Where are you living now, mate? I'm at my mum's, but we don't get on, so hoping to move out any day now. Haven't been able to work for a bit, so things are up in the air. You know when I got back, I left nursing? Yeah, started at a hospital near Reading, but couldn't get along with anyone. Do you find that? It's like people here are so petty and small-minded. I got to thinking that everyone – like *everyone* – should spend a year volunteering in a bush clinic and *then* complain when they've waited three hours for an ambulance. Got a job with Venture Travel, taking backpackers round Cambodia and Vietnam. Start of this year told them I didn't want to do any more tours. Don't know why, really. Didn't feel the same way about it that I felt about nursing, when I started. No enthusiasm. Went to Africa wanting to make a difference. Change the world. But that didn't happen. Instead Africa changed *me*. I'm not who I was and now I don't know who I am. Sorry to lay all this on you, mate, but I think of you guys. How's Sam? What happened with that trouble she had? Did she go to court in the end? Say hi from me. Arnie

---

FROM: Isabel Beck
SUBJECT: Minutes!
DATE: 6 June 2018 at 05:57
TO: Sarah-Jane MacDonald

Hiya SJ! It was lovely to see you, Kevin and Harley last night. Your house is beautifully decorated, like a magazine, and I don't know what herbal tea that was, but it tasted very healthy. I feel so honoured you trust me to do the minutes (attached). I hope they are an accurate reflection of what was said in the meeting, as now and again I lost the thread and had to make something up to fit. Anyway, don't worry if I missed something out; just let me know and I can add it. On another matter, Sarah-Jane, I noticed you were making notes on a plain spiral notepad. Would you like a more decorative notebook? Paperchase have some beautiful designs. I hope you can make Sam's half-marathon on Sunday, but if not, I'll see you at the next rehearsal. Good luck to Harley for his swim. Love Issy xxx

A Cure for Poppy Committee Meeting Minutes, as taken by Isabel Beck

Date: 5 June 2018
Time: 7.33 p.m.
Place: Sarah-Jane MacDonald's house

In attendance: Isabel Beck, Sarah-Jane and Kevin MacDonald, Emma Crooks, Celia and Joel Halliday, Karen Payne.
Apologies for absence: Well, none, but I suppose the Haywards and Reswicks would be here, if they could. Also, I know Sam and Kel Greenwood would love to be involved.
Review of previous minutes: As this is the first-ever committee meeting, we don't have any previous minutes. I'll just leave this section blank. Is that ok, Sarah-Jane?

Matters arising:

1. Fundraising to date
Sarah-Jane spoke about Poppy's Ball and how it raised almost £90,000. That, and all the donations received so far, mean that Martin has made the first payment for Poppy's drugs, so that's wonderful news! All we have to do now is raise the rest.

2. Planned events
The next fundraising event is Sam's half-marathon on Sunday. This wasn't mentioned at the meeting, and I didn't want to interrupt anyone, but I'm very keen she gets a good response. She's got 115% of her target already. I'll be there on Sunday to cheer her across the finish and have even made a banner, which I'm hoping Kel will help me unravel.

Some other events were mentioned at this point, but I got lost when everyone was talking. Harley is doing a swim with his swimming club tomorrow. Someone at Celia's work is cycling from Land's End to John O'Groats. Barry is doing an eating challenge called an Elvis Cookathon, but no one seemed convinced that would make any money.

3. Merchandise

Sarah-Jane had the brilliant idea of making a range of merchandise: T-shirts, badges, pens and keyrings. She must have been very confident the committee would approve this, as she and Kevin have already had samples made and decided which manufacturer to use. They've also picked a logo for the campaign that, if I'm honest, looks like a child's drawing of a buttercup with blood on its petals. Sarah-Jane held up a T-shirt to show us and there was a long moment of shocked silence. The thing is, she's worked so hard I don't think anyone wanted to criticise, so they all said how lovely it looked. I wonder, though: do people who donate realise that some of the money is being spent on merchandise rather than on Poppy's drugs?

4. Ideas-brainstorm

This is where my note-taking skills let me down. Everyone had something to say, and ideas were thrown in, discussed and thrown out at an alarming speed. I think the following is more or less accurate:

1. Karen will hold a race night for her colleagues at work. Apparently, this involves getting old video recordings of horse races for people to bet on. Not my thing at all. According to Kevin, 'those evenings are a licence to print money' and if you 'mark up the bar, you can double profits because drinking and gambling habits go hand in hand'.
2. Emma wants to do a Moonlight Yogathon on Midsummer's Night. She thinks it will be quite popular as it coincides with a full moon. Interestingly, psychotic episodes can coincide with a full moon – ask anyone in A&E.
3. Celia said she will front an *All My Sons* fundraising drive. The profits are already going to the appeal, but she thinks selling merchandise on the nights, taking collection buckets round the audience and handing out leaflets promoting the crowdfunding web link will maximise the potential of our 'captive audience'.
4. A raffle. Sarah-Jane wants to organise a raffle that lasts several weeks to give everyone time to sell lots of tickets. We will all be issued with a set number of tickets to sell to our friends. Hopefully I will be exempt, as all my friends are Fairway Players

too and will be selling their own tickets. I nearly fell off Harley's beanbag when SJ said the tickets would be £10 each.

5. Any other business

Sarah-Jane said Martin was surprised everyone knew about Poppy's eyesight problems, as the family hadn't told a soul. She assured us Poppy isn't totally blind yet, but it's on the cards. I didn't want to interrupt anyone, but I've not heard that chemo causes blindness. If Poppy's eyesight is deteriorating at this stage, I would urge them to have an MRI on her optic nerve. Her doctor has probably got it in hand.

Celia made the point that it's not just money for the appeal that will support the family, but practical, hands-on help too. She reeled off a very long list of things she and Joel are doing on a voluntary basis at The Grange. Poppy has her chemo on Mondays and Thursdays, so they always need extra help then, because Helen takes her to Mount More with Paige. Apparently a lot of building work is about to start at The Grange, plus some long-standing events, as well as the day-to-day classes and catering. Emma is looking after the Reswicks' dog and working extra hours. I felt a bit mean, but with my shifts I know I can't manage anything else, even if I was paid for it, let alone if I wasn't, so I didn't say anything.

Sarah-Jane's personal focus for the next couple of weeks will be to increase the social-media presence of the campaign. She is working on the national news sites and channels, but apparently there are so many people raising money for overseas healthcare there isn't much newsworthiness to Poppy's story. I find that extraordinary. Surely we have the best treatment here for free? I think families feel utterly helpless in the face of serious illness, and raising money gives them a way to feel they are doing something to help.

Sarah-Jane asked if we knew any rich people who might make a more substantial donation. If only! She's heard about a wealthy businessman who paid the whole amount to an appeal like Poppy's once. Well, I don't know anyone that well-off, boo.

6. Next meeting

Sarah-Jane has set the next meeting for two weeks' time. I'll need to check what shift I'm on and get a notebook with lines rather than blank pages.

End of the minutes

FROM: Sarah-Jane MacDonald
SUBJECT: Re: Minutes!
DATE: 6 June 2018 at 09:09
TO: Isabel Beck

Received. Will read in due course.

FROM: Sarah-Jane MacDonald
SUBJECT: Committee meeting
DATE: 6 June 2018 at 10:14
TO: James Hayward
CC: Martin Hayward

Dear James and Martin,
Please find attached the outcome of the committee meeting last night. That insipid girl sent through her minutes, but when I saw the length of the document I lost the will to live and haven't read it. You don't need to know every little detail. In short, we are all on the same page and on course to generate the remaining money. Speaking of which, Martin, please can you confirm the exact amounts raised and required. It's the one question I'm asked all the time, and the only one I can't answer. People like definitive figures to aim for.

A Cure for Poppy Committee Meeting, 5 June 2018

1. Lots of fundraising events coming up in the next few weeks.
2. The merchandising range is designed, approved and ordered; ditto raffle tickets – I'll need a cheque to cover costs.
3. Social-media and national media campaign under way.
4. Next meeting in two weeks.

FROM: Callum McDaid
SUBJECT: The Grange
DATE: 6 June 2018 at 10:23
TO: Martin Hayward

Dear Martin,
As you know, the lads started work Friday. Jonno said the foundations are coming along. Spoke to Pat White this morning. He mentioned a

dispute over a job. It's between you and him, but I need your assurance it has nothing to do with the pool annexe we're working on. This is a small world, and you'll understand we don't take on disputed jobs. Callum

---

FROM: Martin Hayward
SUBJECT: Re: The Grange
DATE: 6 June 2018 at 11:58
TO: Callum McDaid

Dear Callum,
Re: Whites. We withheld payment over the sub-standard fencing they put up around our golf course last year (it's bowing already, you can see for yourself). We were quoted for concrete foundations and posts – they gave us wooden posts and no foundations. We sought a complete replacement of the fencing, Whites refused, solicitors were involved and to this day we remain in deadlock, but I can assure you it has nothing to do with the pool annexe. Regards, Martin Hayward

---

FROM: Joyce Walford
SUBJECT:
DATE: 9 June 2018 at 09:34
TO: Martin Hayward

Well, if no one thinks my Barry's Elvis Cooking Thong is worth doing, then he can always donate the money to something else. Joyce

---

Message from Kevin MacDonald to Sarah-Jane MacDonald on 9 June 2018:

09:52 Kevin wrote:
I'm in the den. It's not a buttercup. It's a Welsh poppy. You remember I wanted the chap to create a bold, stylised illustration of a poppy, but we said red ones remind people of war? Well, I googled it and Welsh poppies are yellow. I then had the bright idea that a ladybird alighting delicately on the yellow petals would add a charming splash of colour. I sketched it out for him as a guide. It was a blob of red, for God's sake! How was I to know the lazy git would just

scan what I'd scribbled and plaster it all over the T-shirts and badges? He'll want another set-up fee if we redesign. A bleeding flower? Is that what they all think?

09:59 Kevin wrote:
Let's say Poppy drew it.

FROM: Sarah-Jane MacDonald
SUBJECT: What!?
DATE: 9 June 2018 at 10:14
TO: Isabel Beck

You sent your committee minutes to everyone in The Fairway Players! No one told you to do that. There's all sorts of nonsense in there that we never even mentioned at the meeting. What's more, it's full of your opinions. That's not the point of the minutes. No one cares what you think.
Sarah-Jane MacDonald

FROM: Isabel Beck
SUBJECT: Re: What!?
DATE: 9 June 2018 at 10:29
TO: Sarah-Jane MacDonald

Hiya SJ! I took the initiative because the document includes details of Sam's half-marathon tomorrow. Don't worry, I removed all mention of the special surprise I'm preparing for her! She's already got 115% of her target, but it's for Poppy's appeal, so I wanted to make sure everyone has a chance to donate. I'm so proud to be trusted with the minutes that I want everyone to know! Thinking about it, I suppose I could have just sent an email about the half-marathon to everyone, but that's not really my place. This way everyone gets the minutes and a reminder to sponsor Sam. How did Harley's swim go? Love Issy xxx

---

FROM: Sarah-Jane MacDonald
SUBJECT: Sorry
DATE: 9 June 2018 at 10:30
TO: James Hayward

Sorry, James, you'll have received a copy of the unofficial minutes last night. Take no notice of them. They are full of rambling nonsense, half of which wasn't even discussed. Please tell your dad and Paige to ignore them, too. I'm sending out my own update today. I think a message from your mum to motivate the fundraising team will be a nice touch – is she still *sans* mobile and email?

FROM: James Hayward
SUBJECT: Re: Sorry
DATE: 9 June 2018 at 10:42
TO: Sarah-Jane MacDonald

Yes, Mum remains firmly in the twentieth century as far as communications go. Poppy had some kind of reaction to her last chemo and they're back at Mount More again today, so call on Paige's mobile – earlier rather than later, so they're not in the middle of their appointment. Yes, those minutes made me chuckle. Isabel is a dark horse. I always thought there was more to her than meets the eye. I doubt Paige or Dad have opened the document, to be honest. Olivia and I are just leaving for St Ann's, as she's been up all night feeling rotten. Thanks, Sarah-Jane, I don't know what we'd do without you. James

---

FROM: Isabel Beck
SUBJECT: Only 22 hours!
DATE: 9 June 2018 at 10:45
TO: Samantha Greenwood

Morning! Just twenty-two hours to go! I hope you're not too worried. If you fancy a chat, then I'm in all day, so just call. It's a shame we don't live nearer each other or I could pop round. I sent the minutes to everyone, like you suggested – when they see your run is tomorrow, they may be spurred into sponsoring you. Sarah-Jane was delighted, as it saved her the job of sending them. I've been refreshing the fundraising page for an hour now. No new sponsors yet. It's still early, though. I'll text if any more donations come in. Is Kel looking forward to spectating as much as I am? My bag is packed – will add my vitamin shake from the fridge on Sunday morning and have set a reminder on my phone for that, so I'm all ready. Thanks for picking me up. I'll wait on the wall outside the block, so you don't have to get out of the car. See you at 7.30 a.m. Love Issy xxx

FROM: A Cure for Poppy
SUBJECT: Fundraising Update
DATE: 9 June 2018 at 11:21
TO: Full mailing list

A Cure for Poppy Fundraising Update

This update replaces the unofficial minutes sent in error last night

Dear Friends,

Thank you for your continued support. We are pleased to say the fundraising committee is now in place, with many planned activities over the next few weeks. If you are able to help at any event, or would like to sell merchandise and/or raffle tickets at your school or place of work, just let us know.

Looking smart for Poppy

Get your beautiful A Cure for Poppy T-shirts, so you stand out when collecting for the appeal. These eye-catching garments feature a sweet little logo drawn by Poppy herself, and the all-important crowdfunding web page, so an excellent awareness-raising opportunity. If you'd like to order your fundraising outfit, complete the form below.

Sponsorship news

- Harley MacDonald successfully swam to Pirate's Island – and back again – with the Otters Swimming Club yesterday.
- Samantha Greenwood is running the Lockwood Half-Marathon on Sunday.
- Gavin Hoyte is cycling from Land's End to John O'Groats next month.
- Barry Walford is holding an Elvis Cookathon that's sure to raise both money and cholesterol.
- Beth Halliday and friends are Baking Off against cancer and selling their showstopper cakes.
- Just click on the fundraising links to donate. And if you are planning a big event and wish to collect sponsorship for us, you will qualify for a merchandising welcome pack of T-shirt, pen and keyring, plus publicity through the campaign's mailing list. Just let us know!

The Big Raffle

With a host of prizes, including membership of The Grange for a month, a golf lesson, a case of champagne and a weekend for two in Paris, the Big Raffle for Poppy will launch next week. Tickets come in books of ten, priced at £10 per ticket. We would encourage everyone to commit to selling at least five books over four weeks. The Big Draw will take place on the final night of The Fairway Players' next production, *All My Sons*, hopefully drawn by BBC Radio 4's Cameron Hilford.

And finally . . .

A message from Helen Grace-Hayward: 'Dear friends, earlier this week Poppy sat on my lap as a tube attached to a port in her chest pumped a toxic soup of chemicals into her body and said, "Granny, I am so happy." I asked what had made her so happy and she said "the sun". My heart leapt there and then. Only our closest friends and family know this, but many years ago I had a beautiful, handsome little boy who died of meningitis at the age of four. Of course Poppy meant the "sun", not "son", but still, there are times when I feel his spirit is with me, and that was one of them. Something I have always hoped for in life is that my daughter Paige never has to endure what I went through all those years ago, and yet here we are. Poor Poppy. The side-effects of her chemo are starting to take hold, and it won't be long before our angel's beautiful hair has all gone. We are also facing the fact that her eyesight will be affected – which makes every day that she can still see all the more poignant. We are so lucky to be surrounded by people who know what true friendship means. What can I say but "thank you"?'

You are receiving this email because you have supported A Cure for Poppy or expressed an interest in joining our mailing list. If you no longer wish to receive these updates, please click here.

FROM: Marianne Payne
SUBJECT: Helen
DATE: 9 June 2018 at 14:21
TO: Carol Dearing

Did you know the Haywards lost a little boy? When Mick and I first moved here and our Karen was born, James was a toddler and Paige a babe in arms. I remember Paige was poorly early on, with asthma first, then a stomach problem. Poor Helen, it must've brought back all that happened with the boy. Luckily, Paige grew out of it and thrived. Nobody mentioned another child, but those were different times and people didn't talk about such things, did they? Poor little mite. Marianne

---

FROM: Carol Dearing
SUBJECT: Re: Helen
DATE: 9 June 2018 at 14:59
TO: Marianne Payne

I didn't know, but it doesn't surprise me. Helen was married before she met Martin. She's mentioned that several times. They must've been very young, and now I suspect a shotgun wedding. If the child died, it's no wonder the marriage didn't last. It's a credit to Helen that she didn't wallow, but moved on and gave Paige and James the happy life her little boy never had. Times were not only different, they were better. No crying on social media or going on telly to sue the hospital. Head up and get on with life. It's no one else's problem or business. That's the way it should be. Carol

---

FROM: Jackie Marsh
SUBJECT: Re: Fundraising Update
DATE: 9 June 2018 at 15:13
TO: A Cure for Poppy

Landed Indonesia. Hot rain! Boom! Hope Poppy's better x

Sent from my Samsung Galaxy S9
Lookie lookie leather bags wallet shoos genuine $10 no-fake www.xclbargain.com today all

---

FROM: John O'Dea
SUBJECT: Re: Fundraising Update
DATE: 9 June 2018 at 17:00
TO: A Cure for Poppy

Are raffle tickets £1 each or £10 a book? You've put £10 each and that can't be right.

FROM: Isabel Beck
SUBJECT: Not long now!
DATE: 9 June 2018 at 13:00
TO: Samantha Greenwood

Hiya Sam! Just 20 hours to go! Just think, this time tomorrow we'll all be celebrating. I've found your name on the Lockwood Half-Marathon website. Did you realise you have a microchip in your race number that gives you an exact time? I've registered for an email, so when you finish I can confirm your actual time. It's a shame we can't have buttercup T-shirts for the day, but Sarah-Jane said they're not ready until next week, boo. I wonder if you'll qualify for a free gift pack, even though your event will be over? Don't mention it yourself. I'll approach Sarah-Jane in my role as committee minute-taker and see if I can swing it for you. Not that you'd want to wear that T-shirt at anything other than a fundraising event, but it'll be ok as a nightie. Gasp! I've had an idea! Once the money's raised – and it won't be long now, surely – everyone will be stuck with T-shirts they'll never wear again. Could we donate them to Africa? I know! Let's collect unwanted T-shirts and take them to Africa together. We can make a little holiday of it. You can show me around and get us from place to place, and I'll look after the paperwork. What do you think? Poor Helen. I had no idea she'd lost a little boy. Meningitis, though. Terrible. Do you ever wonder why some families are dogged by tragedy their whole lives, while others sail through with not so much as a scratch? Well, have a lovely day and I'll see you at 7.30 a.m. tomorrow! Love Issy xxx

PS I'll have a big bag with me. It's got your surprise in it. Just pretend it's not there!

FROM: IPS Marathon Timing
SUBJECT: Lockwood Half-Marathon Results
DATE: 10 June 2018 at 12:23
TO: Samantha Greenwood

You completed the Lockwood Half-Marathon sponsored by Dean Fitzpatrick Motors in

1 HOUR 55 MINUTES 31 SECONDS

This is your official chip time and may differ from independent timing devices.

FROM: Claudia D'Souza
SUBJECT: Well done you
DATE: 10 June 2018 at 18:46
TO: Samantha Greenwood

Dear Sam,

It was lovely to see you and Kel today. You looked completely relaxed as you crossed the line and must be absolutely thrilled to have finished in under two hours, after all. It's a great achievement, especially as you hadn't run seriously for years. So, is it the big 26.2 next?

Had a chat with Kel as we were waiting for you to come in. Who'd have thought his family and mine would both come from the same town in Ireland? He's so easy to talk to and very entertaining! I must say it's good of you both to help your friend Arnie like that. When does he arrive? I'm sure it's not easy to find a new normal after an experience as intense as Africa and, as Kel says, psychiatric staff can be the last to spot danger signs in their own mental health. How long is he staying? If he's a Band 4 ... well, between St Ann's and Mount More there are opportunities all the time, including flexi and maternity cover. Something finite and low-stress, to get him back in the swing. Perhaps I can keep an eye out? I'll stay in touch with Kel about it. Alternatively I can recommend a good supply agency. Of course, only when he's ready.

One last thing, Sam: who on earth was that girl you'd brought? Kel introduced her as your friend from work, so I'm guessing she's the one you were telling me about. If looks could kill, my funeral is any day now. She ignored me the whole time. Then in the Cat & Castle, when you two were at the bar, I tried to strike up a conversation – it was a lesson in one-word answers. I asked what was in that huge bag; she muttered 'nothing' and, as we were leaving, I saw her dump it in the bin outside. I feel sorry for her, but it's no wonder she's falling prey to workplace bullies when she doesn't make the least effort to engage with others. Some people have 'victim' written all over them.

Thanks again for a lovely Sunday and good luck with your post-race muscle recovery programme. One of these days I may join you for a run . . . That is a blatant lie. Well done again and see you in the week. C x

---

FROM: Daniel Bhatoa
SUBJECT:
DATE: 10 June 2018 at 18:59
TO: Tish Bhatoa

Are Mum and Dad ok? I keep meaning to pop back and see them, but haven't managed to get away. Are you still ok to pay for everything? I'm a long way away, but I can tell you're shouldering the responsibility, Tish, and I appreciate it. I heard from Rav a while ago, but he constantly tries to make me feel guilty and I couldn't bring myself to reply.

It's back to normal here in Bangui. Another ebola scare came to nothing, but we're just as full with regular gynae and paediatrics. There's been limited military presence in the area since Christmas, and some days you'd think no conflict had ever happened, then we'll get an influx of injuries from neighbouring regions and it hits home again. Some good news: the FGM lobby is funding our outreach clinic for another year, possibly two. Proof we're over the worst, in terms of our reputation. I'd invite you over, but it's not stable enough right now. Keep me posted on M&D. Dan

---

FROM: Tish Bhatoa
SUBJECT: Re:
DATE: 10 June 2018 at 19:23
TO: Daniel Bhatoa

It's so good to hear from you and know you're safe. M&D are well enough, photos attached. I wish you could see this home. It's in a beautiful setting and so English – Mum loves it! You'd think it was a spa hotel if you didn't look closely. They have a hydrotherapy pool, a nutritionist and extensive cultivated gardens. Mum and Dad live together in their own unit and have 24-hour care. Very reassuring. The staff are excellent. Now Dad's that much worse, they appreciate how lonely it can be for Mum, so they help her socialise with other residents while Dad is looked after. It's not considered the best place in the UK for nothing and not the most expensive for nothing, either, but worth every penny.

Dan, don't feel guilty. You have work to do out there. M&D know and love you for it, and so do I. If Dad hadn't been forced to leave Uganda, he would've done exactly as you're doing. It's just he met Mum and they had the three of us – so his life went in a different direction – but you're living his dream every single day, remember that. Rav can think what he likes, but he visits them twice a week and that's more than I have time for, so let's not be too hard on him, either. Stay in touch. Tish

Transcription from a handwritten notebook found in Isabel Beck's flat:

Dear Sam,

This is the first entry in my Blue Book since you arrived at St Ann's. The last time I even opened it was back in February, when Fucking Frances took everyone for a birthday drink at the end of shift and didn't invite me. I shouldn't have reread that just now. I'm supposed to write it all down, turn the page and pull the elastic band across, so the whole episode is over and done with. Only I wanted to see how far I've come – or thought I'd come – since then. Surely I can't be right back there? WHO IS CLAUDIA? WHO IS CLAUDIA? WHO IS CLAUDIA? WHO IS CLAUDIA? WHO IS CLAUDIA? Kel said she's your friend from work. Well, I'm your friend from work. If she's your friend, why haven't you mentioned her to me? When Kel introduced me, she said in that confident, dismissive way: 'Oh yes, Sam told me about you.' What did you tell her? That we're best friends? That we're inseparable? That we have so much in common it's like we're secret sisters? That we're planning a trip to Africa together and don't need anyone else?

I know the type of person Claudia is. She'll worm her way into your life and then edge out your true friends, so she's the only one left; like a cuckoo chick in a sparrow's nest. She'll isolate you from everyone who cares about you and then you'll be dependent on her, which makes her feel powerful, which is what she wants.

You see this is what I shouldn't do. I shouldn't let my mind race ahead into what may happen. I AM NOT BACK WHERE I WAS IN FEBRUARY. When I've finished this entry I'm going to turn the page, pull the elastic band over it, put the Blue Book out of reach and act as if you haven't hurt me at all. I'm going to be an even better friend to you than I was BC (before Claudia) and make sure you see what a fraud she is. I love life now, Sam, and don't want to live if you're not my friend.

Issy

FROM: Isabel Beck
SUBJECT: Sam!
DATE: 10 June 2018 at 19:40
TO: Sarah-Jane MacDonald

Hi SJ, fantastic news! Sam completed her half-marathon this morning in just 1 hour 55 minutes and 31 seconds. She raised £575 for Poppy, which is absolutely brilliant! It's so kind of her, especially as she's only just arrived here and barely knows us. You said the buttercup merchandise hasn't arrived yet, but when it has, do you agree it would be a good idea to let Sam have a free fundraising pack? It would be such a lovely touch and may better dispose her to do more fundraising work in future. If you could let *me* know rather than Sam, that would be great. Thanks, SJ! Love Issy xxxx

---

FROM: Isabel Beck
SUBJECT: Yay!
DATE: 10 June 2018 at 19:48
TO: Samantha Greenwood

Hiya Sam! I'm *so* proud of my best friend. It's an honour to be her training support executive. Are you feeling sore this morning? My guess is no, because I've read it's the *second* day after a big race that's worse than the first, as lactic acid builds up in the tendons. Apparently blueberries and pomegranate will help heal the muscles. Don't worry, I'll stop off at Tesco on my way to work tomorrow – you can count on me to look after you! Thank you again for the lift. I had a surprise planned, but didn't get a chance to reveal it. It doesn't matter. There's always next time.

I met Claudia, who seems absolutely lovely. She was very friendly with Kel (some women are like that – they relate better to men than other women), so they had a nice chat while we were waiting for you to cross the line. I didn't get a chance to speak to her myself, but she's given up a Sunday to watch you run even though she has two children, so she must have an unhappy home life. Did you notice that before we ate she said she was starving, but only ordered a side-salad and then described herself as having 'stuffed her face'? I wonder if she has an eating disorder. It's very common among women like that.

I've emailed Sarah-Jane and am sure she'll agree to you receiving a free fundraising pack retrospectively. I put forward a good case. Even SJ can't argue with the £575 we've raised. I'll let you know what she says. Congratulations again on your run and we'll catch up at work tomorrow. Splits, boo, but at least we can make rehearsal! Love Issy xxx

---

FROM: Lydia Drake
SUBJECT: Today
DATE: 11 June 2018 at 13:40
TO: Martin Hayward

Dear Martin,
It was a pleasure to meet you today and discuss your granddaughter's appeal. Please find attached my projections, based on the initial investment discussed. As you'll see, I anticipate reaching your goal in approximately four weeks, but this would depend on your committing to the fund and transferring the initial stake by the end of this week, ideally sooner. I'll be in touch.

Yours sincerely, Lydia Drake

FROM: Martin Hayward
SUBJECT: Today
DATE: 11 June 2018 at 13:46
TO: Lydia Drake

Dear Lydia,
Likewise, it was a pleasure to meet you too. As discussed, I have transferred the initial stake and look forward to receiving the funds as soon as possible.

Regards, Martin Hayward

FROM: Isabel Beck
SUBJECT: Poppy
DATE: 11 June 2018 at 13:53
TO: Lauren Malden

When you worked at St Ann's did you ever speak to a woman in HR called Claudia? Dark hair, hollow eyes, looks like a skeleton. She's hanging around Sam, making a nuisance of herself. She ruined her half-marathon day by tagging along to the pub afterwards, when Sam had done so well to get a good time. I was gutted for her. It's funny how some people don't know when they're not wanted. I'm not a confrontational person, but if it gets worse I'll have to say something – out of loyalty to Sam. As you know, I take my friendships seriously.

FROM: Lauren Malden
SUBJECT: Re: Poppy
DATE: 11 June 2018 at 14:03
TO: Isabel Beck

Hello lovely!
Yes, I had Claudia for appraisals a couple of times. She was absolutely awful. Uninterested. Inefficient. Just not very nice. How horrible for Sam. Lucky she's got you to look after her. Did you want to meet up while Josh is away? Let me know, sweetie. Kiss kiss, L xxx

---

FROM: Sarah-Jane MacDonald
SUBJECT: Re: Sam!
DATE: 11 June 2018 at 15:47
TO: Isabel Beck

It's a Welsh poppy, not a buttercup, and the idea is we *sell* the merchandise, not give it away.
Sarah-Jane MacDonald

FROM: Isabel Beck
SUBJECT: Re: Sam!
DATE: 11 June 2018 at 15:52
TO: Sarah-Jane MacDonald

Hiya SJ, of course! I'll pay for Sam's fundraising pack myself. Please don't mention to her that I've bought it, just give it to her at rehearsal tonight as if it's from you. I'll pay you when she's onstage and we're in the green room. I know she'll be so pleased. She'll probably want to do more fundraising events for Poppy. Money well spent. Love Issy xxx

---

FROM: Tish Bhatoa
SUBJECT: Warning
DATE: 11 June 2018 at 18:11
TO: Daniel Bhatoa

I wanted to mention something in my last email, but didn't want to worry you when you were already concerned about M&D. But I've thought some more and decided I should tell you, in case you hear some other way – Samantha Greenwood has popped up again. She's got a job at the big general here. I don't know if that's a coincidence or not, but she's certainly out to cause trouble for me and has made at least two attempts so far – with the BMA and my private patients. This is to let you know I am more than ready and will protect you from her, too. We have the truth on our side, and the truth is strong. Lies are weak, and lies are all she has. Look after yourself. Tish

Charlotte
Are you clear how much money is raised? Is it important? We don't have much time and I don't want to waste it chewing over something that isn't key.

Femi
Tried to keep a running total, couldn't. Let's not worry about it. Tanner would've said if it was that important.

Charlotte
Ok then. Well, no one asks where the money's going, not even among themselves.

Femi
The Haywards are the alpha family. The social status of everyone else depends on being 'in' with them.

Charlotte
Tacit social hierarchy. That bitch.

Femi
Martin is clearly using the appeal to boost his own cash flow. Diverts money from his sick grandchild's appeal. That £20k invoice. The community doesn't know about that.

Charlotte
I'm not cynical or making excuses, but what do they expect? Crowdfunding campaigns are built on trust. You never really know where the cash goes. We've all contributed to friends' campaigns without asking questions.

Femi
Also, Martin contacts Clive Handler despite being assured he's a time-waster. Is that because he's desperate for money or because he doesn't trust Tish Bhatoa? Sam suspects Bhatoa, and I'm inclined to value her view as it's an outsider's perspective.

Charlotte
Sam could be blinded by whatever beef they seem to have had in Africa.

Femi
Yes. But as a wealthy family with a sick child, the Haywards are vulnerable, and fraudsters feed on vulnerability. What are the other points of vulnerability here?

Charlotte
People's fear of cancer, of a child dying. If you donate money it fends off the curse . . . Fear of falling out of favour with the alpha family, being socially excluded? There's a competitive edge to some of this fundraising, no?

Femi
So what happens when fraudsters are faced with someone who isn't vulnerable to this social pressure? An outsider. Someone who threatens their hold on everyone else?

Charlotte
You think fraud is the driving factor in this case?

Femi
Strongly suspect it is.

Charlotte
Then how does Issy fit in? She has no access to funds, no apparent money worries, no power or influence – quite the opposite. Yet there's something strange about her. The Blue Book, what do you think that is?

Femi
An emotional diary? Interesting she abandons it in February, which would be approximately when Sam joins the ward. She goes back to it when she sees Sam getting close to Claudia. It's as if she needs someone to focus on and, if that person fails her, she falls back on this Blue Book.

Charlotte
Focus on or obsess over?

Message from Barry Walford to Magda Kuchar on 12 June 2018:

07:09 Barry wrote:
Can't get in the gate. What's the deal with parking on the street? Already got nine points.

Message exchange between James Hayward and Martin Hayward on 12 June 2018:

07:15 James wrote:
On way to Olivia cranes and trucks in car park can't stop.

07:18 Martin wrote:
Yes builders. They need the car park for their gear but have strict instructions to be considerate to members. Magda and Barry will handle it.

07:22 James wrote:
They need that many JCBs? Driving so this is voice anticipated message ok if it's fine it's fine

---

FROM: Barry Walford
SUBJECT: Hey
DATE: 12 June 2018 at 07:23
TO: Martin Hayward

Hi Boss, the builders won't let us in. Can you get here soon? The guy says he'll only speak to you and he's covered in All-Ireland Boxing tattoos.

FROM: Marianne Payne
SUBJECT: The Grange
DATE: 12 June 2018 at 07:24
TO: Joyce Walford

What's happening at The Grange, Joyce? Mick said it looks like a scene from *Mad Max*. Do you know anything about it?

FROM: Joyce Walford
SUBJECT: Re: The Grange
DATE: 12 June 2018 at 07:35
TO: Marianne Payne

Yes. It's a film about a lot of old jeeps and tanks. Not our thing. You won't believe this, Marianne. I've not seen anything like this in my life. Barry sent me a picture he took with his phone. I'd put it in this email, if I knew how to. Builders have blocked the car park and won't let anyone in or out until they get paid. I told my Barry to tell them Martin has a very sick grandchild, but Barry said this fellow wouldn't be interested in Poppy unless she had the keys to his caravan. How can anyone treat the Haywards like this, when they are already going through so much? It's disgraceful.

FROM: Marianne Payne
SUBJECT: Re: The Grange
DATE: 12 June 2018 at 07:36
TO: Joyce Walford

Stay safe, Joyce. Don't get involved.

FROM: Joyce Walford
SUBJECT: Re: The Grange
DATE: 12 June 2018 at 07:37
TO: Marianne Payne

I won't. I'm on my way there now.

FROM: Callum McDaid
SUBJECT: Payment received
DATE: 12 June 2018 at 11:23
TO: Martin Hayward

Dear Martin,
Your receipt is attached. Again, I'm sorry to cause your staff distress this morning, but when a client has a history of litigation we have to look after our own interests and ensure they don't default. Jonno and the boys are

now stuck into the next stage of the project. On another matter, you're right about the fence Whites put up round the golf course. It won't last five minutes. Callum

---

FROM: Isabel Beck
SUBJECT: Hiya!
DATE: 12 June 2018 at 13:14
TO: James Hayward

Hiya James, hope Olivia and the bumps are ok. Sam, Kel and I are really looking forward to the play. I can't believe it's so soon and will be over so quickly. The trouble is, if this year is anything like last, The Fairways won't meet again until September. That means three months with no rehearsals, boo! I know you and Olivia will be busy for the next few weeks, but perhaps your mum and dad might like to run drama evenings where we act out bits of plays or do exercises (like we did when that drama-teacher friend of Paige's came to the rehearsal during *Blithe Spirit*). I know the three of us would like to do something over the summer. As you can see, I like to plan ahead. Love to Olivia and the bumps. Issy xxx

---

FROM: James Hayward
SUBJECT: Re: Hiya!
DATE: 12 June 2018 at 15:47
TO: Isabel Beck

Dearest Issy, unfortunately Olivia is back in St Ann's with high protein and suspected placental weakness. Chances are she'll have to stay in now, until they can deliver the babies. Not great, but you have to strap yourself in for the ride. Good idea about the drama classes, but can't see anyone being able to organise it. Mum's booked a surprise holiday to Hawaii for Dad's birthday – don't say anything to anyone, he thinks they're going to Boscombe. You could run a drama evening yourself? Paige has a library of plays she'll let you borrow. Pick a few scenes and act them out for each other – that's what the drama teacher did. James

---

FROM: Martin Hayward
SUBJECT: Builders
DATE: 12 June 2018 at 19:42
TO: James Hayward

Don't tell your mum, but I've had to pay the builders up front. In full. What you saw this morning was an attempt to bully money out of us and I'm afraid it worked. I should have called the police, but all I could think of at the time was to get these vehicles out of the car park and the builders back to work. I didn't see it coming. We've had Callum before and he was a decent chap, as well as a good builder. In hindsight, I shouldn't have told him about our legal action against Whites. So, the builders are paid a few weeks sooner than anticipated, but how can I trust Callum again? He could demand more money at any time. Why is everything about money? Regards.

FROM: James Hayward
SUBJECT: Re: Builders
DATE: 12 June 2018 at 19:47
TO: Martin Hayward

For heaven's sake don't get the police involved. You sorted the problem. Forget about it. Not everything's about money. St Ann's is keeping Olivia in, maybe until they can deliver the twins. They suspect her placenta is beginning to fail. Can you take the rehearsal tonight, please, Dad? They're off the book and should focus on Act Two. Mum knows the schedule. James

---

FROM: Martin Hayward
SUBJECT: Re: Builders
DATE: 12 June 2018 at 19:56
TO: James Hayward

Of course. Hope they are all ok. Actually, that is about money too. I remember paying a vast amount on top of already extortionate fees to supposedly get viable embryos that wouldn't cause all this grief. I remember that's where all this started.

FROM: Martin Hayward
SUBJECT: Re: Builders
DATE: 12 June 2018 at 19:57
TO: James Hayward

I didn't mean that to come across as it did.

FROM: Daniel Bhatoa
SUBJECT: Re: Warning
DATE: 12 June 2018 at 20:00
TO: Tish Bhatoa

Hi Tish, only just got our connection back up after a flood at the power plant upriver. I'm seething that she's going for you now. What motivates these people? Tell St Ann's and get rid of her. Don't put up with her bullying. Dan

---

FROM: Tish Bhatoa
SUBJECT: Re: Warning
DATE: 12 June 2018 at 21:03
TO: Daniel Bhatoa

She knows I could click my fingers and she'd be gone in an instant – but I'd rather keep her in sight – for the moment anyway. She's not the only one with a grudge. Tish

---

FROM: Isabel Beck
SUBJECT: Ideas!
DATE: 13 June 2018 at 11:51
TO: Samantha Greenwood

Hiya Sam, I'm queuing in Radiology with Mrs Petit. She hasn't woken up yet. It doesn't look good. I overheard Kel mention his friend from Africa – it's very nice of you to invite him to stay. Perhaps he'd like to join The Fairways? With the play in just three weeks there'll be lots of little jobs he could do. I'll find out from Martin. With all the excitement of your half-marathon, we've neglected our word rehearsals and it's

Act Two tonight, gulp! Shall we spend lunch in the roof garden going through our scenes, just you and me? Then tomorrow we can get back to our jogging sessions. If we alternate jogging and word rehearsals each lunchtime from now until the play, we'll have a perfect balance between mind and body, ready for the whirlwind of play week. You've never been in a play before, so I can't wait for you both to experience it! It's hard work to fit around shifts, and you won't know what's hit you, but so rewarding when you hear the audience applaud at the end and they all come up to you afterwards and say how well you did . . . See you by the lift at 2.30 p.m. Love Issy xxx

---

FROM: Sarah-Jane MacDonald
SUBJECT: Merchandise
DATE: 13 June 2018 at 12:00
TO: Martin Hayward

Dear Martin, the Poppy merchandise has just arrived. The delivery men piled it up in our office, but it can't stay there – do you have room for it at The Grange? There'll be about sixty boxes after I've distributed the stock that people want to sell at their workplaces. Kevin will take some to his Lodge – we desperately need to inspire high-net-worth individuals to make substantial donations. Bring the appeal cheque book tonight, as I've had to pay the merchandising company myself. Samantha Greenwood raised over £500 on her run. She clearly has a great many people who know and trust her. I'd be happy to let her on the committee in future.
Sarah-Jane MacDonald

FROM: Isabel Beck
SUBJECT: Ideas!
DATE: 13 June 2018 at 13:05
TO: Samantha Greenwood

Hiya Sam! You didn't mention your lunch appointment before . . . but that's fine, I'll learn lines on my own. I know no one will talk to me if I stay in the staffroom. We'll start our jogging/rehearsal programme from tomorrow. Good luck at the dentist. Hope you don't need any fillings. Love Issy xxx

---

FROM: Tish Bhatoa
SUBJECT: Phials
DATE: 13 June 2018 at 13:16
TO: Martin Hayward

Dear Martin,
The drug combination is formulated and packaged, ready for transportation to the UK. All I need now is the remaining £125,000 to instigate the exportation process. The contents of the phials will oxidise in two months, so I would recommend paying sooner rather than later, to avoid delays at Customs. Let me know when you're about to transfer the funds – the same account as before, details below. Best wishes, Tish

---

Message exchange between Martin Hayward and Tish Bhatoa on 13 June 2018:

13:24 Martin wrote:
Can we delay our next payment by a few weeks? Cash flow. We've had to invest in merchandise and other unforeseen aspects of the fundraising process. It will start flowing again, I know.

13:30 Tish wrote:
Well, how much *can* you pay now?

13:33 Martin wrote
Nothing. I have absolutely no money at this moment in time.

13:36 Tish wrote:
I'm confused. We need to meet.

DRAFTS FOLDER:
FROM: Isabel Beck
SUBJECT:
DATE: 13 June 2018 at 14:27
TO: Samantha Greenwood

I had lunch in the roof garden and read through the script on my own. I don't have a very big part, though, so I spent some time looking over the rail at the scenery. It's surprising how far you can see from up here: all the way to the terrace at the Orangery. I ate three muffins from the kiosk and felt sick, so I went home. I hate Claudia, I hate myself and I hate

---

Message exchange between Kevin MacDonald and Sarah-Jane MacDonald on 13 June 2018:

16:18 Kevin wrote:
Spent the afternoon with Colin Brasher. Got a tech business. Minted. Google him, he's interesting. His twin brother died of a brain tumour at three. This could be it.

16:27 Sarah-Jane wrote:
Good work. Impress upon him the *urgency*. I'll meet him, if need be. Don't mention it to the Haywards yet – don't want another Handlergate. Make sure you pick Harley up on time – his tutor has to leave dead on five.

FROM: Arnie Ballancore
SUBJECT: Like the old days
DATE: 13 June 2018 at 16:30
TO: Kel Greenwood

Hello mate. Booked my train. Should be at yours by six. If you're not there I'll wait outside. Really grateful to you, Kel, and Sam too. I won't be there for long; it's just I wasn't getting on with Mum, she was doing my head in, you know what family are like. Is Sam ok with talking about what happened in Bangui etc., or should I keep quiet about all that? Don't want to stir up old trauma or the like. Fair enough, if not. Move on, life's too short. See you later, mate.

FROM: Claudia D'Souza
SUBJECT: Thanks
DATE: 13 June 2018 at 16:37
TO: Samantha Greenwood

Dear Sam,
Thank you for that lovely unexpected lunch at the Orangery. I've looked into it and you're right, I can organise intern days in other wards for staff interested in a transfer. It's not something I've ever done before. I don't think people realise they can. Is Isabel that keen on Oncology or are you simply desperate to get rid of her? Either way, I can liaise with my counterpart in HR at Mount More and see what he says. Does it have to be a Thursday? Thanks again for lunch, and hope Kel's friend arrives safely. C x

---

FROM: Isabel Beck
SUBJECT: So low and poorly
DATE: 13 June 2018 at 16:46
TO: Samantha Greenwood

I don't feel well, so I've gone home early. I was gutted not to see you this lunchtime. Really low. Perhaps if we'd had lunch together I'd have felt better. Hardly anyone else in Geriatrics speaks to me, so when you're not there I'm on my own. It gets me down. I'm going to stay in bed tomorrow and read through my lines. Please say we'll have lunch together on Friday. If I've got something to look forward to, it would make me feel life is worth living. How about the Orangery? Issy x

---

FROM: Sarah-Jane MacDonald
SUBJECT: Poppy Reswick
DATE: 14 June 2018 at 15:23
TO: Colin Brasher

Dear Colin, Many thanks for meeting me today and discussing the possibility of donating to Poppy Reswick's appeal. Any substantial

donation like this will make a real difference to a young life. You know yourself the impact of such an illness on those left behind. As we discussed, a previous disappointment with a potential donor who turned out to be a hoax has shaken the family up. I can certainly forward the emails to you and see if your IT people can trace who he is. I'm sure no actual crime has taken place, but if it's someone known to the family, at least they'll be aware and can avoid them in future. In the meantime, if you require any further information to aid your final decision, please do not hesitate to contact me. Yours sincerely,
Sarah-Jane MacDonald

FROM: Claudia D'Souza
SUBJECT: Stuff
DATE: 14 June 2018 at 16:11
TO: Samantha Greenwood

Dear Sam,
I've been looking into this work-placement day and have come up against a problem. How well do you know Isabel Beck? Are you aware she's on disciplinary probation and has been turned down for a transfer already in the last year? I've been speaking to her acting representative, who couldn't say any more as it's confidential. The placement is out of the question for a few months anyway. Hope you're not too disappointed. C x

---

FROM: Claudia D'Souza
SUBJECT: Re: Stuff
DATE: 14 June 2018 at 16:31
TO: Samantha Greenwood

Well, I can speak to Una direct and see if she or a colleague will give Isabel a quick tour, but can't guarantee it'll be a Monday or Thursday. Let me have her email address and they can liaise directly with her. Why the urgency? Is she that unbearable? C x

---

FROM: Isabel Beck
SUBJECT: Re: hello
DATE: 14 June 2018 at 14:48
TO: Samantha Greenwood

Hiya Sam! GASP! Of *course* you can come round! I'd love to see you! That would make me feel sooo much better, thank you! You must've picked up on the tone of my last email. I've been feeling so low. Thank you for supporting me. OMG I can show you my little flat. It's so cosy. If you could come round in an hour, that will give me time to hoover, tidy up and pop to the shop for some biscuits. Yippee! I feel better already! Issy xxxxxxxx

---

FROM: Paige Reswick
SUBJECT: Poppy
DATE: 14 June 2018 at 14:59
TO: Dr Tish Bhatoa

Dear Tish, Poppy is due another chemo treatment on Thursday, but Mum and I are worried, as she hasn't lost her hair. Does this mean the chemo isn't getting through her system? You see children with cancer and not even their eyelashes or eyebrows survive the treatment. I think everyone expects a child with cancer to be completely bald. It seems a bit strange that she's not. We've got a wig from The Little Princess Trust, but she can't really wear it yet, so I've bought some Disney bandanas instead. She looks so sweet in them – photo attached. Paige x

---

FROM: Dr Tish Bhatoa
SUBJECT: Re: Poppy
DATE: 14 June 2018 at 16:18
TO: Paige Reswick

Hair loss is not a common side-effect of this particular chemotherapy. It's nothing to be concerned about. Focus on raising money for the new combination. That's the best use of your energy at the moment.

FROM: Isabel Beck
SUBJECT: Hiya!
DATE: 14 June 2018 at 19:02
TO: Samantha Greenwood

Thank you *so* much for coming round to cheer me up – I've never felt so cheered up in my life! You're the best friend I've ever had. I hereby totally forgive you for lying about the dentist. No one else has ever cared so much about me to do anything like this on my behalf. Did Claudia say she would speak to you-know-who herself? So she'll say 'other members of staff' have noticed how horrible she is to me and have reported her? That way, she won't think it's me. I can't say anything myself. She can turn something round in an instant and make *me* the baddie. Everyone else is automatically on her side. It's only having you working there that's stopped me killing myself these last few months. Because when you stand up for me, it's different. People take notice. I'm walking on air! I can't believe you would do this for me! Wheeeeeeee! That's me doing a little dance of happiness!

Would you consider applying for her job when she goes? We work so well together and make an excellent team, but you'd also be a fantastic ward manager. I'd be working for you – imagine that! A rehearsal for when we take T-shirts to Africa together. You'll be in charge, but I'll be your second in command. I hope Arnie settles in quickly. If your flat gets too crowded with three of you there, you can always come to mine. I'll sleep on the sofa and you can have the bed. I'm not even joking – it would be a pleasure! Thank you for being a wonderful friend. I'm so lucky to have you! Love Issy xxx

---

FROM: Christine Ballancore
SUBJECT: Arnold
DATE: 14 June 2018 at 19:56
TO: Kel Greenwood

Dear Mr Greenwood,
We haven't met, but I'm Arnie's mother. I found your email address on his old laptop, which a neighbour managed to get going. Arnie tells me he will

be staying with you for a while. I very much hope this is true, but sadly I can't trust what he says these days. If you *are* a psychiatric nurse he met in the CAR, I hope and pray you can help my son.

I believe he was the happiest he's ever been as an MSF volunteer and often says he wishes he could go back – the problems began on his return; he found adjusting to life at home very difficult. His mental health has been in decline these last few months and I've had no help from social services, even when his behaviour became aggressive. If you know my son, he is very good at masking his true mental state and even managed to work in Vietnam for a while. Unfortunately, that is where he started using heroin. Please be aware he is self-medicating with opioids and is in desperate need of professional help. It is my hope that you will be able to get him the medical support he needs. Whatever that entails, please, please do it. My contact details are below.

Yours sincerely,
Christine Ballancore

FROM: MAILER-DAEMON Kel Greenwood
SUBJECT: Re: Arnold
DATE: 14 June 2018 at 19:57
TO: Christine Ballancore

[Failure notice] Sorry we were unable to deliver your message. Address unknown.

FROM: The Fairway Players Admin
SUBJECT: All My Sons
DATE: 15 June 2018 at 10:47
TO: Current Members

Dear all,

How time flies! Rehearsals for *All My Sons* are moving into their final phase, as the bleary eyes of anyone in the cast will tell you. We are now rehearsing three times a week, off the book, and running through the whole play each time. All that hard work is not for nothing. If we can clock up three full houses in a row, then each and every one of those late nights and exhausting technical rehearsals will have been worthwhile. So, there is just one word that counts: Tickets!

Tickets are £10 each. All profits will be donated to Poppy's appeal. Your guests will enjoy not only an evening of classic American drama, but also the knowledge they have contributed to an excellent cause so close to the hearts of many long-standing and hard-working Fairway Players.

So, invite your friends, family, neighbours and work colleagues to purchase their tickets as soon as possible. The online link is below, but for those who would rather interact with a human, Celia Halliday is running the box office as usual. Her number is also below.

Meanwhile, as ever, we need all hands on deck to help out on the nights. There's the bar to be tended, programmes to be sold, teas to be made, and chairs and ramps to be set up and taken down at the start and end of every performance. Joel is coordinating front-of-house, so even if you can't attend the performances, an hour or two here and there will still help us.

Finally, we would like to remind everyone that this production is extra-special in that we will be selling merchandise for Poppy, so any help with that will be very much appreciated.

We look forward to seeing you all on, or before, 5, 6 and 7 July.

The Fairway Players Committee

FROM: Isabel Beck
SUBJECT: Re: All My Sons
DATE: 15 June 2018 at 18:44
TO: Joel Halliday

Dear Joel,
Sorry to bother you. I haven't had a chance to speak to you at rehearsals, but before all the jobs are snapped up, I wonder if there's anything Sam and Kel's friend Arnie could do? He's staying with them for a bit and will probably be at a loose end while they're busy with the play. I haven't met him yet, so I've no idea if he's best suited to hauling ramps or selling programmes, but between you and me, he's been a bit low since coming back from Africa. They are keen to get him involved in the local community – and I'm keen to help them help him! Let me know what you think he could do, and I'll pass the details on. Good luck to Beth for her Bake Off. I don't want to spoil my diet, so I'll give it a miss myself, but I'm sure she won't have any trouble selling all the cakes. Love Issy x

---

FROM: Martin Hayward
SUBJECT: Re: Merchandise
DATE: 15 June 2018 at 19:00
TO: Sarah-Jane MacDonald

Dear Sarah-Jane,
Thank you for the merchandise. I stacked some boxes in the extension, then drove the rest to The Grange, where I just managed to squeeze it in. Magda made a display in reception with what doesn't fit in the staffroom. Let's hope it sells quickly.

You'll have heard Olivia is back in hospital, possibly until the twins are born, so I'll be sharing the director's seat with James until play nights. Not ideal, but nothing is these days. That reminds me, I need to get a motivating email out to cast and crew. So much to do. Apologies for forgetting the cheque book last night.

The first dose of Poppy's drug combination has been formulated and is awaiting shipment, so as soon as we've generated another £125k, that can be on its way. I've been working with an investment banker who specialises in raising capital for charity funds. She is very optimistic, but we won't know how much that avenue has raised for another month at least. Hopefully it will make up for the inevitable reduction in fundraising events over the holiday season. Regards, Martin

---

FROM: Sarah-Jane MacDonald
SUBJECT: Re: Merchandise
DATE: 15 June 2018 at 19:03
TO: Martin Hayward

Martin, have you paid money to that woman who claimed to be a friend of Emma's? Because my conservative calculations put the figure raised to date at just shy of £200k, leaving us with around £50k still to raise. Please tell me you haven't given her any money.
Sarah-Jane MacDonald

FROM: Martin Hayward
SUBJECT: Re: Merchandise
DATE: 15 June 2018 at 19:09
TO: Sarah-Jane MacDonald

We met at her office on Upper Thames Street and I was suitably impressed with her portfolio. You would like her too, Sarah-Jane. She's very smart and focused, but creative at the same time; thinks outside the box. I worked in the City myself, so I know the type and they 'get things done', in your words. The trouble with this whole appeal is people have the best intentions, but they can only raise so much doing sponsored walks and selling scones. Poppy's appeal requires a really serious amount of money, and to generate that you have to invest in more productive initiatives. Regards.

FROM: Sarah-Jane MacDonald
SUBJECT: Re: Merchandise
DATE: 15 June 2018 at 19:11
TO: Martin Hayward

How much did you pay her?

FROM: Martin Hayward
SUBJECT: Re: Merchandise
DATE: 15 June 2018 at 19:17
TO: Sarah-Jane MacDonald

Only £80,000. Not the entire pot. It could raise a million in just four weeks. Even if it doesn't achieve its full potential, it will still bring in a comfortable profit. I've seen the figures and they are impressive. Regards.

Message exchange between Sarah-Jane MacDonald and Kevin MacDonald on 15 June 2018:

19:34 Sarah-Jane wrote:
Aaargh! Martin paid £80k of Poppy's fund money to a high-heeled City suit with a livery office and a get-rich-quick scheme. She pretended to know Emma (probably saw the name in the paper when we launched the appeal), said she'd raised millions for sick kids all over the world. Told Martin this £80k will turn into a million overnight. So bloody predatory she probably has a dorsal fin. What was Martin thinking? Poppy doesn't even need that much! When I think how hard it's been to raise that cash in the first place! I'm fuming.

19:49 Kevin wrote:
He's losing it, SJ. Speak to James or Paige or Helen or someone, and either get them to take control of the fund or talk Martin into letting you take control of it. What about their doctor – could she help? We're nearly there: we've told Colin Brasher £50k to buy the drugs, Poppy cured, over and done with – we can't suddenly add another £80k. I'm about to go into this dinner. Speak to James.

19:54 Sarah-Jane wrote:
Olivia's in hospital with whatever problem, so James has bailed out of life.

Paige and Helen are preoccupied with Poppy. The doctor won't know anything. Should I call the police about this woman?

FROM: Ziggy Benjamin
SUBJECT: Tour
DATE: 18 June 2018 at 14:24
TO: Issy Beck

Dear Isabel,
I understand you're visiting us this Thursday for a quick tour of the department. Please report to General Reception at the entrance to Outpatients at 10 a.m. I'll meet you there as soon as I can. As you'll know, Mount More has an extensive Oncology department, comprising inpatient and outpatient wards, as well as specialised units for radioactive, paediatric, young adults, blood cancers, acute assessment and a bone-marrow transplant unit. I'll try to get round all of them, but this may depend on what's happening at the time. I look forward to meeting you and showing you around.

Yours sincerely,
Ziggy Benjamin
Ward Manager, Oncology, Mount More Hospital

***
'ISSYS'
tour

FROM: Issy Beck
SUBJECT: Re: Tour
DATE: 18 June 2018 at 15:53
TO: Ziggy Benjamin

Dear Ziggy,
Thank you for your email. I too look forward to meeting you on Thursday and visiting Oncology. Thank you for agreeing to give me this tour at short notice.

Yours sincerely,
Issy Beck

FROM: Kevin MacDonald
SUBJECT: Charity
DATE: 18 June 2018 at 16:06
TO: Lydia Drake

Dear Ms Drake,
I am the CEO of Cornell Distribution Ltd. I understand you are a fund manager with a focus on the charity sector. My company is interested in donating £100,000 to a good cause and wonder if we could meet to discuss.

Yours sincerely,
Kevin MacDonald

FROM: Lydia Drake
SUBJECT: Re: Charity
DATE: 18 June 2018 at 16:25
TO: Kevin MacDonald

Dear Mr MacDonald,
Thank you for your email. I work exclusively with families raising funds for private medical treatment and do not have any appropriate opportunities at the moment.

Regards,
Lydia Drake

FROM: Martin Hayward
SUBJECT: Re: Merchandise
DATE: 18 June 2018 at 17:17
TO: Sarah-Jane MacDonald

Dear Sarah-Jane,
I should have told you earlier. It's just I hadn't told Helen and it didn't seem right until she knew. She knows now. £250,000 is not the total cost of Poppy's new treatment. She'll need at least four doses of this new combination – over a year or so. It's a shocking amount. More than anyone can raise. That's why I'm keen to explore potentially more lucrative, if more risky, avenues à la Lydia Drake. Please don't tell anyone about this

yet. I want this bloody play out of the way first. It's been a headache for us to keep rehearsals going, but it means a lot to Helen and in many ways has given us all a focus outside the family. Let's just get it over with now. I need to send a rallying email to the troops. James isn't around. Regards, Martin

---

Message exchange between Sarah-Jane MacDonald and Kevin MacDonald on 18 June 2018:

17:24 Sarah-Jane wrote:
See Martin's email. Explains a lot.

17:42 Kevin wrote:
A million quid for a few phials of liquid? I'm in the wrong game. *Now* what do we tell Brasher? 'Sorry, we need £750,000 more.' Why does Martin protect Helen from reality? The woman must live in a wonderland where she's forever centre-stage. As for Lydia Drake . . . I waggled £100k in front of her and she shut me down. I don't understand. Does it occur to the Haywards they could sell The Grange?

17:51 Sarah-Jane wrote:
It's frustrating, but they clearly aren't thinking straight. We've no idea what's going on with the family financially. The Grange could be mortgaged, for all we know. Helen may be emotionally fragile . . . I didn't know about the son who died. Nor did Mum, and she's known them for years. Who knows what else there may be. Let's concentrate on the play and selling the merchandise I'm yet to be paid for. After that, we can lobby to take the appeal out of Martin's hands. One step at a time. Let's get this first batch of drugs over and into Poppy. I want to stay positive, but the reality is it may not work anyway and further doses won't be necessary. Don't forget Harley's match tonight.

17:57 Kevin wrote:
While I'm speaking my mind and no one else can hear: that play is the most depressing we've ever staged. How is that making anyone feel better? Haven't forgotten the match.

FROM: Ziggy Benjamin
SUBJECT: Tour
DATE: 22 June 2018 at 13:39
TO: Claudia D'Souza

Hi Claudia, I'd like to give you some feedback from my tour with Isabel today. I'm afraid it didn't go quite to plan. Perhaps you can shed some light on it.

I showed her around the unit, starting with acute, then moving on to bloods. She was fine up to that point, very chatty and interested, but it was in paediatrics the problem started. She said she needed the loo, so I waited for her on the landing while she popped back to the stairwell washrooms. It was an *age* before she came back. I thought maybe she had an upset stomach and was embarrassed, so didn't want to make a big thing of her absence. It was only later, and quite by chance, that I discovered she hadn't been to the toilet at all, but had retraced our steps back to Paediatric Chemo, asking questions about specific patients. I'm very uncomfortable about it, as the staff there had seen her with me (in her St Ann's uniform too) and gave her the information she asked for without a second thought. It emerged later that she'd spent a good ten minutes alone on the central data system with – theoretically, as any sensitive data is password-protected – access to both staff and patient records. I know you said she's at the end of a disciplinary period: is she likely to do anything with that sort of information?

I think in future if you have staff who wish to be shown around our department, you should be there too. Ziggy

---

FROM: Claudia D'Souza
SUBJECT: Re: Tour
DATE: 22 June 2018 at 14:10
TO: Ziggy Benjamin

Dear Ziggy, I'm *so* sorry you had a problem with Isabel. I've just come off the phone to Sam and there's no need to worry at all. Isabel has a close friend whose daughter is receiving chemo in your department. I know this is true myself, as Sam mentioned it on several occasions. There's an appeal set up for her. Anyway, Isabel is taking the diagnosis very hard, as medical staff can, when illness hits them and theirs. Sam says Isabel was only after very general information about the girl's treatment plan, and in any case was hugely impressed by the department and all the staff there. Please reassure everyone that all is well. Her disciplinary period has nothing to do with misuse of data or anything of the sort. I've always found her rather aloof, but Sam works with her daily and knows her far better than I do. She rates Isabel as a nurse – and I know we can trust her opinion. I'm so sorry you've had this trouble, Ziggy, and of course I'll oversee any other ward visits in future. Claudia

---

FROM: Claudia D'Souza
SUBJECT: Thanks
DATE: 22 June 2018 at 14:14
TO: Samantha Greenwood

Hi Sam, thanks for that. I've reassured Ziggy that Isabel is just a very concerned friend. We want her to make a good impression, don't we! She said she was fine up to that point, so fingers crossed. I can just imagine Isabel wandering off gormlessly. Once her disciplinary period is lifted, I can push vacancies her way; you can say you're planning to move too, but miraculously no job ever materialises for you. It's sneaky, but a means to an end. Once she's settled in over there, she'll find someone else to cling on to and you'll finally be free of her. I'd like a ticket for the Friday night of your play, please. Michael has agreed to stay in and look after the kids. Small victories. C x

---

FROM: Isabel Beck
SUBJECT: Hiya!
DATE: 23 June 2018 at 05:45
TO: Samantha Greenwood

Yaaaaaawn! Earlies after a late rehearsal! How are you? I feel like death warmed up. Did you pick up on a vibe last night? Sarah-Jane seemed a bit off with Martin. It could be nerves. SJ is one of those who likes to be in control. Helen is amazing, though, don't you think? She plays a grieving mother with such sensitivity and conviction. Of course, now that we know she has personal experience you can see where it's coming from. Still, she's a brilliant actress.

Wasn't it lovely of Sarah-Jane to give you a free fundraising merchandising pack even though your half-marathon is over? It shows how much the family likes and respects you.

I've got my stack of raffle tickets, in case I come across anyone to sell them to at work. I'm not confident, though. I'd buy them all myself if I could afford to, just to avoid admitting I couldn't sell them. What will you do with yours?

How are you both feeling, now your first play is almost here? I was so nervous just before *Blithe Spirit*. Luckily, everyone is feeling the same, so we can all support each other. If either you or Kel can't sleep for feeling anxious in the next couple of weeks, message me and we can have a 'chat' – it doesn't matter how late. I'll leave my phone on all night in case you ding me. I was hoping to meet Arnie yesterday, but if he doesn't feel well, then it's best he has an early night. You haven't been out running since your half-marathon. Shall we get back to our lunchtime jogs soon? Going to miss you today. Lots of love, Issy xxx

---

FROM: Isabel Beck
SUBJECT: Hiya!
DATE: 23 June 2018 at 05:52
TO: James Hayward

Hi James, this is just a quick email to see how Olivia and the bumps are. Everyone is thinking about you and crossing their fingers. Also, have you thought yet about what the next play might be? As *All My Sons* is quite serious, perhaps we could do something a bit lighter . . . I saw a banner for *Confusions* by Alan Ayckbourn when the Mendham Players did it. It has a large cast of small roles – so those of us who are a bit less experienced, or newbies like Arnie, can be in it. Let me know what you think. I can order the script from Amazon and have it delivered straight to you, if you like . . . lots of love, Issy xxx

---

FROM: Isabel Beck
SUBJECT: Hiya!
DATE: 23 June 2018 at 10:47
TO: Samantha Greenwood

Hiya Sam, sorry to bother you again. Hope you're enjoying your rest day. Do you know if Claudia has spoken to you-know-who yet? We've just had the admissions and discharge meeting and she was as nasty as ever. She hasn't gone anywhere all morning, either – would Claudia speak to her after working hours or during? I really hope she is true to her word and doesn't *say* she's going to speak to her, just to keep you happy, but really has no intention ... She struck me as a people-pleaser, so it wouldn't surprise me. Perhaps you could mention it to someone else in HR just in case? I'm really missing you. Gaynor is in another mood, boo, and this is Riley's last week, so his mind is elsewhere. I wish you were down to work today. I hate it when our shifts aren't the same. Perhaps once Riley's left, you can ask YKW to tweak the roster so we always work together. We're such an awesome team, it could only be good for the ward. I'll read my script in the roof garden again this lunchtime. I know my lines, but if I don't read them every day I start to believe I've forgotten them. I might pop my head into Maternity on the way home and see if Olivia would like a chat. It must be quite lonely for her as all the attention is on Paige and Poppy. I'll take that box of Maltesers the Somalian family gave me last week. I've been very good and not eaten them. I wonder if they've raised enough money for the drugs yet? In some ways, I hope it takes them longer. Once Poppy's had the new treatment there's nowhere else to go. If it doesn't work, that's it. My nan used to say: 'It's better to travel hopefully than to arrive.' Love Issy xxx

---

FROM: Ravi Bhatoa
SUBJECT: FYI
DATE: 23 June 2018 at 11:31
TO: Tish Bhatoa

I signed off on a permanent night-nurse for Dad. The red-haired manager said Mum's health is suffering because Dad keeps her awake all night. We could get a separate room for Mum, but that would mean Dad is on his own, and he hates that. Rav

---

FROM: Tish Bhatoa
SUBJECT:
DATE: 23 June 2018 at 11:53
TO: Martin Hayward

Martin, the phials are still in Boston and can't be secured until you complete payment. I'm concerned Poppy's health will decline if there's further delay. I understand your situation, but could you take out a loan for the remaining money? Tish

---

FROM: Martin Hayward
SUBJECT: A Cure for Poppy
DATE: 23 June 2018 at 12:42
TO: Full mailing list

Dear all,
I realise you've had no update on Poppy's health for ages and I apologise. Every day feels like a year at the moment. Those of you involved in *All My Sons* will know our daughter-in-law Olivia is in hospital too now, suffering complications with her twin pregnancy, so I have taken over the director's chair from James. At least I get to spend some quality time with my wife, even if she is wearing a wig and speaks with an American accent.

What you will not be aware of is that a few weeks ago our family was dealt a terrible blow by a hoax emailer. This gentleman said he would pay outright for Poppy's life-saving treatment, and although we knew to be wary, we couldn't help but raise our hopes sky-high. As time went by and no money came, we realised he was a time-waster at best, and at worst a fraudster. When he sensed we had rumbled him, he disappeared. It's difficult to believe there are people like that in this world, but there are. Unfortunately, before we realised this was a cruel trick, we ordered the phials from America. As we haven't yet raised the rest of the money, they remain stuck over there. Meanwhile Poppy continues to receive conventional chemotherapy that has resulted in hair loss and blindness.

Luckily, we are not alone. The wonderful Sarah-Jane MacDonald and her fearless fundraising committee continue to keep Poppy's appeal at the forefront of everyone's mind. I know raffle tickets are selling like hot cakes and there are other fundraising activities planned for the summer. This is wonderful, but it is not enough. We need another £200,000 before September – so please, everyone, dig deep, ask friends and family to give all they can and help save our beautiful little girl. Regards, Martin

---

FROM: Joyce Walford
SUBJECT: Re: A Cure for Poppy
DATE: 23 June 2018 at 13:15
TO: Martin Hayward

What a stinking thing to do! If I knew who it was, I'd give them their hoax email with bells on. No wonder you've all had faces like wet weekends these last few weeks – except Helen, of course; the woman's a saint, I've always said it. I've been selling raffle tickets at my walking club, and I know Nick took some to football because I found them the next day in his sports bag, soaking wet from a leaked energy drink. I dried and ironed them, so he'll sell them tomorrow now instead. I've been meaning to tell Sarah-Jane that if they were cheaper, we could sell more. Joyce

---

FROM: Marianne Payne
SUBJECT: Re: A Cure for Poppy
DATE: 23 June 2018 at 13:17
TO: Martin Hayward

Mick says if you ever find out who tried to con you, don't bother going to the police. Just let him know. Marianne

PS I can still get you some Lourdes water, just say the word.

FROM: Denise Malcolm
SUBJECT: Re: A Cure for Poppy
DATE: 23 June 2018 at 13:22
TO: Martin Hayward

God bless you and Helen. I will buy a raffle ticket after all. Denise

---

FROM: Isabel Beck
SUBJECT: Hiya!
DATE: 23 June 2018 at 13:06
TO: Kel Greenwood

Hi Kel! I didn't realise you were working today. I'm in the roof garden on top of West Block – I can see you on the posh tables at the Orangery: look up and to your right, you should just about see my little head above the rail – who are you waiting for? If you're on your own and would rather cram in some last-minute line-learning, I'm up here with just a smoothie and chew bar for company. I'm sure they'd switch your order to a takeaway. Anyway, no problems if not, but would be lovely to see you. I really miss Sam when she's off! Lots of love, Issy xxx

---

FROM: Isabel Beck
SUBJECT: Hiya!
DATE: 23 June 2018 at 13:24
TO: Samantha Greenwood

Hiya Sam! You'll never guess who I've got here with me – Kel! Don't worry, I'm looking after him and we're going through our lines, like the conscientious Fairway Players we are. I spotted him at the Orangery all on his own – just as I'm in the roof garden on *my* own. They say there's no such thing as coincidence; I was meant to see him and drag him up here to learn lines. Are you really going to Emma's Midsummer Yogathon? I've never done yoga myself as it looks so difficult, but if you're both going I'll consider it. I'm sorry to hear Arnie is still under the weather. If he's thinking of getting back to nursing, we know there's a gap in Jelly Antics, now Riley's leaving . . . It's not that I wish it on him, but with three of us there, we can have our own little gang and it might make the days more bearable. I'm really looking forward to meeting him. I'll let you get back to enjoying your day off. Love Issy xxx

---

FROM: Isabel Beck
SUBJECT: Hiya!
DATE: 23 June 2018 at 14:02
TO: Samantha Greenwood

Sorry to bother you again, but as we were leaving I spotted Claudia having lunch by herself at the Orangery. It's a shame when someone doesn't have any friends, don't you think? Love Issy xxx

---

Must have been going on a while?

FROM: Rupert Allardyce
SUBJECT: Invoice due
DATE: 23 June 2018 at 15:18
TO: Martin Hayward

Dear Martin,
Further to our earlier correspondence, the three-month grace on your payment has expired and the full amount is now due. Our invoice is attached. In the meantime Whites' solicitors have re-presented their invoice for the disputed work, along with a final-demand letter. The situation is this: the combined amount you owe is now in excess of the value of the work. If you continue to refuse payment, Whites could (and no doubt will) escalate the case against you, which will involve more and more costs, the further the case goes. I say this as a long-time associate of yours: swallow your pride, pay both invoices and close the case. Repair the fence at a later date.

If you want us to take further steps, we would require full payment of outstanding monies and – because you received a period of grace on a previous bill – advance payment in respect of our work to continue this litigation. I can't advise that course of action. However, it is up to you.

Yours sincerely,
Rupert Allardyce, LLM
Partner, Allardyce & Greene LLP

FROM: Martin Hayward
SUBJECT: Re: Invoice due
DATE: 23 June 2018 at 16:00
TO: Rupert Allardyce

Dear Rupert,
Every penny we have has gone towards my granddaughter's cancer treatment. But in any case I have no intention of paying Whites for their shoddy work and deceitful practices. I find it abhorrent that they are talking about taking *us* to court. I will pull finances from somewhere to pay your bill. Please take whatever steps necessary to resolve this case in our favour. Regards, Martin

---

FROM: Emma Crooks
SUBJECT: Woof
DATE: 25 June 2018 at 14:35
TO: Sarah-Jane MacDonald

Don't want to worry Paige or the Haywards, but Woof hasn't been himself for a couple of days. Lethargic, off his food. He's still drinking, so it may just be the warm weather. I performed a healing mantra and sent him white light, but no change. Do you know which vet they use? I'm sure he's fine, but I'll get him checked over and tell them in a week or two, when things aren't so frantic with Poppy and Olivia. Pop some extra raffle tickets through my door and I'll sell them at my meditation class. You're coming to the Yogathon? Emma

---

FROM: Sarah-Jane MacDonald
SUBJECT: Re: Woof
DATE: 25 June 2018 at 14:41
TO: Emma Crooks

Try the Paws Clinic on St Helen's Road. Emma, thank you so much for the raffle ticket push. I've handed out three books each to the cast and crew of the play, but as not everyone has a wide circle of friends – to put it politely

– I'm sure some of those will be returned unsold. We're offering a prize for the member who sells the most, but at the moment that's Kevin, which would be embarrassing. Yes, we'll both be at the Yogathon. Harley would come if he were old enough – not for the yoga, but just to stay up late.
Sarah-Jane MacDonald

Message exchange between Sarah-Jane MacDonald and Kevin MacDonald on 25 June 2018:

14:44 Sarah-Jane wrote:
Don't forget Emma's Yogathon Saturday night. It's for Poppy, so no piss-taking. You'll have to drop Harley off at Greta's by seven. Mum and Nan are both going, so they can't have him.

14:50 Kevin wrote:
Can't make it: post-golf get-together over Simon's. Take Harley with you. At his age I'd have leapt at the chance to see ladies in Lycra.

FROM: Sarah-Jane MacDonald
SUBJECT: Raffle etc.
DATE: 25 June 2018 at 15:54
TO: A Cure for Poppy Fundraising Committee

Dear all,
Thank you for your continued hard work. Our next big fundraising initiative is the raffle, so let's pull out all the stops to sell tickets. Cameron Hilford will draw the winner on the last night of the play (see below), so we don't have long. Tickets are £10 each or £100 a book, so emphasise both the good cause and the spectacular prizes on offer.

This Saturday, 30 June 2018, is Emma Crooks' Midsummer Yogathon, a delightful evening of Zen calm where participants can balance mind, body and soul on the lawn of The Grange as the sun goes down. Emma will host the class from 7 p.m. until midnight, with plenty of breaks for herbal tea and organic sustainable snacks. Tickets are £10 each. It would be good to see the whole committee there, even if you can only come along for an hour or so.

I propose another committee meeting on the Monday of play week (2 July) to assign fundraising jobs on play nights. Several of us are in the play, so it's important to know who is doing what front-of-house, to keep eyeballs on the appeal and get Poppy's life-saving drugs over here asap. Sarah-Jane MacDonald, Campaign Coordinator

---

FROM: Joyce Walford
SUBJECT: Re: Raffle etc.
DATE: 25 June 2018 at 16:03
TO: Sarah-Jane MacDonald

Dear Sarah-Jane, Did you realise we could sell more raffle tickets if they were cheaper? £10 is a lot of money for one ticket. We sell a strip of five for a pound at the club.

FROM: Sarah-Jane MacDonald
SUBJECT: Re: Raffle etc.
DATE: 25 June 2018 at 16:04
TO: Joyce Walford

Thanks for the feedback, but we need £250,000, not £2.50.
Sarah-Jane MacDonald

FROM: Isabel Beck
SUBJECT: Hiya!
DATE: 25 June 2018 at 16:34
TO: Samantha Greenwood

Hiya Sam! I've just received a group email from Sarah-Jane to the fundraising committee. There's another meeting next Monday. They must want me to take the minutes again – why else would I be on the list? It arrived as I was visiting Olivia and James. I sent them your love. They seem to think she might be allowed home soon, because she only had a minor abruption and the bleeding's stopped. But between you and me, I sneaked a glance at her chart and she's on Dexamethasone, so they are obviously looking to induce in the next few days and certainly won't send her home. I didn't mention it.

She's thirty-one weeks, so it might be ok. Fingers crossed everything goes smoothly and James will be free to take the last few rehearsals. Martin is an amazing director, but he's not himself at the moment.

Do you think Arnie will be better in time for the play? I've already put in a word about him helping, but that was before Kel said he was more poorly than you both expected. I still haven't noticed YKW behaving any different. Can you remind Claudia? I'm sure she hasn't spoken to her. I'm a good judge of people and I've always felt her to be quite two-faced. Love Issy xxx

---

FROM: Arnie Ballancore
SUBJECT: Mum
DATE: 25 June 2018 at 17:00
TO: Kel Greenwood

Woke up in a panic. It's Mum's birthday next week and I need to get her a present. Left my bank cards in my wallet at home. Sam's out. She's been gone all day. Is there any cash in the house I could borrow? I'll pay you back as soon as Mum sends the wallet. Hate asking, but she's been so good to me and deserves something nice. Arnie

---

FROM: Arnie Ballancore
SUBJECT: Re: Mum
DATE: 25 June 2018 at 17:12
TO: Kel Greenwood

Thanks mate. I'll put the card back after and wipe the PIN number from my memory. You saved my life. I owe you one. Ok to take the spare keys?

FROM: Claudia D'Souza
SUBJECT: Raffle tickets
DATE: 26 June 2018 at 10:36
TO: Samantha Greenwood

Hi Sam, hope you enjoyed your rest day. I'll have two raffle tickets, please, and will pay you next time we meet. Sincerely hope I don't win the golf lesson. Still thinking about the Yogathon. Michael has agreed to babysit so I can see the play – don't want to push my luck when he's been willing to compromise on that. I'll forward a couple of vacancies to Isabel shortly. Shall I use the email you sent me or the one on our database? Both positions are at Mount More, and both start after her transfer restrictions expire. When she mentions them, you'll know to be super-enthusiastic. C x

---

FROM: Andrea Morley
SUBJECT: Yesterday
DATE: 26 June 2018 at 10:46
TO: Samantha Greenwood

Dear Samantha,
It was lovely to meet you yesterday. I understand what you're looking for is sensitive, and that your budget is limited, but the more detail I have, the more able I am to source the information you need. May I suggest 'Helen Grace' could be a first and middle name, not first and surname? This would make any local-authority search trickier, as death records are more reliably searchable by surname.

Nonetheless I am happy to help you further, subject to a greater understanding of what you require. My fees are attached. I look forward to hearing from you, should you wish to undertake a wider search.

Yours sincerely,
Andrea Morley
Genealogy & Archives

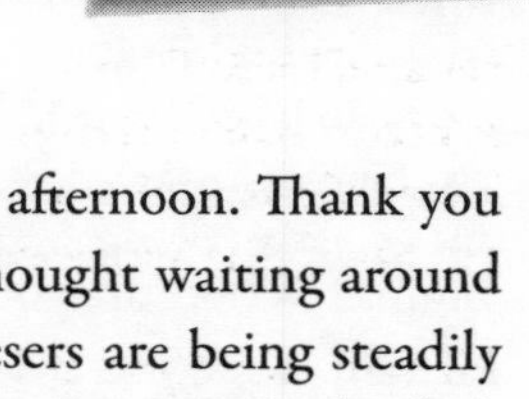

FROM: James Hayward
SUBJECT: Thank you
DATE: 26 June 2018 at 11:49
TO: Isabel Beck

Dearest Issy, it was a pleasure to see you yesterday afternoon. Thank you for popping in and cheering us up. Who'd have thought waiting around in a state of stress could be so boring? The Maltesers are being steadily consumed as I type. Thanks too for the copy of *Confusions*. I had a flick through while Olivia was snoozing earlier. It's a large cast. I'm not sure we have enough men for it. And unless we set it in the 1970s, it could come across as dated. There's no leading female role, so Mum won't like it. I'll show it to Dad, but can't see them going for it at the moment. We've had no news yet about whether Olivia can go home. She says she feels better, but she's still on a drip . . . I doubt I'll be at the committee meeting Monday, so relying on you to take the minutes and report back. Enjoy the Yogathon, and best of luck for the final rehearsals. James

---

FROM: Emma Crooks
SUBJECT: Woof
DATE: 26 June 2018 at 12:04
TO: Martin Hayward

I don't know how to tell you this, but Woof needs emergency abdominal surgery. He was off his food and not himself. I thought it was just the hot weather. The vet says he has a 'major obstruction' in his small intestine. It might be something he's eaten and it might be a tumour. Either way, it's serious. I don't want to worry Paige and Glen, but I'm in such a state. I thought I did everything right . . .

FROM: Martin Hayward
SUBJECT: Re: Woof
DATE: 26 June 2018 at 12:08
TO: Emma Crooks

Oh no. Where is he? I'll come now and drive him to the PDSA.

FROM: Martin Hayward
SUBJECT: Re: Woof
DATE: 26 June 2018 at 12:29
TO: Emma Crooks

Emma? Where are you? Is everything ok? Are you at Paws?

FROM: Emma Crooks
SUBJECT: Re: Woof
DATE: 26 June 2018 at 12:36
TO: Martin Hayward

Sorry Martin, I was just with the lady here. I had a panic attack in the waiting room and she showed me a new breathing technique. I'm much better now. She says we mustn't worry about Woof. He's in theatre and there's nothing more we can do, but trust he's in the best hands. Their group senior surgeon is working on him. Apparently he's a specialist in this type of surgery and we're lucky he's at this practice today. I'm focusing on this as evidence the universe is realigning in our favour. I don't know what to tell Paige. I'd rather wait and say 'Woof's out of danger and on the mend'. But then we risk the total shock of bad news, if things don't turn out well. Heaven forbid. You know what's happening with Poppy at the moment, is it a good time? Emma x

---

FROM: Martin Hayward
SUBJECT: Re: Woof
DATE: 26 June 2018 at 12:42
TO: Emma Crooks

It's not a good time. I'm on my way.

FROM: Emma Crooks
SUBJECT: Re: Woof
DATE: 26 June 2018 at 12:50
TO: Martin Hayward

Do you have Woof's insurance details? The bill is £4,000 so far and they've already asked who will be paying it. Emma x

---

FROM: Isabel Beck
SUBJECT: Re: Thank you
DATE: 26 June 2018 at 13:16
TO: James Hayward

Hi James, it was lovely to see Olivia looking so well under the circumstances. Hopefully she'll be allowed home, but even if she isn't, the Maternity unit at St Ann's is lovely. I'm not just saying that because I work at the hospital – I'd never recommend Geriatrics, but that's another story. What an exciting weekend you're missing! The Yogathon, Big Sunday rehearsal and the committee meeting. That's a shame about *Confusions*, but there are plenty more plays with lots of small parts for less-experienced actors like Sam, Kel and me. I've been looking online and started a list in my committee-minutes notebook. When things settle down, I'll let you know which ones seem most appropriate. I'm sooo looking forward to the Yogathon! I've never done yoga properly before, but Sam has, so we'll put our mats side by side and she'll show me where I'm going wrong. You can't beat a friend like that. I'm also hoping to meet Arnie, whose name is down to help out on play nights. Between you and me, he's been a bit depressed lately. When you're looking for something to take your mind off your thoughts, I can't recommend The Fairway Players enough. Love to Olivia and the bumps, Issy xxx

---

FROM: Sarah-Jane MacDonald
SUBJECT: Yogathon final preps
DATE: 26 June 2018 at 14:00
TO: Emma Crooks

Is there anything more you need me to do for Saturday? I've briefed Magda as to what I think you'll need, but don't be shy asking for anything else, once you arrive. She's Polish and very efficient – she's already got the builders to move their generator around the back. Of course we want to maximise the funds raised, but as the lawn is only so big, we don't want everyone packed in on top of each other. If we end up with lots more people, would you consider moving the Yogathon to the Horizon Room? Sarah-Jane MacDonald

---

FROM: Emma Crooks
SUBJECT: Re: Yogathon final preps
DATE: 26 June 2018 at 14:09
TO: Sarah-Jane MacDonald

Oh SJ, I'm in a bad place. Woof needed major intestinal surgery. Praying it's a tumour and not something he's eaten. Please don't say I've killed the family dog, on top of everything else they're going through. Poor Woof is still in intensive care. I've left Martin paying an eye-watering bill. What a horribly stressful day. At the moment I can't even think about doing the Yogathon. I'll need to re-centre my mind or I simply won't be able to focus. Em x

---

Message exchange between Sarah-Jane MacDonald and Kevin MacDonald on 26 June 2018:

14:12 Sarah-Jane wrote:
Here's the latest: Woof ate something dodgy and needed surgery. Emma is too stressed to do the Yogathon. WTF? I can't be too hard on her when she's done so much to help.

14:20 Kevin wrote:
You can take the Yogathon. It can't be that hard. I mean come on, Paige and Glen have a terminally ill child. They can get another dog.

FROM: Sarah-Jane MacDonald
SUBJECT: Re: Yogathon final preps
DATE: 26 June 2018 at 14:22
TO: Emma Crooks

Oh Emma, that must've been dreadful for you. But dogs are very resilient. Woof is quite young and they bounce back in no time. You've got three whole days to recover and I know you can centre your mind long before then. Woof will be fine. Remember, Paige and Glen have a lot more to worry about and will only be grateful Woof had you there with him in the end.
Sarah-Jane MacDonald

FROM: Emma Crooks
SUBJECT: Re: Yogathon final preps
DATE: 26 June 2018 at 14:23
TO: Sarah-Jane MacDonald

In the end? Oh my God, what have you heard? Has he passed?

FROM: Sarah-Jane MacDonald
SUBJECT: Re: Yogathon final preps
DATE: 26 June 2018 at 14:25
TO: Emma Crooks

No! No, I haven't heard a thing. I mean 'when all's said and done'. Woof will be fine, Emma, there's no need to cancel the Yogathon. Is there anything I can do – anything at all – to make you feel better?
Sarah-Jane MacDonald

FROM: Issy Beck
SUBJECT: Re: Mount More Intranet Portal
DATE: 26 June 2018 at 16:25
TO: Claudia D'Souza

Dear Claudia, Thank you for sending me the link to Mount More's HR portal. I enjoyed my visit last week, but I'm not ready to leave St Ann's, so don't send me any further jobs. Issy

---

FROM: Isabel Beck
SUBJECT: Hiya!
DATE: 26 June 2018 at 16:54
TO: Samantha Greenwood

Hiya Sam, guess what I've just picked up dead cheap in TK Maxx? A yoga mat! £4.99, reduced from £15.99. Its packaging is ripped and it's a bit grubby, but I've already wiped it and it's hanging over the bath. Do you have your own mat? If not, then have this one and I'll see if they've got more in tomorrow. I'm so glad you're going to be there. I'd feel so self-conscious on my own. We can put our mats side by side so that you can show me what to do. Kel can look after Arnie, and you can look after me! Thank you for your offer of a lift to The Grange on Saturday. I'm delighted to accept. I'll finally meet Arnie! Yoga can only be good for his depression, but I'd recommend being in a play to *really* take his mind off things. I can put an extra word in for him at the committee meeting Monday. Love Issy xxx

---

FROM: Claudia D'Souza
SUBJECT: Sigh . . .
DATE: 26 June 2018 at 16:55
TO: Samantha Greenwood

Disaster! Isabel doesn't want to move. You're stuck with her. I wonder if Ziggy put her off when she visited Mount More. I've heard she can be cold. If we leave it a few weeks, then get her together with my friend Una, she may feel more welcome and positive about working there. In the meantime, perhaps you could drop a few hints about how you would like to move there . . . You can tell I haven't given up hope – I hate the thought of you fending off a leech all day. People like that are energy vampires. Obsession is worse than bullying in its insidiousness. I'm going to think positive about the Yogathon and say yes, I'll go. Michael hasn't agreed to stay in yet, but perhaps if I present it as a *fait accompli* . . . How are you fixed for lunch next week? C x

---

FROM: Claudia D'Souza
SUBJECT: Re: Sigh . . .
DATE: 26 June 2018 at 17:04
TO: Samantha Greenwood

Oh poor you! If you've got a cold, you definitely shouldn't do yoga! Don't feel bad. I wasn't dead set on going and, even if I were, there would still have been the Michael hurdle to overcome. If you're better next week, drop me a line and we can meet up over one of the Orangery's delicious Super Salads. I hope you're better for your play next Friday. I hardly ever go to the theatre. If I'm honest, I find it boring and my mind wanders. But it won't when you're onstage, I promise! Hope you're better soon and don't spend the whole weekend coughing and sneezing! C x

---

FROM: Glen Reswick
SUBJECT: Pet insurance
DATE: 26 June 2018 at 17:30
TO: Martin Hayward

Don't tell Paige. She's at a chemo kids' picnic (it's not called that – something the hospital does) with Poppy. Helen asked me to give you our pet insurance details, and I said I would, but the truth is I didn't bother with it after the first few months. It was extortionate. Yet another expense every month. Have they said how much? If it's over £100, tell them to put him down. I'll tell Paige he couldn't be cured. It will be the best thing all round, given how much he costs to feed, plus what we're giving Emma to look after him. We can't afford this at the moment. My interview yesterday was a no-go, but at least they told me there and then. Thanks for dealing with this, Martin, appreciated.

FROM: Martin Hayward
SUBJECT: Re: Pet insurance
DATE: 26 June 2018 at 17:57
TO: Glen Reswick

The obstruction was a calcified amalgamation of synthetic fibres, woodchip, polystyrene beads and a cushion cover in the shape of Vishnu. They also found a small plastic dinosaur, a golf tee and a coin, which I told them to put towards the bill. This they refused to do because it was a euro and they don't accept foreign currency. Woof is in intensive care, groggy and unrepentant. I've already paid them. Martin

---

FROM: Emma Crooks
SUBJECT: Re: Woof
DATE: 26 June 2018 at 18:46
TO: Sarah-Jane MacDonald

Woof has pulled through! I'm so pleased. Bless Martin, he knew how worried I was and made a special trip to see me on the way back from the vet. It was nothing we'd done. Woof had simply got a blockage or something. What a relief! I'll see you 6 p.m. Saturday at The Grange. Em x

---

FROM: Lauren Malden
SUBJECT: Hiya!
DATE: 28 June 2018 at 06:29
TO: Isabel Beck

Hello lovely! It's been *ages*, how are you? Any news, any gossip? Mum says the play is soon. We hope to get back for it, but we've got so much on we might have to send our good luck instead. How are rehearsals? I know you'll knock 'em dead! How's Poppy? Mum says they're still raising money and have even had a hoaxer promise to pay the bill. She's surprised anyone would do such a thing, but after working at St Ann's, I'm not. Please tell me you're moving on, Issy. You shouldn't stay there just because of your friend. I know you love working with her, and that you don't want to even contemplate this: but she might not feel the same way about you and could leave any time. I don't know when I'll next be up there, but let's meet when I am. Will let you know when I'm free. In the meantime, keep me updated on all the news. Kiss kiss L x

---

FROM: Isabel Beck
SUBJECT: Re: Hiya!
DATE: 28 June 2018 at 06:44
TO: Lauren Malden

Sam feels exactly as I do. We could be sisters. She isn't like you and me. She doesn't put up with you-know-who like we did. She's already spoken to Claudia in HR, and between them they are going to make sure YKW is either moved or moves of her own accord. One way or another, she'll be gone soon. It hasn't happened yet, but I've watched Sam and she doesn't let anything slide. She'll keep on, and people listen to her. Anyway, we're planning to go to Africa together and distribute T-shirts. It was Sam's idea. She said we work together so well, we'd be ideal for that sort of trip. It'll take a while to plan, so we're not too career-focused at the moment. I don't know when I'll have time to meet up. Issy

---

FROM: Sarah-Jane MacDonald
SUBJECT: Yogathon tomorrow
DATE: 29 June 2018 at 09:32
TO: Martin Hayward

Martin, Helen has agreed to say a few words at the start of the Yogathon. Please can she talk about the raffle and say tickets are available from reception at The Grange and from any of the committee members (who should all be there at one point or another). I've mentioned it to her at rehearsal, but I'm relying on you to keep reminding her. Until the play, this is our main source of fundraising, so I'm keen for it to be a success. We're entering the point of saturation, where everyone who knows us has already donated. We need to keep reinventing the appeal, so to speak. I'm not counting your venture with Lydia Drake. You know I have reservations about that, but am happy to be proven wrong. Look forward to seeing you tomorrow for some Zen calm on the lawn.
Sarah-Jane MacDonald

FROM: Martin Hayward
SUBJECT: Re: Yogathon tomorrow
DATE: 29 June 2018 at 10:18
TO: Sarah-Jane MacDonald

Helen is duly briefed. Paige, Glen, Poppy and I are all hoping to be there for the start, if not the end. Regards, Martin

---

Message exchange between Sarah-Jane MacDonald and Kevin MacDonald on 29 June 2018:

10:22 Sarah-Jane wrote:
I'm still in Martin's bad books, but if that stops him gambling with any more appeal money, then so be it. Harley must go directly from cricket to rehearsal on Sunday, is that clear?

10:30 Kevin wrote:
Dear Kevin, please can you get up early on your only day off to take our sports-averse son to cricket, squint at him across a vast plain while he fields for two hours, a mile from the crease, then drive him straight to an all-day rehearsal without passing a sanitary toilet or a dinner plate. Thank you so much. Your loving wife.

10:32 Sarah-Jane wrote:
You know that's what I meant.

FROM: Paige Reswick
SUBJECT: Poppy
DATE: 29 June 2018 at 10:49
TO: Dr Tish Bhatoa

Dear Tish, It was lovely to see you at the Teddy Bears' Picnic. Thank you for inviting us. It means a lot that you came too. I know all the parents were delighted to see you. Poppy had a wonderful time. Since all this happened her social life has shrunk, so it's good to see her interacting with other children in a normal way, and not from a hospital bed. There were two other little girls there: Millie and Caroline, both Poppy's age and both on their first course of chemo. Poppy is twice their size. Is that right? What I mean is, despite all she's going through, Poppy is hitting her growth and development targets. I'm still concerned the drugs she's on aren't working. I suppose I just need a bit of reassurance. Thanks so much again, Tish, Paige x

---

FROM: Dr Tish Bhatoa
SUBJECT: Re: Poppy
DATE: 29 June 2018 at 12:01
TO: Paige Reswick

Dear Paige, I can't comment on other patients' treatment or their reactions to it. If it would set your mind at rest, I can drop by when you're in on Monday and give Poppy a quick examination. Dr Tish Bhatoa

---

FROM: Tish Bhatoa
SUBJECT: Dan
DATE: 29 June 2018 at 14:37
TO: Ravi Bhatoa

Have you heard from Dan? I've sent emails and texts – no reply. Nothing since 12 June. We've had no reports of renewed fighting there, but why would we? No one is reporting it. It's rare to go this long without any communication from him. I'm considering contacting the Foreign and Commonwealth Office, but am mindful he wants to lie low as far as the authorities are concerned. It's at night I can't stop thinking about him. Have you heard anything? Tish

---

FROM: Ravi Bhatoa
SUBJECT: Re: Dan
DATE: 29 June 2018 at 15:01
TO: Tish Bhatoa

I'll worry about Dan precisely as much as he worries about us. He helps strangers on the other side of the world while his family fends for themselves. Does it never rile you that we bust a gut for Mum and Dad, and they take us for granted? He's barely sent them a card in fifteen years, yet he's their golden boy. No, I haven't heard from him and if he's disappeared, then he's probably seen the latest invoice from Edenfield. Rav

PS And don't get me started on the other stuff. If you spend your time and money picking up the pieces for him, that's up to you.

PPS If you really want him to get in touch, stop sending the monthly allowance you pretend to me you know nothing about.

PPPS And if you want to know why it's you he stays in contact with, not M&D, see above.

FROM: Tish Bhatoa
SUBJECT: Re: Dan
DATE: 29 June 2018 at 15:25
TO: Ravi Bhatoa

Whatever you think of him, he's our little brother and he is doing important work that we would all do if we could. If something's happened . . . I can't even think about it. The 'other stuff' was made up by an attention-seeking liar and I'll prove it. Let me know if you hear anything.

FROM: Arnie Ballancore
SUBJECT: Where am I, mate?
DATE: 30 June 2018 at 17:53
TO: Kel Greenwood

I'm stuck in Lockley Bois and I've never even heard of it. There are no more trains today and it's not remotely dark. Things are different out in the sticks, no? I want to get back for Sam's yoga thing but can't see it happening. Arnie

---

FROM: Arnie Ballancore
SUBJECT: Re: Where am I, mate?
DATE: 30 June 2018 at 18:11
TO: Kel Greenwood

Thanks mate. You don't have to do that, but it's really kind. See you soon.

FROM: Isabel Beck
SUBJECT: Re: lift to yoga
DATE: 30 June 2018 at 18:12
TO: Samantha Greenwood

Hiya! No problem, I'll get the bus to yours, so Kel can rescue Arnie. I'm only watching yoga videos on YouTube and listening to this guru speak about energy flow. Lucky Arnie having a friend in Lockley Bois! There are huge houses out there. Just think, this time next week we'll have done two shows and only have the last night to go! Can't wait to see your flat! It looks lovely on Street View, but I notice the pictures were taken three years ago, so you didn't live there then. Once the play is over, we can start planning our trip. I think about you and our journey to Africa every time I pick up my rehearsal bag, and my heart jumps a little bit. I'll definitely take it with me when we go. I expect we'll have to launch a separate appeal to collect old T-shirts. It might be awkward if everyone is still raising money for Poppy, but I'm sure they'll have reached their target soon enough and then we can start ours. In any case, we'd be asking for T-shirts in the first instance, rather than money. I hope Kel and Arnie get back in time for the Yogathon. If not, we'll have to make our own way to The Grange. Don't worry if we do – I know the buses. See you soon! Love Issy xxxx

Midsummer Yogathon

Saturday 30 June 2018
7 p.m.–midnight

Join Emma Crooks at The Grange for an energising evening of karmic renewal under the waning gibbous moon.

Decongest spiritual channels, manifest deep gratitude and awaken your calm.

£10 per person (no concessions)

Organic herbal refreshments available to purchase

All proceeds in aid of A Cure for Poppy

FROM: Paige Reswick
SUBJECT: Poppy
DATE: 30 June 2018 at 19:40
TO: Glen Reswick

I've taken that scary voodoo thing away from Poppy. It gave me the creeps, but more because it's made of hair and dirty cloth or something and her immune system shouldn't be exposed to germs. I don't know who gave it to her, but if anyone asks after it, tell them she loves it, won't put it down, etc. xx

---

Message exchange between Kevin MacDonald and Sarah-Jane MacDonald on 30 June 2018:

21:23 Kevin wrote:
With Simon and the rest. Gonna be an all-nighter. Sorry. Good news. Colin says yes to £50k! Instructed his PA to make the transfer while I was there, so he's as good as his word. But you won't believe who Clive Handler is. Was. Is or was? Hope yoga going well. Talk later, must go – in toilet.

21:35 Sarah-Jane wrote:
GET A TAXI HOME. Harley is due at cricket 9 a.m. Yoga nightmare. Fuck!

Message exchange between Sarah-Jane MacDonald and Magda Kuchar on 30 June 2018:

21:35 Sarah-Jane wrote:
Are there any more clean towels?

21:36 Magda wrote:
No. That is all. Delivery from laundry tomorrow. There bag dirty towels. You want?

21:37 Sarah-Jane wrote:
Anything. Anything to stifle the smell.

Message exchange between Emma Crooks and Sarah-Jane MacDonald on 30 June 2018:

21:39 Emma wrote:
I know he says not to call an ambulance, but do you think we should? That was some punch. He may have, er, lost control of himself because he lost consciousness.

21:44 Sarah-Jane wrote:
The three people with him are all nurses, so they should know. Let's see how he is after this break. Emma, you're a trouper. Thank you for carrying on and keeping control of the class. At least Joyce got Barry out before he threw a punch at anyone else. When he sobers up, I expect him to buy a whole book of raffle tickets.

FROM: Joyce Walford
SUBJECT: My Barry
DATE: 30 June 2018 at 22:43
TO: Sarah-Jane MacDonald

That chap started it. He swore blind he'd given me a tenner and was waiting for change. He hadn't even paid! That trick's as old as the hills, but so am I, and I told him so. He properly squared up and, if the trestle table wasn't between us, I don't like to think what he might have done. My Barry only went to have a word with him, but he does martial arts and doesn't know his own strength. What a nasty piece, trying to rob from a charity. I take it he's a friend of those nurses. Anyway, my Barry is sorry to disturb the yoga and hopes everyone is ok. Joyce

---

FROM: Sarah-Jane MacDonald
SUBJECT: Re: My Barry
DATE: 1 July 2018 at 08:44
TO: Joyce Walford

I said to Joyce Walford. I said I'm dictating this because I'm driving Harlem to cricket. I don't know what happened, but it was literally message. When people take pinches in films they don't sow them hitting themselves. Harlem! Language. Lucky we had ne'er share who said apparently it's Norman. I have no idea who that man was nor how he is now. Barry should be aware there may beagle implications. I'll find out more the snoring. Send. Send now. Be quite Harlem I can do it. Send!

Another handsfree speech2text from KrystalCleer – up to 90% accuracy guaranteed

---

FROM: Joyce Walford
SUBJECT: Re: My Barry
DATE: 1 July 2018 at 08:50
TO: Sarah-Jane MacDonald

I've just received a very strange message from your email address, Sarah-Jane. Is it a virus or did you drop something on your keyboard?

Message exchange between Kevin MacDonald and Sarah-Jane MacDonald on 1 July 2018:

08:53 Kevin wrote:
I'm ill. Not flu. Something worse. Was Martin pleased about Colin's £50k? Think he might want to do a news piece for the local.

09:05 Sarah-Jane wrote:
Thanks for not getting in until 7 a.m. This is all I need this morning. Am in a queue of 4x4s trying to get into the car park. Harley jumped out and met the others at the clubhouse. The police have cordoned off a house that backs onto the green and are only letting us in one at a time.

09:07 Sarah-Jane wrote:
Didn't tell Martin about Colin because of almighty punch-up in middle of yoga field. I didn't see it, but Barry took offence to something Kel's friend said to Joyce and confronted him. Martin was in the middle of it for some reason. Probably ambled over, made it worse and the next thing anyone knew, Barry floors this man. Blood everywhere.

09:09 Sarah-Jane wrote:
That's not the worst. The man lost control of his bowels. According to Kel, who spoke to Mum, this is a normal reaction (you learn something new every day). Emma carried on with Sun Salutations, but the smell became critical. The Grange ran out of towels. Celia Halliday was sick because she has coprophobia, aka fear of faeces. The man was effing and blinding, about not going to hospital. Luckily Kel, Sam and that dopey girl managed to bundle him away. It was a disaster. Didn't even raise much money. Plus, Harley now wants to ditch cricket and take up yoga. I'm next into the car park, thank God.

09:12 Kevin wrote:
Whoah! Wish I'd been there. Something in the herbal tea or did the guy turn up pissed to a Yogathon?

FROM: Sarah-Jane MacDonald
SUBJECT: Last night
DATE: 1 July 2018 at 09:31
TO: Martin Hayward

Dear Martin,
Well, the Yogathon was livelier than expected, but there is some excellent news: we have a £50,000 donation from Colin Brasher! He owns a tech company and is a Lodge friend of Kevin's. The money should be in the appeal account this morning and, if my understanding is correct, the first dose of drugs can now be released from the States. Please confirm this, so I can communicate the good news to the committee. We need some serious motivation after last night – the details of which I am still unclear about. In the melee I neglected to compliment Helen on another wonderful speech. I'll thank her this afternoon at rehearsal, but there's never enough time to speak properly, so for the record, she did a great job of focusing everyone – well, almost everyone – on Poppy's plight.

Message from Kevin MacDonald to Sarah-Jane MacDonald on 1 July 2018:

09:33 Kevin wrote:
I never knew Celia had a 'fear of faeces'. Fear of shit? That's ridiculous. How does she live?

FROM: Sarah-Jane MacDonald
SUBJECT: Re: My Barry
DATE: 1 July 2018 at 09:34
TO: Joyce Walford

Someone else's shit. Apparently her own is tolerable.

FROM: Sarah-Jane MacDonald
SUBJECT: Re: My Barry
DATE: 1 July 2018 at 09:37
TO: Joyce Walford

No! Sorry, Joyce, I meant that for Kevin. I'm switching between apps on my phone . . . Yes, yes, yes, that other message shouldn't have been sent. Harley was holding the phone and I was using a voice app he'd downloaded. I haven't heard how that man is – or even who he is, as I've never seen him before. I need to find out how badly he's injured. Barry should be aware that he may sue. I've never been assaulted myself, but if I ever were, then I would sue for sure.
Sarah-Jane MacDonald

Message from Sarah-Jane MacDonald to Kevin MacDonald on 1 July 2018:

09:40 Sarah-Jane wrote:
Someone else's shit. Apparently her own is tolerable.

FROM: Sarah-Jane MacDonald
SUBJECT: Number
DATE: 1 July 2018 at 09:41
TO: Isabel Beck

I need to contact Sam about last night. What's her number?

FROM: Martin Hayward
SUBJECT: Re: Last night
DATE: 1 July 2018 at 09:45
TO: Sarah-Jane MacDonald

Yes, that fellow was spouting unintelligible nonsense. Inebriated, no doubt, or a raving madman. Luckily, Helen and Paige had already left. How much money was raised? Excellent news about Mr Brasher. Another £50,000 would be even better. By the time Lydia reports back on the fund, it'll be all systems go. So, it's Big Sunday rehearsal today. The start of play week. I need to organise a few things for the set-build this afternoon. Regards, Martin

---

Message exchange between Kevin MacDonald and Sarah-Jane MacDonald on 1 July 2018:

09:45 Kevin wrote:
Balls! That's not a phobia. That's a get-out-of-poop-scooping excuse!

09:46 Sarah-Jane wrote:
Stop messaging me! I'm dealing with 101 things on phone in car while Harley crickets. Go to sleep. Big Sunday, remember.

FROM: Carol Dearing
SUBJECT: Last night
DATE: 1 July 2018 at 09:55
TO: Margaret Dearing

Mum, you were right next to them: what did that chap say to Martin? Whatever it was, Martin turned white as a ghost. Carol

FROM: Margaret Dearing
SUBJECT: Re: Last night
DATE: 1 July 2018 at 10:18
TO: Carol Dearing

Didn't hear a thing. The man whispered in Martin's ear, but Barry flattened him before Martin could reply. Ask Sarah-Jane, if you can get her to stand still for five minutes – I can't. Mum

---

Message exchange between Carol Dearing and Sarah-Jane MacDonald on 1 July 2018:

10:20 Carol wrote:
Are you bringing Harley round today? We've got his favourite: a lovely beef roast. Mum

10:29 Sarah-Jane wrote:
It's Big Sunday. We have to go straight from cricket to The Fairways and won't be home till late. I told you last week. Anyway, you saw Harley yesterday. I found out why Barry hit that man. He'd had an altercation with Joyce over payment for herbal tea. It could only happen here.

10:41 Carol wrote:
Your nan hardly saw him last night. Bring him round for an hour. He isn't needed onstage for the *whole* day! And that wasn't what the fight was about. The man said something to Martin. That's why Barry hit him. See you later. Mum

---

FROM: Martin Hayward
SUBJECT: Lydia Drake
DATE: 1 July 2018 at 14:19
TO: Glen Reswick

We need to tell people about Lydia Drake. I'll accept the blame, but people will be angry with me, so I'll need family backup and, with James at the hospital all hours, he can't do it. When can you come round?

FROM: Isabel Beck
SUBJECT: Re: Number
DATE: 1 July 2018 at 09:42
TO: Sarah-Jane MacDonald

Hi SJ, I was involved in the whole thing and know all about it, so you needn't worry Sam. I can't type too much at the moment. I slept on Sam's settee as we got home so late. I'll send you an email once I'm home and can get my laptop out. I hope Harley wasn't too upset by what happened. I'll write later. Love Issy xxx

---

Messages from Isabel Beck to Samantha Greenwood on 1 July 2018:

09:43
Are you awake yet?

09: 59
Are you awake now?

FROM: Isabel Beck
SUBJECT: Hiya!
DATE: 1 July 2018 at 10:29
TO: Samantha Greenwood

I don't want to get up until I know you're awake. Thank you for letting me sleep on the settee. I've barely slept at all, so I know Kel and Arnie aren't back from the hospital yet. You have lovely decor. But nothing from Africa . . . I was expecting you to have mementos of your time there, like the little doll Arnie gave Poppy. It's very thoughtful of him, although I can't say I believe it has any healing properties as such. I hope he's ok. On balance, I don't think he's ready to help out at the play. I'll email Joel and let him know, although as he was there last night I imagine he's put two and two together. I overheard Arnie mention Claudia. Did you suggest he looks for work at St Ann's, like I said? It's just . . . I didn't realise he would be quite as agitated and jittery as he is. I'd say he's not ready to go back to work yet.

I would love a desk like this. I recognise it from the Ikea catalogue. Your laptop is even older than mine! I keep meaning to upgrade, as new laptops are more secure than these older models, but it's so expensive, and my phone does everything much faster.

I've always fancied a balcony. Imagine eating breakfast on it in the summer. Orange juice, mixed berries and a croissant (so long as I'd reached my ideal weight), followed by black coffee – even though I don't like coffee much, and especially not without milk. I'm going to see if I can open the sliding doors very quietly. I watched them building this block and wondered what the view would be like from the upper floors. Does Arnie know Martin? I don't understand why he said that to him . . .

It's lovely out here – a beautiful sunny day again. Pity we'll be inside rehearsing. You said you'd drop me off so I can have a shower and get changed before rehearsal, but would you mind waiting for me, so we can both go into the hall together? After last night . . . we don't want people thinking we have aggressive friends or we may not be cast in the next play. Perhaps we could decide together what we tell people. I don't mean lie, but whatever's wrong with Arnie, it's subject to patient confidentiality. Then again, after last night, people deserve to know what happened. The yoga was so badly interrupted. I only hope it didn't affect the amount of money raised . . . How long is Arnie staying with you? Whether he's on the wrong medication or has an undiagnosed psychiatric condition, it's probably best he moves to where he can be monitored and supported. Hopefully Kel will sort that out. Does he know the bus route back? It's so high up here. I can see Topps Tiles. Let me know when you're awake. Lots of love, Issy xxxx

---

FROM: Isabel Beck
SUBJECT: Hiya!
DATE: 1 July 2018 at 10:33
TO: Samantha Greenwood

Sorry to email you again, but should we volunteer to clean up the lawn at The Grange today before rehearsal? We're so used to ringing for a contractor when accidents happen – plus we were preoccupied with getting Arnie to A&E . . . Thinking about it, for most people there the poo would be the worst aspect of the whole thing. If nothing else, working in Jelly Antics gives us a high tolerance of bodily waste. For me, though, the worst thing is what he said. Why would he accuse Martin of being a rapist? I'm in the kitchen very quietly making a cup of tea. I'll make two cups, in the hope you'll be awake soon. Lots of love, Issy xxxx

---

Message exchange between Nick Walford and Barry Walford on 1 July 2018:

12:02 Nick wrote:
What's Mum banging on about? Have you been nicked again?

12:09 Barry wrote:
Just some tosser getting on my tits. He got pissed at Mum, then started on Martin, so I knocked the shit out of him. Literally, the guy shat himself. Sick! Mum says he'll squeal, but he won't. It's nothing. Reckon we can get off Big Sunday and see the match?

FROM: Martin Hayward
SUBJECT: Curious incident
DATE: 1 July 2018 at 12:21
TO: Tish Bhatoa

Dear Tish,
We are about to embark on a new phase of fundraising – hopefully one that will prove more productive than the current appeal, which has plateaued. You were asking about Samantha Greenwood a while ago. Well, a curious incident occurred last night at a charity event for Poppy. Sam was with a scruffy man I'd never seen before. He was rubbing people up the wrong way, and I had to step in when things threatened to get punchy with a lad in our drama society. I'd never seen him in my life, Tish, but he seemed to know me – and you. He said I was 'Bhatoa's bitch' and then something about 'protecting a rapist'. He was quite obviously mentally unstable, but how did he know your name? Regards, Martin

---

FROM: Tish Bhatoa
SUBJECT: Re: Curious incident
DATE: 1 July 2018 at 12:49
TO: Martin Hayward

Dear Martin,
Whoever this was, Samantha Greenwood is behind it. It's a long story, but he doesn't mean me. My younger brother runs a specialist clinic in the Central African Republic. From time to time he clashes with other aid agencies and individuals, largely due to the nature of his work and the struggle for funding. You would hope volunteer charities would all pull in the same direction, but the continent defies our logic and reason. It's hard for us to imagine, but that part of the world is war-torn and lawless. Where life is worth so little, the truth has no chance. For some, this existence can scrape away their veneer of civilisation until all that's left is a base instinct for survival. Samantha Greenwood is one of them. Don't trust anything she says. I'm sorry you've been drawn into this, but please don't worry. Concentrate on the appeal, and I will deal with her. Tish

---

FROM: Tish Bhatoa
SUBJECT:
DATE: 1 July 2018 at 12:53
TO: Samantha Greenwood

I know what you're trying to do and it's futile. You're not in Bangui now. As long as I live, you will *never* get to him.

FROM: Isabel Beck
SUBJECT: Re: Number
DATE: 1 July 2018 at 12:55
TO: Sarah-Jane MacDonald

Hi SJ! I hope you're well and looking forward to Big Sunday. Not long now until we're back onstage and under the spotlight! Sorry for the delay in emailing you. Sam has just dropped me off to get changed. She's parking and waiting in the car, so I can't be long. I know Sam and Kel are mortified by what happened with Arnie. He's their friend from Africa – well, he's not from Africa obviously, but he worked there with them – and they're helping him come to terms with being back home. I can't say too much because, of course, his medical status is confidential, but please don't worry – whatever he said to anyone last night, it wasn't really him. He'd been stuck at a friend's house earlier in the day. Kel picked him up and drove him straight to the Yogathon, so he missed his medication and that sent him haywire. Also, it was a full moon last night and, while this sounds mad, tempers are more likely to fray at that time of the month, which accounts for Barry's response too, I suspect. I've probably already said too much, but I hope it explains Arnie's outrageous language. We took him straight to St Ann's rather than wait for an ambulance. He'd had a blow to the head, so there was a chance he could be more badly injured than it appeared. You can't be too cautious about blood clots and neck injury. Sam and I got in at two and will be at the hall for one, but Kel will be late as he's only just back from the hospital. Arnie's neck is fine, but they are keeping him in until they have a discharge meeting. I hope he can access more appropriate care, as his behaviour was worrying even before the altercation on the lawn. But that's between you and me. We are all keen to make up for what happened. Would it help if we volunteered to clean the lawn? It was Sam's idea, and she always knows what's best. I so hope Harley wasn't scared by what happened. See you at one, Love Issy xxx

---

FROM: Sarah-Jane MacDonald
SUBJECT: Re: Number
DATE: 1 July 2018 at 13:00
TO: Isabel Beck

That explains it. Magda cleared the lawn as best as. Perhaps she'd like some flowers? We'll have to ensure fundraising events do not coincide with a full moon in future. Harley is fine.
Sarah-Jane MacDonald

FROM: Isabel Beck
SUBJECT: Hiya!
DATE: 1 July 2018 at 13:05
TO: Samantha Greenwood

Hiya! Thanks for waiting for me. Hope you've sent all your emails. Ah! I can just about see you from the bathroom window – you're on the phone. You're welcome to wait in the flat, but I won't be long now anyway. I've sent SJ a quick message to let her know it was Arnie's medication talking, not him. Apparently the Polish girl Magda cleaned the lawn. It would be a lovely idea to send her some flowers: what do you think? I can order them from Blooms and have them delivered to The Grange on Monday – split the cost three ways.

I've been thinking about what Kel said on the phone. That Arnie missed his meds. Well, if missing his medication has that effect, don't you think he'll need proper help? I don't mean what he said to Martin, or the thing with Joyce; he wasn't right before then. You're far cleverer than me and you must've noticed it, too. I'm sure Kel isn't like this, but I've read that sometimes people who work with psychiatric patients all day can start to regard disrupted behaviour as normal. Almost ready for Big Sunday! Love Issy xxxx

---

Messages from Sarah-Jane MacDonald to Kevin MacDonald on 1 July 2018:

12:59 Sarah-Jane wrote:
You never said who Clive Handler was. I forgot to ask in the literal shitstorm of the Yogathon. Who was it?

13:14 Sarah-Jane wrote:
Your phone's off and you're asleep, aren't you? Wake up! Don't keep me in suspense! Typical! And now Martin's here to open up the hall. Big Sunday begins. Don't be late or I'll send Joyce to wake you up. I mean it.

Femi
Are you clear what happened at the Yogathon?

Charlotte
Yes, all good.

Femi
Great. Just checking.

Charlotte
Thanks.

Femi
Could you possibly summarise it for me? Please.

Charlotte
Sam, Kel, Issy and Arnie are at the Yogathon. At some point in the evening Arnie has a run-in with Joyce at the tea counter. Her incensed son Barry follows him to the lawn, where the yoga is in full swing, and confronts him. Martin tries to calm them down, but Arnie turns on him. What he says causes Barry to knock Arnie to the ground. A momentary loss of consciousness etc. ends in Sam, Kel and Issy taking Arnie away to hospital.

Femi
He accuses Martin of protecting a rapist and of being 'Bhatoa's bitch'.

Charlotte
And it baffles everyone who overhears it. Because they don't know what we know. We know it refers to what happened with Sam, Tish and Dan in Africa, plus it reveals that Sam has spoken to Arnie about her suspicions re the appeal.

Femi
For the record, I disagree with Bhatoa's view of Africa: 'Where life is worth so little, the truth has no chance.' It's a Western perspective that defines a continent by its most troubled regions.

Charlotte
While we've taken a break: in his update on 23 June Martin states categorically that Poppy is going blind. But that's just what SJ said to get the band to play for free – am I right?

Femi
Yes. Martin is a desperate man. His granddaughter is seriously ill. He feels responsible for curing her. Doesn't share the burden of stress with his wife.

Charlotte
I'm inclined to agree with Tish and Kevin. The Haywards are successful, wealthy landowners. Why don't they pay for Poppy's treatment themselves?

Femi
They've had numerous outgoings, referred to throughout the correspondence. Are they as wealthy as we assume?

Charlotte
So the community – people far worse off than them – are asked to empty their pockets.

Femi
We're back to the alpha family again. Vulnerability to social pressure. Anyway, the Haywards are lynchpins of the community. They employ a lot of these people. It makes sense to support them.

Charlotte
Sam, Kel and Arnie have all spent years living and working in troubled regions of Africa. Witness to goodness-knows-what. The first letter in our pack: 'eye removal', FFS! Might their experiences influence how they interpret perfectly ordinary events?

Femi
That and Sam's 'trouble', which seems to have preceded their return home. Whatever happened over there between her and Dan, it was Sam who had to return, not him. She lost.

FROM: Isabel Beck
SUBJECT: Hiya!
DATE: 1 July 2018 at 14:22
TO: Samantha Greenwood

Are you ok in the green room? I'm backstage behind the trellis. They're taking ages on this scene. Helen is the only one hitting her cues. Martin is being curt with everyone. Kevin, SJ and John are all over the place. I noticed you and Kel haven't spoken a word to each other. All I can say is: don't worry. Big Sunday is always like this. Everyone's tired and worried. We've been rehearsing for weeks and just want to get out there and do it. No audience, no atmosphere and everyone is tired. Not only that, but I think Barry is hungover ... has anyone mentioned last night to you? Luckily, to anyone who was out of immediate earshot, Barry was the aggressor. I overheard Marianne and Denise talking and they said Barry should've been arrested and that 'the nurses took him to hospital themselves', in a tone that suggested we were the heroes of the evening! Phew! Let's hope whoever casts the next play thinks the same. Apparently the yoga only made £500. That seems like a lot to me, but SJ sounded disappointed. She's barely spoken to Kevin since he arrived (late). See, everyone is feeling the pressure of play week. Hope you're ok. See you onstage! Love Issy xxxx

---

FROM: Sarah-Jane MacDonald
SUBJECT: Update
DATE: 1 July 2018 at 14:28
TO: Emma Crooks

Emma, how are you this afternoon? I hope you slept better than I did and that you didn't have to drive out to Lockley Bois at dawn to watch under-elevens cricket. Anyway, first the good news. The man who felt the full force of Barry's right hook is fine. Apparently he's a friend of the nurses, forgot his Valium and one thing led to another. Been given a clean bill of health and will be discharged later. Barry is here at Big Sunday rehearsal as if nothing happened. To him, it probably didn't, as I suspect he'd been drinking before the Yogathon. Not that Joyce will accept that. Now the bad news: Kevin has charmed a £50k donation out of a Lodge friend. Great,

I know, but he's a tech bod and has discovered the identity of our appeal hoaxer. I know I can trust you not to let on, Emma, but it's someone in the play, and I can't say anything to anyone until it's all over and done with. We want it to go well, so it raises as much cash as possible. It's appalling, but I'm not rocking the boat till it's safely in the harbour.
Sarah-Jane MacDonald

FROM: Emma Crooks
SUBJECT: Re: Update
DATE: 1 July 2018 at 14:35
TO: Sarah-Jane MacDonald

Oh SJ, you poor thing! Who is it? Do I know them? Go on, I won't tell. I slept like a baby, thank you, which is more than I'll be doing for a while because Woof is back tomorrow. Martin's picking him up from Paws first thing and bringing him straight round. He's up and about, but I'm not confident I can look after a poorly pup. I really want to say he should go to Paige's, but how can I when Poppy is at the hospital on Monday? James is with Olivia, Martin and Helen are running The Grange . . . I thought it was Big Sunday today? Emma x

---

FROM: Sarah-Jane MacDonald
SUBJECT: Re: Update
DATE: 1 July 2018 at 14:41
TO: Emma Crooks

It is. We're simulating the interval, to see if everyone can get changed in time. If Woof is under the weather, you're excused the committee meeting tomorrow night. I'll take minutes and send them through. Yes, you know the hoaxer. We all do. I don't understand why they did such a thing, but I should let them explain themselves first – after the play.
Sarah-Jane MacDonald

FROM: Martin Hayward
SUBJECT:
DATE: 1 July 2018 at 14:43
TO: Glen Reswick

Tuesday. After their committee meeting and before the play. Don't email. Come round if you need to speak. Regards.

FROM: Isabel Beck
SUBJECT: Don't worry!
DATE: 1 July 2018 at 23:31
TO: Sarah-Jane MacDonald

Hiya SJ! Sorry to bother you so late at night – and after Big Sunday, too – but I just want to say: don't worry. Everyone knows how good you are and the fact you've had another off-day only means you'll be motivated to up your game for the technical and dress rehearsals Tuesday and Wednesday. You can be sure no one thinks badly of you. I'm just emailing to remind you that Sam is still interested in being on Poppy's fundraising committee. It would be rather late notice for the meeting tomorrow, but I can always relay any information back to her. I've got my notebook and pen all ready by the door. See you tomorrow! Love Issy xxx

---

FROM: Sarah-Jane MacDonald
SUBJECT: Re: Don't worry!
DATE: 1 July 2018 at 23:32
TO: Isabel Beck

Don't come tomorrow. I'll take the minutes.
Sarah-Jane MacDonald

FROM: Isabel Beck
SUBJECT: Re: Don't worry!
DATE: 1 July 2018 at 23:33
TO: Sarah-Jane MacDonald

Hi SJ, it's no bother. I'm all ready for it, and James has said he'd prefer me to take notes for him. I'll see you at seven. Love Issy xxx

---

FROM: Sarah-Jane MacDonald
SUBJECT: Re: Don't worry!
DATE: 1 July 2018 at 23:34
TO: Isabel Beck

I SAID DON'T COME. We don't want or need you there.
Sarah-Jane MacDonald

FROM: Claudia D'Souza
SUBJECT:
DATE: 1 July 2018 at 23:45
TO: Samantha Greenwood

Kel's told me what Arnie said, and that you know now. Oh, Sam, I'm so sorry you had to find out this way. I don't want to give you a reel of excuses. I didn't want it to happen. Nor did Kel. I haven't told Michael. He's had to dash to Edinburgh with work and is very stressed. I need to find the right time. He doesn't suspect a thing and I genuinely don't know how he'll react. I've got the kids to think about. Please, please, Sam, don't say anything yet. I am so, so sorry. C x

---

FROM: Ciara Savage
SUBJECT: Arnold Ballancore
DATE: 1 July 2018 at 23:49
TO: Kel Greenwood

Dear Mr Greenwood,
I understand you are taking responsibility for Arnold Ballancore. He will be discharged tomorrow morning, but the department will not release his

prescription without an appropriate adult to monitor his medication. I will also issue a letter for his GP. In it we recommend the Community Mental Healthcare Team assesses his needs, alongside Addiction Support. You should be able to arrange an initial consultation within the next six to eight weeks. You will find all the details you need in his discharge letter. If you have any further questions please do not hesitate to call me.

Yours sincerely,
Ciara Savage
Emergency Mental Health Care Nurse, St Ann's Hospital

FROM: Isabel Beck
SUBJECT: Why?
DATE: 1 July 2018 at 23:52
TO: James Hayward

Oh James, I'm so upset. Sarah-Jane sent me a nasty email telling me I'm barred from the committee meeting tomorrow. I told her you'd asked me to take the minutes for you. But she still said I can't come. I was with you and Olivia when I received the email, so you know I was invited. I don't understand why she'd say something like that. I only want to help. I haven't stopped crying since, and I need to get up at six for work. Issy x

---

Message exchange between James Hayward and Sarah-Jane MacDonald on 1–2 July 2018:

23:54 James wrote:
What's this about Isabel being barred from the committee meeting?

23:57 Sarah-Jane wrote:
For crying out loud, will I get any sleep tonight? She was sent the invitation email by accident. I'll take the minutes. Last time she was next to useless anyway. I don't know why she's upset – I'd kill for a night to myself at the moment.

23:59 James wrote:
I understand what you're saying, SJ, but Issy is very sweet. She's helped out with the appeal, she always asks after Olivia and has even visited us in hospital. Go on, it can't hurt, can it?

00:03 Sarah-Jane wrote:
Yes, it can. I won't address this subject until the play is over, but I *do not* want Isabel anywhere near the appeal. Don't ask me any more, James, or mention this to *anyone* else, least of all Isabel.

00:04 Sarah-Jane wrote:
I hope Olivia is as well as can be hoped.

Was Issy Clive Handler?

Transcription of a handwritten note found in Samantha and Kel Greenwood's flat:

To the couple in Flat 5a:

The whole block is sorry to <u>hear</u> you're having relationship problems, but some of us have to get up early and need our sleep. It would be great if, after 11 p.m., you could switch your arguments to text, messenger or email.

Thanks.
Your hard-working neighbours

FROM: Ravi Bhatoa
SUBJECT: Edenfield
DATE: 2 July 2018 at 09:54
TO: Tish Bhatoa

Is there a problem with payments to Edenfield? The bursar just called: this month's Swift transfer hasn't arrived and they need it by close of business today or extra fees apply. Mum's been asking about Dan. I've said he's fine.
Rav

FROM: Tish Bhatoa
SUBJECT: Re: Edenfield
DATE: 2 July 2018 at 11:49
TO: Ravi Bhatoa

The FCO say electricity has been patchy in that region for weeks, but that if anything had happened to a Western aid worker they'd have heard about it. They tried to be reassuring, but Dan isn't involved with the big organisations and I don't know how quickly we'd hear if anything *did* happen. I'm so worried I can't think straight. Tell Mum I've heard from him and he'll write to her soon. I've had to do payroll this week and there's a cash-flow issue. I'll put the payment through again. Tish

A letter found on Samantha Greenwood's desk. It is thought to have arrived around 2 July 2018:

Samantha Greenwood
c/o Médecins Sans Frontières
Orion Building, 3rd Floor
49 Jorissen Street
Braamfontein 2017
Johannesburg
South Africa

27 June 2018

Dear Ms Greenwood,

I was part of the WaterBorn task force in DRC when you were there with MSF. We didn't meet, but I heard about you from other aid workers. I'm sending this letter via MSF in the hope someone there knows a current address for you. I hope you do not find my news too upsetting.

Two weeks ago we were forced east by a rebel clash with the militia. We found ourselves in Faradje, on the border with South Sudan. It was a barren rural area, so we were surprised to find an encampment that looked like a clinic. It's on the main refugee route from South Sudan, so that would make sense. Yet it was deserted. We moved in and set up emergency water-purifying facilities and basic medicals. It's a divided area between Lingala and Swahili, but by chance our leader, Selima, could speak both. Bit by bit she found out what had happened there. I doubt very much anyone else knows and, even if they do, they may not think to tell you. I don't want you to hear it through the media – that's why I'm writing to you now.

The locals said aid workers built the clinic at a time of heavy traffic between South Sudan and DRC. They tried to establish a medical centre, but there were tensions with the community. It may have been general unrest, or the surge of refugees across the border, but the clinic suffered random raids and the aid workers struggled to stay in control. The fact that they were not pulled out indicates they were working independently and didn't have access to key information.

The man in charge was referred to as Daniel Bangui, but the custom here is to call people by their first name and where they're from (everyone here is from somewhere else). I believe this was Daniel Bhatoa, driven east when he found himself unable to work in the CAR.

After a particularly violent clash, they fled south but were hijacked by militants and driven across the border into South Sudan. Word of mouth is as tricky here as anywhere . . . but Selima says news came back they were taken to a militant camp, where they were held for as long as their medical supplies lasted. A week at most. Once they were of no further use, and I will spare you the details, they were all killed.

I've wrestled with whether to write this letter or not. You may be angry he was never brought to justice. Resentful that he will likely be hailed a hero. Or you may think he deserved that fate on some level. I don't know how it will affect you, but I feel you should know. We've tried to pass the news on, but there's no one here to get a team across the border to confirm the deaths, or retrieve the bodies, so I have no idea whether even his family are aware of his fate yet. He wasn't married. The sister who came to Bangui and paid for the trial is his next of kin.

I hope you are settling into life back home. It isn't easy, especially when you had to leave the way you did. Something else you should know is that you have a great deal of respect among the aid workers in Bangui and beyond. The irony is, it's changed. You won't believe how many have been quietly reassigned to admin jobs in the cities. You can't tell me those changes took place because they didn't believe something was going on. Wherever there are vulnerable people, there are those who will exploit them, and others who will protect the abusers – because to expose them is to expose their own tacit complicity. Maybe they turned a blind eye to the suffering it caused, because the suffering it alleviated was deemed so much worse . . . whatever is ultimately behind the changes, none would have happened without you speaking up. Thank you.

Yours sincerely,

Martha Diaz
c/o WaterBorn, Pretoria, South Africa

FROM: Isabel Beck
SUBJECT: Hiya!
DATE: 2 July 2018 at 13:07
TO: Kel Greenwood

Hi Kel, aw, so sorry to hear Sam's under the weather. I'm hoping and wishing her a swift recovery for the tech rehearsal tomorrow. Let's hope there isn't a bug going round the cast! Gulp! Of course I won't disturb her while she's trying to get some rest. But I'm surprised Arnie is allowed home today. Is that ok with you? I mentioned to Sam that he seemed agitated long before things got out of hand at the Yogathon. I'm not as experienced as you are, but he seems to need more help than you and Sam can provide. What on earth did he mean about 'seeing Claudia'? Surely he's not ready to go back to work yet.

I'm at work and feeling like a zombie after two sleepless nights either side of Big Sunday. In fact I'm so tired I've told Sarah-Jane I won't be able to make the committee meeting tonight. It's a shame, because James wanted me to take the minutes, but I've got to think of my performance in the play and have an early night. Between you and me, SJ should think about doing the same, as she was abysmal onstage yesterday – there's no kind way of putting it. How are you enjoying play week so far? I couldn't help but notice you and Sam were quieter than usual. Don't worry. As play week goes on, we'll all pull together, and by opening night The Fairway Players will be working as one slick team. Love to you both, Issy xxx

---

FROM: Paige Reswick
SUBJECT: Thanks
DATE: 2 July 2018 at 15:50
TO: Tish Bhatoa

Dear Tish, I just want to let you know that whatever you gave Poppy today it's worked! She's been sick and running a temperature since we arrived home and has been in bed ever since. Finally – evidence the chemo drugs are getting round her system! I've taken the plunge and decided to shave her head. We made it into a game and she loves wearing her wig. All in all, that was less traumatic than waiting for it to fall out naturally. Thank you so much, Paige and Poppy xxx

Message exchange between Martin Hayward and James Hayward on 2 July 2018:

18:00 Martin wrote:
So you know: Tomorrow. Glen's agreed to come round.

18:02 James wrote:
I should think so. He's done nothing so far. Olivia not so good today. They are talking about operating 'soon'.

18:05 Martin wrote:
Don't message any more. I'll visit you at home or the hospital if there's anything you need to know. Mum and I send our best wishes to Olivia.

FROM: Sarah-Jane MacDonald
SUBJECT: Committee meeting
DATE: 2 July 2018 at 21:59
TO: Martin Hayward
CC: James Hayward

Dear Martin and James,
We held a brief committee meeting this evening to finalise our fundraising strategy for play nights. A brief outline is attached. Regarding the raffle. We have so far raised £3,870. I expect that figure to rise above £4k by the Saturday night. Add to this the proceeds from the box office, merchandise, etc. and I'm confident the play will raise in excess of £5k. I know Colin has transferred his £50k to the fund's account. Please can you confirm the first batch of drugs is on its way? He would also like to place a news piece about his donation in the press and has a journalist friend ready to write it. I said you'll be busy up to and including the play nights, and he's happy for you to do that next week. I know it's a pain, but that type of coverage can lead to 'me too' donations from other high-net-worth individuals. I'll liaise with Paige to see when Poppy will be able to take part in another photoshoot.
Sarah-Jane MacDonald

FROM: Martin Hayward
SUBJECT: Re: Committee meeting
DATE: 2 July 2018 at 22:17
TO: Sarah-Jane MacDonald
CC: James Hayward

Thank you, Sarah-Jane. I'll email everyone tomorrow. Regards, Martin

---

FROM: Dr Sonja Ajanlekoko
SUBJECT: Re: help
DATE: 2 July 2018 at 23:30
TO: Samantha Greenwood

Dear Samantha,
I am sorry to hear that. I really am. You deserve every happiness God can provide. Yes, I can make a case for you to return to the CAR in some manner. Perhaps when a year has passed. If you can get to Johannesburg under your own steam, then so much the better. I have heard only unconfirmed reports of the news, but it does not surprise me. We no longer make a presence in that region, due to the dangerous nature. Independent workers fare badly in those circumstances. Leave me to look into things here and I will keep you in the loop.

Blessings, Sonja

Dr Sonja Ajanlekoko, MBBS (Nigeria) 2008, DRCOG
Project Coordinator, Médecins Sans Frontières

* Sam driven to Africa by the affair? Running away or back... What's the difference?

FROM: Lauren Malden
SUBJECT: Well done!
DATE: 2 July 2018 at 23:41
TO: Isabel Beck

Oh. My. God. Mum told me what happened at the Yogathon. She said you were the hero, tackling a drunk and violent man and saving the day. Clever girl! Go on, spill the beans, what happened? New boyfriend? Only joking! Hey, guess what? I saw a spiritual counsellor the other day. She said I am an intensely passionate woman with a block. So something is stopping me achieving my full potential and reaching the degree of spiritual fulfilment I crave. I told her about what happened and how badly it affected me, but that I got out and it's the bravest thing I ever did. We won't make the play, but let me know all the hot goss. Kiss kiss, L xx

---

DRAFTS FOLDER:
FROM: Isabel Beck
SUBJECT: Re: Well done!
DATE: 2 July 2018 at 23:45
TO: Lauren Malden

What do you mean 'how badly it affected me'? It didn't affect *you* because they blamed *me*. We were friends, so I didn't want to snitch on you. I thought we could share the blame to the outside world, but between us, we'd know you did it. I thought you'd be so grateful you'd be my friend forever. I was so shocked when you told them it was *me*. You knew I wouldn't be able to tell them the truth then, because it would mean admitting to them I lied before. Even if I did, it wasn't as bad a lie as you telling them I did it. Now you believe it yourself – that I'm the one who made the mistake. Do you really believe I did it, or are you just rewriting history in my head as well as your own?

FROM: Isabel Beck
SUBJECT: Re: Well done!
DATE: 2 July 2018 at 23:53
TO: Lauren Malden

It was nothing really. I can't say too much as it's confidential, but yes, I helped sort everything out, take the man to hospital and get him the help he needs. Sam and Kel didn't realise how poorly he was, but I could see there was something wrong with him from the moment I got in the car. It's funny how when someone is in an extreme state they tell the truth. You know what a good judge I am of people. Well, I was right about Claudia. Issy

---

FROM: Kevin MacDonald
SUBJECT: H
DATE: 3 July 2018 at 08:15
TO: Sarah-Jane MacDonald

How is he? I kissed him goodbye, but it was so early he was still asleep. If he's no better, he can miss the tech rehearsal. Martin will understand. A Julian Maher will contact you at some point: be charming – it's Colin's journalist friend.

FROM: Claudia D'Souza
SUBJECT: Appraisal
DATE: 3 July 2018 at 08:59
TO: Samantha Greenwood

Dear Ms Greenwood,
I need to organise an appraisal for you. Please see the list of available time slots below and tick the most convenient one. I will book the Gladstone Room in HR, where we can talk privately and won't be disturbed.

Yours, Claudia D'Souza
Human Resources Manager
St Ann's Hospital

Police Incident Report

Date: 1 July 2018
Location: 42 Victoria Gardens, Lockley Bois
Reporting officer: Constable Warwick Turner
Details of crime: Breaking and entering, theft, assault, ABH, false imprisonment
Crime number: 11346778-08

On the morning of 1 July officers arrived at the premises following a 999 call made by the owner, Mr Robert Green, 63. On arrival, they found Mr Green in a distraught state in the front garden, being comforted by neighbours. He told officers he had been the victim of a burglary/assault during the course of which he was tortured regarding the whereabouts of an artwork he had sold some years before. On failing to find the artwork, three masked assailants commenced a messy search of the house, stealing money, jewellery and other small valuables. They left the victim blindfolded, gagged and tied to a radiator. He indicated that the perpetrators gained access to the house on the afternoon of the previous day - Saturday 30 June 2018. He says they broke in through French windows and spent around an hour there before fleeing. It took the victim sixteen hours to work his way free and raise the alarm.

Perpetrator descriptions:
Male 1 - white, medium build, dark hair, London accent
Male 2 - white, stocky build, gravelly voice, London accent
Male 3 - white, light build, slow voice (like a drawl), indeterminate accent

Notes: The victim gave officers the names of people who might believe he was still in possession of the artwork. As he had been due to travel away from home that weekend, he suggested the intruders were not expecting to find him in. They did not seem to be armed; however, they used items in the house as weapons, including a wooden figurine and a long metal antique shoehorn. Despite being bruised, the victim repeatedly declined officers' polite suggestions that he should go to hospital. The victim has an extensive collection of African crafts. Male 3 correctly identified and then stole a Healing Doll, picture attached, meaning he must have some knowledge or experience of such cultural artefacts.

* The victim requests the violent nature of the attack remain out of the media. Initial press releases should give only sparse details of items stolen, until possible dispersal channels are ruled out.

FROM: Priti Panchal
SUBJECT: Query IB23436008 978 PP
DATE: 3 July 2018 at 09:43
TO: Samantha Greenwood

Dear Ms Greenwood,
I've examined the activity on your accounts and notice that a series of withdrawals were made using your husband's debit card and the correct PIN. It seems maximum withdrawals were made until the current account reached its overdraft limit and the savings account was empty. As the card isn't reported stolen, could anyone in your household have used it? We often find people forget they've made withdrawals, only to remember at a later date. I do hope you understand I can't sanction a time-consuming search of CCTV footage without more evidence a crime has taken place. I'm sorry not to be of any further help.

Yours sincerely,
Priti Panchal
Customer Services

FROM: Martin Hayward
SUBJECT:
DATE: 3 July 2018 at 09:59
TO: Tish Bhatoa

Dear Tish, I understood the active ingredients will be good for at least another month. Regards, Martin

---

FROM: Tish Bhatoa
SUBJECT: Re:
DATE: 3 July 2018 at 11:48
TO: Martin Hayward

Martin, I have a lot on my plate at the moment. The phials will last a bit longer, but I am concerned the delay will prove detrimental to the integrity of the contents. Please consider taking out a loan against your assets. The conventional chemotherapy drugs are now making Poppy very ill and I don't want her immune system to slip below the strength required for the new combination. Keep me informed. Tish

---

FROM: Ian Levy
SUBJECT: Daniel Bhatoa
DATE: 3 July 2018 at 12:58
TO: Dr Tish Bhatoa

Dear Dr Bhatoa,
Further to your calls regarding the last-known whereabouts of your brother Dr Daniel Bhatoa, I can only tell you that reports on the ground confirm he moved from Bangui several months ago and has not been seen since. He left shortly after funding for his women's health clinic was refused. I have no idea why he led you to believe he was still there, but the possibility that he travelled east into remote and war-torn territory is a very real one. Perhaps he did not want you to worry.

As you know, that region suffers from violent clashes as well as sparse electricity and water, so few aid agencies maintain a presence there. Furthermore, the local populations, such as they are, tend to be displaced peoples, migrants and refugees fleeing fighting elsewhere, so there are cultural and language barriers to the transmission of information. Having said that, I understand Daniel Bhatoa has a reputation for not only surviving the most adverse situations, but also thriving in them. He is experienced in the field, with good local knowledge and language skills. We need not assume the worst just yet.

I have made enquiries where I can and you are welcome to make your own via your contacts at DfID and any other source you think may have more information. If I have any confirmed news, of course I will let you know immediately.

Very best of luck,

Ian Levy
Africa Directorate
Foreign & Commonwealth Office

FROM: Ravi Bhatoa
SUBJECT: Re: Fwd: Daniel Bhatoa
DATE: 3 July 2018 at 13:32
TO: Tish Bhatoa

Thanks for forwarding the email, Tish. Fuck it. I've told Mum he's in touch with you. This guy says not to assume the worst . . . Look, we know Dan. He falls in shit and comes up smelling of roses. The email practically says as much. Why didn't he mention he'd left Bangui? I thought he said his funding had been renewed? He sure as shit wasn't thinking of us, because he's never thought of anyone else in his whole life. Did they make it hard for him in Bangui after the accusations? Perhaps, for once, it stuck to him. Look, sit tight. We've known for years this could happen at any time. He'll be in touch as soon as he can. Rav

Item published in the *Lockwood Gazette* online 3 July and in print 6 July 2018:

HEARTLESS THUGS BEAT MAN, 63, IN DAYLIGHT BURGLARY

Three men wearing face masks and anoraks ambushed retired art and antiques dealer Robert Green, 63, in his home in Victoria Gardens, Lockley Bois on Saturday afternoon (30 June). Police say the men gained access to the house from the rear, probably via the cricket ground on Green Lane, and spent around an hour in the property before making off with various small antiques, jewellery and African crafts. Police are appealing for witnesses who saw anything suspicious in the area on Saturday afternoon, and especially those houses and businesses with CCTV cameras. The three men were all white with English accents and appeared knowledgeable about art and antiques.

FROM: Isabel Beck
SUBJECT: Hiya!
DATE: 3 July 2018 at 13:40
TO: Samantha Greenwood

Hiya Sam! Aw, sorry to see you're not in work again. I'm really going to miss you today and hope your tummy's getting better. If not, then let me know and I'll pick up some Imodium from Boots on my way home. You know what we say: the show must go on! It's tech rehearsal tonight, dress tomorrow and then opening night on Thursday. Gulp! Yikes! And yay! One minute I feel sick with nerves and the next so, so excited. Then I remember this time next week it'll all be over and my heart sinks. I've decided to make a new list in my committee notebook about all the things we can do over the summer. Jogging and yoga come to mind, but we can have a chat about other things. Perhaps lunch at the Orangery tomorrow? I'm attaching a link to a little story in the *Gazette*, just in case Arnie saw anything when he visited his friend on Saturday. It's about a nasty burglary in Lockley Bois – an old man was beaten up. I'm glad to hear Arnie's new medication is working. I hope you agree it's still a bit too soon for him to come to the play. Let me know about the Imodium. Lots of love, Issy xxxx

---

FROM: Julian Maher
SUBJECT: Colin Brasher
DATE: 3 July 2018 at 13:59
TO: Sarah-Jane MacDonald

Dear Mrs MacDonald,
I'm writing an article for the *Gazette* network about Colin Brasher's donation to some little girl's charity. I'll take a photograph of Colin with the girl and her mum, ideally in a hospital bed. Is she bald? Great, thanks for organising. Jules

---

FROM: Martin Hayward
SUBJECT: Mea Culpa
DATE: 3 July 2018 at 14:08
TO: Full Mailing List
CC: A Cure for Poppy

Dear all,

I start every letter with an apology, but this apology is far more soul-destroying and humiliating than I ever imagined writing. It chokes me to tell you that, after all your hard work and dedication to raising money for Poppy, I have lost £80,000 of it. I could blame the fraudster who posed as an investment banker and promised to raise significant funds in a very short time, but it was I who desperately wanted to believe her and handed the money over. I did this despite warnings from those around me, so *mea culpa*.

They say you can't con an honest man and every victim of fraud is at least guilty of greed. After this experience, I have to agree. For some time I've been aware that the £250,000 we need for the new drug combination is only the start of Poppy's cure. We will need at least four batches if she is to make a long-term recovery, bringing the total figure required to £1 million. I wanted to raise those funds quickly, and without relying on the relentless hard work of so many good people who have more than enough to worry about in their own lives. Then, just as I despaired we would ever reach our target, along came a woman who said she could help.

Please be aware that those who knew what I was considering tried to talk me out of it. This includes the lovely Sarah-Jane, whose firm advice I bitterly regret ignoring. My son James and son-in-law Glen were also sceptical, but while James has been at Olivia's side in hospital, Glen has been my rock. Indeed, it was Glen who finally uncovered the fraud when he returned to his old workplace in the City yesterday and, with the help of some ex-colleagues, tried to uncover the fund we had supposedly invested in. I am afraid there is no doubt. The £80,000 has disappeared, along with the woman who targeted our family in the coldest, most calculating way possible.

There is no more to be said. I am so, so sorry. Regards, Martin

---

FROM: Sarah-Jane MacDonald
SUBJECT: Re: Mea Culpa
DATE: 3 July 2018 at 14:22
TO: Martin Hayward

Dear Martin,
I'm so sorry. While it is not a total surprise, I had hoped you were right about Lydia Drake and we would see a motivating increase in funds, due to her involvement. I assume you have told the police or are going to? I wasn't intending to mention this until after the play, but Colin recently helped us identify the device used to send the Clive Handler emails. He may be able to help you discover who is behind Lydia Drake (which I'm assuming isn't her real identity).
Sarah-Jane MacDonald

Message from Kevin MacDonald to Sarah-Jane MacDonald on 3 July 2018:

14:23 Kevin wrote:
Shit! What a plonker. Have the police said anything? Presumably this isn't the first time she's done it. We'll have to tell Colin. It'll sound like we're fishing for more cash. Would be great if he stumps up to replace the money lost, but can't expect him to. Harley is forwarding promotional emails for a new PlayStation game, so take it he is feeling better?

FROM: Sarah-Jane MacDonald
SUBJECT: Re: Colin Brasher
DATE: 3 July 2018 at 14:46
TO: Julian Maher

Dear Julian,
Further to your email, there have been some developments in this story. Colin may not be aware of them yet and, quite frankly, after his generosity and support, I am dreading the moment I tell him. The appeal has been scammed to the tune of £80,000. A woman who called herself Lydia Drake promised Martin Hayward, Poppy's grandfather, that she could provide inflated returns on his money by investing in high-risk, high-return funds.

He was vulnerable, as you can imagine, and handed over money raised by the campaign. I am fuming with anger that someone is callous enough to steal from a sick child, and a distraught family, like this. Would you be able to expose this fraud in such a way as to warn other potentially vulnerable people? It may also be a way to raise replacement funds for the appeal and help it reach a wider audience. Any ideas you may have, or help you could give us, would be very much appreciated.
Sarah-Jane MacDonald

FROM: Martin Hayward
SUBJECT: Re: Mea Culpa
DATE: 3 July 2018 at 15:02
TO: Sarah-Jane MacDonald

You know who Clive Handler was? Who is it? Someone we know? Why haven't you said? Regards.

FROM: Joyce Walford
SUBJECT: Re: Mea Culpa
DATE: 3 July 2018 at 15:10
TO: Martin Hayward

Dear Martin, if something sounds too good to be true, it probably is. Joyce

---

FROM: Marianne Payne
SUBJECT: Re: Mea Culpa
DATE: 3 July 2018 at 15:26
TO: Martin Hayward

Dear Martin, Why would anyone do something like that? A woman as well! She must have no kids of her own, if she's prepared to steal from a sick child. Mick can't believe it, and I know Karen will be shocked when she hears. What have the police said? They'll trace where the money's gone and can seize it back, too. We know, because Mick's cousin got in with the wrong crowd a few years ago and that's what they did to him. Of course that was nothing like this. He only stole off other drug dealers, and even then just for revenge. Oh, Martin, please don't blame yourself. You did what you thought was best at the time. It's not your fault there are these people in the world. All our love, Marianne, Mick and Karen x

---

FROM: Isabel Beck
SUBJECT: Re: Mea Culpa
DATE: 3 July 2018 at 16:27
TO: Martin Hayward

Dear Martin, I am so sorry to hear this. I can't even imagine having that amount of money, let alone having it and losing it. Don't worry. With the play this week, we could raise at least some of it back. And even if it takes longer than you thought to get Poppy's new drug, she is at least still having chemotherapy and the Oncology department at Mount More is very well respected. I did a placement there during my training and haven't been back since, but St Ann's is part of the same Healthcare Trust and you get to hear the strengths and weaknesses of all the different departments. I'm sure no one is blaming you for trying to increase the funds quickly. Anyone would, in your situation. Hopefully this won't affect *All My Sons*, as the whole group has been working so hard to make it the best it could ever be. I know Sam, Kel and I are soooo excited and proud to be part of it. You know what they say: the show must go on! Love Issy xxx

---

FROM: Isabel Beck
SUBJECT: Hiya!
DATE: 3 July 2018 at 16:36
TO: Samantha Greenwood

Hi Sam! Gasp! Have you read Martin's email? £80,000 down the drain. That's sooo much money! Fancy Martin falling for a confidence trick! He always comes across as so rational and in charge. It just goes to show how stress and desperation can lead people to behave out of character. I've sent him a rallying email, assuring him we're all behind the play. The last thing we need is to disrupt the performance nights. I pointed out that Poppy is having chemo anyway, so it's not as if she's not being treated. I didn't want

to say, in as many words, but these new drugs may not be a cure anyway. The first thing I thought, all those weeks ago, was that they would be no better than existing treatment. You get carried away on a tide of hope, don't you? Really looking forward to the technical rehearsal tonight. Don't worry: it's not really for us. It's just to get lights, sound and backstage all cued up and clued up. Although the full dress isn't until tomorrow, I'm going to wear my costume anyway. I feel much more in character when I'm dressed in the right clothes! Just think – the day after tomorrow it'll be opening night and I'll be frantically emailing you all day to tell you, time and again, how nervous I am . . . and you'll tell me time and again that nerves give your performance an edge, and that'll make me feel better – for a few minutes! Hope you and Kel are looking forward to it as much as I am! Lots of love,
Issy xxxxx

FROM: Jackie Marsh
SUBJECT: Re: Mea Culpa
DATE: 3 July 2018 at 16:54
TO: Martin Hayward

need my donation to Poppy's appeal back now. You know about stuff – reverse the transaction or something. I didn't mean to odnate so much anyway so it's not like I want it back It's rea;;y important.
Sent from my Samsung Galaxy S9

Ooops no more! Magic pee-proof pants peeproofpants.eu. No more leaks or stains with Order now and love two pairs for the pirce of one peeproofpants.eu you won't believe it

Item published in the *Lockwood Gazette* online 3 July 2018:

HUNT FOR £80K CANCER CHARITY FRAUDSTER

by Julian Maher

A charity raising money for a toddler's cancer treatment has been conned out of £80,000. Two-year-old Poppy Reswick, shown here with her mother Paige and local crooner Tony Zucchero at the launch of the appeal, was diagnosed with Medulloblastoma earlier this year and her best chance of a cure was said to be a new drug only available in the US. Friends and family set up A Cure for Poppy to raise £250,000 for the first round of treatment, and the cash rolled in. Then an investment banker calling herself Lydia Drake approached Poppy's grandfather, Martin Hayward, 59, and promised to increase the funds to £1m in as little as three months. 'I wanted to raise funds quickly, and without relying on the relentless hard work of so many good people who have more than enough to worry about in their own lives,' he explains. 'Just as I despaired we would ever reach our target, along came a woman who said she could help.' It wasn't until weeks later the family realised Ms Drake had disappeared, along with the £80,000 she had been paid. More information about the appeal can be found at www.wefund.com/acureforpoppy

FROM: Julian Maher
SUBJECT: Re: Colin Brasher
DATE: 3 July 2018 at 17:18
TO: Martin Hayward

Here's a link to the story about your missing £80,000. I'm updating it live online, so let me know asap:

- Name of the police team dealing with the case and their public contact details.
- Description of Lydia Drake and any info she gave you about herself: e.g. CV, office address – anything.
- A recent photo of yourself, Poppy and her mum looking sad.
- Donation details for readers who want to send money to replace the stolen funds. I've put the website at the bottom of the online story, but a postal address is better for our print edition.

Cheers, Jules

FROM: Martin Hayward
SUBJECT: Re: Mea Culpa
DATE: 3 July 2018 at 17:29
TO: Sarah-Jane MacDonald

I've been contacted by a journalist. There's an article online about Lydia Drake. I'm just this minute reading it.

FROM: Sarah-Jane MacDonald
SUBJECT: Re: Mea Culpa
DATE: 3 July 2018 at 17:36
TO: Martin Hayward

Brilliant! Hopefully this will help us: a) find Lydia Drake; and b) publicise the fraud, so we can raise the money back that much quicker. I'm impressed by Julian's speed. Very efficient. What have the police said? Do they know Ms Drake?
Sarah-Jane MacDonald

FROM: Martin Hayward
SUBJECT: Re: Mea Culpa
DATE: 3 July 2018 at 17:40
TO: Sarah-Jane MacDonald

Sarah-Jane, this article must be taken down NOW. I DO NOT want this episode in the public domain. It won't do us, or the appeal, any good at all. For goodness' sake!

FROM: Sarah-Jane MacDonald
SUBJECT: Re: Mea Culpa
DATE: 3 July 2018 at 17:49
TO: Martin Hayward

Martin, I know you're ashamed and humiliated to have fallen for a confidence trick, but this is how criminals like Drake are caught. It's also how other people avoid falling for similar scams in future. However embarrassed you are, this is all for the best – check the appeal page – new donations have been rolling in steadily since the story went live. Think of this as another stage in the fundraising process. Surely the police have advised you to tell as many people as possible . . . You have reported this to the police, Martin?

FROM: Martin Hayward
SUBJECT: Re: Mea Culpa
DATE: 3 July 2018 at 17:53
TO: Sarah-Jane MacDonald

No. I don't want this out there. Contact them and get the article taken down, removed from searches, whatever it is they do. We can't have the police poking into everything. I'm sorry, but this is a family matter now. I'm blocking Julian Maher, and don't want you to tell him anything, either. Let this story die.

Message from Kevin MacDonald to Sarah-Jane MacDonald on 3 July 2018:

18:02 Kevin wrote:
I know, but what can we do? Colin's happy to run a check on Lydia's email codes, so I've forwarded the message she sent to me. He thinks she'll be part of a larger operation and will have covered her tracks, but he'll let us know if anything comes up. If it identifies an individual, we'll go to the police ourselves – after the play.

FROM: Claudia D'Souza
SUBJECT: Appraisal
DATE: 3 July 2018 at 18:02
TO: Samantha Greenwood

Dear Sam,
I take it, from your lack of reply, that you don't want to meet with me. I understand, I really do. You must be feeling terrible, and that's only to be expected. Kel told me all about what happened in Africa and I'm sorry. I just want to let you know how difficult this is for us, too. Both Kel and I have been going through hell these last few weeks. Believe me, if we could walk away from each other, we would. Our feelings are stronger than both of us. Kel wanted to tell you himself and was waiting for your play to be over. He didn't have anyone to talk to, and confided in Arnie before his condition was apparent. If he thought there was a danger he'd blurt it all out like that, he'd never have mentioned it. What's done is done. We are all just passengers now. I'm going to tell Michael and the kids this week, I promise. He's back tomorrow and I have to find the right moment. Claudia

---

FROM: Isabel Beck
SUBJECT: Hiya!
DATE: 3 July 2018 at 18:05
TO: Samantha Greenwood

Hiya Sam! Glad you're feeling better for the tech rehearsal tonight. I'm outside the hall now, but it's all locked up. That'll teach me to get here half an hour early. Still, it's a nice warm evening, so I can sit here and watch the world go by. I've been thinking about Claudia and the fact she's not returning your messages. Do you think she's friendly with YKW, so hasn't said anything to her? It's just, I was in the staffroom on afternoon break and Gaynor asked how the play was going. YKW literally stepped in front of me and said, 'Gaynor, I want to know all about your spa weekend . . . ' and cut me off completely. (Gaynor could have said, 'Excuse me, Frances, but Issy is telling me about her play. I can speak to you about the spa weekend in a minute' – like I know *you* would've done – but she didn't.) I just had to stand there and wait while Gaynor told her about the spa and YKW gasped and cooed, as if Gaynor had stayed on the moon or something, not just a hotel with a swimming pool (which we all know she can't afford). Perhaps there's something wrong with Claudia's email address? Did you realise her husband works in the PR office at St Ann's? His name's on the Intranet. So if we need to, we can always go through him.

Ah, here's Martin to open up. Between you and me, he looks very pale. I won't mention anything about the fund money. He probably wants to forget. See you and Kel soon. Lots of love, Issy

---

Handwritten inside a cheap condolence card sent to Tish Bhatoa at her Mount More work address:

RIP The Banqui Baba

FROM: Tish Bhatoa
SUBJECT: Card
DATE: 3 July 2018 at 18:14
TO: Ravi Bhatoa

First pic is the front of the card, second pic inside. Arrived at MM with a first-class stamp, local postmark. I haven't told anyone Dan's missing. If it's true, then how does anyone know, if *we* don't? Who would send something like this?

FROM: Ravi Bhatoa
SUBJECT: Re: Card
DATE: 3 July 2018 at 18:16
TO: Tish Bhatoa

I'm on my way over. Callous as it is, someone obviously knows something. We have to prepare Mum for bad news. Don't do anything yet. We'll ring round together when I'm there.

FROM: Sarah-Jane MacDonald
SUBJECT: Woof
DATE: 3 July 2018 at 18:00
TO: Emma Crooks

How is Woof? I keep meaning to pop in and say hi, but work, the play and the appeal keep getting in the way. You didn't miss much at the committee meeting. We just ascribed fundraising roles for play nights. I'm sitting in the car outside the hall, but can't go in yet because drippy Issy is hanging around outside. James wanted her to take the minutes last night, but she's friends with Sam, so I didn't want her anywhere near the committee. Ah, the Hallidays have just pulled up. If you need my mum to watch Woof when you come to the play, just ask.
Sarah-Jane MacDonald

FROM: Emma Crooks
SUBJECT: Re: Woof
DATE: 3 July 2018 at 18:05
TO: Sarah-Jane MacDonald

Woof is rocking a giant cone of shame and has not adjusted his spatial awareness in any way. He's already destroyed a pair of my best tights (£18 in the vegan shop) and chipped paintwork all over the ground floor. Needless to say, he seems to be feeling better. I would LOVE to see the play and bless your mum for offering to Woof-sit. Can I call her to arrange? I'm behind on the goss – why is Sam *persona non grata*? I thought she was lovely. Emma

---

FROM: Sarah-Jane MacDonald
SUBJECT: Re: Woof
DATE: 3 July 2018 at 18:07
TO: Emma Crooks

Yes, you can give Mum a call. It's water under the bridge now, but we traced the hoax emails to Sam Greenwood's laptop. I'm not rocking the boat till after the play, though. Keep it to yourself. Poor Martin and Helen have enough to deal with at the moment.
Sarah-Jane MacDonald

FROM: Emma Crooks
SUBJECT: Re: Woof
DATE: 3 July 2018 at 18:08
TO: Sarah-Jane MacDonald

Oh my God! That nurse conned £80k out of the appeal? And she's still in the play? I can't believe it! Why don't you say something, SJ?

FROM: Sarah-Jane MacDonald
SUBJECT: Re: Woof
DATE: 3 July 2018 at 18:10
TO: Emma Crooks

No, she didn't steal the money. That was Lydia Drake. Sam emailed us under a fake name and said she would pay for Poppy's treatment, then didn't. No idea what her motivation was. It was devastating at the time, but pales into nothing next to this latest shitstorm. That was all down to Martin, by the way – chat when I can pop round.
Sarah-Jane MacDonald

FROM: Carol Dearing
SUBJECT: Play
DATE: 3 July 2018 at 18:31
TO: Sarah-Jane MacDonald

Did you tell Emma I'd look after that smelly dog while she sees the play? I thought you wanted me to sell tat and raffle tickets . . .

FROM: Sarah-Jane MacDonald
SUBJECT: Re: Play
DATE: 3 July 2018 at 18:33
TO: Carol Dearing

Sorry, Mum, do you mind? Emma's stuck with a poorly Woof. He can't go home because of Poppy's compromised immune system. Thank you.
Sarah-Jane MacDonald

PS Not tat. Official 'A Cure for Poppy' merchandise.

FROM: Carol Dearing
SUBJECT: Re: Play
DATE: 3 July 2018 at 18:35
TO: Sarah-Jane MacDonald

I don't need your full name and surname at the end of every bloody email.
Carol Rose Dearing

FROM: Sarah-Jane MacDonald
SUBJECT: Re: Play
DATE: 3 July 2018 at 18:36
TO: Carol Dearing

It's an automatic signature. I try to delete it when the email's personal, but I usually forget. Have to switch my phone off now – tech rehearsal about to start.
Sarah-Jane MacDonald

FROM: Isabel Beck
SUBJECT: Hiya!
DATE: 3 July 2018 at 21:39
TO: Samantha Greenwood

I'm still in the green room. They're taking so long over Act One I don't think I'll get onstage before ten. What did Sarah-Jane want? Did she mention the committee meeting? Love Issy xxxx

---

FROM: Isabel Beck
SUBJECT: Hiya!
DATE: 3 July 2018 at 21:49
TO: Kel Greenwood

Hi Kel! Well done! I heard what Martin said about your characterisation. He's not dishing out compliments tonight, so consider yourself lucky. Where's Sam? Love Issy xxxx

---

Message exchange between James Hayward and Martin Hayward on 3 July 2018:

22:00 James wrote:
An emergency scan this evening. Touch and go for a bit, then all relax again. They want to wait another day at least. Every moment we keep them inside gives them a better chance. How's it going?

22:03 Martin wrote:
Don't message. I'll call in the morning.

22:04 James wrote:
I meant the tech rehearsal. Ok, speak tomorrow.

FROM: Jackie Marsh
SUBJECT: Re: Mea Culpa
DATE: 3 July 2018 at 22:22
TO: Martin Hayward

Did you get my last message? The p[olice have my passport and want $200. Its really really important I get my money back. Don't understand why you haven't refunded it?

Sent from my Samsung Galaxy S9

Feeling lonely lovely horny girls for you waiting for you now online and in personal sexy girls

---

Message exchange between Kevin MacDonald and Sarah-Jane MacDonald on 3 July 2018:

22:32 Kevin wrote:
Ok? You looked upset when I left to take Harley back. Rehearsal not that bad, was it? Where are you?

22:50 Sarah-Jane wrote:
Leaving now. Wasn't intending to speak to her, but Sam cornered me when we were offstage. Started talking about Martin and Helen. Told her I've known them all my life, they are my family's closest friends and the loveliest people one could ever hope to meet. She . . . well, it's not important what she said. I ended up blurting out that we know she was the hoax benefactor. That we're only keeping quiet because we want the play to go well for Martin and Helen, but that we want nothing more to do with her. She was about to say something else, but that insipid Isabel appeared out of nowhere, and that was the end of that. I needed time to think, so helped Martin and Joel put props away. Helen's only just left. Apparently Poppy has lost all her hair and is wearing a wig now. Can you imagine how we'd feel if that was Harley? The stress is written on their faces. Martin was right. Sam is trouble.

FROM: Isabel Beck
SUBJECT: Hiya!
DATE: 3 July 2018 at 23:28
TO: Kel Greenwood

Hi Kel, hope you don't mind me emailing you, but I just want to make sure Sam's ok. She barely spoke to me at all after rehearsal and I wonder if Sarah-Jane said anything? I really *did* decide not to go to the committee meeting yesterday, even though SJ said not to bother anyway. I know James wanted me there, but apparently it was only a quick meeting. Anyway, we should consider the dress rehearsal as a play night, so that means it all starts tomorrow! This is what we've been working towards, thinking about and worrying over for months. It's all down to these last few days. I am so excited and nervous and elated and scared . . . I know you both must be feeling the same, so it's understandable you're feeling the pressure. I am so tired I could sleep for a week, and yet I know I'll be lying awake for hours trying to drop off. What I mean is, please tell Sam not to worry, everything's fine and this is how it should be at this stage in the play! I hope everything's ok. Love Issy xxx

Extract from Constable Warwick Turner's notebook:

Date: 3 July 2018

Time: 23:35

Crime number: 11346778-08

A woman walked into Lockley Bois police office with information about the above crime. She did not wish her identity to be recorded, but claimed an individual named Arnold Ballancore was in possession of an African Healing Doll on Saturday 30 June, shortly after the above crime took place. She witnessed him give the doll to a two-year-old child who has been unwell. The woman claims her suspicions were only raised when she read press reports stating that African crafts had been stolen during the aggravated burglary above. She recognised the doll as being of genuine Central African origin, an area she claims Mr Ballancore also knows well. She further suspects Mr Ballancore's involvement, as he was stranded in Lockley Bois on the afternoon of 30 June. She claimed Mr Ballancore recently took money from two of her bank accounts after discovering her PIN numbers. Mr Ballancore was recently discharged from St Ann's Hospital and is now living with her and her husband by the green in Lockwood. She describes his general behaviour as consistent with psychotic episodes and/or opioid addiction and fears for the safety of those he is in contact with.

FROM: Isabel Beck
SUBJECT: Hiya!
DATE: 4 July 2018 at 05:14
TO: Samantha Greenwood

Good morning! Just imagine how we'll feel this time tomorrow! Sometimes I think Kel is lucky to get these few days off, but on the other hand I would just sit at home getting more and more nervous. I like to have my mind taken off things. I'm so relieved we both managed to get on earlies this week – thanks to you. Do you remember way back, when we first knew we were in the play, we both put in for earlies and YKW approved yours but not mine? It was only when you lobbied for me that she changed it. You would make a fantastic ward manager, Sam. Have you thought any more about applying? If Claudia really can get rid of YKW, you could be in post by autumn. Then we can start planning for our trip to Africa. Do you think a year is enough to arrange something like that? We can fly out after next year's summer play, so we're back before rehearsals start for the November play. See, I'm already doing the admin! How is Arnie? Kel said last night he probably won't come to see *All My Sons*. Phew! I'm sure he wouldn't enjoy it. If you're not a regular theatregoer, it can be a chore to sit through a play as serious as that. I love acting in it, but there aren't many laughs. *Blithe Spirit* was very funny. I'm so glad you came to see it before joining. I've made a list of comedy plays with large casts and will send it to James as soon as he and Olivia are out of the woods with their new babies (fingers crossed). Comedies are so much more fun to do, and if there's a large cast we will have a better chance of getting parts in it. What did Sarah-Jane say to you yesterday? You were very quiet after speaking to her, and I wonder if it was about me? She's been working very hard on the appeal lately and she can get the wrong end of the stick at the best of times. I'm sure she's just worried about the play. Well, time to start work! I need to take my mind off what lies ahead, so I don't even care if I get discharges today! See you at break! Love Issy xxxx

---

FROM: Marianne Payne
SUBJECT: Police
DATE: 4 July 2018 at 07:43
TO: Joyce Walford

What's happening, Joyce? Karen says there are police outside the new flats.

FROM: Joyce Walford
SUBJECT: Police
DATE: 4 July 2018 at 08:12
TO: Marianne Payne

They've been there since six. Two big vans and a car parked on the green. They all piled in, in their riot gear, but no one's come out yet. Wait ... they're bringing someone out. It's that swampy who tried to con me out of tea money at the Yogatron! I knew there was nothing good about that one. He's shouting and swearing and only wearing a pair of shorts! I've opened the window to see if I can hear exactly what he's saying. They're putting him in the van. He must be staying with those nurses on the fifth floor. No wonder the police took so long, if they had to run up all those stairs with their shields! Yes, there's that male nurse now. He's talking to a policewoman ... Ah, the police are going, I wonder if he's tried to diddle money out of someone else this time. Not that the police will do anything. He'll get a slap on the wrist and counselling. I'm not being funny, Marianne, but my Barry had the right idea. Have you got all your baking things ready? My poppy-seed cakes are in the oven now. Joyce

---

FROM: Martin Hayward
SUBJECT: Clive Handler
DATE: 4 July 2018 at 08:23
TO: Tish Bhatoa

Dear Tish, Well, some good news at least. We've got to the bottom of who 'Clive Handler' really was. It was your 'friend' Samantha Greenwood. Looking back over those emails, she was clearly trying to glean information about the provenance of the drugs. Obvious, when you look at it. Any idea why she might have done such a thing? Regards, Martin

---

FROM: Tish Bhatoa
SUBJECT: Re: Clive Handler
DATE: 4 July 2018 at 08:29
TO: Martin Hayward

Samantha Greenwood is responsible for the death of my brother. She accused him of unspeakable things. Of abusing those he cared about most: the women and children who walked miles – hundreds of miles in some cases – to be treated and healed by him. They gave him a nickname, meaning 'father', to demonstrate what he meant to them. He dedicated his life to making the world a better place. But she spread lies about him, destroyed his reputation, made him an outcast in the place he loved and that loved him, until he was forced to move somewhere so godforsaken he had no chance of survival. But that was her mistake. Now I have nothing left to lose.

FROM: Martin Hayward
SUBJECT: Re: Clive Handler
DATE: 4 July 2018 at 08:34
TO: Tish Bhatoa

Dear Tish, I am so sorry to hear about your brother. Our thoughts are with you at this difficult time. Regards, Martin, Helen and family

---

FROM: Robert Green
SUBJECT: Thank you
DATE: 4 July 2018 at 09:33
TO: Warwick Turner

Dear Constable Turner, I am feeling much better now, thank you. My partner has just returned from his business trip to Oman, so I am no longer in the house alone and that makes a big difference. Many thanks for visiting and keeping me in the loop re the burglary. I hope the man you arrested can shed light on the gang. I am intrigued he knew about the Healing Doll and gave it to a young girl who is unwell. Behaviour quite at odds with the savagery he exhibited during the attack, as he was easily the most aggressive of the three. That particular example is thought to be an effigy of an ancestral spirit and is very old. Yes, it is a direct antecedent of the 'voodoo' we know from cultures in Haiti and other regions where Africans have settled. However, far from the 'spooky' connotations we associate with anima belief systems, the doll would have been made when a girl was born, to keep negative energy, spells and ill health at bay. It must have done its job because if she had died, the doll would have been destroyed. In other words, the original owner reached adulthood – usually deemed to be the point when she has her first child – and gave this one away, or even sold it, as a doll with proven protective powers. Some dolls 'live' for years, protecting one person after another for generations. As you can imagine, there is a bucolic approach to healthcare in central African regions and the power of these dolls is taken seriously by the rural population. In short, I would like the little girl to keep the doll. It has positive energy and, at the very least, I am sure she will enjoy playing with it. Best wishes, Robert Green

Transcription of a 999 call made at 13:44 on 4 July 2018:

Operator: Emergency, which service?
Caller: Police.
Operator: Hello, police emergency. What address?
Caller: St Ann's Hospital, Geriatric Ward.
Operator: What's happening, Caller?
Caller: She's being attacked.
Operator: Is the attacker still there?
Caller: Yes.
Operator: Are they hurt?
Caller: [*inaudible*]
Operator: Do you need an ambulance?
Caller: No, we're in the hospital already. We need the police.
Police radio: St Ann's Hospital.
Operator: Explain what's happened?
Caller: Pushed her into Isolation and shut the door.
Police radio: Is she still there?
Caller: Who's that?
Operator: The police. They can hear you and are on their way. What's happening now?
Caller: They're in Isolation. I can hear, but the window [*inaudible*].
Operator: So this is two nurses fighting?
Caller: No. She came in, pushed her into Isolation . . . I can hear them. She's jammed the door shut. Can you open the door? Push . . . I can hear her hitting her. Oh my God . . .
Police radio: Two minutes. Is Geriatrics easy to find, Caller?
Caller: Er . . . I don't know. Are you at the main entrance or Clyde Bank Way?
Police radio: We're at the bus terminus.
Caller: By Clyde Bank Way?
New voice: *Who's in there, Isabel?*
Caller: Sam. It's Sam. I've called the police.
New voice: *We don't need the police! Give me the phone. You're hopeless. Give it to me!*

Caller: [*new voice*] A woman is arguing with one of our staff nurses. They're locked in a side ward. I'm sure we'll sort it out.

Police radio: We're here now, at the bus terminus.

Caller: [*new voice*] Ok then. Come to the side entrance of St Ann's on Clyde Bank Way behind the bus station. Straight down the long corridor, then up the stairs at the end. Geriatrics is on the third floor.

Operator: Did you get that?

Police radio: Yep, we're at the entrance. Can someone let us in at the door?

Caller: [*new voice*] Go on, Isabel – you called them, you let them in. Now, yes, go on.

Operator: Thank you. What's your name please, Caller?

Caller: [*new voice*] Frances Turner. The dimwit you spoke to first was Isabel Beck.

Message exchange between Glen Reswick and Martin Hayward on 4 July 2018:

14:19 Glen wrote:
The police are outside. Shit, what's going on?

14:20 Martin wrote:
Surely they'd come here first. Is Paige there? Can you hide?

14:20 Glen wrote:
She's in the kitchen with Poppy. What shall I tell her? They've rung the bell . . . Shit, she's answered.

14:58 Martin wrote:
Everything ok? Have they gone?

15:16 Martin wrote:
Everything ok?

15:45 Glen wrote:
And breathe. You won't believe this. Someone gave Poppy a rag doll at the Yogathon (the drunk guy you had words with). We put it out of the way – it's so obviously second-hand. Well, it had been stolen from a private art collection

and could be valuable! They took photos of it and a statement from Paige. The owner was told it had been given to a little girl and said she could keep it. It has healing properties. Sorry about that.

15:49 Martin wrote:
All's well that ends well. How much is the doll worth?

FROM: Isabel Beck
SUBJECT: What on earth happened?
DATE: 4 July 2018 at 14:26
TO: Samantha Greenwood

Oh my goodness, Sam, are you ok? I dialled 999 as soon as Gaynor said you were being attacked. I have a sixth sense, when it comes to the seriousness of things. YKW tried to take over the call, but I didn't let her. She's sent me down to X-ray with a new admission because she knows how much I want to go to A&E with you. Who did that to you? I didn't see her come through reception, just heard the door slam. I only knew it was a woman because Gaynor said so. Is she a bereaved relative? We've had that before, although nowhere near as violent. Have you told Kel? Shall I email him for you? He'll want to come and pick you up. Oh my goodness, do you think you'll be ok for the play? Hope you're not too badly hurt. Lots of love, Issy xxxx

---

FROM: Isabel Beck
SUBJECT: Sam attacked!
DATE: 4 July 2018 at 14:30
TO: Kel Greenwood

Kel, something terrible has happened. A woman burst into the ward and attacked Sam! I didn't see it myself, but she pushed Sam into Iso and jammed the door shut. If I hadn't called the police, anything might have happened. I don't know who on earth she is. Who would attack Sam? They took this woman off the ward straight away, according to Gaynor. I'd been sent down to X-ray by then, and our ward manager took Sam to A&E (she always wants to be at the centre of any drama, covered in glory), so I've no idea how she is now. Can you bring the car? I really hope Sam is ok and that she'll be fine for the dress rehearsal tonight. I'm so worried. Love Issy xxxx

---

FROM: Paige Reswick
SUBJECT: Drama!
DATE: 4 July 2018 at 15:14
TO: Emma Crooks

Hi Ems, how's my baby Woof doing? We had the police here today. The man who punched Barry at the Yogathon has been arrested for a burglary over at Lockley. But there's more! He gave Poppy a *horrible* grubby doll. We thought nothing of it at the time, except that we took it straight off her in case it was covered in germs. Well, the doll is a valuable artwork and was stolen in the burglary. Luckily, Poppy charmed the policemen and they said she could keep the doll. Or was it the owner who said she could have it? Anyway, it's lovely of them. Even though the doll is shocking, pic attached, apparently it's called a Healing Doll. So glad we didn't bin it on sight. Love to Woof! P x

---

FROM: Emma Crooks
SUBJECT: Re: Drama!
DATE: 4 July 2018 at 15:30
TO: Paige Reswick

Ew! It looks shamanic. Careful it doesn't walk around the house at night. Do they have healing dolls for dogs? Woof is lying across the doorway, panting in the heat and occasionally woofing, cantankerously, at me. His scar looks quite angry still, but he's eating anything that lands in his bowl, so he must feel ok. Carol's offered to Woof-sit so I can see the play Friday. Will you be there? Emma

---

FROM: Paige Reswick
SUBJECT: Re: Drama!
DATE: 4 July 2018 at 15:36
TO: Emma Crooks

Yes, I'll be there all three nights while Glen babysits. It's more to support Mum, Dad and the appeal. I hope it goes ok for them, but it's no fun when you haven't got a part. I really wish I could be in it. I had no intention of dropping out when Poppy was diagnosed. After all, Mum didn't have to. But Dad insisted it would look odd if both of us continued in the play. I'm sure I could have fitted rehearsals around her treatment. Oh well, sulky face, I'll have to wait for the next one. Let's sit together on Friday. P x

Extract from Constable Josie Thompson's notebook:

Date: 4 July 2018
Location: St Ann's Hospital, Geriatric Ward
Time: 13:55
Crime number: N/A

Following a 999 call, Constable Liam Albutt and myself found alleged assailants barricaded into a side room. Liam forced the door – inside, two women were fighting on the floor – a nurse and another. We separated them and I took the other woman out of the ward. She was unhurt. Would not say what happened or why. Liam spoke to the nurse, who was bleeding from nose and forehead. The nurse admitted she knew the other woman, said the attack was unprovoked, yet 'understandable'. Neither wanted to press charges and, having established no one was badly hurt, we left a colleague to take the nurse to A&E and escorted the other woman from the premises. No further action was taken.

Femi
Is Sam 'trouble', like Bhatoa says, or simply a principled person unafraid to speak out if it will help put something right?

Charlotte
That's it, though, Femi. What she sees as right isn't necessarily what *is* right.

Femi
And Kel? They clash with Dan in Africa, then turn up at the same healthcare trust where his sister works . . . surely no coincidence.

Charlotte
There's a conspiracy somewhere here. It's a case of who's in on it . . .

Femi
Bhatoa is the hardest to fathom. She detests the Haywards, yet seems coldly dependent on them. Strange.

Charlotte
Bhatoa marches into Sam's work and attacks her. Pure passion.

Femi
Bhatoa attacks Sam in the hospital? That isn't Bhatoa.

Charlotte
Tish blames Sam for her brother's death. Who else would it be?

Femi
Claudia. Because Sam told her husband, Michael, about the affair with Kel.

Charlotte
Have I missed something? When does Sam tell Michael this?

Femi
She doesn't.

Charlotte
Well, who does?

Femi
Isabel. Let's read to the end. We haven't got long, and we can explore our theories in the document for Tanner.

Charlotte
Ok. I knew I'd be shit at this.

FROM: Isabel Beck
SUBJECT: Sam!
DATE: 4 July 2018 at 17:12
TO: Martin Hayward

Dear Martin,
I'm sorry to bother you when you're so busy with the play and everything else. I just want you to know that Sam had an accident at work today and has a swollen mouth, a black eye and a cut to her forehead. Who'd have thought the geriatric ward could be so perilous! As you know, Sam is dedicated to the play and is still planning to come to the dress rehearsal tonight. I just wanted to warn you, as Denise will need to work miracles on the make-up. I have to fill in an Incident Report for HR, so I'll stay after my shift, but hopefully it won't make me late. Kel came to collect Sam, so I had a word with him, and he told me categorically not to worry and that they will both be there tonight. He looked so worried. Between you and me, their friend Arnie is back in their flat and, in my opinion, he needs more help for his personal issues than they can give him. Still, we've got *All My Sons* to keep us busy this week. I can't wait to be back onstage in the spotlight, in front of an audience again! Thanks, Martin! Love Issy xxx

County Police Interview Report

Extract from police interview with Arnold Ballancore, arrested on 4 July 2018:

Sgt Cooper: So take us back to when you met this gentleman.

A. Ballancore: Sharkey took me to him. Said he was all right, a proper mate. I took his word for it.

Sgt Cooper: Sharkey the heroin dealer . . . ?

A. Ballancore: Yeah. But he was so wrong. He robbed every bit of money off me. Over six grand. But he said I had to get him more.

Sgt Cooper: This is some of the money you owed Sharkey for heroin.

A. Ballancore: Yeah.

Sgt Cooper: And you yourself had taken the money from Sean Greenwood's account?

A. Ballancore: Who?

Sgt Cooper: Your friend Sean Greenwood. Although I doubt he's a friend now.

Sgt Crowe: The account of Sean Kelly Greenwood and Samantha Greenwood.

A. Ballancore: Oh. Kel. Yeah, Kel Greenwood. He's not . . . he *is*, he's a friend, but you know when a friend does something you hate? So he's not your friend, but he still is?

Sgt Cooper: Right.

A. Ballancore: No one should treat Sam like that, after all she did.

Sgt Cooper: So Sharkey took you where?

A. Ballancore: I don't know, man. Out in the sticks. A gnarly old place like in *Withnail and I*. Sharkey says if I do a job with this Corey and another dude called Gray, they'll pay off my debt to him and he'd leave me alone.

Sgt Cooper: So you had a choice. Pay off your drug debt or – in your words – 'do a job' with these men?

A. Ballancore: Yeah. No. I could do the job or . . . I dunno. I couldn't pay the money. There was nothing left in my account.

Sgt Crowe: In the Greenwoods' account. In fact, two accounts. A current account and savings account. You cleaned them out, didn't you?

Ms Anand: May I have another word with my client?

– Interview suspended –

Ms Anand: My client would like to make another statement.

Sgt Cooper: Go ahead.

Ms Anand: Sean Greenwood, who I know as Kel, gave me his card and PIN number, along with permission to access funds in his name.

Sgt Cooper: Did you tell him you would be taking every penny he and his wife had, to pay your drug debt?

A. Ballancore: No comment.

Sgt Cooper: So, via Sharkey, you meet two men known only to you as Corey and Gray.

A. Ballancore: No comment.

Sgt Cooper: They brief you on a burglary they are planning, during which they intend to steal a painting called *World* by Irma Stern, while its owner is abroad.

A. Ballancore: No comment.

Sgt Cooper: They need you to help carry it.

A. Ballancore: No comment.

Sgt Cooper: On the afternoon of 30 June this year, they take you to 42 Victoria Gardens, Lockley Bois, where the three of you break into the house, via the rear doors, and search for the painting.

A. Ballancore: No comment.

Sgt Cooper: However, upon entry you all discover that the home owner Mr Robert Green, who you believed to be absent, is still there. You proceed to assault Mr Green, tie him up and beat him.

A. Ballancore: Not me.

Sgt Cooper: What did you do?

A. Ballancore: Not that. No way.

Sgt Cooper: So I take it you're saying Mr Corey and Mr Gray did the beating up and torture while you stood and watched?

Sgt Crowe: For the benefit of the transcript, Mr Ballancore has pushed his chair away from the table and has his head in his hands.

Sgt Cooper: Take your time, Arnie, but the sooner you tell us what happened, the sooner we can identify who *did* torture Mr Green, and the sooner you can go home.

Sgt Crowe: Mr Ballancore, where were you when sixty-three-year-old Mr Green was being beaten by two men armed with blunt objects?

A. Ballancore: Looked around. Pointed my eyes elsewhere. You know. Keep it out of sight.

Sgt Crowe: Again, for the benefit of the transcript, Mr Ballancore now has his hands over his ears.

Sgt Cooper: Is that what you did while it was going on? You looked away and covered your ears, so you didn't have to hear it? I think Mr Ballancore is nodding. Take a tissue. There you go.

Sgt Crowe: Is that a nod, Arnold?

A. Ballancore: Uh-huh. Yeah.

Ms Anand: My client would like a break.

– Interview suspended –

Sgt Cooper: So, Arnie, we've spoken about what happened when you arrived at 42 Victoria Gardens on the afternoon of 30 June. Let's move on. Now at some point Mr Corey and Mr Gray realise the painting is not there. What happens then?

A. Ballancore: No comment.

Sgt Cooper: Do you join them in a violent and messy search of the property, during which you help them steal cash, watches, antique rings, ornaments and an African Healing Doll?

A. Ballancore: No comment.

Sgt Cooper: You spent three years working in Africa, didn't you? Do you know what a Healing Doll is, Arnold?

A. Ballancore: I didn't steal anything. I took the doll, but it wasn't theft. Sam and Kel know a kid who's really sick. They're raising money to get help for her. But money won't cure a thing. Not a thing. That doll was old. It's powerful. It didn't belong to him. They protect little girls. I took it for the kid. It belongs with her.

Sgt Crowe: Unfortunately for you, it belongs with Mr Green. He's the one who bought it.

A. Ballancore: I thought if I gave it to the kid, it would make me better too. Heal me. Instead of all that blood and anger. This sick feeling all the time.

Ms Anand: My client is quite distressed.

Sgt Crowe: Careful! Mr Ballancore has fallen to the floor. You ok?

Ms Anand: Fine. No, I'm ok, thanks. He's just . . .

A. Ballancore: They said I shouldn't have spoken to him about the doll. That I still owe them . . . Chucked me out the van. Left me by the road.

Sgt Cooper: Ok, Arnold, let's have a break there. And get you a doctor.

– Interview suspended –

FROM: Isabel Beck
SUBJECT: Sam!
DATE: 4 July 2018 at 17:31
TO: Claudia D'Souza

Dear Claudia,
Sorry to bother you. I found your email address on the Intranet. I know what a loyal friend you are to Sam, so thought I'd inform you that she was attacked on the ward today. I know – it's scarcely believable! I can't imagine who would have done such a thing.

I wasn't there, but our ward manager saw the whole thing and is preparing a full Incident Report for HR. She described the woman as 'a mad screaming witch' and said Sam had no choice but to defend herself. As soon as I heard the commotion, I called the police. Hopefully they'll take the necessary legal action. But even if they don't, St Ann's has a zero-tolerance policy when it comes to violence between staff. Plus acts of violence in the workplace result in instant dismissal, which quite frankly is no less than this woman deserves. I'm contributing to the Incident Report and intend to give a comprehensive account of everything. Sam and I are *very* close – she's my best friend, on the ward and off. Of course you know her yourself, although I've heard you're much closer to Kel these days. Issy

---

FROM: Claudia D'Souza
SUBJECT: Re: Sam!
DATE: 4 July 2018 at 17:44
TO: Isabel Beck

Don't lie. You were there. I saw you. Hiding behind everyone else. That's how you work. You keep your mouth shut, while slyly making trouble behind people's backs. If you think you've got Sam to yourself now, you're mistaken. Your 'best friend' Sam has been plotting for months to get you off the ward and out of her life. She calls you clingy, a leech and a vampire. It was Sam who begged me to organise that tour around Mount More, in the hope you'll transfer there. It was her idea. She literally can't stand you. Your only friend wants you as far out of her life as you can go. But she's a kind, generous person. She sees you're a sad, lonely loser that no one likes, and she doesn't want to add to that. But I'm not a kind, generous person, and I'm happy to tell you the truth. Does she know you nearly killed someone? You'd be long gone by now, if your colleague hadn't stepped in and resuscitated them. I bet you've never told Sam, because the one thing you have in common with her, the only thing, is your job – and you're not even any good at that.

FROM: Isabel Beck
SUBJECT: Re: Sam!
DATE: 4 July 2018 at 17:47
TO: Claudia D'Souza

A tour around Mount More? I don't know what you're talking about. I haven't been there since a training placement in 2009. Clearly you are jealous of my friendship with Sam and are trying to break us up with a stream of lies. But we're stronger than that. Issy

---

FROM: Isabel Beck
SUBJECT: Hiya!
DATE: 4 July 2018 at 18:02
TO: Samantha Greenwood

Hiya Sam, I rushed down to A&E after my shift, and was relieved to hear you'd been discharged and gone home. I spoke to Kel when he arrived, and he said you were definitely coming to rehearsal tonight. Yippee! What a trouper! Now, I hate to say I told you so, but I'm a good judge of character and I've always been wary of Claudia. From the moment I first met her at the half-marathon, to the second I saw the policewoman lead her out of Iso. But why did she attack you? I know she's always pretended to be friendly and helpful, but she's neurotic and unstable, so her behaviour can turn in an instant. Perhaps we'll never know the reason. You must be feeling rotten, but our focus now is the play. I know Martin, Helen and Sarah-Jane will be so impressed you're still at rehearsal, even when you've been the victim of mindless violence. It shows how committed we are to The Fairway Players and *All My Sons*. It will only go in our favour when they're casting the next play. We can start planning our trip to Africa now. Just you and me. Kel can do what he likes. This time next year we'll be finishing our final preparations and working out where to distribute the T-shirts – Claudia's psychotic attack will be water under the bridge. I can't wait for the dress rehearsal tonight! Just think, we'll only perform the play four more times and then never again. It's so intense, yet so finite. I'm just getting my things together ready to leave the flat. See you in a minute, Love Issy xxxxx

---

FROM: Isabel Beck
SUBJECT: Hiya!
DATE: 4 July 2018 at 18:08
TO: Samantha Greenwood

Sorry to email you again so soon. It's just occurred to me. Have I ever mentioned why I'm stuck in Jelly Antics for eighteen months? It's nothing really. I worked with my ex-friend Lauren in Ortho. She had appalling attention to detail and one day she accidentally added Bupivacaine to a saline IV. The patient went into shock. Luckily, I spotted the problem just in time. Thing is, she was already on watch for a few other slip-ups and this would have meant instant dismissal. I said I'd share the blame with her . . . only when we were interviewed for the Incident Report, she blamed me entirely. Said she wasn't even there! I was so shocked she'd done that, but she knew I couldn't go back in and tell them I'd lied the first time. Then a few weeks later she got together with Josh and left anyway. I was high and dry in Jelly Antics with YKW and the dregs of St Ann's. I thought she was my friend and she betrayed me. That's why it was so important to me when you arrived, Sam. You changed my life. Suddenly I could see a future stretching in front of me instead of nothingness. You're the best friend anyone could have, but not only that: you've changed how people see me. Usually they ignore me. But when I'm with you, they respect me because they respect you and you respect me. Neither of us needs anyone else. Ever. Lots of love, Issy xxxxx

---

Message exchange between John O'Dea and Martin Hayward on 4 July 2018:

18:12 John wrote:
Who's playing Sue Bayliss now? It's not good to change cast this late.

18:15 Martin wrote:
Sam is playing Sue. I understand she had a minor accident at work today, but was told she's fit and well enough to be in the play. Is there something I don't know?

18:18 John wrote:
After ripping you off to the tune of £80k, I'd assumed she was out of the play. It's up to you.

FROM: Joyce Walford
SUBJECT: The cheek
DATE: 4 July 2018 at 18:23
TO: Martin Hayward

I can't believe it, Martin. The cheek of it! Stealing money from little Poppy and then getting up onstage and acting with us all as if nothing's wrong! And bringing that nasty piece of work to disrupt the yoga, too. If that's the company they keep, I'm not surprised they can rob a cancer appeal of all that money. And people say *my* boys are trouble! I hope the police will be taking action. Joyce

---

FROM: Martin Hayward
SUBJECT: Fwd: The cheek
DATE: 4 July 2018 at 18:29
TO: Sarah-Jane MacDonald

It seems rumours are flying about and wires crossed. See Joyce's email below. Several Fairway Players seem convinced Sam is Lydia Drake. Please can we keep such tittle-tattle under wraps until after the play? Obviously I do want a word with Sam about why she strung us along re Clive Handler, but let's do it after *All My Sons* is over. Regards, Martin

---

FROM: Sarah-Jane MacDonald
SUBJECT: Fwd: The cheek
DATE: 4 July 2018 at 18:34
TO: Martin Hayward

Of course. I can't think how those rumours came about. I'll have a quick word with them and put them straight.
Sarah-Jane MacDonald

FROM: Martin Hayward
SUBJECT: Fwd: The cheek
DATE: 4 July 2018 at 18:43
TO: Sarah-Jane MacDonald

Coincidentally enough, Sam was in Africa with Poppy's doctor's brother and, from what Tish has said, there was bad blood between them (this brother died recently), so I suspect Sam had her own reasons for contacting Tish under an assumed name. Perhaps we were caught in the middle of something that's now over. In any case, I am happy with Sam and Kel being in the play, so let's ensure the dress rehearsal goes smoothly. Regards,
Martin

FROM: Isabel Beck
SUBJECT: Arnie?
DATE: 4 July 2018 at 19:27
TO: Kel Greenwood

Hi Kel, sorry to message you when you're backstage waiting to go on, but I've just heard Joyce tell Denise that Arnie was arrested this morning. Is that right? She said he and Sam stole £80k from Poppy's appeal and Sarah-Jane traced them through their emails. I didn't say anything, but I know Sam wouldn't do that, even if Arnie did. Just thought you'd like to know what people are saying. Don't worry, I'll put Sarah-Jane right myself. Love
Issy xxxx

FROM: Isabel Beck
SUBJECT: Sam?
DATE: 4 July 2018 at 20:11
TO: Sarah-Jane MacDonald

Hi SJ, sorry to bother you. I noticed people were ignoring Sam, then overheard a few things. I assure you Sam would *never* be involved in anything like the theft of Poppy's appeal money. We spend *lots* of time together, in work and out, and if she'd been planning anything like that, I'd know. She is the most honest person I have ever met. Unfortunately, I can't say the same for Arnie, who I believe is in police custody as we speak. Between you and me, I'm relieved. I hate the idea of him staying with Sam when he seems so disturbed. I hope you can have a word with everyone and tell them she's innocent. Issy xxx

---

FROM: Sarah-Jane MacDonald
SUBJECT: Re: Sam?
DATE: 4 July 2018 at 20:12
TO: Isabel Beck

You were standing right here only moments ago. Why not just speak to me?

Message from Kevin MacDonald to Sarah-Jane MacDonald on 4 July 2018:

21:01 Kevin wrote:
I feel like death. Typical. Had a cold for *Blithe Spirit* and now for *All My Sons*. Only hope you and H don't catch it. Sam looks like she's spilled a docker's pint. Tried to strike up a convo with Kel but he walked away. Then caught them having words behind the trellis. He told her not to 'dare say anything, or she'd never see him again'. She said she has 'no choice now'. You know I don't gossip, but do you think he knocks her around?

Message from Joel Halliday to Celia Halliday on 4 July 2018:

21:32 Joel wrote:
Don't come to rehearsal. Martin's called it off and sent us home. I'm locking up now. You won't believe what happened.

Message from Martin Hayward to Glen Reswick on 4 July 2018:

21:39 Martin wrote:
Come to the house now. Don't call.

Message from Martin Hayward to Sarah-Jane MacDonald on 4 July 2018:

21:40 Martin wrote:
Thanks for your support. Helen is crushed. She so rarely cries . . . That's why I called it off. We go into opening night without rehearsing half the play, but Helen is so upset I could see she couldn't go on. I'll cc you in on my email to Sam. Thanks again from all of us.

Message from John O'Dea to Martin Hayward on 4 July 2018:

21:40 John wrote:
Is Helen ok? Never seen her in such a state.

Message from Marianne Payne to Martin Hayward on 4 July 2018:

21:45 Marianne wrote:
Poor Helen. Tell her to take no notice of that awful woman. How could anyone accuse Helen of such a thing? She must be mad. Wait till I tell Mick.

Message exchange between James Hayward and Martin Hayward on 4 July 2018:

21:30 James wrote:
I don't want to worry Mum, but they're prepping Olivia for surgery. They think the babies are distressed and may have to be delivered now.

21:31 Martin wrote:
Ok. Call when you can. Dress rehearsal not great. Don't worry about it now. Love to Olivia.

Message from Sarah-Jane MacDonald to Emma Crooks on 4 July 2018:

21:39 Sarah-Jane wrote:
Emma, I know it's late, but could I pop round?

FROM: Denise Malcolm
SUBJECT: Helen
DATE: 4 July 2018 at 21:36
TO: Joyce Walford
CC: Marianne Payne

Oh ladies, I'm so upset for Helen. Shall we club together for some flowers from Blooms? I can order them tomorrow morning and drop them into The Grange on my lunch break. It's a small gesture, but it'll show her how much we all love her. God bless. Denise

---

FROM: Martin Hayward
SUBJECT: This evening
DATE: 4 July 2018 at 22:44
TO: Samantha Greenwood
CC: Sarah-Jane MacDonald

Dear Sam,
We are all reeling from your outburst this evening. Not least because until that moment you seemed to be a hard-working team player committed

to the group. It is unusual for a new member to be cast in a play without working backstage first, but such was our generosity, we waived this convention and welcomed you and Kel in. Amateur drama requires commitment, dedication and cooperation, but most of all it requires trust – and until tonight I felt we could trust you. I am only sorry you did not express your true thoughts sooner.

While I can only apologise for the fact some Fairway Players seem to think you took money from the appeal – I have corrected anyone and everyone who mentioned this to me – the rumour arose precisely because you hoaxed us early on with the promise that the drugs would be paid for. You must therefore take some responsibility for the confusion. I know both Sarah-Jane and I want to discuss that issue privately with you, and are prepared to hear your side of the story. We were also prepared to wait until the play was over. However, you left us with no choice but to thrash it out in public this evening. For the record, the Clive Handler episode was a cruel and heartless deception that heaped more agony on a family already suffering the unimaginable. You say you did it to investigate a potential fraud elsewhere, but that is no excuse, I'm afraid.

Tonight was meant to be a chance for everyone to rehearse *All My Sons* for the last time. Now, thanks to you, the whole cast and crew have been denied this vital element of the process, not to mention the stress and duress you put Helen through.

My wife has endured a great deal and does not have to defend herself to you. You may well believe Poppy's appeal to be poorly run, but we are doing the best we can under difficult circumstances. As for the very personal accusations you made against Helen, I will not dignify them by discussion. Except to remind you that most Fairway Players have known us both for many years. If what you said were accurate, others would connect the dots and believe you. You saw yourself how few allies you had – not even your own husband supported you – an indication of how wide of the mark you were.

A great many people have put in months of hard work to bring *All My Sons* to the stage. If you do not intend to play any further part in the production, you will be letting them all down. However, if you do not return tomorrow, as with every hurdle we face, we will get over it. I only ask that you let us know your intentions, as they were not clear from the manner in which you left the rehearsal. Regards, Martin

---

Message exchange between Martin Hayward and Paige Reswick on 4 July 2018:

22:47 Martin wrote:
Ructions at Fairways. Hysterical, paranoid cast member. Please call Mum, she's still very upset. If we lose cast member, could you step in? The part is smallish and doable for an actress of your talent, but you'd need to carry the script.

22:49 Paige wrote:
I'd *love* to be in the play. Poor Mum. I'll call her now. How exciting!

22:55 Martin wrote:
No reply from James, so Olivia's probably gone into surgery, but don't tell Mum after all that went on tonight.

FROM: Sarah-Jane MacDonald
SUBJECT: Re: This evening
DATE: 4 July 2018 at 22:51
TO: Martin Hayward

Thank you for copying me in on Sam's email. However, she described the appeal as much more than 'poorly run'. She said it's a 'financial conspiracy', that there are no experimental drugs, that Poppy is having regular chemo at Mount More. That her notes are kept on her doctor's private record system, not at the hospital. That you're exploiting your granddaughter's illness. That certain other things we've been told to engage us with the appeal are complete and utter fabrications. That if you really were the victim of a fraud, then you deserve to be beaten at your own game. That's what she said.
Sarah-Jane MacDonald

FROM: Martin Hayward
SUBJECT: Re: This evening
DATE: 4 July 2018 at 22:59
TO: Sarah-Jane MacDonald

The 'other things' being Helen's little boy. Well, did you see Helen's face when she said that? Was that the face of someone conducting a cynical fraud against their friends and family, or was it the face of someone genuinely devastated by distressing accusations? When she lost her little boy, it was the single most catastrophic event in her life. It affects her every day, even now. It happened before I met her, and long before Paige and James were even born, but such is the legacy of tragedy, it is something that we feel happened to us all. Sam summarily dismissed it as a deliberate lie for financial gain. In public. In front of our lifelong friends. On the very stage Helen feels safest and most at home. It's not the accusation itself – we can produce the relevant proof, if anyone is interested, which I doubt – it's the utter betrayal by someone we had embraced as a friend. Regards,
Martin

FROM: Sarah-Jane MacDonald
SUBJECT: Re: This evening
DATE: 4 July 2018 at 23:11
TO: Martin Hayward

You said yourself she had no support among the people who know and love you both. As you point out, not even Kel seems to think what she said is true. When she stormed out, only that Isabel went after her. I saw them in the car park – Sam was even shouting at *her*; grabbed her arm and was snarling in her ear about something. The girl is mousy enough as it is, but she looked even more crushed than usual. It does leave us with a dilemma about Sam's role in the play. I know you've left the door open, but I don't see how she can ever come back after this.
Sarah-Jane MacDonald

FROM: Martin Hayward
SUBJECT: Re: This evening
DATE: 4 July 2018 at 23:29
TO: Sarah-Jane MacDonald

Paige is on standby to play Sam's role. She'll have to carry the script, but John did that in *Absent Friends* and it was fine. We haven't worked this hard on the production to cancel it at the eleventh hour, all because Sam is deluded and paranoid. I blame myself – I should've listened to Tish. Regards.

Message exchange between Kevin MacDonald and Sarah-Jane MacDonald on 4 July 2018:

23:03 Kevin wrote:
Where the hell are you? I nodded off. Just woken up and you're not here.

23:06 Sarah-Jane wrote:
Round Emma's. Chatting about things. Go back to sleep, you're not well. I'll be home later.

23:07 Sarah-Jane wrote:
Thanks for taking Harley back.

23:07 Kevin wrote:
Ask her about Helen's kid. Does she know if it's true or not?

23:08 Sarah-Jane wrote:
Dealing with Martin and Emma. Will send email.

FROM: Sarah-Jane MacDonald
SUBJECT:
DATE: 4 July 2018 at 23:57
TO: Kevin MacDonald

That's why I'm here. Can't imagine the Haywards making up a story like that, but why would Sam say it, if there weren't some foundation? I needed to chat with someone who's known them even longer than I have, and

thank goodness I did. Yes, Helen *is* telling the truth. Emma says as far back as primary school Paige spoke about a big brother who died before she was born. She also remembers a teacher talking about bereavement when a classmate's father died. Emma asked Paige why she didn't mention her brother, but Paige said, 'Shush, it upsets Mummy', as if she'd been told not to speak about it – which explains why Helen hadn't even told Mum about him, and she's one of her oldest friends. So that's that. Sam is nothing but a troublemaker, and I'm only sorry I was taken in by her myself.
Sarah-Jane MacDonald

FROM: Kevin MacDonald
SUBJECT: Re:
DATE: 5 July 2018 at 00:07
TO: Sarah-Jane MacDonald

Well, if she wanted us to take that as evidence the appeal is a 'financial conspiracy', then it's worked the other way. The dead kid is true, so the appeal must be true. No wonder she's got a black eye, if she goes around saying things like that. Can't believe we're heading for opening night with no proper dress rehearsal. Like play week isn't stressful enough. Kev

---

FROM: Claudia D'Souza
SUBJECT:
DATE: 5 July 2018 at 00:09
TO: Kel Greenwood

I'm outside the Travellers' Inn. It's at the crossroads of Honeypot Lane and the road by the big Tesco's. No one seems to know anything and I couldn't get through to him. C xxx

---

FROM: Martin Hayward
SUBJECT: Kel?
DATE: 5 July 2018 at 00:11
TO: Sarah-Jane MacDonald

It's only just occurred to me that Kel may also be out of the play. It didn't cross my mind earlier, as he so obviously disapproved of what she was saying. But they drove away together, not speaking . . . so I don't know. What will we do if he pulls out, too? We don't have any spare men. There's Joel, but he's far too old to play Frank. And anyway, having two people reading from a script would be awful. We'd look like the Fowey Light Operatic Society. Regards, Martin

---

FROM: Arnie Ballancore
SUBJECT: Hello?
DATE: 5 July 2018 at 00:11
TO: Kel Greenwood

Are you awake? Sorry about all that this morning. I've got bail, so outside the police station now. Do you know how I get back to the flat from here? There's a bus stop, but it's got graffiti over the timetable. Buses, do they run at night here? I might walk it. Nice and warm. Man, the cops were hard as. Way tired. Going straight to bed. Got my key, so don't wait up.

FROM: Lauren Malden
SUBJECT: Hiya!
DATE: 5 July 2018 at 00:15
TO: Isabel Beck

Hello lovely! Mum heard the dress rehearsal turned into a slanging match between 'the new girl' and Martin. I said that would be your friend Sam. Were you there? Go on, what happened? Mum said she accused Helen of lying. Of telling everyone she had a child years ago who died of meningitis, when apparently she didn't – it was all to get everyone to raise money – not for Poppy's chemo, but to rescue The Grange. You're a good judge of character, Issy, what do you think? Could she be right? Kiss kiss, L xx

---

FROM: Isabel Beck
SUBJECT: Re: Hiya!
DATE: 5 July 2018 at 00:20
TO: Lauren Malden

I was there and saw it all. It was nothing really. Sam's been under a lot of pressure. I can't go into detail, but she had an accident at work during the day and I think it may have affected her. She said some things – some horrible things I'm sure aren't true. Concussion can be insidious and change mental processes in subtle ways. It can turn someone against the very people they are closest to. They say things they don't mean or believe. Sam will be fine in the morning. I'll email Martin and Sarah-Jane and tell them not to worry. Issy

---

FROM: Martin Hayward
SUBJECT: Sam Greenwood
DATE: 5 July 2018 at 00:18
TO: Tish Bhatoa

Dear Tish, I hope you are as well as can be expected, given your recent bereavement. I feel you ought to know our mutual friend Samantha Greenwood has accused you and us together of a 'financial conspiracy'. She did this in front of our amateur drama group of around twenty people. The proof she offered turned out to be circumstantial at best. While our friends and family trust us implicitly, I cannot guarantee the allegations will not get back to you and feel you should be prepared. For the record, I bitterly regret welcoming Ms Greenwood into our social circle. You were quite right about her. I suggest we delay shipping of the phials until this latest furore has blown over. Regards, Martin

---

FROM: Tish Bhatoa
SUBJECT: Sam Greenwood
DATE: 5 July 2018 at 00:19
TO: Martin Hayward

[Out of Office AutoReply]
I am overseas on a personal matter until further notice.

Transcription of a call on Samantha and Kel Greenwood's untimed landline message service:

Hi Sam, it's Andy. Are you there? No. Well, you mentioned something about the mum being ill. I know it seems like a by-the-by detail but . . . I took a gamble across the pond and found something. It's *really* interesting. Explains the other stuff and more. But it's one of those things you can't un-know and if you can verify it, you *must* tell someone. Look, call me when you can. You're obviously out now so . . . Bye.

FROM: Isabel Beck
SUBJECT: Hiya!
DATE: 5 July 2018 at 00:34
TO: Martin Hayward
CC: Sarah-Jane MacDonald

Dear Martin and Sarah-Jane, Sorry to bother you. I couldn't speak after the rehearsal this evening, but just want to say: don't worry. Sam suffered a blow to the head during her accident at work this afternoon – perhaps more than one blow. Chronic concussion can affect a person's clarity of thought. I'm sure this explains her out-of-character behaviour and the outrageous things she said. Things I don't believe, and I'm certain no one else will. The good news is: it's a transient symptom. I know she will regret the whole thing and am in no doubt she will apologise in the morning. Sam is always true to her word and hates to let anyone down, so I'm sure she'll return tomorrow and the play will go ahead as planned. But if she decides she no longer wishes to be involved, I would just like to remind you I've been rehearsing with her for *months*. I can easily slip into the role of Sue.

Then perhaps Emma, Beth or Paige could read the part of Lydia? It's such a small role, I'm sure they would easily pick it up. If Kel doesn't wish to be involved, perhaps, Martin, you could play Jim Bayliss? It's unlikely either of them will let you down, but I'm always thinking ahead. You can't be too prepared for the future. Love Issy xxx

---

Social-media status update from James Hayward at 12.09 a.m. on Thursday 5 July 2018:

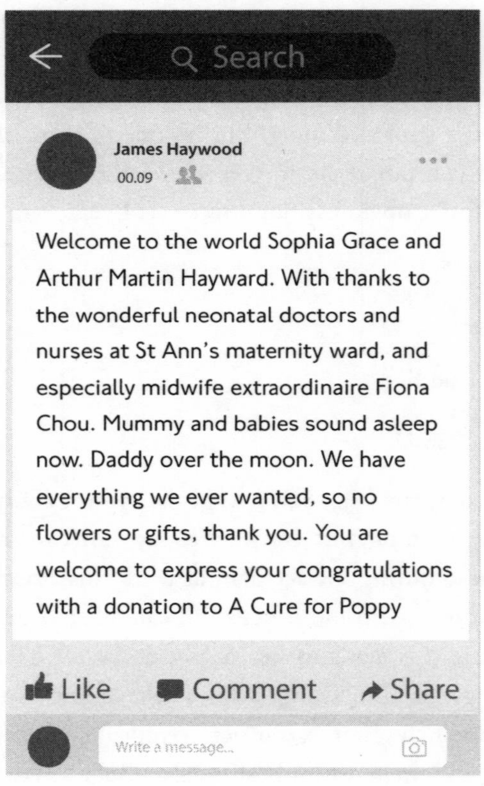

Olufemi Hassan
Charlotte Holroyd

Dear both,

Please note: this is the recovered correspondence we believe to have been written *before* the murder, which took place between 11 p.m. on 4 July 2018 and 4 a.m. on 5 July 2018. However, as the body remained undiscovered for almost twenty-four hours, the following correspondence is vital. Therefore, going forward, you must ask: who already knows Samantha Greenwood is dead and who doesn't?

Yours,

RT

Roderick Tanner, QC
Senior Partner
Tanner & Dewey LLP

Femi
So this is it. Tanner trusts us with a murder. Let's nail it.

Charlotte
I feel sick. Not sure if it's because Sam's dead or because of the responsibility.

Femi
We can't do anything about the crime itself. Let's just do what we can to uncover the truth now.

FROM: Isabel Beck
SUBJECT: Hiya!
DATE: 5 July 2018 at 07:14
TO: Samantha Greenwood

Hi Sam, sorry to bother you. Are you coming in today? I said to Frances I'd find out. I told her you were taken ill at last night's rehearsal. It's more or less true. I emailed Martin and Sarah-Jane to let them know you had a bump on the head yesterday. It's quite possible you had a touch of concussion. After everything you've been through in the past couple of days, it would be no surprise to anyone if you felt very low and in a bad place right now. Anyway, Frances isn't in a good mood, so if you could let me know whether you've gone sick today, that would help us. Thanks. Love Issy

---

FROM: Isabel Beck
SUBJECT: Hiya!
DATE: 5 July 2018 at 07:18
TO: Kel Greenwood

Hi Kel, sorry to bother you. Do you know if Sam is coming to work today? She hasn't arrived and the ward manager is asking where she is. I said I would find out. Love Issy

---

FROM: Sarah-Jane MacDonald
SUBJECT: Congratulations
DATE: 5 July 2018 at 08:45
TO: James Hayward
CC: Martin Hayward

James, congratulations on the births of Sophia and Arthur. Lovely news. I imagine Martin told you what happened at rehearsal last night. If Kel doesn't turn up tonight, could you read the part of Jim? It may not come to that. I'm open-minded about whether Sam shows up – she has enough brass neck. Having slept on it, I now believe it would be best for the play if she does, and the play is all I'm concerned about at the moment. Let's line up replacements, but see what happens.
Sarah-Jane MacDonald

FROM: Martin Hayward
SUBJECT: Re: Congratulations
DATE: 5 July 2018 at 08:59
TO: Sarah-Jane MacDonald
CC: James Hayward

Thank you for your input, Sarah-Jane. That's what we're doing. Regards, Martin

---

FROM: Martin Hayward
SUBJECT: Play
DATE: 5 July 2018 at 09:05
TO: Paige Reswick

Mum says she'll take Poppy to the little zoo, so you can learn as much of Act One as you can. Act Two would be good as well, of course, but I'm realistic about how much you can cram in such a short time. It's best to be off-book for your early scenes, while the audience are still warming to the characters. Later on they'll be glued to Mum and John anyway. Thanks again. Regards, Dad

---

FROM: Paige Reswick
SUBJECT: Re: Play
DATE: 5 July 2018 at 09:11
TO: Martin Hayward

Aw, bless Mum. Poppy loves it there – especially the big pig. Glen woke me up at four to go through Act One. It's not just the words, Dad, it's the accent. When Mum brings Poppy back from the zoo, can she stay and give me some help with pronunciation? Glen can take Pops for a Happy Meal. Oh my God, this is so exciting! Paige x

---

FROM: Nick Walford
SUBJECT: Urgent
DATE: 5 July 2018 at 09:43
TO: Joyce Walford

Mum, when you iron my stage shirt, remember to put the folded-up paper on the mantelpiece in the top pocket. It's my cue lines, so it's *very important*. Everything else I'll need is in the Adidas bag already – *don't* forget it. Leave it in the green room in the corner by the props table. I should be there by seven. I know you like all the gossip – well, I was called out to the Travellers' Inn, two o'clock. Did you know Kel is staying there with a woman, not Sam? They walked through reception while I was resetting the pressure. Didn't know what to say after the slanging match at rehearsal, so kept my head down till they'd gone. They looked *terrible*, like someone had died. Let me know if you hear anything else. See you tonight. Nick

PS Don't forget the paper or the bag.

FROM: Emma Crooks
SUBJECT: Everything ok?
DATE: 5 July 2018 at 09:50
TO: Sarah-Jane MacDonald

Did you get home ok? It was so late, but I could see you needed to talk after such a traumatic rehearsal. *So* glad I wasn't there. I'd have absorbed all that negative energy like a sponge. Poor Helen. Her little boy's death is the one thing she hates to speak about. To hear it brought up in front of everyone must've been awful, and amid such horrible accusations, too. But I've been going over what you said, and it's clear to me why Sam did it. Think about it, Sarah-Jane, she's only a nurse. No money, no house, no kids. She envies the Haywards; wants them to suffer, in return for the lovely family they have and the privilege they enjoy. She doesn't want Poppy to get better, so she tried to turn us all against the appeal. Only she waited until the eve of the play, so she could ruin something else they care about, too; that we all care about. Jealousy is a very destructive emotion. Speaking of destruction, Woof says hi. A flock of crows landed in the garden this morning and he barked his head off, so he must be feeling better. Is your mum still happy to look after him while I see the play tomorrow? I know Paige is super-excited – she can't wait to get back onstage! Emma x

---

FROM: Sarah-Jane MacDonald
SUBJECT: Re: Everything ok?
DATE: 5 July 2018 at 10:01
TO: Emma Crooks

Thanks again, Emma. You're right, I did need to chat. But we don't know yet whether Sam and/or Kel is/are in or out of the play. I hope they both come back and deliver the best performances they can, as they committed to do all those weeks ago when they auditioned. Things might be a bit frosty in the green room, but our priority is the play now, especially as it's a key fundraising event. We needn't have anything to do with the Greenwoods again, but we need *All My Sons* to go ahead and go well. You may be right about Sam's motivation. On the positive side, it's a lesson to us all to be wary of strangers in future. On a happier note, it's lovely to hear the twins have been born safely – and it means James can more easily get away for a few hours, if Kel doesn't show up for the play. Yes, Mum is very much looking forward to Woof-sitting tomorrow. Thanks again, Emma. Sarah-Jane MacDonald

---

FROM: Joyce Walford
SUBJECT: Last night
DATE: 5 July 2018 at 10:16
TO: Marianne Payne

You'll never guess what's happened: Kel and Sam have split up! My Nick saw him with another woman at the Travellers' Inn at two o'clock this morning. Thought it was strange I hadn't seen either of them leave for work. That'll be why she said all that about Helen and the appeal money. I know, from when the boys' dad left, you're not thinking straight. She'll be angry with him and his fancy woman, so she took it out on someone else. Do you think he hits her? That black eye and cut lip looked terrible until Denise covered them with make-up – work accident, my foot! Now

I know it wasn't her who robbed the appeal, I might go over later and see if she's all right. There's some good news, though, Marianne: it looks like the police let that swampy off and he's gone – came out with his rucksack at five this morning, left the place like he wasn't coming back – well, good riddance. Joyce

PS James and Olivia's twins have arrived. A boy and a girl.

FROM: Marianne Payne
SUBJECT: Re: Last night
DATE: 5 July 2018 at 10:22
TO: Joyce Walford

Thank God! I hope they're both healthy, for everyone's sake. The twins, I mean. Sam and Kel, well, I noticed they were very cool with each other these last few rehearsals, Joyce. Are you *sure* it wasn't them robbed the appeal? She could've pointed the finger at Helen because she'd done it herself. Mick says it's the first thing you do, when they accuse you of something you've done bang to rights. Be careful getting involved with her. Marianne

---

FROM: Isabel Beck
SUBJECT: Yay! Congratulations!
DATE: 5 July 2018 at 10:33
TO: James Hayward

Hiya James, congratulations! I'm delighted the bumps are safely here. I see from your profile photo they are both in neonatal, but neither needs respiration, which is an excellent sign. I wonder if your dad has mentioned what happened at last night's rehearsal? I expect he has. I thought it would blow over, but Sam wasn't at work this morning and, between you and me, I now don't think she'll turn up for the play tonight, or the remaining nights. I've got a sixth sense when it comes to these things. I've already said I'm happy to step in to the role of Sue Bayliss, leaving the smaller part of Lydia for a stand-in. Perhaps Paige? I'm so sorry Sam has let you down, especially as she and Kel were my friends and I was so keen they settled in at Fairways. Please don't think I believe anything Sam said about your mum and dad. I am fully committed to the play and want you to know that if there's anything I can do to help, just ask. Love to Olivia, Sophia and Arthur, Issy xxx

---

FROM: James Hayward
SUBJECT: Re: Yay! Congratulations!
DATE: 5 July 2018 at 10:40
TO: Isabel Beck

Dearest Issy, Thanks for your good wishes. The family is doing well. Olivia is a bit sore after the Caesarean. I wasn't allowed to see her or the babies for a while after the op, which was rather lonely and worrying at the time, but thankfully it's all over now. We've asked Paige to play Sue and she's feverishly learning the role, with the help of Mum (or should I say Grandma Helen) all day today. Thanks again for your support. You're a vital member of our team. See you tonight, James

---

FROM: Lauren Malden
SUBJECT: Any news?
DATE: 5 July 2018 at 10:45
TO: Isabel Beck

Hello lovely! What's the latest? Mum says surely they won't want Sam in the play after all the things she said, regardless of whether it's true or not. How big is her part? Can you take it over? You're easily good enough. Josh says they won't cancel as they'll have spent too much on set and props, and not to worry that it won't go ahead, because it will. I so wish I could come up and see it now. Not that I want to watch things go wrong – just to support everyone. Still, I know you'll do a great job! Break a leg for tonight and let me know everything that happens. Kiss kiss, L xxx

---

FROM: Isabel Beck
SUBJECT: Re: Any news?
DATE: 5 July 2018 at 10:59
TO: Lauren Malden

The latest news is Sam has gone back to Africa. After she left rehearsal, she came to tell me specially, as we'd been such close friends. We had a long chat in the car park, which was nice. She said goodbye and wished me well, etc. It's a bit sad, as we were planning to go together and do charity work, but I've realised all my friends are here at Fairways, so I decided to stay. Work isn't so bad, either. As soon as I can, I'll apply to move. I quite fancy Maternity or Haematology. But there's the play to get over first. I'm not that nervous now. I know my lines and my cues. Paige will read in for Sam and everyone will soon forget her. I've decided to start jogging again Monday lunchtime instead of eating. My diet is going so well I don't want to spoil it. I'll let you know how *All My Sons* goes, but I doubt there'll be any more gossip. Issy

---

Message exchange between Kevin MacDonald and Sarah-Jane MacDonald on 5 July 2018:

08:02 Kevin wrote:
On a scale of one to ten, I'm minus three. Maybe four.

08:03 Kevin wrote:
Banging headache, blocked sinuses, sore throat and the genesis of a cough.

08:04 Kevin wrote:
Daren't shout down the stairs in case it gets worse. Have to preserve what's left of my voice.

08:05 Kevin wrote:
The flu virus has mutated after the stress last night. It's a new strain. I'm Patient Zero.

08:06 Kevin wrote:
Thanks for sleeping on the sofa and getting H up when it was my turn. You're the best wife anyone could have.

08:07 Kevin wrote:
What would help me feel a bit better would be a mug of warm (not hot) blackcurrant juice.

08:08 Sarah-Jane wrote:
Ok. On a scale of one to ten, I'm a two. Hardly slept worrying about the play, the appeal, Harley's education and by 5 a.m. trifling little things from twenty years ago. Why do we do this when it's so stressful? It's meant to be a hobby.

08:12 Sarah-Jane wrote:
Before I forget to tell you: last night I overheard Martin say the man who disrupted the yoga has been arrested for theft. He was a friend of the nurses. This was also going through my head: I wonder if they *were* involved in the Lydia Drake scam, after all. The Clive Handler thing could have been a dry run, or a diversionary tactic. They'd only need a friend to play Lydia. Anyway, I blame that little grey mouse, Isabel: it was her who brought them to Fairways.

08:13 Kevin wrote:
And some Nurofen please. Not too hot, remember.

Message exchange between Martin Hayward and James Hayward on 5 July 2018:

08:11 Martin wrote:
I'm sorry. I didn't think it would ever come to it. I should have listened to you. It got out of hand and now this. Bloody mess.

08:21 James wrote:
Dad, it's ok. Don't message. You're meeting your new grandchildren this afternoon – we'll have a chat then. We'll get through it together. Don't bring us anything – it's just you and Mum we want to see.

FROM: Selima Kenya
SUBJECT: Daniel Bhatoa
DATE: 5 July 2018 at 11:57
TO: Dr Tish Bhatoa

Originally written in French – Google translation

Madame Bhatoa,
The Africa Branch in London gave me your details. I understand you enquired about the last known location of your brother, Daniel Bhatoa. I can only tell you what was said to me. An independent activist, Daniel Bangui, was kidnapped by a militia alongside three other humanitarian workers in an area near Faradje and taken across the border into southern Sudan, where they all perished. You have my condolences. Be blessed. Selima Kenya

---

FROM: Dr Tish Bhatoa
SUBJECT: Re: Daniel Bhatoa
DATE: 5 July 2018 at 12:23
TO: Selima Kenya

Dear Selima,
But what was he doing in Faradje? He was based in Bangui. That's where his clinic was. He'd been there nine years. That's the area he knew, the people he knew. He told me he was still there. I need to find out what happened to make him quit Bangui for such a dangerous new region. I am trying to discover the truth. Please help me. Dr Tish Bhatoa

---

FROM: Selima Kenya
SUBJECT: Re: Daniel Bhatoa
DATE: 5 July 2018 at 12:58
TO: Dr Tish Bhatoa

Originally written in French – Google translation

Madame Bhatoa,
I am sorry for your loss. You may not like what I say. Daniel Bhatoa and his companions were discovered to have behaved inappropriately with the

women and children in their care. I met several aid workers who knew him, and his good reputation was well deserved, but some very, very bad things. I met myself with migrant women with children who visited his clinic at the Sudanese border. They could claim food, shelter and medical care for their sexual activities. I believe this behaviour was not new. It was investigated at a point, but only one person spoke, another humanitarian worker, which was considered a poor piece of evidence. However, the people he knew and supported him in his area are all gone. I believe the clinic also saw money worries. He and his associates then moved. Once again, I am very sorry for your loss. Be blessed. Selima Kenya

---

FROM: Dr Tish Bhatoa
SUBJECT: Re: Daniel Bhatoa
DATE: 5 July 2018 at 13:13
TO: Selima Kenya

Are you telling me those accusations were *true*? I don't mean rumoured to be true, or what someone who once knew someone else heard might have happened. I mean *actually* true? This is very important, Selima, because I can't have any doubt at all.

FROM: Selima Kenya
SUBJECT: Re: Daniel Bhatoa
DATE: 5 July 2018 at 13:29
TO: Dr Tish Bhatoa

Oui, Madame, yes it is true for me without doubt. The ladies have no benefit to lie. Sadly, it is a problem here. One problem among many. *Soyez bénis*. Selima Kenya

---

FROM: The Fairway Players Admin
SUBJECT: All My Sons
DATE: 5 July 2018 at 13:39
TO: Current Members

Dear all,

It's here: the first night of *All My Sons*. We've built the set, learned the lines, imbibed the tea, rehearsed until our loved ones suspected we had left home and, at 8 p.m., with a swish of the curtain, it will all have been worthwhile. It hasn't been an easy production. There have been a number of glitches to overcome along the way, but tonight, tomorrow and Saturday night there *will* be a performance, and an audience to enjoy it. For a few fleeting hours we take the same thrilling, elusive journey that generations of players have been undertaking for centuries, one that transcends time, place, language and creed.

Paige Reswick and James Hayward will play any roles that require an understudy, so for their benefit we will run through the play, in its entirety, as best we can, from 6 p.m. Please arrive as soon as possible. Our dress rehearsal was unfortunately curtailed last night, so this will be the final opportunity to iron out those last-minute niggles. Please do not forget any costumes or props you need to bring from home.

As ever, our usual Green Room Rules apply:

- Cast must remain in the green room whenever not on stage. No greeting guests in the auditorium, as it ruins the illusion that we work so hard to create onstage.
- No smoking, vaping or drinking alcohol in the green room, or at all, until after the play.
- Mobile phones must be switched off or (if you have family issues and absolutely *must* remain connected) switched to silent. Yes, the mobile-phone ban includes a ban on texting, messaging, playing games, surfing the web, emailing and checking social-media feeds.
- No talking in the green room during the performance. During quiet moments onstage, every sound we make will carry.
- Please avoid flushing the backstage toilet during the performance.

Finally, there are still a few tickets left for each night, so if any family or friends haven't bought theirs yet, they are welcome to come along and pay on the door. All that remains for me to say is: enjoy! Remember: if we enjoy performing the play, our audience will enjoy watching it.

The Fairway Players Committee

FROM: A Cure for Poppy
SUBJECT: All My Sons
DATE: 5 July 2018 at 13:46
TO: Current Members

Dear all,
As a swift adjunct to Martin's email, I would like to remind everyone that The Fairway Players' production of *All My Sons* is a *very* special one, because it is in aid of A Cure for Poppy. As we have suffered the loss of £80k recently, we need to claw back those funds and set Poppy's life-saving drug treatment back on track.

Raffle tickets
Please, please, please keep up the good work selling raffle tickets, ideally by the book. Radio 4's Cameron Hilford will conduct the draw during our interval on Saturday night, so there are still a few days left to bump up sales.

Merchandise and cakes
Celia, Joel and the fundraising team will be selling the full range of Poppy merchandise and Joyce's specially baked poppy-seed cakes, alongside a tasty array of other edible produce, all in aid of our appeal.

In short, please ensure friends and family bring their appetites, and especially their money, when they come to see the play. Thank you.

Sarah-Jane MacDonald
Campaign Coordinator, A Cure for Poppy

Femi
I like Sarah-Jane, but her positive energy and commitment could be used by others. Is she an unwitting enabler?

Charlotte
She's on my list of suspects. Out late the night of the murder. Sleeps on the sofa. Don't forget how easily she lies to Zucchero about Poppy's blindness.

Femi
What's her motivation for killing Sam?

Charlotte
She's the backbone of the appeal, its public face. She involves all her personal and work contacts. If Sam is right, then she must admit to them all that she's part of a massive fraud *or* so stupid she's been fooled by her oldest friends.

Femi
She's too practical, too fair. She's the only one who takes Sam's accusation seriously, investigates it, via Emma, decides it's not true – and moves on.

Charlotte
Yes, SJ decides *something*, but does she decide it *could be* true? Then she's in the frame herself – unless she ~~silences~~ discredits the accuser.

Femi
Bhatoa is a hotter suspect. Or someone employed by her. She blames Sam for Dan's death. Vows to get revenge. Has Sam killed, then realises Dan was guilty all along.

Charlotte
Issy changes most after the murder. Goes from reassuring everyone Sam is fine and didn't mean what she said, to 'Sam's gone to Africa and won't be back'.

Femi
Because Sam is rejected by the group? Issy is desperate to stay in favour, more so than she is to stay friends with Sam. Overnight she decides where her loyalties lie.

Charlotte
Issy is one of those quiet, grey, seemingly inept people, but a massively underhand player. Destroys Claudia, then gloats.

Femi
Let's think about Paige. Paige gets what she wants. She wants to be in the play. Next thing, there's a part needs filling and she's 'so excited' to do it. A princess. A chip off the old block.

Charlotte
This isn't about a part in a play. Sam is killed because she could destroy someone or something. Who stands to lose the most from what she said?

Femi
Who is Andy, the voice on Sam's answerphone on 5 July? What is it that no one can 'un-know'?

FROM: Marianne Payne
SUBJECT: Cakes
DATE: 5 July 2018 at 15:51
TO: Joyce Walford

We're leaving in ten minutes. Bring your crate of cakes to the door – Mick can't park on the bend, so he'll leave the engine running. Did you speak to that Sam? Are you ok?

FROM: Joyce Walford
SUBJECT: Re: Cakes
DATE: 5 July 2018 at 15:59
TO: Marianne Payne

No, Marianne, she wasn't in. The lift didn't come, so I had to huff and puff up all those stairs on my clicking ankle. When I finally reached their door, there was no answer. Put my ear against it and listened, but it was quiet as the grave. You can tell when a place is empty, and I swear no one was in. Couldn't hang around. I had another batch in the oven. Doubt she even went home last night. Wouldn't surprise me if she'd cleared off already. Tell Mick to leave a bigger space in the van – I've got three crates this time – we need to raise that money for Poppy. Joyce

---

FROM: Martin Hayward
SUBJECT: Tonight
DATE: 5 July 2018 at 16:02
TO: Paige Reswick
CC: James Hayward

Good news. I bumped into the curate and talked the spare keys out of him, so we can access the hall at 4.30 p.m. now. I won't email the group again; let's go through Paige's scenes on our own, as we know she's definitely going on. At 6 p.m. we'll see if Kel turns up – if not, then James is on, too. I've called and messaged Kel, no reply, so quite likely you'll both be onstage tonight. Dad

---

FROM: Paige Reswick
SUBJECT: Yippee!
DATE: 5 July 2018 at 16:08
TO: Emma Crooks

Yes! I'm definitely on tonight as Sue Bayliss. Can't believe my luck: just as I was pining for the stage and feeling jealous of everyone on it. Is this what you mean by asking the universe and waiting for it to reply? If it is, I intend to ask for a lot more in future! Paige x

---

FROM: Sarah-Jane MacDonald
SUBJECT: Tonight
DATE: 5 July 2018 at 16:11
TO: Kel Greenwood

Dear Kel, are you planning to turn up for the play tonight? It's not only the culmination of months rehearsing, but also a big fundraising initiative for Poppy. Whatever you think of the group and its members, there is a very sick little girl at the heart of our community and if you care about healing her, then please, please come down tonight and play your roles to the best of your abilities. I'll personally ensure no one holds against you what was said last night. The play and the appeal are what count now.
Sarah-Jane MacDonald

FROM: Sarah-Jane MacDonald
SUBJECT: Re: Tonight
DATE: 5 July 2018 at 16:29
TO: Kel Greenwood

Kel, I assure you I *was* listening. I don't want to get into this argument now, but Sam was *wrong*. I've known the Haywards all my life. My mother was expecting my sister when she met Helen, pregnant with James. Martin was still working in the City at the time – they only bought The Grange when he sold his company a few years later. They started The Fairway Players when Paige was a toddler. We watched them build up their business from scratch, alongside a valuable community group, through good times and bad. These are more than friends. They would *never* con us, even if they

had lost their money, which they haven't. Admittedly they don't have a spare million hanging around, but who does? I can put Sam's outburst down to stress. She had clearly been assaulted at work, you're having a relationship break – yes, people talk, I'm afraid – and now you say your friend stole money from you; well, that's no surprise after his behaviour at the Yogathon. But the fact you've fallen for a con yourselves doesn't mean we have. Please, so many people have put in so much work to make this play the best it can be. Even if you never see us again, please, both of you, come down tonight and make this the best performance you've ever given.
Sarah-Jane MacDonald

FROM: Sarah-Jane MacDonald
SUBJECT: Grrrrr
DATE: 5 July 2018 at 16:34
TO: Kevin MacDonald

Grrrrrrr! Just had an email spat with Kel. He seems to be on Sam's side, even though he said he tried to stop her speaking out and has left their flat. What's going on with them? Says he doesn't know where she is or whether she's coming tonight. And listen to this: he justified their accusations against Martin and Helen by citing the fact that their lovely friend who swore, fought and shat his way through the yoga has now stolen a lot of money from *them*. *Quelle surprise!* I'm fuming. At myself more than him – I thought a friendly email would convince them both to turn up this evening. Now I fear we'll have two understudies onstage for opening night.
Sarah-Jane MacDonald

FROM: Kevin MacDonald
SUBJECT: Re: Grrrrr
DATE: 5 July 2018 at 16:46
TO: Sarah-Jane MacDonald

Colin called. His people traced Lydia Drake's email codes to a device called 'Magda' on a network at The Grange. An inside job. Using my cold as an excuse to leave early. Home soon. I'll be ecstatic when this play is over. Kev

FROM: Sarah-Jane MacDonald
SUBJECT: Lydia Drake
DATE: 5 July 2018 at 16:52
TO: Martin Hayward

We've found Lydia Drake! Colin traced her emails to a computer called 'Magda'. I'm sorry. This means your lady at The Grange is behind it. Did you have any suspicions about her? I always thought she was very accommodating and efficient. Now we know why. She's probably operating as a mole for a much larger gang. But at least now the police have something to go on. I haven't asked Colin if he's happy to liaise with them, but assume he is. Whether they'll get our money back is another matter. I won't say anything tonight. We don't want anyone turning vigilante. This play has been a rollercoaster ride, as it is.
Sarah-Jane MacDonald

Message exchange between Martin Hayward, Glen Reswick and James Hayward on 5 July 2018:

16:53 Martin wrote:
One problem subsides as another rears its ugly head. Forwarded SJ's email.

16:56 James wrote:
Glen, can you answer SJ. Dad's rehearsing with Paige and Mum, so can't discuss it now. Just tell her to keep it quiet – we'll deal with this as a family after the play etc., etc. Keep it light. Cheers.

FROM: Glen Reswick
SUBJECT: Fwd: Re: Lydia Drake
DATE: 5 July 2018 at 17:00
TO: Sarah-Jane MacDonald

Dear Sarah-Jane, It's nice of Colin to look into it for us, but Magda is a very common Polish name, so not necessarily our Magda. Don't tell anyone. We'll deal with this as a family after the play, etc. Thanks, Glen

---

FROM: Sarah-Jane MacDonald
SUBJECT: Re: Fwd: Re: Lydia Drake
DATE: 5 July 2018 at 17:11
TO: Glen Reswick

It's definitely your Magda. The computer is on a network at The Grange. I've told Martin I won't say anything, but *please* be wary of her. She's part of a sophisticated gang that has the wherewithal to set up an office in the City and employ someone skilled enough to fool him. Does she have access to accounts at The Grange? Kevin suggests keeping her *in situ* and not letting on to her that you know what she did, but monitoring her online activity and daily movements. See if you can identify other individuals in this gang. The fact she's still working there, after they embezzled the fund money, means they may have further scams planned.
Sarah-Jane MacDonald

FROM: Glen Reswick
SUBJECT: Re: Fwd: Re: Lydia Drake
DATE: 5 July 2018 at 17:13
TO: Sarah-Jane MacDonald

It's fine, SJ, we're dealing with it. They've had a receptionist dip their hand in the till before. Martin knows what to do with them.

FROM: Sarah-Jane MacDonald
SUBJECT: Re: Fwd: Re: Lydia Drake
DATE: 5 July 2018 at 17:19
TO: Glen Reswick

It's rather more than someone's hand in the till. This is the woman who stole £80,000 from your daughter's appeal. But ok, it's fine. Let's get on with the play.
Sarah-Jane MacDonald

Message exchange between Denise Malcolm and Joyce Walford on 5 July 2018:

18:26 Denise wrote:
Kel is here! He's parking the car now. He's on his own. He looks very down. Can you tell Martin? I haven't finished my cigarette, or I'd tell him myself.

18:29 Joyce wrote:
I will. Where's Kel now? What's he doing?

18:35 Denise wrote:
He's parked the car, but is just sitting there, staring through the windscreen at a brick wall. Poor man. I wonder if that Sam has been giving him grief. Hell hath no fury. Ah! He's getting out. Well, I've never noticed he walks with a limp before. Don't tell me he's got an injury for opening night! Right, I'm done here. Put the urn on, Joyce, we've got a lot to talk about.

FROM: Isabel Beck
SUBJECT: Hiya!
DATE: 5 July 2018 at 18:46
TO: James Hayward

Hiya James, sorry you won't get to tread the boards after all. Still, we're all glad Kel is here. I haven't had a chance to speak to him myself yet, but I've watched him and he seems a bit preoccupied. Don't worry. I have no doubt he'll deliver a decent performance. His friend Arnie was arrested early yesterday for stealing and, between you and me, he's best out of Kel's life. Still, I think Kel sees it as a failure on his part. But there's no helping some people – they have to find their own way. Isn't Paige brilliant! To learn her lines and master the accent in a matter of hours demonstrates what an exceptional actress she is. Helen must be so proud. I saw them both onstage earlier and was struck by how alike they are. We're so lucky to have them, and to have you all. Without the Haywards there would be no Fairway Players, and I'd have nothing if the group weren't in my life. Sorry to ramble, but I'm getting nervous now, even though my bits went well during the run-through earlier. It's a good sign. Nerves give your performance an edge. I'm allowing myself one poppy-seed cake from Joyce each play night, but only after I've finished onstage. It's a treat for getting through the play. The audience will be coming in soon and there's that frisson of anticipation in the green room. Like Martin says, this is exactly how it is at the National Theatre or when *Coronation Street* does a live episode. It's what actors felt like in Shakespeare's plays (when he was alive), and back in ancient Greece where theatre started. It doesn't matter that we're just a little amateur drama group in a church hall. An audience is an audience. It's times like this I don't know if I love this or hate it. Or both. What a shame Olivia won't see the play, but she'll need two days' rest minimum after a C-section. Love to all four of you, Issy xxx

---

FROM: James Hayward
SUBJECT: Re: Hiya!
DATE: 5 July 2018 at 18:50
TO: Isabel Beck

Dearest Issy, I was more than relieved to see Kel. I know Dad was, too. Break a leg for your performance tonight. As I'm not needed now, I'm popping back to the hospital, probably in the next half-hour. If Olivia's discharged on Saturday (as we hope) I might be able to see the play that night, but otherwise I'll rely on you to tell me how it goes and if there's any other news. You haven't seen Sam, have you?

FROM: Isabel Beck
SUBJECT: Re: Hiya!
DATE: 5 July 2018 at 18:51
TO: James Hayward

No.

FROM: Sarah-Jane MacDonald
SUBJECT: T-shirts
DATE: 5 July 2018 at 19:18
TO: Joel Halliday
CC: Celia Halliday

I'm in the green room and not allowed out, as the audience has started to arrive. This is just to wish you all the best for the fundraising drive this evening, and especially selling raffle tickets. We've still got hundreds left, so please try to flog at least one to every punter. If you need more merchandise, there's plenty in storage at The Grange. Ask Martin to pick it up rather than bother Magda. Thinking about it, I wish I'd ordered XXL T-shirts as well as XL. People like baggy. I'll call the supplier in the morning.
Sarah-Jane MacDonald

FROM: Joel Halliday
SUBJECT: Re: T-Shirts
DATE: 5 July 2018 at 19:22
TO: Sarah-Jane MacDonald

Don't worry, SJ. You can concentrate on the play now. Everything's in hand. We've got a captive market and we're in for the kill. Break a leg. Joel

---

FROM: Lauren Malden
SUBJECT: Break a leg!
DATE: 5 July 2018 at 19:25
TO: Isabel Beck

Hello lovely! Break a leg, sweetheart. I'll think of you at curtain up – is it still 8 p.m.? You've probably got your phone switched off by now (I remember Martin's strict green room rules), but I'll send you positive vibes over the psychic airwaves. Has Paige learned the role of Sue Bayliss? It's a big part for someone to memorise at short notice. With all the rehearsing you've done, I'm sure you would have slipped straight into it. Paige could have read your lines. Still, Martin knows best, and you'll smash any part you play. Mum's got a ticket for tonight, so she'll say hi afterwards if she can find you among your crowd of well-wishers. Kiss kiss, L x

FROM: Isabel Beck
SUBJECT: Re: Break a leg!
DATE: 5 July 2018 at 19:28
TO: Lauren Malden

Thanks. Hope your mum enjoys the play. Still got my phone on. I'm hiding between the props cupboard and wardrobe rail, so no one's noticed me using it. I'm really nervous now. Everyone's in costume and make-up. Helen is incredible. I'd be terrified if I had a role as large and demanding as Kate Keller, but she's chatting to Denise, Paige and Kevin as if nothing is out of the ordinary at all. John is pacing the green room. You can tell he wants a cigarette. The Walford boys are out by the toilet, watching football on Kevin's phone and secretly vaping like mad, so there's a fruity smell in the air. Sarah-Jane is sitting opposite. She's pretending to read her script, but every now and then I catch her watching me over the top of it. I'll have to switch my phone off after I've sent this. Harley is very sweet. He's happily doing his homework, as if he doesn't have to be onstage in a few minutes. Paige is laughing and chatting to everyone as if she's been in the play from the beginning. Between you and me, she doesn't suit that dowdy costume as well as I would have. Marianne had to alter it to fit her, which took ages. Still, as you say, Martin knows best. Well, SJ's just given me another look, so I'd better go. Deep breath and . . . this is it. Issy

Review of the first night of the play, published online 6 July 2018:

All My Sons by The Fairway Players

Deep trouble in the deep south 🖐🖐🖐👇👇
by Amanda Basham

Arthur Miller constructs a play the way a sculptor creates a three-dimensional image from an amorphous chunk of clay. He shows us a basic shape. Then bends and stretches its contours, turns it for us to view alternate angles, gradually reveals its finer details until, finally, we can see for ourselves what it really is.

Miller's *All My Sons* debuted in 1947. In the heart of small-town America, Joe and Kate Keller enjoy a comfortable lifestyle, thanks to their aviation business and the money they made from the Second World War. While their son Chris returned from the Western Front a hero, their other son Larry has been 'missing in action' for three years. Kate refuses to believe he is anything but alive and well and will be on his way home soon. When Larry's girlfriend, Ann Deever, returns with her brother George, we see a different side to the Kellers, as the awful truth about Joe's business practices comes to light.

Fresh from their breezy production of Noel Coward's *Blithe Spirit* earlier this year, The Fairway Players, under co-directors Martin and James Hayward, treat Miller's classic with all the reverence it deserves. More talking than action means greater pressure on the actors to deliver on pace and emotion. Helen Grace-Hayward, whose perfect comic timing as Elvira made *Blithe Spirit* such a treat, here shows us that her talent for drama is every bit as well honed.

Her Kate Keller is a woman happy to exist in a state of delusion, remote from the uncomfortable realities that gradually close in until, in a shockingly tragic twist, she must face them head-on and alone. I barely dared breathe during Kate's final scenes, such was Grace-Hayward's onstage charisma and intensity of commitment to this demanding role. Her impeccable performance was almost matched by John O'Dea, a superficially jovial Joe, who sinks into awful realisation as the truth is unveiled. Of course mastering an American accent is key to delivering this play and if I were told both leads were genuinely from the region, I would happily believe it.

Unfortunately, the same cannot be said for every performer in this amateur production. I noticed several slips of intonation and the odd English vowel here and there. Sarah-Jane MacDonald played Ann, a woman on a painful and angry mission, with a faltering, distracted edge I wasn't entirely convinced by. Nick Walford as Ann's brother George, a newly qualified lawyer spoiling for a fight with Joe, could have been better rehearsed. His most convincing scenes were those where he clashed with the Kellers' surviving son Chris, played by his real-life brother Barry.

The Kellers' neighbours provide both insight and (minimal) light relief for the audience. Kevin MacDonald was solidly convincing as Jim Bayliss, a doctor with a perpetual streaming cold. Paige Reswick shone as his wife Sue, a performance all the more commendable as she took on the role with half a day's rehearsal, when the company was let down by the original cast member.

On the other side of the Kellers is the Lubey family. Newcomer Kel Greenwood, in his inevitably nervous stage debut, plays amateur astrologer Frank as a limping nuisance. This outwardly bumbling dolt is clever, selfish and cowardly enough to dodge the draft to raise a family with George's homely ex-girlfriend Lydia.

Mention must be made of young Harley MacDonald, who delighted everyone with his sensitive portrayal of local cheeky-chappie Bert. His word-perfect performance and convincing accent lead me to suspect he is a starring Fairway Player of the future.

The simple set, designed by Joel Halliday, did not distract from the actors' work, while delightful 1940s costumes and make-up, thanks to Marianne Payne and Denise Malcolm, helped transport us in time and place.

Finally, no one could miss the brightly clad fundraising team who were out in force all evening, reminding us that this production has a very important purpose. The players are raising money for sight-impaired Poppy Reswick, who needs life-saving brain-tumour treatment in America. I wish them luck for their appeal and the final two nights of *All My Sons*.

FROM: Celia Halliday
SUBJECT: Ooops
DATE: 5 July 2018 at 22:39
TO: Sarah-Jane MacDonald

Was that a dramatic pause or did you forget your words? It's awful when that happens. You feel as if you've let everyone down. You didn't seem yourself, SJ, are you ok? Helen was breathtaking, so it wasn't as if you were going to outshine her in that tiny role anyway. Kevin did well, considering. Bless Harley! He looked like a little girl up there onstage. Anyway, tonight's sales are listed below. I focused the team on raffle tickets and it's paid off. I don't need any more merchandise for tomorrow night, except cakes. Celia

---

FROM: Carol Dearing
SUBJECT: First night over with
DATE: 5 July 2018 at 22:43
TO: Sarah-Jane MacDonald

Bloody Celia drives me up the wall. I do not want my every move micromanaged and criticised, my mistakes pointed out to everyone in earshot – then the credit for *my* sales stolen from under my nose. I go to work for all that, and get paid. I know she says what she thinks and this is considered an attribute, but I don't bloody care what she thinks, especially when it's not true. She's always been jealous of my friendship with Helen. It comes out in her attitude to me. Whatever she says, I single-handedly shifted seventeen raffle tickets – more than any other seller. I don't care how smelly Woof is, I will dog-sit him tomorrow with pleasure. You were brilliant onstage, by the way. The best up there. Mum

---

FROM: Sarah-Jane MacDonald
SUBJECT: Re: First night over with
DATE: 5 July 2018 at 22:52
TO: Carol Dearing

Thanks. I barely felt in character at all. We've had a lot going on. I'm absolutely exhausted. Celia means well, Mum, and has worked hard for the appeal. She doesn't intend to be offensive. I don't think. Anyway, it's

Joel we need. He's a brilliant set designer and they come as a package. Must get Harley home. Thanks for tomorrow. SJ

FROM: Joel Halliday
SUBJECT: Lift?
DATE: 5 July 2018 at 23:01
TO: Isabel Beck

Where are you, Issy? Celia and I are waiting to lock up. I didn't realise you don't drive until I saw the car park was empty. The buses are hair-raising this time of night. We'll give you a lift. Don't want to lose another cast member . . . Did all your people leave soon after the curtain call? I didn't see anyone waiting to congratulate you. Joel

---

FROM: Isabel Beck
SUBJECT: Re: Lift?
DATE: 5 July 2018 at 23:04
TO: Joel Halliday

I would *love* a lift – thank you so much! I'm in the wings, stage right, behind the trellis. Just enjoying some quiet time before I set off. I'm coming now. I didn't have anyone in tonight. I expect my people will all come tomorrow or Saturday. I don't mind. It takes the pressure off – a bit. Luckily, it all went quite well for me. Kel was shaky on his words. Sarah-Jane looked like a ghost and her accent dropped several times. She's been working too hard on the appeal, not concentrating on her role, and it showed. I'm coming now . . . Love Issy xxx

---

FROM: Beth Halliday
SUBJECT: Where are you?
DATE: 5 July 2018 at 23:39
TO: Joel Halliday

Where are you? Thought you and Mum were coming straight home after locking up. x

---

FROM: Joel Halliday
SUBJECT: Re: Where are you?
DATE: 5 July 2018 at 23:44
TO: Beth Halliday

On our way. Gave that quiet girl Issy a lift to save her taking the bus and now wish we hadn't. We felt sorry for her. Since Sam's gone she doesn't speak to anyone, and no one she knew came to see the show. Well, we thought she would want to go home, but she asked to be dropped off at Sam's flat, right over the other side of Lockwood, at this time of night! Said she had something for Kel. Your mum told her he'd left and was at the Travellers' Inn with another woman. I said whatever it is he's left behind, she can give it to him tomorrow night, but she was adamant that's where she wanted to go, so that's where we left her. We're just at the big traffic lights, home soon. Love Dad xx

PS Don't worry: I'm not breaking the law. Mum's driving.

Transcription of a 999 call made at 00:12 on 6 July 2018:

Operator: Emergency, which service?
Caller: Ambulance.
Operator: Who's injured?
Caller: Sam.
Operator: Are they breathing?
Caller: [*inaudible sound*] Lower Lockwood Heights. Behind the new flats. Park in front and come round the side.
Paramedic: I know it. We're on the way.
Operator: Can you tell me what's happened there?
Caller: She's under a hedge.
Operator: Is she breathing? Check if she's breathing.
Caller: No. She's dead.
Operator: If there's a chance she's breathing, you need to check. It's very important.
Caller: She's been there a whole day. She hasn't moved.
Paramedic: Three minutes now.
Operator: What's happened to her? Can you tell me?
Caller: She fell off the balcony.
Operator: How high?
Caller: [*inaudible sound*] High.
Operator: And what's your name, please?
Caller: It's . . . You can see Topps Tiles from up there.

Olufemi Hassan
Charlotte Holroyd

Dear both,

That is all the correspondence submitted at the original hearing. Remember: these 'conversations' were only ever intended for the person(s) to whom they were addressed. We might assume no one else, much less a court of law, was ever meant to hear them – but would we be correct? Wittingly or unwittingly, all these people gave evidence. They did so freely, in their own words and without the intimidation of the witness box – yet without ever committing to tell the truth. I believe somewhere in there is the key to why Samantha Greenwood was found dead, under her fifth-floor balcony, on 6 July 2018, where she had lain for around twenty-four hours. Cause of death was multiple injuries, consistent with a fall from that height, but incompatible with life. In addition, her body exhibited minor injuries to the face and torso, but according to the coroner, these were most likely caused the previous day in the assault at St Ann's. So . . .

1. Who killed Samantha Greenwood?
2. In the hours before her death, she told three people three things. Who and what?
3. Who knew it was going to happen?
4. Who knew about it before her body was discovered?
5. Who is erroneously imprisoned and why?

We must submit our case to the Court of Appeal this week, so time is not on our side.

I need a single document that explores these questions. Please put forward evidence, plus clearly reasoned arguments, for or against particular theories and suspects. Your role as fresh young eyes on this is crucial. I believe there is an innocent person in jail, but I'm no maverick – I need you to see it, too.

If you can solve these further riddles, then it's more than I could at the original hearing: three people are not who they say they are. Three masquerade as others. One does not exist at all. To help you here, Sandra has completed a full list of participants in this case. It is attached. She has placed them in their main social groups rather than alphabetical order. I am reluctant to request a change as I gather from her demeanour it was a long and laborious job as is.

Finally, some facts available to the court and not clear from the correspondence:

1. Officially, Sam was forced to resign from her overseas volunteer post due to ill health.
2. Both Sam and Kel were prescribed Interferon and Ribavirin to control the effects of chronic Hepatitis C, contracted during their time in the Central African Republic. Neither disclosed this to St Ann's. Sean 'Kel' Greenwood was subsequently suspended and resigned.
3. Isabel Beck was on disciplinary probation for eighteen months following an incident in the orthopaedic ward at St Ann's, where she attached the wrong intravenous bag to a patient who then had to be resuscitated.
4. There were no signs of forced entry to the Greenwoods' flat the night Samantha Greenwood died.

I look forward to receiving your document before 9 a.m. tomorrow.

Yours,

RT

Roderick Tanner, QC
Senior Partner
Tanner & Dewey LLP

PS One further fact you should be aware of. Topps Tiles is *not* visible from the Greenwoods' balcony.

List of Individuals

The Fairway Players

Martin Hayward, 59, chairperson of The Fairway Players and joint owner of The Grange

Helen Grace-Hayward, 62, secretary of The Fairway Players and joint owner of The Grange

James Hayward, 36, their son

Olivia Hayward 33, his wife

Paige Reswick, 33 (née Hayward), their daughter

Glen Reswick, 31, her husband

Poppy Reswick, 2, their daughter

Woof, 3, their dog

Sarah-Jane MacDonald, 34 (née Dearing)

Kevin MacDonald, 37, her husband

Harley MacDonald, 10, their son

Carol Dearing, 61, Sarah-Jane's mother

Margaret Dearing, 88, mother of Carol and Shelley, grandmother of Sarah-Jane

Shelley Dearing, 63, Carol's sister, Sarah-Jane's aunt

Isabel Beck, 29, staff nurse, Elderly Care at St Ann's Hospital

Lauren Malden, 29, former staff nurse, Elderly Care at St Ann's Hospital

Josh, 30, her boyfriend

Lauren's mother, *c.* 57

Kel Greenwood, 34, staff nurse, Mental Health, St Ann's Hospital

Samantha Greenwood, 34, staff nurse, Elderly Care, St Ann's Hospital

Joyce Walford, 63, tea lady at The Fairway Players and retired receptionist at The Grange

Nick Walford, 33, her son

Barry Walford, 28, her son

Harry, 62, Joyce's partner

John O'Dea, 56, treasurer

Denise Malcolm, 59, wardrobe and make-up
Steve Malcolm, 60, her husband

Marianne Payne, 48, wardrobe and make-up
Mick Payne, 51, her husband
Karen Payne, 26, their daughter

Jackie Marsh, 23, currently travelling

Joel Halliday, 54, set designer
Celia Halliday, 55, his wife
Beth Halliday, 16, their daughter

The Grange Golf and Country Club
Magda Kuchar, 24, receptionist

Emma Crooks, 32, yoga teacher, Paige's best friend

Chris Wilkinson, 68, member
Marion Wilkinson, 67, his wife

Gavin Hoyte, 30, member

St Ann's Hospital
Frances Turner, 39, ward manager, Elderly Care

Gaynor, 27, staff nurse, Elderly Care
Riley, 25, staff nurse, Elderly Care

Claudia D'Souza, 36, Human Resources
Michael D'Souza 37, marketing manager, her husband
Sophie, 11, their daughter
Marco, 9, their son

Hilary Mulvey, 26, human resources manager (maternity cover)

Ciara Savage, 40, nurse, Mental Health

Mount More Hospital

Dr Tish Bhatoa, 51, consultant oncologist
Ravi Bhatoa, 53, her brother
Dr Daniel Bhatoa, 43, their brother

Una, 32, Claudia's friend in Human Resources

Ziggy Benjamin, 39, ward manager, Oncology

Overseas volunteer community

Dr Sonja Ajanlekoko, 34, project co-ordinator, Médecins Sans Frontières
Arnold 'Arnie' Ballancore, 33, former volunteer nurse
Christine Ballancore, 64, his mother
Dr Alicja Szkatulska, 37, former volunteer doctor
Dr Tanya Strickland, 34, former volunteer doctor
Alasdair Hynes, 47, former volunteer logistics manager
Martha Diaz, 35, current volunteer outreach worker
Ian Levy, 39, Africa Directorate, Foreign & Commonwealth Office
Selima Kenya, 27, current volunteer outreach project leader

Police/legal representatives

Constable Liam Albutt, 22
Constable Josie Thompson, 25
Sergeant Cooper, 37
Sergeant Crowe, 43
Ms Anand, 33, duty solicitor
Rupert Allardyce, 53, solicitor for Martin Hayward

Miscellaneous

Nigel Crowley, 57, band leader, aka Tony Zucchero
Stella Cornwall, 33, string quartet leader
Cameron Hilford, 67, Radio 4 quiz host
Ben Taylor, 50, CEO, Robinson EcoField Ltd.
Clive Handler, age unknown, local entrepreneur

Callum McDaid, 44, local builder
Lydia Drake, age unknown, financial advisor
Colin Brasher, age unknown, local entrepreneur
Julian Maher, 44, local journalist, friend of Colin Brasher
Andrea Morley, 32, genealogist
Robert Green, 63, antique dealer
Priti Panchal, age unknown, customer services, local bank
Graham Oxshott, 61, local community volunteer
Noel Burton, 54, corporate intelligence consultant

Femi
We can work on the doc together. Whizz it back and forth.

Charlotte
Why's Tanner so keen on this case? Guilt trip.

Femi
I propose we amalgamate our suspects, create a profile for each, with thoughts, observations, evidence for and against.

Charlotte
And relationships between them. Something odd about Issy and Sam.

Femi
The Haywards. They're up to something, but is it relevant to Sam's murder? Bhatoa. The same. I don't trust her.

Charlotte
One person doesn't exist. Two, surely? Clive Handler and Lydia Drake.

Femi
Three masquerade as others. Sam pretends to be Handler. Magda pretends to be Drake. Who's the third?

Charlotte
Sam pretends to be Issy to visit Mount More. Given that Issy is not particularly clever, the question is: were they working together?

Femi
Issy's no dimwit. Devious when motivated.

Charlotte
How about: this isn't an exercise but a game. Sam wasn't murdered. It's an accident or suicide.

Femi
I'm starting the doc now. Give me an hour.

The murder of Samantha Greenwood

Exploratory document for Roderick Tanner, QC, School of Law, Year One
Contributors: Femi Hassan, Charlotte Holroyd

Introduction
After eight years of living on the precipice of human experience Samantha Greenwood arrives 'home', only to fall victim to violence as savage as any she can have witnessed in war-torn Central Africa. She is described as 'an honest and hard-working lady of principle who is not afraid to speak'. It seems such fearlessness could have led to her murder. In this document we will examine events leading up to Ms Greenwood's death, and the complex relationships between those witnesses who knew her and those who assumed they did.

Before we consider our suspects, we would like to identify five interlocking microcosms:

- The Fairway Players and their production of Arthur Miller's classic drama *All My Sons*.
- The medical staff at St Ann's and Mount More.
- The appeal to raise money for Poppy Reswick's cancer treatment.
- Two intertwined dynasties: the Haywards and Reswicks, the Dearings and MacDonalds.
- The Africa connection, and how something a world away can have such a profound influence.

Samantha Greenwood
Sam arrives in Lockwood as an outsider on a number of levels. Thanks to Isabel, she and Kel find themselves at the bottom of a strict, well-established social hierarchy. Their experience as humanitarian volunteers is so remote from that of everyone else that it counts for nothing. Here, life revolves around two interlocking family dynasties: the Haywards and Reswicks, the Dearings and MacDonalds. A person's closeness to the alpha family – the Haywards – determines their social status. For example, Shelley Dearing is not high enough to be seated on the top table at the ball.

A large, wealthy, influential family is a powerful unit. The Haywards are successful, intelligent business people. They employ many locals and run a high-profile drama society. They are well respected in the community and by their employees. Sarah-Jane mentions how hard everyone works, unpaid, during Poppy's Ball. Meanwhile, Celia and Joel volunteer at The Grange, while Emma takes in Paige's sick and troublesome dog. Celia and Carol compete for friendship with Helen. Being of value to the alpha family can lead to increased social standing and subsequently greater confidence and self-respect within the community.

We see how someone not part of this social hierarchy – like Nigel Crowley – isn't as sympathetic or keen to go the extra mile. Meanwhile we also see, initially at least, that Sam and Kel want to be part of this world. They join The Fairway Players despite having no interest in theatre, and as soon as they learn about Poppy's illness, they mine their medical contacts for information to help her (27 April). Sam quickly commits to run a sponsored half-marathon and tries to help the family when she suggests on 30 April that Martin lobbies Parliament (which later leads him to construe that she is paranoid about authority).

We should consider Sam's behaviour in the context of what has gone before. In Bangui, she tried to bring the truth out into the open, but was discredited and silenced. We suspect her accusations against Dan Bhatoa could be behind her discharge from frontline medical volunteering, even if her health was cited as the reason.

When she arrives at St Ann's, it seems Sam's commitment to putting right what she sees as wrong is undimmed by her recent experience. During her first meeting with Claudia on 22 April she lists everything she thinks is wrong with the Elderly Care ward. She either hasn't learned the fate of the whistleblower, or she's learned it but is strong enough to put herself on the line again. By her second meeting on 18 May, she's using Claudia for information about Tish Bhatoa.

Martin concludes that Sam is paranoid about authority, but is that any surprise when she has challenged authority, only to have it close ranks and let an injustice go unpunished? It surely cannot be a coincidence that they have arrived in Dan Bhatoa's sister's Healthcare Trust. If Sam's intention is to discredit Bhatoa, in revenge for defending Dan in Bangui, then can her actions be viewed in that light and her accusations dismissed? Does she see things that aren't there and stir up trouble where none exists? Early in this correspondence, Issy observes that the UK 'probably seems very dull in comparison' to the Greenwoods' life abroad. Is Sam subconsciously generating excitement and drama to replace all she lost over there?

As it is, Sam reports Tish to the BMA on 18 May and follows up her accusation with evidence in the form of the Poppy's Ball programme on 5 June. She's out to get Tish in whatever way she can.

We also noted that Sam is not afraid to lie and deceive when the aim is to uncover a deeper, more significant truth. While we have no access to Sam's personal emails here, we *do* in fact hear directly from her. In the 'voice' of Clive Handler on 30 May, she describes the suggestion that he use an offshore account as 'not "quite legitimate", it is a loophole, but one I am prepared to jump through for the greater good'. Through the course of this correspondence Sam deceives the Haywards, Claudia, Isabel and others, all in pursuit of a 'greater good'. By the time she confronts the Haywards at the dress rehearsal on 4 July she has clearly amassed what she believes to be strong evidence that they have deceived and defrauded their loyal friends in order to preserve their own businesses and lifestyle. But is she right?

What did Samantha tell the drama group, and could she be correct?

There is no question Samantha Greenwood hits a nerve when she addresses The Fairway Players at their dress rehearsal for *All My Sons*. Helen, who 'so rarely cries', exhibits inconsolable distress, and Martin is so disturbed – possibly by Sam's accusations, possibly by the uncharacteristic reaction of his wife – that he abandons the crucial rehearsal completely. The community is firmly on Helen's side. We believe the key to Sam's murder lies in what she revealed that night. But how right is she, and who stands to lose the most from what she says?

From Sarah-Jane we discover that Sam claims to know the following:

- The appeal is a 'financial conspiracy'.
- There are no experimental drugs. Poppy is undergoing a course of conventional chemotherapy at Mount More.
- Poppy's notes are not kept at the hospital.
- Helen did not have a little boy who died of meningitis, as she claims – it is a story to engage the community with the appeal. There is no mention of it here, but as we will see below, Poppy's 'sight loss' is exactly this.
- That if he *really were the victim of a fraud*, then Martin deserves to be beaten at his own game. Sam seems to doubt the Lydia Drake story.
- Martin later distils what Sam says about the appeal into the phrase 'poorly run', as if to dilute the power of her accusations.

We would like to explore Sam's claims.

To what extent is the appeal being used for personal gain, and by whom? We are unanimous that *someone* is using Poppy's fund money for their own purposes, but is it Martin, Tish or both? If it's both, then are they in collusion or not? At this point we cannot rule other members of the Hayward and Reswick families in or out of the deception.

Both Martin and Tish have onerous financial responsibilities. But which came first: their money worries or the appeal? The appeal raises a great deal of cash very quickly. Did they see this and *then* realise they could solve their financial issues – confident the cash flow would continue? If so, then we can see how it might subsequently be difficult to *stop* taking money from the fund, especially as they can hide behind Sarah-Jane while she lobbies friends and family. The curse of easy money . . .

If we chart the progress of the 'lie' that Poppy is going blind, we may find some clues. It starts with good intentions. On 18 May, Sarah-Jane must convince Nigel Crowley to play at Poppy's Ball for free. There is no time to find another band and she wants to spend as little of the fund money as possible on event expenses. Initially she tells him Poppy is a fan of his music and listens to it while having her cancer treatment. This innocuous untruth does not convince Crowley to change his mind. The more emotive lie about Poppy losing her sight is blurted out just as he seems out of reach. Having pulled this 'fact' from thin air, Sarah-Jane is then honest with the Haywards about what she's done, expressing horror at telling such a 'whopper'. The Haywards find this predicament amusing, with Martin content to continue the 'lie' for the benefit of the event. At no point does anyone suggest revealing the truth to Crowley.

Inevitably, word gets around about Poppy losing her eyesight. Isabel believes the family has 'the wrong end of the stick'. Meanwhile Sam sources information that suggests the family is simply focusing on the side-effect they fear most. Both have enough medical knowledge to doubt the claim.

It does not escape the family that any mention of blindness increases donations to the appeal. In fundraising updates, Poppy's sight loss is continually alluded to: 'We are also facing the fact her eyesight will be affected – which makes every day that she can still see all the more poignant' (9 June). Having said that, a few days earlier Glen questions what people will think when they see Poppy is obviously not blind: 'We don't want anyone feeling they've been conned, when they've been kind enough to support us' (3 June). Is this something he would say if it were a premeditated deception? We suspect that, after the lie works so well with Nigel, the family comes to regard such 'fibs' as an acceptable part of the fundraising process.

By the time Martin sends his update telling their fundraising community about the Clive Handler hoax on 23 June, he categorically states that Poppy's chemo has 'resulted in hair loss and blindness'. We are unanimous in the belief that Poppy is not losing her eyesight – we later learn she has not lost her hair, either, yet Paige shaves her head on 2 July because people 'expect' a child with cancer to be bald – are they cynically manipulating their friends, or is it simply a convenient lie they now believe themselves?

Martin becomes increasingly vague about how much money has been raised and how much is needed. He is otherwise pedantic and efficient, yet we can see throughout this correspondence how reluctant he is to engage with Sarah-Jane's requests for a definitive figure. His son James refers to his 'petulant vagueness' in response to stress. Yet on occasions when we might assume Martin is under pressure, such as after Sam's outburst at the dress rehearsal on 4 July, he displays great clarity of thought and measured calmness in his correspondence with both Sam and Sarah-Jane. Could it be that he is undertaking a 'financial deception' that is the source of far greater stress and anxiety than anything concerning the drama group?

We also have another train of thought. That the Haywards are acting in good faith, but that Tish Bhatoa is deceiving *them*. Samantha Greenwood exercises suspicions early on that Tish is not being honest with them about the drug treatment Poppy needs. The whole Clive Handler hoax throws doubt on the entire premise of the appeal. In Bangui, Sam witnessed Bhatoa work to get her brother off charges of inappropriate behaviour. This could easily colour Sam's perception of anything Bhatoa says or does, but just because Tish is prepared to bend the truth to protect her brother does not mean she is guilty of defrauding the Haywards, or of Sam's murder. Similarly, the fact that Sam harbours a grudge against Tish does not mean the doctor is innocent of defrauding the appeal.

We both agree on one thing: by the time Martin reveals the truth about Lydia Drake on 3 July, he, James and Glen are all on the same page, all in on some sort of conspiracy – apparently in isolation from Helen, Paige and Olivia. It seems the Hayward women are spared any stress and financial responsibility. Martin tells James and Glen on several occasions to keep facts from Helen.

Martin very clearly calculates a time to tell the drama group about the Lydia Drake fraud: 'Tuesday. After their committee meeting and before the play. Don't email. Come round if you need to speak' (1 July). This is also one of many occasions when Martin tells his son and son-in-law not to email, apparently mindful that this evidence could be used against them. We also note a curious one-line email from Martin to James on 2 June: 'I know what you mean. Thank you', in response to a bland statement about making memories with Poppy. We think Martin thanks him for the reminder that this correspondence could be used as evidence in their favour, should they be found out.

Speaking of evidence, we see Glen's panic when the police visit on 4 July. Martin says: 'Surely they'd come here first. Is Paige there? Can you hide?' There is palpable relief when the police only want to see the Healing Doll. What are they hiding?

Finally, on 3 July Sarah-Jane MacDonald says to Kevin: 'The stress is written on their faces.' But is it solely the stress of Poppy's illness, or also a financial fraud that has spiralled out of the family's control?

Do the experimental drugs exist at all?

This is the question behind Sam's deception of the Haywards when she poses as Clive Handler on 20 and 30 May. Why does she play such a cruel trick on a family already under enormous emotional pressure? It seems out of character for her. If we follow the correspondence, its primary aim is to discover where in the US the drugs originate. On 2 May Sam asks Martin and Tish, but can't get an answer; she asks her medical contacts, no luck there either. So she resorts to this underhand way to find out, perhaps not appreciating how much it will hurt the family.

Speaking as Handler on 30 May, Sam tells Tish that the fund is a lie to manipulate the Haywards. If she has hit the nail on the head at this point, surely Tish would bail out there and then, knowing she's been found out – and by someone unafraid to speak. Therefore if the appeal is a fraud, the Haywards *must* be in on it to some degree.

Sam's success as Clive Handler serves another, unanticipated function. It leads her to construct a more sophisticated deception later, when she poses as Isabel to trawl through the medical records at Mount More.

Poppy is having conventional chemo at Mount More – so why are her notes not kept at the hospital?

We can say for sure: Poppy's drugs are administered by Hickman line into her chest on a twice-weekly basis at Mount More's Paediatric Oncology department. By manipulating Claudia, Sam poses as Isabel to infiltrate the system there on 22 June. She fails to find Poppy's medical notes. While we have no idea how typical this is, or if there could be an innocent explanation – Poppy is one of Tish Bhatoa's private patients, after all – the fact that Sam identifies it as unusual has to be taken into account. We are not entirely in agreement that, having been out of the country for eight years, Sam could know what current treatment pathways are, or that her professional experience would qualify her to judge the decisions of a senior consultant in Oncology.

Did Helen have a little boy who died of meningitis or is this a story to engage the community with the appeal?
Sam is consulting a genealogist about Helen on 25 June, so presumably she is the source of the information that Helen did not have a child before James. What led Sam to go down this route of enquiry we don't yet know, but Andrea Morley is likely to be the 'Andy' we hear on the answering service the night Sam is killed. Sam often goes missing from work through illness or days off. But is she ill with the condition that we know she has, or is she meeting Andrea, or both?

This question is one that seems to play on Sarah-Jane's mind after Sam's outburst at the dress rehearsal. Emma's corroboration convinces Sarah-Jane and, on the whole, us too. However, with no further evidence, we do not feel able to explore this point fully.

Is there any mileage in the accusation that Martin fabricates the Lydia Drake 'fraud'?
As we've seen, the 'financial conspiracy' accusation is very likely true, to one extent or another. However, Sam throws doubt on the Lydia Drake fraud here, and we can't see why Martin would pretend to have been conned. We are more inclined to believe greed convinced him to fall for Lydia Drake's promises – whether that 'greed' is for Poppy's cure or his own financial gain remains to be determined. It does beg the question: who is Lydia Drake?

What is the relationship between Sam and Issy?
With only one side of this correspondence available to us, nonetheless we can see how Isabel Beck quickly becomes a needy, high-maintenance friend. However, through her we learn some key facts about Sam, especially when James – one of the few characters sympathetic to Issy – asks her what Sam is like. From Issy's answer we deduce that: people

listen to her, she gets on with everyone and she gets things done. These qualities all backfired in Bangui, and again at the dress rehearsal. We were interested to observe that when Isabel 'speaks', as she does through the committee minutes she sends to the whole group on 6 June, for the most part people take very little notice. Sarah-Jane even says to her 'no one cares what you think'. Issy is simply not high enough up the social ladder to have a voice. We are also bemused to note that Issy is the only cast member of *All My Sons* not credited by name in the online review published on 6 July. Even onstage, Issy goes unnoticed.

Sam tells Claudia she's desperate to be rid of Issy, but is that true? Sam uses Claudia and Isabel to conduct an audacious deception that leads directly to her making the accusations that very probably lead to her death. Sam asks Claudia to arrange a tour of Mount More for 'Isabel'. Only the email address she gives her is a false one. Sam, as Isabel, accepts the invitation and meets Ziggy for the tour, where she absconds to look up Poppy Reswick's treatment plan and medical records. Our primary evidence for this is how Ziggy describes the 'Isabel' she meets as 'chatty and interested'. The Isabel we know is the exact opposite of that.

We wonder why Sam doesn't simply organise a tour of the department under her own identity. We think she is wary of Tish Bhatoa hearing her name and feels safer undercover.

This deception is one Sam finds herself having to shore up repeatedly. She must tell Isabel she was speaking to Claudia about having Frances (you-know-who or YKW) moved from Elderly Care. Isabel then nags her about this on 23 and 25 June. Sam must also lie to Claudia on 26 June and say that she's ill, in order to keep her away from the Yogathon, where she'll meet Isabel – who knows nothing about the tour. After the Mount More visit, Sam must keep them apart. When Sam's relationship with Claudia threatens to undermine her relationship with Issy, Sam is obliged to foster Issy's flagging friendship. As much as Sam might find Issy a drain, she wants to keep her onside, to use her and avoid her becoming vengeful.

We believe Sam fails to appreciate the long-term consequences of her actions when she has her mind set on a higher truth.

It is easy to focus on what Sam thinks of Issy, but we should also take into account how Issy feels about Sam. Her neediness borders on obsession, and where obsession is concerned, isn't there a fine line between love and hate? Obsessive love – if it can be described as 'love' at all – can change direction in a flash. When Issy spots Sam having lunch with Claudia in the Orangery on 13 June, she types an unsent email that ends 'I hate Claudia, I hate myself and I hate . . . ' The missing word, we think, is 'you', meaning Sam. Issy feels dependent on Sam for her own social status and self-respect, but dependence breeds resentment.

We discussed at length Issy's curious inaccurate observation on 1 July that Topps Tiles is visible from the Greenwoods' balcony and have the following theory to expound. There is a moment, the morning after the Yogathon, when Issy wanders around the Greenwoods' lounge. This is when Issy has hands-on access to Sam's life.

During the altercation between Arnie and Barry, when Kel and Sam separate their troubled friend from the affray, Arnie blurts out to Sam that Kel has been seeing Claudia. We believe Issy hears this, too. Isabel describes herself as someone who likes to plan ahead. But we can see she is just as much an opportunist. Therefore we think it possible that, when the opportunity arises, Issy uses Sam's laptop – an old one, so old it does not feature a security password – to send an email to Michael D'Souza. She impersonates Sam to tell him about the affair, to hammer the final nail into Sam's friendship with Claudia and stir up trouble for her nemesis. We are going to assert that Topps Tiles is visible from *elsewhere* in the flat, where Issy was situated at the exact time she pretended to be out on the balcony.

Issy could not have guessed her email would lead Claudia to attack Sam on 4 July. We believe Claudia probably reproached Sam during the attack for telling Michael when she had begged her not to, for the sake of their children. This could be the moment Sam realises Issy is behind it all. We know Sam has harsh words with Issy after the dress rehearsal, leaving even Sarah-Jane feeling sorry for her. But what does she say? Perhaps that she knows Issy sent the email to Michael. Or that she has never liked her and was only pretending to be her friend. Whatever it is may be devastating, but is it enough to turn Issy's toxic 'love' for Sam into hate and ultimately murder? By the next morning Issy's loyalties are firmly with the community, whose attitude to her is at best indifferent.

What were Sam's intentions?
We believe that at the point she discovers Kel is having an affair with Claudia, Sam decides to return to the Central African Republic. Only she is unable to do so because Arnie stole their money after Kel gave him their PIN number on 25 June. Does frustration over this, the end of her marriage, her attack at the hands of Claudia and her constant management of Isabel's obsession lead to Sam's outburst? We are certain her outburst leads to her downfall.

Femi
I'm worried about the time this is taking. We're not even halfway through. Are we getting wrapped up in the minutiae and missing the bigger picture?

Charlotte
I don't think so. I like it so far. It's just a bit wordy. We need to show we've discussed all the possibilities.

Femi
We need to answer the fucking questions. Go back to Tanner's letter. He asks five questions, then some random shit.

Charlotte
If we just A the Qs, we barely touch the surface of the underlying relationships.

Femi
Here goes. Who killed Samantha Greenwood? Kevin MacDonald. Sam tells three people three things: the drama group about the appeal, Issy that she knows she told Michael about Claudia, and Kel that she's returning to Africa. Sarah-Jane knew it was going to happen. Emma knew about it before the body was discovered. Kel is imprisoned because it's always the nearest and dearest in the frame.

Charlotte
The message from Andy telling Sam something she can't un-know? It's left while she's at the dress rehearsal on the evening of 4 July.

Femi
Red herring. Kevin wants Sam gone because he's involved so many masonic contacts in the appeal. He confronts her in the flat, they fight, Sam dies. SJ flees to Emma's for an alibi but, phew, Kel is charged.

Charlotte
Would SJ cover for murder the way she lied for the Haywards?

Femi
Yes. So, three are not who they say they are: Handler is really Sam, Drake is Glen and Kel is Sean. Three masquerade as others: Sam as Issy, Issy as Sam, Arnie as Kel. One does not exist: don't know. Handler and Drake both.

Charlotte
Glen is Drake? Conning his father-in-law and defrauding his own daughter's appeal or are they all in it together?

Femi
He was prepared to have Woof put down on 26 June and then lie to his wife about it. Harsh.

Charlotte
You are so fucking good at this. I feel like a spare part.

Femi
Not at all. Ok, new angle for the doc. Prime suspects, plus reasoning behind each.

Charlotte
Hope we're right about the Topps Tiles thing. Otherwise it looks like we're making things up to fit the facts. Why would Issy bother to tell Michael, when Sam knows already that Claudia has betrayed her and is unlikely ever to be friends with her again?

Femi
To turn Claudia against Sam. It works, too. Initially better than Issy ever thought it would – it leads Claudia to attack her. But then it turns Sam against Issy. That's what I believe informs their final convo in the car park after the dress rehearsal.

Comment [Femi1]:
Charl, here it is with your amends. Prime suspects, followed by outside suspects.

Who killed Samantha Greenwood?
We have four prime suspects. They are presented in no particular order.

Sean 'Kel' Greenwood
Most women who are murdered are killed by their husband or partner. Kel was forced to return from his dream job as a medical aid worker and has found it difficult to readjust to life in England. His relationship with Claudia has been dragged into the open. His confidant, Arnie, betrayed him by stealing all his money, embarrassed him in front of his new social circle and revealed to his wife, in the cruellest way possible, that he is having an affair with her friend. Yet he can see Arnie is unwell and feels responsible for him. Added to this: Kel is ill himself with Hepatitis C, which he keeps secret from his employer. We know Sam and Kel have been arguing in their flat at night, from a note sent by their neighbours on 2 July. Kel did not want Sam to say anything at the dress rehearsal and threatened her with consequences if she did – that she would never see him again.

Kel and Claudia are seen entering a local motel together after 2 a.m. on 5 July by Nick Walford, looking 'like someone had died'. The next day Kel is off-radar, only replying to an email from Sarah-Jane. He arrives for the first night of the play limping. His performance is described as 'nervous'.

Interestingly, Kel's email to Sarah-Jane suggests he agrees with what Sam says at the dress rehearsal, but felt she should not have said anything. Is he mindful of how speaking out has destroyed their lives once already? He doesn't want it to happen again.

After the dress rehearsal Kel and Sam return, argue, fight and – whether premeditated or not – Sam falls from their balcony to her death. Kel flees, meets Claudia, herself reeling from Michael's shock discovery of the affair, and the couple hole up at the Travellers' Inn. Despite everything that's happened, Kel honours his commitment to the play. Is he a man of his word, or simply mindful that fleeing completely would draw attention to him as a suspect in his wife's murder?

Tish Bhatoa via an associate

Bad blood between Sam Greenwood and Tish Bhatoa runs through their interconnected stories like a polluted river. Tish won the day in Bangui and, while she harbours resentment towards Sam for what she 'tried to do', there would be scant motivation for her to have Sam killed at this stage. Sam is openly antagonistic towards Tish – writing to her under her own name, questioning what Tish has told the Haywards, as if letting Tish know she is close and watching her. Nonetheless, Tish seems confident that truth is on her side and that Sam is not a threat.

However, the death of Dan Bhatoa in South Sudan changes that. Suddenly there is a reason for Tish to want deadly revenge. In Bangui, she supported her brother's defence against Sam's accusations of impropriety, and saw those charges dismissed, potentially having paid to make them go away. But as a result of the case, he was forced to move to less stable areas, where he perished. Dan and Tish won the battle, but lost the war. It is not without foundation that Tish blames Sam for his death.

But this is not all. From very early on in the Haywards' appeal, Sam suspects Tish is not being honest with them. If the experimental drugs exist, and if Tish were intending to import them for Poppy, why would she not be open about where they came from? Tish has oppressive financial responsibilities. She pays for her parents' expensive care home. Her businesses have cash-flow problems and she helps support Dan's clinic. We believe that if Sam is right about Tish lying to the Haywards, then the threat of this being exposed, plus revenge for Dan's death, could have led Tish to hire a mercenary to kill Sam while she is safely out of the country. This hitman climbed up the outside of the block and was waiting in the flat, or on the balcony, for Sam to return. Kel dropped her off and left to meet Claudia, without entering the flat. When Sam arrived home, she was confronted by the intruder and thrown off the balcony in a bid to make the death appear accidental or a suicide.

As for the identity of the intruder, we suggest Nick Walford, who is in the area the night of the murder, and the next day has very firm instructions for his mother regarding what to do with his bag.

Kevin MacDonald

Kevin and Sarah-Jane MacDonald have ploughed their time, energy and professionalism into Poppy's appeal. If Sam is right, then they have been conned by their oldest friends, and have been instrumental in further conning their families and everyone in their professional and friendship circles. That they fell for such a scam would be an appalling admission to make to everyone whose opinions matter. The shame is almost unimaginable.

It is after she tries, and fails, to confide in Sarah-Jane that Sam decides to spell out the situation to the entire Fairway Players. We believe this failure to engage Sarah-Jane is a direct result of Sam having posed as Clive Handler, a deception that counts against her from the moment the MacDonalds discover it.

While most members refuse to believe Sam's accusations and take the Haywards' side without question, once they are out in the open, Sarah-Jane *does* take them seriously. However, she focuses on what we believe to be the least likely or relevant of the accusations: that Helen lied about having a child before James, who died of meningitis. When Emma corroborates Helen's claim, Sarah-Jane and Kevin cling to this as evidence that everything Sam says is a lie. This is not necessarily the case . . .

Kevin, aware that Sam could be accurate in her interpretation of the appeal, and having involved so many of his Lodge associates, went to Sam's flat on the night of the dress rehearsal and killed her. This is while Sarah-Jane is at Emma's. She believes he is home in bed. We also believe he tells her afterwards. The MacDonalds have almost as much to lose as the Haywards if Sam's accusations go further than their immediate circle of friends.

Arnie Ballancore

Arnie is a lost soul long before he arrives in Lockwood. He has given up his nursing career, drifted around the world, become addicted to heroin and estranged from his family. However, the Greenwoods do not receive his mother's warning email. By the time they realise the extent of his problems, he has already stolen £6,000 – apparently most of the money they possess. As Kel gave him their PIN number on 25 June, it seems likely they would not be able to recover those funds from the bank. This prevents Sam fleeing back to Africa as soon as she discovers Kel's affair.

From his emails, Arnie comes across as a languid drifter, lost and lazy perhaps, but not a danger to anyone. However, we believe there is another side to him – the side that leads his mother to warn the Greenwoods how much he has changed since they knew him in Africa. We see how he attempts to swindle Joyce at the tea counter during the Yogathon on 30 June, and riled Barry and Martin with uncontrolled verbal aggression. Yet the most telling observation on the character of Arnie comes on 4 July from Robert Green, the burglary victim who describes his 'savagery' and says he was 'easily the most aggressive' of his three attackers.

On 3 July Sam informs the police that Arnie was in possession of an African Healing Doll of the type stolen in the burglary, and also informs them he has taken their money. On the night of the murder, Arnie is released from police custody and makes his way back to the Greenwoods' flat. We believe he lets himself in, confronts Sam over informing on him or is confronted by her for stealing their money. In the midst of this confrontation we believe Arnie is unable to control his aggression, and the result is Sam's tragic death. He is seen leaving the next morning, with his rucksack, at 5 a.m.

These may be our prime suspects, but we have identified others – all with possible motives to kill Sam. Again, they are in no particular order.

Isabel Beck

As soon as they arrive in Lockwood, Isabel targets Sam and Kel as potential new friends. It is easy to use emotive language to describe her strategy: she 'sinks her claws' into them or 'latches on'. Yet much of her ensuing correspondence *does* denote obsession rather than true friendship. Isabel is socially isolated, lonely and lives for The Fairway Players. Much of her self-respect comes from her work, and we can see she's a dedicated nurse who likes to help and reassure others, even when that help and reassurance are not requested or valued. She proves herself to be very perceptive when she immediately identifies that Arnie is trouble. Of all the emails the Haywards receive following Poppy's diagnosis on 21 April, we feel Isabel's is the most appropriate.

Isabel has lost her friend Lauren – both emotionally, after Lauren's betrayal over the IV mistake, and literally, when Lauren left St Ann's and moved away with Josh. We believe Isabel sought to replace Lauren with Sam. Once she realises how much better her life is with Sam in it, she goes into overdrive, as if terrified she will lose her new friend, too. The arrival of Claudia makes Isabel take up her Blue Book again on 10 June and express negative and aggressive emotions that do not find their way out through her other, copious correspondence.

Isabel is immature and socially awkward. She seems to experience difficulty talking to people, and others do not warm to her. She soon becomes emotionally dependent on Sam and attempts to isolate her from other potential friends, like Sarah-Jane and Helen. Therefore when Sam finally withdraws her friendship and support – in the car park after her outburst at the dress rehearsal – Isabel is distraught and incensed. Is this a case of 'if I can't have Sam, no one else will'? We believe Isabel follows Sam home that night and, Kel having left to meet Claudia at the Travellers' Inn, enters the flat, where the pair fight and Sam is killed. Isabel's correspondence in the twenty-four hours following Sam's death is markedly different to all that's gone before. To say nothing of her 999 call the following night, in which she seems to know precisely how long Sam has been lying under her balcony. Also telling is the swiftness with which Isabel seems to move on and look forward to life without Sam. She even offers to step into Sam's role in *All My Sons*.

The Haywards: Martin, James, Glen

The men of the Hayward–Reswick dynasty are driven by three things: family, money and keeping their women in an infantile state of carefree bliss. If they are behind Sam's murder, then we must assume that when she describes Poppy's appeal as a 'financial conspiracy', Sam is right. If they are using the appeal money to support their failing businesses and maintain their lavish lifestyles, then their motivation for killing Sam would be to limit her accusations to their loyal social circle, where they are summarily dismissed.

If we assume this trio has a motive for wanting Sam out of the way, we need to consider where they all are the night she dies. James is with Olivia as she gives birth in St Ann's. Martin cuts short the ill-fated dress rehearsal. Later that night he exchanges emails with Sarah-Jane, after which he writes to Sam, setting out his position on what she said and her future with The Fairway Players. We cannot say whether or not Glen was at the dress rehearsal. However, Paige says 'Glen woke me up at four to go through Act One'. So Glen is up at 4 a.m. and knows then that Paige needs to take over Sam's role in the play. However, we cannot be sure this is because he knows she's dead, or because he knows she is likely to be out of the play. Either way, he's up at that key time.

The burglars

Sam informs on Arnie, who then gives the police the names of his criminal associates. Arnie may be an addict coerced into taking part in the crime to pay off a drugs debt, but the men behind it certainly appear to be bigger, more organised criminals. They plot to steal a painting, which means they have connections to the global criminal underworld, and this would place Sam in a dangerous position if they found out who went to the police. We are certain Arnie could be made to tell them who informed on him and where she lived. This may or may not have some co-relation to the fact that Arnie returns to the flat at some point during the night Sam is killed, and is seen leaving for good very early the next morning.

Suicide/accident

Like Kel and Arnie, Sam has struggled to settle since her return from Africa. She is ill with Hepatitis C, which she must keep secret from her employer. She is stuck in a failing ward with a poor atmosphere; her work colleague is needy, clingy and obsessed; her husband is leaving her for someone she thought was a friend; and a man she tried to help has stolen her money, making her escape impossible. She has tried to fit into a community that turns on her the moment she attempts to stop them falling for a fraud. And there is one other major factor we discovered: the drug Sam is taking – Ribavirin – has a rare side-effect: 'thoughts of suicide'. Did Sam return to her flat the night of the dress rehearsal, full of despair over her personal life, as well as her thwarted attempts to help others and put right what is wrong in the world? If so, then the influence of Ribavirin could have contributed to her final, fatal, impulsive decision.

Meanwhile, any of the above suspects may have caused Sam's death, but purely by accident. The night of the 4–5 July was warm and balmy. If the balcony doors were open, then it is quite possible any fight could have ended up there, with tragic consequences for Sam.

Comment [Femi1]:
Have we missed anything? Good call re Ribavirin btw.

Charlotte
Why are Martin/James/Glen only outside suspects? Should be near the top.

Femi
See Martin's emails to SJ and Sam after her outburst. He sounds so open, honest, fair. Not running scared, or defensive because he's just been found out.

Charlotte
You still think Bhatoa is behind the fraud behind the appeal?

Femi
Yes. But Nick Walford? Tenuous.

Charlotte
Sam is on to *something*. Her outburst is a catalyst, but to what?

Femi
'One does not exist at all.' Well, someone who doesn't exist in this correspondence is Helen.

Charlotte
Sam and Kel too . . .

Femi
Sure, but we know they send emails, as we have replies addressed to them.

Charlotte
Ok. Where are you going with that?

Femi
The Haywards, the play they're putting on. Despite everything – from Poppy's illness to Sam's accusations – *nothing* gets in the way of the play and it's all about Helen. Helen this, Helen that, everyone loves Helen. Martin: she's our leading lady onstage and off. James: if there isn't a significant female role, The Fairway Players won't choose that play. His mum 'belongs onstage'. Issy: she's so larger than life that if she's in a scene, no one else is. Kevin: she lives in a wonderland where she's forever centre-stage. If Helen is such a brilliant actor who delivers an 'impeccable performance' with such 'intensity of commitment' to her 'demanding role' – then WHO IS THIS WOMAN?

Charlotte
Good point. Sam suspects Helen of something . . . Why consult a genealogist?

Femi
The character who 'does not exist at all' could be Helen's little boy, like Sam says. She tells Martin she's a bereaved mother when she meets him, then lives the lie. Paige and James believe it.

Charlotte
Her emotional reaction to Sam's revelation could be a genuine response to her lie being exposed. Or just another act. Would this give her a motive to kill Sam?

Femi
Don't forget Paige. She and Helen are 'so alike'. Both obsessed with themselves and the stage. Both protected from reality by their partners. Both in it together?

Femi and Charlotte's Breakdown of Theories

Theory One

Who killed Samantha Greenwood? **Glen Reswick** to stop her spreading the accusations.

Who knew it was going to happen? **Martin** and **James Hayward** because they're in on it.

Who knew about it before her body was discovered? **Paige** and **Helen** because they need to re-cast and rehearse the play.

Who is erroneously imprisoned and why? **Kel Greenwood** because nearest and dearest.

Theory Two

Who killed Samantha Greenwood? **Kel Greenwood** in a tragic fight.

Who knew it was going to happen? **Claudia D'Souza** because she is there.

Who knew about it before her body was discovered? **Arnie Ballancore** because he returns to the flat afterwards, but flees in the morning.

Who is erroneously imprisoned and why? **Isabel Beck** because the object of her obsession has rejected her.

Theory Three

Who killed Samantha Greenwood? **Someone hired by Tish Bhatoa** to limit the impact of Sam's accusations.

Who knew it was going to happen? **Rav Bhatoa** because Tish is with him in Central Africa, dealing with Dan's death.

Who knew about it before her body was discovered? **Martin Hayward** because Tish tells him.

Who is erroneously imprisoned and why? **Kel Greenwood** because nearest and dearest.

Theory Four

Who killed Samantha Greenwood? **Kevin MacDonald** to preserve his professional pride.

Who knew it was going to happen? **Sarah-Jane MacDonald** because they are in it together.

Who knew about it before her body was discovered? **Isabel Beck** because she goes to Sam's flat and finds the body shortly afterwards. However, whether through shock or some other reason, she returns home and carries on as normal the next day.

Who is erroneously imprisoned and why? **Kel Greenwood** because nearest and dearest.

<u>Theory Five</u>

Who killed Samantha Greenwood? **Arnie Ballancore** in a tragic fight.

Who knew it was going to happen? **Samantha Greenwood** because she knew he'd want revenge for informing on him.

Who knew about it before her body was discovered? **Kel Greenwood** and **Claudia D'Souza** because they return to the flat, but say nothing for fear of being seen as guilty, but . . .

Who is erroneously imprisoned and why? **Kel Greenwood.**

<u>In the hours before her death, Sam told three people three things. Who and what?</u>

1. The drama group that Helen and the appeal are frauds.
2. Issy that she has never liked her and no longer wants to be her friend, because she used her email address to tell Michael about Claudia.
3. Kel that she's returning to Africa.

Three people are not who they say they are. Clive Handler, Lydia Drake, Magda Kuchar.

Three masquerade as others. Sam as Clive Handler, Sam as Issy, Issy as Sam.

One does not exist at all. Helen's little boy.

Femi
I'll merge the docs, so Tanner gets the intro and suspect profiles, plus the summary of the five theories. Can you add something to wind it up? E.g. 'Samantha Greenwood is not afraid to speak. Nor should we be.' Acknowledge the fact that we *only* have the correspondence. Without it sounding like an excuse.

Charlotte
'In a small community such as this, the social hierarchy is strict, allegiances are strong and grudges magnified. Strangers are regarded as suspicious and you are judged by who your friends are. In such a microcosmic world, ordinary rules do not automatically apply. From this correspondence alone, we know Samantha Greenwood is committed to the truth. She would not want an innocent party imprisoned for her murder, as much as she would want those guilty brought to account. We can only address the tragedy of her death by ensuring justice is done, and is seen to be done.'

Femi
Brilliant.

Charlotte
It's sent. Let's get to bed.

Olufemi Hassan
Charlotte Holroyd

Dear both,

I am in receipt of your document and will peruse in due course. Do not doubt that I am agog. As is mentioned in the correspondence, there are some things you can't un-know. The opportunity for unbiased interpretation is soon lost.

Meanwhile, here are some scraps of recovered correspondence that you may find interesting. None were available at the first hearing, so they have no bearing on your initial response. Some date from before the murder and some after, but again they are broadly chronological.

I will be back in touch before I have to submit this appeal.

Yours,

RT

Roderick Tanner, QC
Senior Partner
Tanner & Dewey LLP

FROM: Noel Burton
SUBJECT: Can we help again?
DATE: 3 May 2018 at 10:10
TO: Tish Bhatoa

Dear Ms Bhatoa,

We recently undertook a successful period of work for CloudRegal SA and trust the service we provided was beneficial for you and your business.

** Priority rates for existing clients in May, June and July **

We specialise in all forms of corporate intelligence, from digital forensics to pre-litigation. We work closely with a network of international investigators who can track and trace individuals across the globe, including historical criminal-record searches and financial profiling. We would be delighted to work with you again, so please do not hesitate to call.

Yours sincerely,

Noel Burton
RedHawk Consulting Ltd

FROM: Tish Bhatoa
SUBJECT:
DATE: 13 June 2018 at 14:55
TO: Martin Hayward

Martin, whenever I enter into business with anyone I am thorough in my due diligence. I do not believe for a moment you have no money at all. In any case, a man of your means and intelligence can always find a way to make more. If you do not fulfil your promise to pay each monthly instalment, I will say the word. Poppy's drugs will oxidise.

FROM: Martin Hayward
SUBJECT: Re:
DATE: 13 June 2018 at 15:02
TO: Tish Bhatoa

I've never promised to pay monthly. We can only raise funds so quickly. You know how difficult our family situation is. You *will* get your money – that I can guarantee.

FROM: Tish Bhatoa
SUBJECT: Re:
DATE: 13 June 2018 at 15:10
TO: Martin Hayward

We all have difficult family situations. You have plenty of assets to sell, and that is something you should do if the appeal is not delivering funds quickly enough. I only agreed to this because you gave me cast-iron assurances.

FROM: Martin Hayward
SUBJECT: Re:
DATE: 13 June 2018 at 15:13
TO: Tish Bhatoa

Cast-iron? Everything is mortgaged to the bone. I have no assets left now. You know what that's like. Why do you think I suggested this in the first place? You think it was simply chance I came to *you* when Poppy fell ill? I, too, have a thorough approach to due diligence.

FROM: Graham Oxshott
SUBJECT: Hi
DATE: 11 June 2018 at 20:34
TO: Martin Hayward

Dear Martin,
We haven't seen you for a few weeks now, and trust that means all is well. I write to see if you feel ready to sponsor a new member, just starting out

on their journey, as I did for you all those months ago. The role is one of healthy friendship. It offers active support, especially during times of stress when difficulty sticking to the twelve steps is most likely to be felt. It is a one-to-one relationship between individuals at different stages of recovery, and will help you both help yourselves. It is not compulsory, but you have made such good progress that you were the first potential new sponsor who came to mind. We have one new member in particular who I believe would be an excellent match for you. If you'd like to attend the meeting Thursday, I will introduce you both.

Let me know how you feel,
Graham
Fowey GA

FROM: Claudia D'Souza
SUBJECT:
DATE: 5 July 2018 at 08:58
TO: Michael D'Souza

Michael, please tell Sophie and Marco 'Mummy's fine and she'll see you very soon'. I'm sorry, M. I really am. I wanted to tell you myself, but she got there first. She says she didn't, but who else would it be? I need you to know I completely understand why you've done this, but it's not right taking it out on Soph and Marco. They have all their friends here, their school work, their clubs and hobbies, and they barely speak Portuguese. Let them have a few days with your mum and then come home and we'll all sit down and discuss this together: you, me and Kel. We'll work something out that suits everyone, and talk about where we go from here. Please. C x

---

FROM: Arnie Ballancore
SUBJECT: See ya
DATE: 5 July 2018 at 09:53
TO: Kel Greenwood

Just to say goodbye really. Feel I should get away and make a new start somewhere. The police think I'm at yours, so they might want to know where I went. Just say you don't know. I don't know myself, maybe the Far East or South America? I'm on bail, so it's gonna be tricky without my passport. I might chill with a couple buddies up North for a bit. See if I can get back to normal or something. Hope you and Sam are ok and sorry if I made things awkward. Hoped it would be like Bangui. Guess you can't go back. Everything changes. I love you guys. Arnie

---

Message from Glen Reswick to James Hayward on 5 July 2018:

05:00 Glen wrote
Told Paige. She's stoked. Only saying the other day she missed being in the play.

FROM: Dr Tish Bhatoa
SUBJECT:
DATE: 5 July 2018 at 21:24
TO: Samantha Greenwood

Dear Samantha,
I never imagined I would write this letter. I've been in Bangui for days at most, but I'm already changing. It's been so long since I had to adapt to anywhere. The place is the same. It's the people who are new. Dan is dead. We need a taskforce willing to travel across the border and bring him back, but no one will agree to anything so risky at the moment. While I wait here, people come and talk to me about him. You remember how they do that when someone dies. There's no announcement, but one person tells another and that person tells someone else, and so on. I'd forgotten.

You were right about him. I didn't want to believe it. I still don't. But I've seen too many people now. All knew him better than I did. The man they talk about is not the brother I had. Perhaps life here changed him, but I fear it did not – he could mask his darkness before, but this place gave it permission and opportunity. Yet in his letters to me he was always the same. It seems there's only so much you can know from letters. A man can hide a world behind words.

I'm sorry you were not taken seriously last year, and that you had to go through the trial – if that's the correct word for such a fiasco. Please understand I was only protecting my family, and did so in good faith. I will not be back in the UK yet. In the meantime, stay away from the Haywards. Dr Tish Bhatoa

---

FROM: Magda Kuchar
SUBJECT: Computer
DATE: 6 July 2018 at 07:54
TO: Martin Hayward

Hi Martin, this morning I have a problem. My computer starts as normal, but my email history is all gone. Sent and received, empty. Even the trash empty. Can the system corrupt and be restored? I lose records of talk with builders, suppliers and members. I don't know what happen. Magda

---

FROM: Martin Hayward
SUBJECT: Re: Computer
DATE: 6 July 2018 at 08:58
TO: Magda Kuchar

I believe there is a virus that wipes email records. I'll have the tech firm look into it. Regards, Martin

---

FROM: Sarah-Jane MacDonald
SUBJECT: Isabel
DATE: 7 July 2018 at 12:03
TO: Kevin MacDonald

She was hiding behind the rail, furiously tapping on her phone. Who was she texting? Not a friend. She doesn't have any. Hasn't sold a single ticket for the play, according to Celia. Plus she returned nearly all her raffle tickets unsold. I don't know why James insisted on casting her in *Blithe Spirit* or this. I told you I saw Sam have words with her that night. What do you think?
Sarah-Jane MacDonald

FROM: Kevin MacDonald
SUBJECT: Re: Isabel
DATE: 7 July 2018 at 12:44
TO: Sarah-Jane MacDonald

She followed Sam around, seemed to hang on every word she said, didn't have any other friends. When Sam blew up, Issy followed her out of the dress rehearsal. You popped out and saw them argue outside. I was rallying around Helen at the time. Then I took Harley home and went to bed with a cold, while you went round Emma's to discuss the appeal and see how Woof was. That's what I told the officer anyway. Sound plausible?

A decorative card printed by the Maternity Unit at St Ann's Hospital:

> The Stork Reports
> A very special delivery for Olivia and James Hayward
>
> Sophia Grace Hayward
> Born 4 July 2018 at 10.25 p.m.
>
> Arthur Martin Hayward
> Born 4 July 2018 at 10.27 p.m.
>
> Signed by Fiona Chou on behalf of The Stork
> Maternity and Neonatal Unit, St Ann's Hospital, Lockwood

FROM: Isabel Beck
SUBJECT: You
DATE: 6 July 2018 at 05:18
TO: Lauren Malden

I won't write to you any more. I don't even know why I started. It's not as if you were ever my real friend. My only real friend has left and I'm making a new start. That means cleansing my life of people who don't nurture or fulfil me. I'm going to sign up for a yoga course – a proper one this time, at a real gym, not just online. I'm going to keep up my healthy-eating plan and twice-weekly lunchtime jogging. As soon as I can apply to move wards, I will. By the time The Fairway Players meet up again in September I'll be a whole new me, ready for the winter play. It doesn't matter if I'm cast or not. I'll go to rehearsals anyway, perhaps make the tea with Joyce or help the actors learn their words. If Paige is in the play, I could babysit Poppy. They will probably prefer someone with medical training to take care of her if she's still poorly. There are lots of great things waiting for me in my future. So I won't be writing to you again. Issy

Femi
So Martin's an addict.

Charlotte
Gambler. Letter on 11 June from Gamblers Anonymous. There's a reference on 21 May to him betting. Reacts badly when James makes a casual remark. He's a man with debts.

Femi
And a risk-taker. Despite seeming cautious and level-headed. He has a City background, and the financial world is just gambling, no? Also, could be a response to stress.

Charlotte
Debts are not always paid in money. Like Arnie and Sharkey. Bhatoa covers her back by jetting to Bangui while she blackmails Martin into doing her dirty work re Sam.

Femi
Their convo is *not* about Poppy's drugs. A code?

Charlotte
Her remorse seems genuine. But is it for not believing Sam over Dan, or for having Sam killed when she was right all along?

Femi
'Stay away from the Haywards.' Threat or warning? Or insurance if/when the police come knocking?

Charlotte
Claudia doesn't include Sam in her family 'chat' about the future. She must know she's dead.

Femi
Claudia and Issy each claim to be Sam's bestie, but move on immediately once she's gone. Literally don't look back.

Charlotte
Arnie is out of the frame IMO. I think he goes back to the flat. It's empty. Sam's dead outside, the killer gone. He stays the night, leaves early. None the wiser.

Femi
So who was it?

Charlotte
The MacDonalds. Kel wrongly convicted.

Femi
Martin, acting on behalf of Bhatoa. MacDonalds wrongly convicted.

Charlotte
MacDonalds guilty. Issy wrongly convicted. They frame her.

Femi
Claudia guilty. Kel wrongly convicted, because he confessed to protect her.

Charlotte
Arrrghh! Where's the evidence? We're supposed to analyse the correspondence, not just make up stories.

Femi
Let's see what Tanner says about our doc. Really wish I hadn't put 'precipice' in the first line. Too emotional, melodramatic. Should have said 'edge'. Words are so important.

Olufemi Hassan
Charlotte Holroyd

Dear both,

I have read your document. There is a prize waiting for whoever solved the riddle of Topps Tiles. Yes, you are correct. That venerable ceramics emporium is visible from the small, north-facing window of the Greenwoods' lounge, situated in a recess above their Ikea desk, which Isabel admires so much. When she muses 'I can see Topps Tiles' she *must* be sitting down at the desk to see the sign. Her email coincides with a message Michael D'Souza claims he received from Sam's email address, informing him that his wife Claudia is having an affair with Kel Greenwood. Isabel deleted the sent file immediately and blocked Michael's email address, so that Sam would not receive any further emails from him. Michael deleted the received file, so this correspondence is not available.

A close second prize goes to whoever discovered the side-effects of Ribavirin.

However, you need to go back through the correspondence and think again about who does not exist at all. It's a matter of corroboration.

Overall, good work, but there is one angle you did not touch upon. The question of who *benefits* most from Sam's death. I believe this is more important than who stands to lose the most from her revelations. There are four primary motives for murder: love/sex, money, silence and revenge. Revenge is fourth for a reason. A murder motivated purely by revenge is uncommon, because the *benefits* are vague, intangible, of negligible worth. Most people who plan and – pardon the pun – execute the death of another do so in *anticipation* of something positive occurring as a result, rather than as an empty *reaction* to something already in the past.

We will discuss these matters tomorrow.

Yours,

RT

Roderick Tanner, QC
Senior Partner
Tanner & Dewey LLP

PS I should tell you who is imprisoned – I believe, erroneously. It is Isabel Beck.

Femi
So it seemed, beyond reasonable doubt, to be Isabel. That's curious. Apart from appearing to be an empathetic personality, how does she benefit from Sam's death?

Charlotte
Hardly anyone *likes* Issy. We only see her emails. There has to be *something* about her. Something we don't pick up on, through the correspondence.

Femi
Lauren likes her. James likes her. As far as we can tell, Sam likes her at first. The Fairway Players like her enough to cast her in two plays.

Charlotte
The community turns on the least-popular, least-integrated individual and makes them fit the crime? We see Sarah-Jane and Kevin do just that, perhaps because they killed Sam, but not necessarily. They *want* it to be Issy because they see everyone else as a friend.

Femi
Could Issy's fixation with Sam lead a jury to believe she could have killed her to move on in her life, free of the obsession? She moves on instantly, we can see that.

Charlotte
I still think the MacDonalds frame Issy. They grow closer as a couple over the course of events, don't you think? Something sinister in the way SJ watches Issy text Lauren in the green room.

Femi
So, the person who doesn't exist at all *corroborates* something and we haven't spotted it. Any thoughts?

Charlotte
Emma corroborates Helen's story for Sarah-Jane.

Femi
Emma must be real. Martin emails her about Woof.

Charlotte
Woof! Does Woof exist? Fuck, is that whole thing about the vets a code for something else?

Femi
If it is, then Sarah-Jane must be in on it. And her mother. No, both are mentioned by other people.

Charlotte
A code! Code, code, code. I made a note of this when you mentioned it before. Give me a minute. Don't message, I'll get distracted.

Femi
Ok. Go for it.

Charlotte
This is it. A code. A simple one between Tish and Martin *only*. Imagine that when they talk about 'phials' they mean 'files'. 'The contents of the phials will oxidise in two months, so I would recommend paying sooner rather than later.' The contents of the files will be exposed (things 'oxidise' when exposed to the air) in two months. So pay up.

Charlotte
On 23 June: 'The phials are still in Boston and can't be secured until you complete payment. I'm concerned Poppy's health will decline further if there's any more delay.' Secured – kept closed, out of sight. There will be consequences if you don't pay.

Charlotte
'The phials will last a bit longer but I am concerned the delay will prove detrimental to the integrity of the contents.' She's prepared to wait, but whatever is in the files will be worse when exposed.

Charlotte
Martin's only reference to the 'phials' in his correspondence with Tish comes after Sam has accused them of a financial conspiracy: 'I suggest we delay shipping of the phials until this latest furore has blown over.' He wants to suspend their arrangement until Sam is out of the way. Shit! Blown over – over the balcony . . .

Charlotte
I say this: there are no experimental drugs. Poppy is having NHS treatment at Mount More via Bhatoa's private practice. However, there is no financial conspiracy, either. Tish is blackmailing Martin. She's helping him raise funds, and is colluding in the deception of the community, but all the money is going to her. That's why Martin is in such a fucking financial mess.

Femi
Charl, you're on fire. Bhatoa has form here. In her email on 3 May she threatens to tell St Ann's the 'real reason' Sam had to return from Africa. She knows she has Hepatitis C. What could Tish know about Martin? That he's a gambler?

Charlotte
The Haywards arrive at Tish's private practice with a very sick little girl and a determination to cure her. Tish does her research into Martin's business affairs via Noel Burton from RedHawk Consulting and spots an opportunity. What does she dig up? A dodgy deal, tax evasion, debts, an affair maybe? My main point is: Lydia Drake is a scam, but it's *Martin* scamming *Tish* – to divert at least some of Poppy's appeal money back to himself. At first he tries to reconnect with Clive Handler behind Tish's back, but Sam has already deleted the email account. So Lydia Drake is born. He sends the emails from Magda's computer at The Grange – to give him something to forward on to SJ. Only Martin isn't particularly creative. He gets the name Lydia from *All My Sons*; Drake from the script publisher – look back at SJ's message to him on 20 April. She complains about the cost of the Drake Classics version of the script. When he realises SJ and Kevin can trace emails, he panics and early next morning deletes them to cover his tracks – to the dismay of the entirely innocent Magda.

Femi
Good work. See, you *can* do this, Charl.

Charlotte
Let's say I'm correct. Tish knows something inflammatory about Martin. Well, James and Glen must know it, too. Helen and Paige, as ever, in the dark. Surely he'd want to keep it from James and Glen too, if it were 'just' an affair or gambling? Must be something bigly illegal . . .

Femi
So, park SJ and Kevin. That makes the Haywards our main suspects – Sam doesn't know about the blackmail, but if she exposes the appeal as a fraud, then she will inadvertently expose whatever Tish knows about the Haywards.

Charlotte
How does Issy end up in jail?

Femi
The MacDonalds could still frame her. They don't necessarily know what's in the 'files' or that the files exist. But they are tight with the Haywards. They will protect the alpha family on instinct.

Olufemi Hassan
Charlotte Holroyd

Dear both,

Something has come up. I'm stuck in the City all day. However, the last thing I want is to cancel our meeting. It's time I learned to use the speech-bubble messaging function you have on your phones. Please, one of you, kindly liaise with Sandra and help her input it to my phone. Thank you.

Yours,

RT

Roderick Tanner, QC
Senior Partner
Tanner & Dewey LLP

Charlotte
For God's sake, start a new group, don't add him to this one. He'll see everything we've ever discussed.

Femi
Spoke to Sandra. She calls WhatsApp 'a program'.

Roderick Tanner, QC
Dear

Roderick Tanner, QC
Both

Roderick Tanner, QC
Thank you for

Roderick Tanner, QC
It disappears

Roderick Tanner, QC
What are the three dots no question mark

Roderick Tanner, QC
]

Charlotte
Don't press return until you're ready to send the message. You see three dots when someone else is typing.

Femi
It's an informal medium Mr Tanner. Don't worry too much about punctuation.

Charlotte
You'll get used to it.

Roderick Tanner, QC
This is Sandra. Mr Tanner will dictate. I'm new to this myself. Bear with me now. So, did the remaining correspondence alter your perspective on the case?

Femi
Yes, Martin Hayward is now our prime suspect. Glen and James his accomplices. Isabel framed and convicted because she's a relative outsider obsessed with the victim.

Charlotte
We believe the appeal is a financial conspiracy, in so far as it's a vehicle for Tish Bhatoa to blackmail Martin. Martin makes up the Lydia Drake fraud to divert £80k of the appeal money away from Tish. He has to pay his builders sooner than expected, on top of which he has legal fees and a gambling habit.

Roderick Tanner, QC
Good. Who benefits from Sam's death?

Charlotte
The Haywards, Tish, the MacDonalds all benefit from Sam's silence.

Femi
Kel. He's free to be with Claudia. Vice versa. Isabel. She's free from her obsession and can move on.

Roderick Tanner, QC
I said three people pretend to be others. You correctly identify one as Sam – she pretends to be Isabel to access Mount More's treatment records. Also, Isabel sends an email as Sam. I believe there is another, pivotal masquerade, in plain sight, much later on. Clive Handler and Lydia Drake are not who they say they are – along with one other. Which brings me to the one who does not exist at all.

Charlotte
Can I ask: how did 'who's who?' affect the original case?

Roderick Tanner, QC
It contributed to the miscarriage of justice. I believe. Posing as someone else betrays a propensity to deceive.

Femi
So it involves Isabel, one of these deceptions?

Roderick Tanner, QC
Yes, one of them.

Femi
Mr Tanner, is there something we should know about Isabel? From her correspondence, she has an empathetic personality. She's kind, friendly, optimistic and simple, in a good way. She's shy and lonely and suffers from depression, she's socially awkward, but even so, why would she ever be considered a suspect, let alone convicted?

Charlotte
Her major 'crime' is her obsession with Sam. But she's not serious stalker material.

Femi
She's not intelligent enough to plan a murder.

Roderick Tanner, QC
Really? Well, she's intelligent enough to fool both of you.

Roderick Tanner, QC
Go back and read through the correspondence again. This time, bear in mind that Lauren Malden is really Isabel. See how that changes your perspective.

Femi
Lauren? Wasn't she at the ball? What about her mum and Josh?

Charlotte
Just to be clear, Mr Tanner: there was *never* anyone called Lauren? Not working at St Ann's, not in The Fairway Players?

Roderick Tanner, QC
Never. Lauren Malden does not and never has existed. Nor anyone related to her. Call it an alter ego, if you like.

Femi
Isabel emails *herself* as an imaginary friend she's fallen out with? Someone who betrayed her and then jogged off with a boyfriend?

Charlotte
Man, that's fucked-up.

Roderick Tanner, QC
She's a complex creation.

Charlotte
Sorry, Mr Tanner. I didn't mean to use that language, I'm on voice.

Roderick Tanner, QC
We believe Lauren replaced the Blue Book for Isabel. Look at the emails and see if you can understand why. Well, I've given that away, but won't tell you anything else. Go back and see how this new information influences your list of suspects. Don't forget the masquerade you haven't seen yet.

Charlotte
So she's created Lauren. It's weird, but there are others with more credible motives; it still doesn't make Isabel an obvious suspect in Sam's murder.

Roderick Tanner, QC
Indeed. Quite possibly she wouldn't have been, if it were not for one thing. She confessed.

Roderick Tanner, QC
What's more, she maintains to this day that she did it. I'll forward the transcript.

Femi
Is there evidence she is innocent?

Roderick Tanner, QC
That's what I'm asking you.

County Police Interview Report

Extract from police interview with Isabel Beck:

Ms Anand: I'd like to read a prepared statement.

Sgt Cooper: Go ahead.

Ms Anand: My name is Isabel Beck. On the night of 4–5 July 2018 I was responsible for the death of Samantha Greenwood. After The Fairway Players' dress rehearsal for *All My Sons* I caught a bus to Sam's flat, with the intention of discussing our forthcoming trip to Africa. When I arrived we argued and she fell over the balcony. I panicked and ran home. I hoped she was ok, but noticed she did not come in to work the next day. Nor did she arrive at the church hall for the performance of the play that night, 5 July. After the play I was given a lift to Sam's flat by Joel and Celia Halliday. There, I discovered Sam's body lying under the balcony and called 999.

Sgt Cooper: Thank you. Isabel, did Samantha Greenwood know you were coming to the flat on the night of the 4th, after the dress rehearsal?

Ms Beck: No comment.

Sgt Cooper: Only, you were seen with Ms Greenwood after the rehearsal. In the words of this witness, 'Sam snarled in Isabel's ear as if she were furious with her. Sam marched off and Isabel was left alone in the car park. She [meaning you] looked utterly devastated.' Is that correct?

Ms Beck: No comment.

Sgt Crowe: What did Sam say that was so bad you pushed her over the balcony?

Ms Anand: That isn't in the statement. Ms Beck does not say she pushed Ms Greenwood over the balcony.

Sgt Crowe: What did you argue about that was so bad Ms Greenwood ended up falling over the balcony?

Ms Beck: No comment.

Sgt Cooper: You say your intention, in going to Ms Greenwood's flat that night, was to discuss a trip to Africa with her. Only there was no trip planned, was there?

Ms Beck: No comment.

Sgt Cooper: Ms Greenwood was making her own plans to return to Africa as a volunteer with Médecins Sans Frontières. You were not part of that.

Ms Beck: No comment.

Sgt Cooper: Is that what she told you in the car park?

Ms Beck: No comment.

Sgt Cooper: Or was it something else?

Ms Beck: No comment.

Sgt Cooper: As we've seen from the CCTV footage, you took the bus, at night, all the way across Lockwood for a reason. There was no trip. So why go?

Ms Beck: No comment.

Sgt Cooper: Why not text or email?

Ms Beck: No comment.

Sgt Cooper: You could speak to her at work the next day. Why go to her flat, there and then?

Ms Beck: No comment.

Sgt Cooper: If you won't tell us, then we might assume you went there intending to cause harm to Ms Greenwood, because that's what it looks like. Can you see our problem?

Sgt Crowe: Did you go to Ms Greenwood's flat on the night of 4 July with the intention to kill her?

Ms Beck: No comment.

– Interview suspended –

Charlotte
People confess all the time. They aren't convicted.

Femi
Exactly. *Corpus delicti*. There must be evidence she did it.

Charlotte
Tanner implies there's no evidence she didn't.

Femi
If there's a murder and someone who has opportunity and motive holds their hands up and says they're guilty, how much effort does anyone put into finding out if they really are?

Charlotte
So, if we say Isabel is innocent – what's her motive for confessing?

Femi
Attention. Her name linked to Sam's, part of her ongoing obsession.

Charlotte
Covering for someone else?

Femi
Who and why? And when does she decide to cover for them? Right after the murder she's looking forward to the future . . . She hasn't factored in ten years of jail time.

Charlotte
Shock. It happens. People experience something terrible, like killing their best friend, and then carry on as normal.

Femi
We need to go back and read Issy's email exchanges with Lauren.

Charlotte
Denial! That's the word. Yes, let's reread . . .

Charlotte
Finished yet? I can't believe we didn't see it. On 17 April 'Lauren' says 'all-nighters at my age, boo'. Boo! Issy says that all the time.

Femi
When you know Lauren is really Issy, you can see how she plays on her own fears and allays them.

Charlotte
She's created someone to hold a grudge against. For dropping her in favour of a boyfriend; for betraying her at work; for only contacting her when she wants gossip; for leaving. Those early emails between them – Issy is so offhand and cool.

Femi
She creates someone even lower down the social ladder than she is.

Charlotte
Lauren tells Issy things her 'mum' has heard, when really Issy overheard them. So instead of eavesdropping, Issy gives herself the higher status of being told: e.g. builders at The Grange. Issy mentions watching yoga on YouTube in an email to Sam on 30 June, and by 2 July Lauren is suddenly writing to Issy about spiritual issues.

Femi
With Lauren she has conversations she doesn't have with anyone in real life. We don't even know if Sam converses with her at this level of intimacy. Most have no time for her.

Charlotte
Lauren boosts Issy's confidence by reinforcing what she wants to be true. Like having friends or being right for a part in the play. She blames Lauren for the mistake she made at work. So instead of feeling a failure, she convinces herself she's a martyr.

Femi
It's weird. Yet nothing in Lauren's emails makes me think Issy is or isn't guilty.

Charlotte
That could be the problem. It just doesn't look good. Someone who emails an imaginary friend could be seen as unstable enough to kill someone who rejects them in real life. Especially when they confess to it.

Femi
Do we know why Tanner is so keen on this case? Seems personal.

Roderick Tanner, QC
Acting on evidence available at the time, he was instrumental in convincing Isabel to plead guilty to murder. He now needs to reach the truth. So yes, it's personal. Thus far we are looking to reduce her sentence to manslaughter. However, I believe she is entirely innocent. But I need bright, intelligent people to see what I see before I can act.

Femi
Sorry, Mr Tanner, I didn't realise you were still here.

Charlotte
Mr Tanner. Can I ask, what is Isabel like, as a person?

Roderick Tanner, QC
I would describe her as a survivor. We tend to consider survivors as strong and heroic. The reality is never as pretty or noble. Some survive because they deceive, some because they delude themselves. Others refuse to engage with reality.

Femi
Which is Isabel?

Roderick Tanner, QC
I'll send through some correspondence from after Ms Greenwood's body is discovered. We'll meet Friday as usual.

FROM: Martin Hayward
SUBJECT: Sad news
DATE: 6 July 2018 at 14:10
TO: Current Members

Dear all,
It is with great shock and sadness that I must report the sudden death of Samantha Greenwood. I am unaware of the details, but as many of you already know, Sam was very distressed on Wednesday and left the rehearsal quite distraught. We wondered why she did not arrive for the play last night, and it now seems she passed away suddenly, very shortly after leaving us. I know everyone will join me in sending our heartfelt condolences to Kel.

While Paige replaced Sam in the play before we realised what had happened, it now seems only right to continue with the production, both in the spirit of 'the show must go on' and as a tribute to Sam and the work she put into rehearsals over the last few months. She was a new member, so we did not know her well, but she was a friendly and enthusiastic person who showed great promise as an actor. She will be sadly missed.

Kel has valiantly agreed to continue in his role for the remaining production nights. May I extend our sincere thanks to him, and urge all our members to rally round and support him, as I know you all will, at what must be a most sad and challenging time. Regards, Martin Hayward

---

FROM: John O'Dea
SUBJECT: Re: Sad news
DATE: 6 July 2018 at 14:32
TO: Martin Hayward

Thank God we already re-cast her in the play. John

FROM: Sarah-Jane MacDonald
SUBJECT: Sam
DATE: 6 July 2018 at 14:44
TO: Joyce Walford

Joyce, what's happening at the Greenwoods' now?
Sarah-Jane MacDonald

FROM: Joyce Walford
SUBJECT: Re: Sam
DATE: 6 July 2018 at 14:51
TO: Sarah-Jane MacDonald

Oh Sarah-Jane, it's terrible. They put up a white tent. People are saying she jumped. But he could have pushed her. The state of her at that last rehearsal. Black eye, bruises, cuts. And him off with another woman. Doing her in is cheaper than divorce. Joyce

---

FROM: Sarah-Jane MacDonald
SUBJECT: Re: Sam
DATE: 6 July 2018 at 14:57
TO: Joyce Walford

Well, I saw Sam argue with that quiet girl, Issy, just as she left the hall on Wednesday. It could have been her, don't you think?
Sarah-Jane MacDonald

FROM: Joyce Walford
SUBJECT: Re: Sam
DATE: 6 July 2018 at 15:02
TO: Sarah-Jane MacDonald

Issy? Oh no, she wouldn't say boo to a goose, that one. If it wasn't him, then Sam probably killed herself. I had an uncle do it. Very upsetting, and I didn't even like him. When you get to my age, life is one sad thing after another. Joyce

---

FROM: Andrea Morley
SUBJECT: Hello
DATE: 6 July 2018 at 15:09
TO: Samantha Greenwood

Dear Sam,
I can't stop thinking about it. Let me know what he said. Is it possible he doesn't know all the details himself? If medical professionals are fooled to that degree, then anyone can fall victim. It might be wise to tread carefully.
Andy

FROM: Martin Hayward
SUBJECT: Sad news
DATE: 6 July 2018 at 15:13
TO: Tish Bhatoa

Dear Tish, I'm sorry to email you with more bad news when you are dealing with enough yourself. However, I feel you should know our mutual friend Samantha Greenwood has passed away, apparently by her own hand. I understand you were at odds with her in the past, but feel you ought to know. Regards, Martin

---

FROM: Tish Bhatoa
SUBJECT: Re: Sad news
DATE: 6 July 2018 at 15:47
TO: Martin Hayward

That is truly terrible news. I sent her a message recently. It seems she didn't receive it. I am in the Central African Republic and do not intend to return yet. Martin, I wish you were here to see what the world is. You would appreciate that you are not the centre of it. It would make you grateful. You might just value what you have, not what you want. The longer I'm here, the more strongly I feel I belong. The truth is I may never return. Tish

---

FROM: Martin Hayward
SUBJECT: Re: Sad news
DATE: 6 July 2018 at 15:53
TO: Tish Bhatoa

But, Tish, there is the matter of Poppy's drugs. What will happen? Will she continue to receive chemotherapy at Mount More?

FROM: Tish Bhatoa
SUBJECT: Re: Sad news
DATE: 6 July 2018 at 15:54
TO: Martin Hayward

Is that what you want?

FROM: Martin Hayward
SUBJECT: Re: Sad news
DATE: 6 July 2018 at 15:59
TO: Tish Bhatoa

You know it isn't. I am managing a situation, no more. But Poppy needs treatment of some sort. What should I tell Helen and Paige?

FROM: Tish Bhatoa
SUBJECT: Re: Sad news
DATE: 6 July 2018 at 16:00
TO: Martin Hayward

Tell them whatever you have to tell them. You'll think of something.

FROM: Martin Hayward
SUBJECT: Re: Sad news
DATE: 6 July 2018 at 16:03
TO: Tish Bhatoa

Tish, please don't desert me now. I need your help. Whether you stay out there or not, you'll still need money.

FROM: Tish Bhatoa
SUBJECT: Re: Sad news
DATE: 6 July 2018 at 16:04
TO: Martin Hayward

I don't need your money.

FROM: Martin Hayward
SUBJECT: Re: Sad news
DATE: 6 July 2018 at 16:05
TO: Tish Bhatoa

Then send the phials to me.

FROM: Tish Bhatoa
SUBJECT: Re: Sad news
DATE: 6 July 2018 at 16:07
TO: Martin Hayward

No. The phials will remain securely in Boston . . . unless you contact me again. Goodbye, Martin

---

FROM: Sarah-Jane MacDonald
SUBJECT: Sam
DATE: 6 July 2018 at 15:43
TO: Emma Crooks

Emma, I need your advice, and it's deadly serious this time. Martin's email implies Sam killed herself, but I think she was murdered. You remember

Issy, the quiet girl at the committee meeting? She worshipped Sam, followed her around, bought things for her, latched on with an iron grip. Well, when Sam stormed out of the dress rehearsal, Issy followed her. Moments later I went outside myself and saw them. Sam had a hold of Issy's arm and was snarling in her ear. I couldn't hear what was said, but Issy looked devastated. She went back inside, collected her bag and left. The next day she emails Martin, all bright and breezy, and offers to play Sam's role herself! I think Issy followed Sam home that night and killed her. Should I go to the police?
Sarah-Jane MacDonald

Femi
Again, Martin is very calm in the face of a crisis.

Charlotte
Tish withdraws from their arrangement. But Martin calls it a desertion. Was it really blackmail? He seems a willing victim.

Femi
It's an exchange of some sort, but with a power imbalance. Martin needs Tish more than she needs him.

Charlotte
SJ wants everyone to see Issy as guilty.

Femi
I'm going to say that the final person 'not who they say they are' is Helen. I think Sam found out who she really is and that somehow led to her death.

Charlotte
Where's the evidence?

Femi
Sam was consulting Andrea specifically about Helen. Andrea 'Andy' says 'tread carefully' because even doctors can be fooled. They 'have to say something'. Sam was killed when she said something.

Charlotte
Just like in Africa. Only there she's sent away. Here, where it's supposedly more 'civilised', she's killed.

Femi
Two communities, one raising money to cure a sick child, the other healing victims of war. Both so kind and caring, so intent on doing what they believe is right. Yet both refuse to see what's wrong. Their solution is to silence the person pointing it out.

Femi
Because the alternative is to acknowledge the shame. Of enabling abuse, of hailing an abuser as a hero, of reducing a continent to a primitive war zone, of falling for a scam, of being conned by friends, or conning your friends in turn. All these things are not easy to acknowledge.

Charlotte
I know you have strong feelings about Western aid in Africa. Don't let it affect your impartiality in this case. What do you always say to me about letting emotions get in the way?

Femi
Because what do you do, once you've acknowledged it? How do you atone for something like that? It's not a simple case of paying the money back. Pouring cash into aid, or trying to pick up the pieces. The damage is done. Money won't repair broken trust. There are some things you can't un-know, says Andy. Well, there are some things that cannot be forgiven.

Charlotte
Let's see what Tanner says on Friday.

Femi
We've nearly got this. There's just something we haven't seen yet. I'll read through everything again tonight.

Femi
Wake up!

Femi
Come on, wake up!

Femi
Charl, are you awake? I've got it – what Tanner was talking about. This changes everything.

Charlotte
Yep. What?

Femi
That night of the dress rehearsal Sam tells the whole Fairway Players everything she's found out about Helen and Martin, plus everything she's discovered, courtesy of her own medical knowledge and that of her acquaintances. It shocks everyone. Not what she says, but *because* she says it. This community is not in the habit of questioning the Haywards. Whatever they may know or suspect, they would rather continue enabling the deception than challenge it. They all reject Sam there and then, except Issy. Sam rejects Issy outside in the car park. From that moment Sam is alone. That evening Martin emails Sam and Sarah-Jane. He addresses Sam's outburst and discusses the play.

Charlotte
Ok, we've established all that.

Femi
He's calm, he's fair, he's in charge – because Sam has shown her hand and she *doesn't* have the one thing he fears everyone seeing. Sam arrives home to the message from Andy, calls her back and discovers what it is. She has to tell *someone*. She calls Martin and tells him. More about this in a second. Go back a few weeks . . .

Femi
Sam is hot on the case of a suspected 'financial conspiracy', courtesy of her inherent distrust of Tish Bhatoa and, quite possibly, her outsider's perspective on this little community and the Haywards' status at the top of it. She engages Andy to find out if Helen is lying about having a little boy who died. But she can't afford a full search, so asks her to check records of death only. No record of his death *in the UK*. Sam takes from this that the little boy never lived, that it's an emotive lie to raise sympathy and money. She's almost right, but wrong.

Femi
Andy is intrigued by the case, or maybe she just likes Sam – who knows. For some reason she continues to look into Helen's history. But she's not the first. Remember Tish and her due diligence? We assumed she dug into Martin's business history, but Helen is co-director of The Grange, and the company Tish employed to investigate their finances automatically studies *her* background, too. Andy looks 'across the pond' and, like Tish, discovers that Helen had a little boy who died – only he didn't have meningitis: he had a mother who made him ill deliberately to gain attention for herself, until one day, tragically, she killed him.

Charlotte
Munchausen's by proxy? They call it 'Fabricated or Induced Illness' now. It would be less well known then . . . not spotted until it was too late. That is so fucking tragic.

Femi
This is what's in the 'files' Tish Bhatoa has: files from the US, where Helen was born and where she was arrested for the murder of her eldest child. Like the newspaper review says, her American accent is so convincing it could be real.

Charlotte
Femi, are you saying what I think you are?

Charlotte
Was she tried and convicted?

Femi
Perhaps, perhaps not, but there is enough evidence in the 'files' to throw a whole new light on this charismatic woman everyone loves, respects and protects.

Femi
Not only are there *no* experimental drugs, but also Poppy isn't ill *at all*.

Femi
And whatever Helen tried to do to her first child, she started doing to Poppy.

Charlotte
SHIT! Where's the evidence?

Femi
It all hinges on what Sam is doing when she accesses the database at Mount More. Only she doesn't realise it at the time. Also, check out the words Martin uses to describe the effect Poppy's cancer will have on their family. He repeats the phrase 'legacy of tragedy' that will 'scar' his family forever. Both are direct quotes from a genuine letter describing the death of a child from cancer. Given that his granddaughter does *not* have, and never has had, terminal cancer, it's his only source of reference for such emotion. I've got pages of notes – sending you an email . . .

TO: Charlotte Holroyd
SUBJECT: New theory continued
FROM: Femi Hassan

Tanner told us the person who doesn't exist is a matter of corroboration. When we heard it was Lauren, we assumed it related to Isabel. Her existence as an imaginary friend *is* a character witness for Isabel after all, and probably led her to be found guilty. However, I believe he meant us to notice what Lauren corroborates about *Poppy*. I've been through this entire correspondence again and again – there is *no* independent evidence that Poppy is ill and actually having chemotherapy, other than from Lauren on 24 April and 31 May, or to put it more accurately, what Isabel, with her better-than-average medical knowledge, has *made up*. The Haywards, Reswicks and Tish Bhatoa are actively involved in the deception – there's no corroborative reference to her Hickman line, chemo sessions, nothing. In fact we know Paige shaves Poppy's hair off on 2 July so she can wear her wig.

When Sam gains access to the treatment records at Mount More, she is gone a long time. Only she doesn't find Poppy's notes, because there are none, so something *else* must keep her at that database. I believe it is Paige's notes. She discovers that, as a child, Paige was hospitalised multiple times with minor complaints and conditions. Others have mentioned this in their correspondence, too: on 9 June, Marianne Payne tells Carol Dearing that 'I remember Paige was poorly early on, with asthma first, then a stomach problem'. Sam mentions Paige's medical history in passing to Andy, who struggles to find records for Helen under the name we know her by. It isn't until Andy broadens her search and tracks her to the US that the truth starts to emerge. 'You mentioned something about the mum being ill . . . I took a gamble across the pond and found something.'

Sam's mistake is to assume Martin doesn't realise his wife has a history of this psychological condition. I believe he not only knows, but uses it to create a situation he and Tish can exploit financially. We've seen how the family shelters Helen from the stress of reality – I think this is to keep her symptoms at bay. When Martin is in a dire situation himself, with his gambling addiction, financial worries from Olivia's IVF and legal issues at

The Grange, he can't keep that stress from Helen. Imagine that she starts to act out again, this time with Poppy.

As Helen fabricates Poppy's symptoms, Martin must do something and fast. Seeking help for his wife doesn't occur to him, because it means acknowledging the awful truth of her condition and her history. So he looks for a doctor with overwhelming financial commitments, because they are more likely to be seduced by the promise of easy money. He finds Tish; with her parents in a five-star care home, her brother in Africa draining her finances and a fluctuating business income, she's the ideal collaborator. He asks her to 'pretend' to treat Poppy, yet ensure Helen doesn't damage the child's health. In return for compromising her professional integrity, Tish will benefit from the fundraising appeal that he intends to use as a solution to his financial problems, too.

On 6 July he describes himself as 'managing a situation'. I believe he's managed this situation for years, since he found out about Helen's condition when Paige was a child. Sarah-Jane says they started The Fairway Players when Paige was a toddler, and according to Marianne, this is the point when her health apparently improved. Once Helen had a place to be centre-stage, where she could express her attention-seeking side, she stopped making her daughter ill. The Fairway Players is an important community group, but its significance to the Haywards is far greater: it keeps them functioning as a close and loving family.

This situation doesn't occur to Sam. Why would it? She's heard from Issy that Lauren and her mum have seen Poppy being treated at Mount More. Who would make their own child or grandchild ill anyway? Which brings me to Paige. We've seen how close mother and daughter are. Could they suffer from the same psychological make-up? Did the fact Paige was abused like that – made ill by her own mother as a child, in an environment where that situation was not challenged or addressed – somehow inform a pattern of behaviour now? She certainly shares a love of the spotlight with Helen, and similarly she's kept in her own happy world by the rest of the family.

So Martin nurtures a scenario that Helen and Paige play into. It's all so that he can start the appeal for non-existent experimental drugs and raise the cash he so desperately needs. Only it soon becomes more than he can handle. Martin does not realise quite how far the community will go to help him and his family. The appeal explodes into a flurry of activity and a deluge of cash. With this comes more lies, more deception, even more stress, and more problematic management issues, not least Tish.

Martin confides in Tish about his wife's condition, but she does her own 'due diligence' and turns this wealthy family's explosive secret to her own advantage. She probes their background using RedHawk Consulting, discovers Helen's true identity and secures evidence of her involvement in the death of her first child. It is the one thing the family does not want their friends to know.

Knowledge is power, and Tish uses hers to ensure she is the sole beneficiary of the appeal. They are soon dependent on each other in the worst way. For the record, I don't believe Poppy is given drugs when she goes for 'chemo' – Tish fabricates the whole process. She even makes Poppy feel poorly on 2 July to reassure Paige the chemo is working. When she withdraws her participation, Martin says, 'Poppy needs treatment of some sort' as if Helen and Paige will not be happy unless the little girl is having medical care.

So is Martin acting alone, or are James and Glen part of this, too? I suspect they know about it from the off. Glen, who believes the meningitis story, is on board with what he thinks is a quick fix to bail the family out of their temporary financial straits – of which his failure to find work is key; on 22 May he is emailed by Ben Taylor, saying that his contract will not be renewed. Meanwhile James is reluctant. I wonder if he would prefer his mother to seek professional help for her condition? In their early correspondence James and Martin are cool with each other, as in ice-fucking-cold. On 19 May James says to Issy: 'I never wanted to be a part of this. I tried to talk them out of doing it in the first place.' We thought he meant the play, but it's the appeal – the deception – he is drawn into against his will.

James refuses to attend Poppy's Ball. The family lies about the reason. They say he and Olivia are babysitting Poppy, when Beth Halliday is doing that. I've tried to identify the moment James is forced to engage with his father's plan. It's when Sam visits Martin with her theory that Tish is lying to them. On 1 June Martin says, 'I don't know what to do or which way to turn. I'm sorry about everything else. I know how you feel but we need you on our side.' For a man like Martin, that is serious emotional stuff. James is a part of it from then. It's against his better judgement, but he's aware his IVF is part of the problem and that his whole family's health, wealth and future happiness now depends on the deception, the appeal and the play.

It's James who insists Sam and Kel are excluded from the fundraising committee, and James who says, 'Don't reply, Dad, leave it to me' when Sarah-Jane objects. That's it. Martin now relies on James for emotional support and practical help. But when James is called away to an ailing Olivia on 5 July, the somewhat less-articulate Glen is required to do his bit for the family and email Sarah-Jane. So, having said all this:

Who killed Samantha Greenwood? **Martin Hayward**, to stop the family secret being exposed.

Who knew it was going to happen? **Glen Reswick**, who helps Martin and effectively takes James's place while James is with Olivia at the hospital.

Who knew about it before her body was discovered? **James Hayward**, because Martin tells him once the twins are born.

Who is erroneously imprisoned and why? **Isabel Beck**, because she is a quiet, awkward outsider at the bottom of the social hierarchy, with a well-documented obsession and a complex psychological life. For some reason, she also happened to be at Sam's flat that night.

Charlotte
There's no suggestion Helen made *James* ill as a child?

Femi
No. But Martin had a job in the City at that time. Let's say Helen felt secure enough then to function normally. It's when things get rocky that she starts again.

Charlotte
Ok. But the actual murderer could be any combination of the Martin/Glen/James triangle.

Femi
Theoretically. But James is at the hospital with Olivia and the twins. He's out of the picture the whole night. Glen wakes Paige at 4 a.m. with news she's got Sam's part in the play. But I don't believe Glen has Martin's motivation. We can't account for Martin after he's sent the emails to Sam and SJ. He describes the whole thing as a 'bloody mess' to James the next day. But I also don't think they know for sure Sam is dead at that point – even if they suspect it.

Charlotte
James asks Issy if she's seen Sam. She says 'no'. A one-word email from Issy? That says more than any of her rambling missives. Why was she at Sam's flat that night? She doesn't tell the police the reason.

Femi
This is what we need to establish. Perhaps she intends to speak to her about what they discuss in the car park. The next day she tells Celia and Joel she has something for Kel.

Charlotte
That's a lie. She wants to 'discover' the body and call the police. We keep hearing how Helen loves to be centre-stage. Well, so does Issy. Even says she can't wait to be 'back onstage in the spotlight'.

Femi
Has she arranged with the Haywards to find the body? James and Issy are closer than they themselves realise. They have quite a bond. He confides in her when he wants info about Sam, when he says 'I never wanted to be a part of this.' He defends Issy several times, to Sarah-Jane and Martin. James is an outsider in his family – does he identify with Issy, the social outsider? Tanner describes Issy as 'a survivor', but not in a good way. Does she delude herself that she's acting for the best, for the benefit of her friend James and the alpha family?

Charlotte
What is it James says to Issy after the murder? 'Thanks again for your support. You're a vital member of our team.'

Femi
We're no nearer the 'who's-who' thing Tanner is so keen on. If the third person 'not who they say they are' is Helen, then I have no idea 'who pretends to be who' later on. No idea.

Charlotte
We need to think on that, and why Issy is at Sam's the night of the murder.

Femi
Let's see what Tanner says. We may have got there without needing the who's-who thing.

Femi Hassan
Charlotte Holroyd

Dear both,

Further to our meeting today: thank you. You have identified what I believe to be the crux of this case and now we can move forward. To recap: Helen is the final character not who they say they are. Records are patchy, but we know she was born Helen Macauley-Grace in Boxborough, a well-to-do suburb of Boston, Massachusetts, in 1956. She marries a Kenneth Anderson in February 1973. In August 1973 David Kenneth Anderson is born. The child dies in October 1978 of renal failure and breathing complications. Helen Anderson is charged with Voluntary Manslaughter after doctors report their suspicions to the coroner, whose Open Verdict stands to this day. The trial takes place in 1979. Evidence is overwhelming, yet circumstantial. Helen's display of grief in the witness box is, by all accounts, riveting. Doubts fester. Sympathy flows. A technicality is raised. The judge stops the trial. Helen is a free woman, but there is too much evidence for her reputation to survive in that small community. Her marriage is dissolved in 1979 and she makes a new start, in a new country.

By 1980 a Helen Anderson is living not far from here in Lymbridge, although it is Helen Grace who marries Martin Hayward in 1981. James is born in 1982 and Paige in 1985. Do they know their mother has a past life in America? Clearly the subject of the older brother has arisen, but whether they know the full story is yet to be established. When did Martin discover the truth? Probably years after falling in love and starting a family with a woman whose act he believed. By then it was too late.

You've worked hard, and I feel we are very nearly there, but not quite. As promised, attached is the explanation Isabel gave for her journey to the Greenwoods' flat the night of the dress rehearsal. It explains much about how the relationship between Samantha and

Isabel ended. As usual with this case, the meat is all between the lines.

Isabel's conviction for murder hangs on whether she intended to kill Samantha or not. There is a quiet confidence we'll commute to manslaughter. However, I believe Isabel did not even enter the Greenwoods' flat that night. Someone else did. That's why this appeal is so crucial.

You've put forward a good argument for Martin Hayward, but read his statement attached and see if you feel the same way. As you've come this far in the dark, to a degree, I've included a few other statements you will find interesting. I have not relinquished my quest for you to see the final masquerade. I believe it is crucial.

I cannot meet up again before the deadline, so please use The What's Up to communicate your thoughts. Thereby, please liaise with Sandra.

Yours,

RT

Roderick Tanner, QC
Senior Partner
Tanner & Dewey LLP

County Police Interview Report

Extract from police interview with Isabel Beck:

Ms Anand: I'd like to read a further statement.
Sgt Cooper: Good. Go on.
Ms Anand: I have remembered the reason I visited Samantha Greenwood's flat on the night of 4 July. I was in possession of some property of Ms Greenwood's and wanted to return it. This property is a colourful fabric shoulder bag, decorated in a traditional African style. Ms Greenwood lent me the bag some weeks earlier, and afterwards said I could keep it.
Sgt Cooper: Thank you. Why did you want to return it, if she said you could keep it?
Ms Beck: No comment.
Sgt Cooper: And why go there so late at night? You could have given it to her the next day at work.
Ms Beck: No comment.
Sgt Crowe: Where is this bag now? For the benefit of the transcript, Ms Beck is trying to communicate with the duty solicitor.
Ms Anand: My client would like a break.

– Interview suspended –

Ms Anand: My client would like to make a further statement.
Sgt Cooper: Go on.
Ms Anand: As Ms Greenwood left the dress rehearsal, she voiced her regret at having given the bag to me. I was shocked and upset, so did not think to return it to her immediately. She left. I then wanted to return the bag as soon as possible, so took the bus to her flat. When I arrived there, we argued as per my previous statement.
Sgt Crowe: Thank you, Ms Anand. So this bag is at Ms Greenwood's flat now?
Ms Beck: No comment.
Sgt Crowe: You go to the flat to return the bag. Sam lets you in. 'Here's

the bag' – you give it to her . . . then you argue and Sam ends up . . . as we all know. Is that accurate?

Ms Beck: No comment.

Sgt Crowe: There's no bag that matches this description in Sam's flat. We have officers searching your flat now. So let's wait and see.

Sgt Cooper: Meanwhile we can move on. In your original statement you say you 'panicked and ran home'. Yet you closed and locked the balcony doors after you. That's not the action of someone in a panic, is it? It's calm, calculated.

Ms Beck: No comment.

Sgt Cooper: Was it *your* suggestion you both move to the balcony? Seems strange to go out there at night.

Ms Beck: No comment.

Sgt Cooper: And you ran all the way home? Over five miles.

Ms Beck: No comment.

Extract from a later police interview with Isabel Beck:

Ms Anand: My client would like to make a further statement.

Sgt Cooper: Go ahead.

Ms Anand: While Ms Greenwood and I were talking, she suggested we move to the balcony, as her neighbours had complained about loud voices in the flat. I must have automatically closed and locked the doors afterwards. I have been running regularly for several months and ran home in a panic.

Sgt Cooper: Thank you. Do you recognise this, Ms Beck? [Ref. no. 000967] It's 'a colourful fabric shoulder bag, decorated in a traditional African style'.

Ms Beck: No comment.

Sgt Cooper: We found it hung behind your bedroom door. If you had this bag with you when you went to Samantha Greenwood's flat, then you certainly took it home again, didn't you?

Ms Beck: No comment.

Sgt Cooper: Maybe you decided to take it back after you'd killed her, but if you really wanted the bag *that* much, you'd never have gone there to return it in the first place. I don't think you went to the flat to return the bag. I think you went there to kill Ms Greenwood. You lured her out onto the balcony, where you pushed her over it to her death. Afterwards you locked up and calmly walked home.

Ms Beck: No comment.

County Police Interview Report

Extract from police interview with Martin Hayward:

Sgt Cooper: Thank you for coming in, Mr Hayward. I understand your solicitor would like to make a statement on your behalf.

Mr Allardyce: Thank you. My name is Martin Hayward and I am volunteering a statement in relation to the death of Samantha Greenwood on the night of the 4–5 July 2018. I am taking this step because Ms Greenwood and I had a public falling-out shortly before she was found dead, and I am keen to set the record straight. On the evening of 4 July I was at St Joseph's Community Hall from 6 p.m., conducting a dress rehearsal for The Fairway Players' production of *All My Sons*, for which I am director. However, I was forced to terminate the rehearsal early, at around 9.15 p.m., because Samantha Greenwood publicly accused my wife and I of using inappropriate means to raise money for our granddaughter's life-saving brain-tumour treatment. Her accusations were inaccurate and unfounded, but they upset my wife, as well as our long-standing friends. I wanted to defuse the situation, so I cancelled the rehearsal and sent everyone home. After locking up at the hall, my wife and I arrived home at 9.45 p.m. She went to bed to read. I emailed Samantha Greenwood and Sarah-Jane MacDonald, further to the disastrous rehearsal, as well as checking on our son, James, who was with his wife at St Ann's Hospital. Their twins were born that night. I also emailed our daughter, Paige, and asked her to call my wife as she was upset. Distressed by what had happened and anxious over whether or not I had handled it well, I spent much of the night playing poker via my account with StarlightPoker. My hard drive and other devices are available to the police, if required. I understand several of The Fairway Players mentioned in passing to police officers that my granddaughter's appeal has been defrauded of £80,000 by a woman called Lydia Drake. I am pleased to put the record straight that this is untrue. It is, however, an honest misunderstanding on their part and is not a police matter.

Sgt Cooper: Thank you, Mr Allardyce. Mr Hayward, when did you discover Ms Greenwood was dead?

Mr Hayward: Friday, when Joyce Walford, who lives opposite the Greenwoods, called my wife.

County Police Interview Report

Extract from police interview with Sean Greenwood:

Sgt Cooper: Thank you for coming in, Sean.
Mr Greenwood: It's Kel.
Sgt Cooper: Why's that?
Mr Greenwood: Lots of Seans. My dad, his dad, my mum's dad, my uncle, an older half-brother – that's complicated. I've always been Kel.
Sgt Cooper: We appreciate this is a difficult time, so won't keep you long. Can you tell me when and where you last saw your wife, Samantha?
Mr Greenwood: Outside our block. I . . . we left the hall about nine, nine-thirty. Drove home. We sat in the car outside for a little bit. Then she got out and went in.
Sgt Cooper: Did you go in with her?
Mr Greenwood: No.
Sgt Cooper: Why not?
Mr Greenwood: We split up.
Sgt Crowe: You ended your relationship. When?
Mr Greenwood: Right then. She said she would go back to CAR – er, Central African Republic – as soon as she could. I drove away and . . . that was it.
Sgt Cooper: You didn't go inside to collect your clothes or . . . ?
Mr Greenwood: No.
Sgt Crowe: Why not?
Mr Greenwood: Couldn't face it.
Sgt Cooper: That seems sudden.
Mr Greenwood: It wasn't.
Sgt Cooper: You worked for Médecins Sans Frontières, didn't you? Why did you come back?
Mr Greenwood: We'd seen too much.
Sgt Crowe: Violence?
Mr Greenwood: We saw monsters conspire to protect each other. You don't get over that. Sam couldn't. But she couldn't let it go, either.

She came here to watch her. To see who she was. Who would do something like that. There must be something else rotten in their life. Sure enough, there was. But when I sent her a card, she said it was spiteful and vindictive. I said we're helpless. Spite is all we have left. Then the neighbours complained.

Sgt Cooper: When was this?

Mr Greenwood: Weeks ago.

Sgt Cooper: On *Wednesday* night, where did you go?

Mr Greenwood: The Travellers' Inn. Claudia. Her husband knew. He'd known for days, but didn't let on. He arranged air tickets to Portugal for him and the kids. Changed the locks, texted her from the airport when she was at work. Said the house is on the market and they aren't coming back.

Sgt Cooper: Claudia is your girlfriend, who earlier that day attacked your wife at her place of work? For the benefit of the transcript, Mr Greenwood is nodding.

Mr Greenwood: Sam emailed Claudia's husband and told him about us. Spiteful and vindictive, huh? She doesn't know when to keep her mouth shut. Sorry. But if she hadn't said anything, she'd be alive now. You don't have to speak, do you? You can leave things be. Even if they're wrong. Even if they stink the place out. It's not your problem, or your business, or your place to put them right.

Sgt Crowe: Take a tissue . . .

Mr Greenwood: I told her: let it go. I said people don't always want to know the truth. It's too complicated or painful or whatever . . . It was my last shot at saving us. I can't go through it again. When you take a stand like that, no one else will stand with you, believe me. I told her: if she said anything, she'd never see me again. But it wasn't enough. She had to go and say it.

Sgt Crowe: Say what? What did Sam say that she shouldn't have?

Mr Greenwood: All that about the appeal.

Sgt Cooper: So she was wrong?

Mr Greenwood: Wrong? No! They're rinsing that kid's cancer for all it's worth. God only knows how much they've made, but . . . so what? So what. If people want to throw money at the Haywards, let them.

Sgt Crowe: So . . . correct me if I'm wrong. You told Samantha that night that if she spoke her mind about the appeal, you would leave the relationship. She did. So when you both arrived back at your block of flats that night, you dropped her off and drove away to be with Claudia instead.

Sgt Cooper: Mr Greenwood is nodding.

Mr Greenwood: If I'd gone in with her, she wouldn't have done it.

Sgt Crowe: Kel, can I ask how you injured your foot?

Mr Greenwood: Claudia needed clothes. Her keys didn't work. We had to break in through an upstairs window. Lost my footing. Fell off the garage roof. Woke the neighbours. Didn't get back to the motel till gone two.

Sgt Cooper: And the following day. Thursday. What did you do?

Mr Greenwood: Went to a solicitor.

Sgt Cooper: To see about a divorce?

Mr Greenwood: No. With Claudia. To find out how she could get the kids back if Michael stayed in Portugal.

Sgt Cooper: You appeared in the play for all three nights, I believe?

Mr Greenwood: Yes. For what that was worth.

Sgt Cooper: In the circumstances, if you'd felt unable to continue, they would have found someone else. Why did you go through with it?

Mr Greenwood: Didn't want to let them down. They've all worked hard. And it raises money for the kid.

County Police Interview Report

Extract from police interview with Nicolas Walford:

Sgt Cooper: Thanks for coming in, Mr Walford. You know why you're here?

Mr Walford: Yep.

Sgt Cooper: A woman was found dead across the green from your address and, under those circumstances, we speak to anyone in the vicinity with convictions for comparable crimes, just to eliminate them.

Mr Walford: I never killed anyone.

Sgt Crowe: We know . . .

Sgt Cooper: We know. But you have a conviction dating back to 2007 for ABH against your then-girlfriend . . .

Sgt Crowe: And you were acquainted with the deceased.

Mr Walford: She was in the drama group. I didn't know her.

Sgt Cooper: Amateur drama a strange hobby, isn't it?

Mr Walford: Not really.

Sgt Cooper: What I mean is, you don't strike me as a thespian, Nicolas.

Mr Walford: We do it for Mum. She says it keeps us out of trouble.

Sgt Cooper: When did you last see Samantha Greenwood?

Mr Walford: At the dress rehearsal.

Sgt Cooper: Anything unusual about her behaviour?

Mr Walford: No.

Sgt Crowe: Apparently she had a verbal altercation with Martin Hayward. Did you see that?

Mr Walford: No.

Sgt Cooper: The rehearsal was abandoned as a result. You didn't know why?

Mr Walford: Just glad of the early night.

Sgt Cooper: What did you do when you left the church hall?

Mr Walford: Went back home. Logged on for work at midnight. Was called out just before two.

Sgt Cooper: That's right, you were at the Travellers' Inn. Why was that?

Mr Walford: Gas escape. Leak at boiler. I was there an hour. It's all on my works system.

Sgt Crowe: Your mother, Joyce, told us you saw Kel Greenwood there with a woman not his wife – the deceased – and that they looked distressed.

Mr Walford: Nah. It might have been him. I couldn't swear to it. Mum puts two and two together and makes ten.

Sgt Cooper: Did Kel see you?

Mr Walford: *If* it was him. I don't know.

Sgt Cooper: Did this person who may have been Kel say anything to you, or you to him?

Mr Walford: No.

Sgt Crowe: That'll be all for now. Thank you for your help.

Mr Walford: Pleasure.

County Police Interview Report

Extract from police interview with Arnold Ballancore:

Sgt Crowe: That's a fat lip you're rocking there, Arnie. How did you get that?

Mr Ballancore: When the police came. Must've fallen or something.

Sgt Crowe: That's a shame.

Sgt Cooper: We won't keep you long. You can go back to Fowey clink in a bit.

Mr Ballancore: Thanks.

Sgt Cooper: When did you last see Samantha Greenwood?

Mr Ballancore: Can't remember. Why?

Sgt Cooper: It's very important. When did you last see Samantha Greenwood?

Mr Ballancore: Probably . . . last week. I been smoking, so . . . why?

Sgt Crowe: Sam died on Wednesday night. She fell from the balcony of her flat.

Sgt Cooper: Ah. Ok.

Sgt Crowe: [*to duty officer*] Can we have a bucket, please?

– Interview suspended –

Sgt Cooper: All right? Happy to continue?

Mr Ballancore: Uh-huh.

Sgt Cooper: You didn't know? Mr Ballancore is shaking his head.

Mr Ballancore: Kel?

Sgt Cooper: Kel is very upset, as you can imagine.

Mr Ballancore: That man. He didn't know what he had.

Sgt Crowe: When were you last at Sam's flat, Arnie?

Mr Ballancore: Walked back, took a wrong turn somewhere, but got in . . . dunno when.

Sgt Cooper: You were released from here at just after midnight on Thursday 5 July. Are you saying you walked *seven* miles back to the flat?

Mr Ballancore: Yeah.

Sgt Crowe: You've got your own key? Mr Ballancore is nodding.

Sgt Cooper: What time did you get there?

Mr Ballancore: Late. Where was Kel? Sam. Oh no. She didn't . . . to herself?

Sgt Cooper: Was Sam in the flat when you got there? Not again. Take a tissue. Arnie, concentrate and you'll help us find out what happened to her.

Mr Ballancore: Place was empty. I thought, 'They're on nights.' I lay down a while. Got my things together. Left when it was light.

Sgt Crowe: Was the flat messy when you arrived? No.

Sgt Cooper: Did you notice anything – *anything* out of the ordinary? No.

Sgt Crowe: Did you see anyone around, maybe in the car park or on the green? No.

Sgt Cooper: Were the balcony doors open or closed?

Mr Ballancore: Closed. Didn't touch 'em. Not my place. Just lay on the couch.

Sgt Cooper: And when it was light you left, even though you were on bail and had a pending court appearance for aggravated burglary? Mr Ballancore is nodding.

Mr Ballancore: Sorry.

Sgt Cooper: Someone grassed you up for that. Do you know who it was? Mr Ballancore shrugs in reply to that question.

Sgt Crowe: Arnie, did you kill Samantha Greenwood?

Mr Ballancore: What? Oh, the fuck? No! So that's where it's going. I'm not saying any more. I want the duty solicitor. Kel . . .

Sgt Crowe: [*to the duty officer*] Can you call Ms Anand, please.

Sgt Cooper: Kel? What about Kel?

Mr Ballancore: No comment.

County Police Interview Report

Extract from police interview with Isabel Beck:

Sgt Cooper: After Sam falls over the balcony, what do you do then?

Ms Beck: No comment.

Sgt Cooper: Do you look over to see where she's landed, whether she's ok or not?

Ms Beck: No comment.

Sgt Cooper: Call an ambulance?

Ms Beck: No comment.

Sgt Cooper: You do in fact call an ambulance, but almost twenty-four hours later. The following evening, 5 July, Joel and Celia Halliday drive you to Sam's flat. You want to go there you say, because you 'have something for Kel'. They tell you he's not home, but you insist. What is it you want to give Kel?

Ms Beck: No comment.

Sgt Cooper: Or is that a lie?

Ms Beck: No comment.

Sgt Crowe: You don't have anything to give Kel, but you want to be the one to find Sam. You deserve your little moment in the spotlight, after all that planning and execution.

Ms Anand: Sergeant . . .

Ms Beck: No comment.

Charlotte
The police interview Nick Walford, but not Glen Reswick or the MacDonalds?

Femi
Notice Kel and Issy mention Sam returning to Africa on her own. It must be one of the things she told people before she died. It means Kel and Claudia have no motivation for Sam's murder. They're 'free' now anyway.

Charlotte
The bag Sam gives Issy at the ball comes out of the blue here. If Issy really does go to the flat to return it – and I think she does – then Sam must have said something earth-shattering to her after the rehearsal.

Femi
Exactly my thoughts. 'You emailed Michael D'Souza, said you were me. I don't like you, never did. Going to Africa without you. Don't want to speak to you again' – Issy says earlier the bag reminds her of Sam, so once Sam rejects her, she wants it out of her life. So what stops her handing it over?

Charlotte
We know now why Claudia attacks Sam. And why Sam describes it as 'understandable'. During the attack they exchange accusations. Claudia: 'You told Michael when I asked you not to . . .' Sam: 'It wasn't me.' Claudia doesn't believe her, and nor does Kel. It must influence his final ultimatum.

Femi
Kel sent the condolence card to Tish, telling her Dan is dead. Yet Sam is angry with him for it. Despite all Tish is guilty of, she won't do that to her. It explains why she's so angry with Issy for telling Michael about Claudia and Kel.

Charlotte
She really is 'a lady of principle'.

Femi
Tanner thinks Issy didn't enter Sam's flat that night. It could still be an attention-seeking confession.

Charlotte
Her fingerprints are found, but she sleeps there the previous Saturday night, when we know she snoops around the lounge.

Femi
And does she really run five miles home? Both Martin and Kel have credible statements, if not cast-iron alibis. Nick Walford doesn't give the police anything. But that doesn't mean he did it.

Charlotte
Arnie? He must take at least two hours to walk seven miles – and take at least one wrong turn. By the time he arrives, Sam is dead and the murderer has closed the balcony doors, locked them and gone. That places Isabel, who arrives at 10.30 p.m. or a little later, in the right place at the right time.

Femi
Sam arrives home to Andy's message. Do we think she responds to it immediately, even though her husband has just ended their relationship and driven away? We need a timeline. Give me a minute.

Charlotte
Isabel travels to Sam's flat, but doesn't go in. Confused. Distressed. She hangs around outside. Out of sight. Sends emails about everything being ok in the morning. Waits. Watches. Rides out her dark night of the soul. That's where she meets the murderer.

The murder of Samantha Greenwood

Timeline of events

In the absence of exact times, I've approximated. All based on statements and correspondence.

<u>Wednesday 4 July 2018</u>

Before 6 a.m.	Sam leaves her flat to start the early shift. Isabel is also on the early shift. Kel is off work this week, so he's home.
After 6 a.m.	Arnie is arrested by the police at the Greenwoods' flat and taken away.
	At some point during the morning, Michael texts Claudia to say he's on his way to Portugal with their kids.
1.44 p.m.	Claudia attacks Sam in the ward. Issy calls the police.
2.20 p.m.	Police arrive at the Reswicks to take photographs of the Healing Doll.
	Kel picks Sam up from the hospital and takes her home.
6 p.m.	The Fairway Players arrive for dress rehearsal.
Between 6 and 9 p.m.	A message is left on Sam's answering service from Andy, telling her that if she can verify something, they will have to tell someone about it.
9 p.m.	Sam confronts Martin and Helen in front of the whole drama group. The rehearsal is abandoned. Sam leaves, followed by Issy, but Sam confronts Issy in the car park. Issy returns to the hall, devastated.
9.15 p.m.	Sam and Kel leave the hall by car and drive to their flat.
	Issy leaves the hall and catches the bus to Sam's flat.
	Kevin MacDonald takes Harley home and goes to bed with a cold.

9.30 p.m.	Sarah-Jane visits Emma to discuss Sam's accusations; she arrives home so late she sleeps on the sofa.
	Martin and Helen arrive home; Helen is distraught and goes to bed.
	Martin spends the next two hours sending emails and messages to Sam, Tish, Sarah-Jane and Paige; he claims then to play online poker for 'much of the night'.
9.45 p.m.	Sam and Kel arrive at the flat. Kel drives away without going in. Sam enters and picks up Andy's message.
	Olivia is taken to surgery.
10 p.m.	Issy claims to arrive at Sam's flat, where she argues with Sam and accidentally pushes her off the balcony. Then Issy claims to run – or at least walk – five miles home.
10.30 p.m.	James and Olivia's twins are born.

<u>Thursday 5 July 2018</u>

12 a.m.	James announces his babies' births. Arnie is released from police custody on bail; he walks back to the Greenwoods' flat, taking at least one wrong turn. We have no confirmation of the exact time, but we are confident it is well after the event.
	Issy sends emails assuring everyone Sam will be fine, didn't mean what she said and will be in the play the following night.
2 a.m.	Nick sees Kel and Claudia arrive at the Travellers' Inn. They have been at Claudia's house trying to break in to collect her belongings.
4 a.m.	Glen wakes Paige to tell her about her part in the play.
5 a.m.	Joyce sees Arnie leave the Greenwoods' flat.

6 a.m.	Issy arrives for her early shift.
	Kel spends the day with Claudia, consulting a solicitor.
	Helen takes Poppy to the zoo, then helps Martin and Glen prepare Paige to take on Sam's role in the play.
4.30 p.m.	The Haywards arrive at the hall to rehearse.
6 p.m.	The other Fairway Players arrive at the hall. Kel turns up late, limping, and is not himself.
8 p.m.	Curtain up.
11.30 p.m.	Celia and Joel drive Issy to the Greenwoods' flat.

<u>Friday 6 July 2018</u>

12 a.m.	Issy calls 999 to say she's found Sam's body and that it's been there a whole day.

Roderick Tanner, QC
Thank you for the timeline. If you consider it alongside the final masquerade, you will, I hope, reach the same conclusion I did.

Femi
We don't have an alibi for Glen, except he's home by 4 a.m. to tell his wife she's in the play. How does he know that? Nothing points to him *not* being involved in the murder.

Charlotte
Sam dies between 11 p.m. and 4 a.m. Isabel and Arnie claim to be in the flat between those hours. Yet Arnie must arrive later, after the murderer has gone. This narrows the murder to earlier: 11 p.m.–1 a.m.

Femi
The twins are born at 10.30 p.m. That's early. Earlier than I realised. Mr Tanner, is the final person who pretends to be someone else Olivia?

Charlotte
Olivia? We haven't even heard from her. She's having a baby – two babies – by Caesarean. She's out cold.

Femi
She's probably had an epidural. By midnight she posts – as James – to announce the births. Describes herself as 'fast asleep'. James has left his phone with her at the hospital. He's at Sam's.

Charlotte
Sam doesn't call Martin to tell him about Helen – she calls James!

Femi
Yes! Why would she call Martin, after their fight at rehearsal? She suspects him of knowing about Helen. She doesn't suspect James. She trusts him. But what she has to tell him – that his mum killed his older brother and is now making his niece ill – is super-sensitive. She doesn't want to tell him on the phone. She calls him at around 10 p.m., says, 'There's something you have to know about your mother.' I think she mentions that Kel has left, that she's only just discovered this herself.

Charlotte
James is terrified. He's heard the rehearsal went badly, he knows Sam's on to them. He also knows from Isabel how dogged and tenacious Sam is. That people listen to her, that she doesn't let anything slide. He could try lies, bribery or threats, but with a child's health at stake, he knows Sam will be impossible to silence.

Femi
Once the babies are born, he enlists Olivia to help. She knows about the murder before it happens, because she has to post as James while it is taking place!

Charlotte
James drives from the hospital to Sam's flat. Arrives 11.30 p.m.–12 a.m. She lets him in, tells him what she and Andrea have discovered. But he already knows the truth about his mum. Paige doesn't, but he does – and he must protect his family's reputation, social standing and internal cohesion.

Femi
Sam suggests they talk on the balcony, because the neighbours have complained . . . James listens to what she has to say, establishes that no one else knows and then pushes her off the balcony, calmly closes and locks the doors, makes his way back to the hospital.

Charlotte
The police look into Sam's phone records.

Femi
And James says she called to tell him she won't be in the play the following night. Outside the flat he meets Issy. She's been sitting there, in the shadows, sending emails to say Sam will be fine in the morning, that she didn't mean what she said – especially what she said to Issy. He realises she is a witness to him being at the scene of the crime, so must get her onside. He tells her what happened, convinces her *not* to call the police, carry on as normal and, ultimately, confess to the killing. But what does he promise for her, to do that?

Charlotte
He confides in her. Doesn't tell her everything – not about Helen or the appeal. Says it happened by accident. Sam suggested they move to the balcony because of the neighbours and, while they fought, she fell. Issy has never been the confidante of the alpha family before. She agrees to keep his secret. Remember the scenario she imagines with Lauren – that if they keep a secret together, they'll be friends forever? He drives her home.

Femi
James returns to the hospital, calls Martin, tells him Sam is dead. Martin calls Glen to say Paige needs to learn Sam's part. I don't think Glen knows the real reason why. It's Issy and Martin who know about the murder before the body is found. These phone records simply reflect a family telling each other the happy news of a birth. If they triangulate the phones, James's is at the hospital all night, Issy's is at Sam's flat. Does James ask Issy to find the body the next night?

Charlotte
If he wanted that, surely he would drive her there himself? They could easily explain that away as checking on a friend. No, I think once Issy comes to terms with Sam being dead, which she does very quickly because her obsession was never about Sam, only about herself, she places herself centre-stage for a taste of the spotlight. Just as she does when Claudia attacks Sam.

Femi
James can't realise Issy will take the blame. He must pin his hopes on a verdict of suicide. Why *does* she confess? Why admit to a crime you didn't commit?

Charlotte
Go back to the Lauren thing again. Issy imagines a situation in which she feels sympathy for a friend who has made a terrible mistake. A friend who will suffer horribly if she is found out. She agrees to share the blame, meaning the friend is now in debt to her. Their friendship is guaranteed. She confesses in order to guarantee her status with the alpha family.

Femi
James is a new father. He's always been supportive of Issy. Meanwhile Sam has totally rejected her. Kel has left with Claudia. Lauren doesn't exist. Give me a moment . . .

Femi
Here it is. Correct me if this is wrong, but:
Who killed Samantha Greenwood? James Hayward.
In the hours before her death, she told three people three things. Issy that she no longer wants to be her friend, Kel that she's returning to Africa, James that she knows Poppy is not ill at all.
Who knew it was going to happen? Olivia Hayward.
Who knew about it before her body was discovered? Isabel Beck and Martin Hayward.

Femi
Who is erroneously imprisoned and why? Isabel Beck, because she took the blame in a misguided effort to protect the alpha family.
Three people are not who they say they are: Clive Handler, Lydia Drake, Helen Grace-Hayward.
Three masquerade as others: Sam as Issy, Issy as Sam, Olivia as James.
One does not exist at all: Lauren Malden.

Charlotte
Mr Tanner, are we close to your theory with this?

Femi
Are you having problems with WhatsApp?

Charlotte
Close the app and open it again if it freezes. You may have an old phone.

Femi
Are you still there, Mr Tanner?

Roderick Tanner, QC
This is Sandra. Mr Tanner has stepped away for a moment. He'll compose himself now and will return shortly.

Posts written by the user SueB on a community message board for *The Association of Overseas Volunteers*

10 April 2018

SueB

Dear OV friends, back in the UK after medvol in CAR, DRC, S. Sudan. OH and I had to leave, thanks to me, and I want this to work. It's not easy. We joined a local drama group to help us settle in, but a woman there makes me uneasy and I don't know why. The moment we met, I had shivers down my spine. No obvious reason. It's like she's putting on an act all the time. Hiding something. Tricky to put in words. No one else can see it. They all love her. Do you find your time as an OV means you can't relate to certain people now?

17 April 2018

SueB

Been busy and can't look at this message board often, but thanks and love to everyone for your kind words and messages. It's good to know others have had issues too. Determined to chill out and just accept readjusting takes time. *Soyez bénis.*

26 April 2018

SueB

Medical friends. Does anyone know of any new therapies or research into Medulloblastoma? Heard there's a new combination being tested in the US.

27 April 2018

SueB

Thanks all – me neither. If anyone hears anything, let me know. A friend's child is just diagnosed. Cheers.

29 May 2018

SueB

City and finance friends: do you know how someone v rich might donate a lot of money to a crowdfunding campaign? Looking for terminology and understanding of the options and process, etc. PM me.

30 May 2018

SueB

Urgently need info on an overseas bank account. Got a long number, IBAN and BIC codes plus other references. Can you tell me what it reveals about the owner, legality, etc.? *Anything*. PM me.

9 June 2018

SueB

Can anyone recommend a researcher? Need info on someone's background to see if they had a child thirty years ago or more. Not an adoption thing. Is it a researcher or something else? Not too expensive. PMs only. Cheers.

4 July 2018

SueB

Thanks, OV friends, for your help and support. Sorry not to reply by PM to you all. Too much has happened here. For all those who helped: I found what I was looking for. My heart is so heavy, but better to know the worst-ever truth than be happy only because you believe lies. I don't belong here. I'm going home.

The user **SueB** deleted their account at 21:51 on 4 July 2018.

Phone records reveal a call from Samantha Greenwood's phone to James Hayward's phone that went straight to message at 21:52 on 4 July 2018.

FROM: The Fairway Players Admin
SUBJECT: Night Must Fall
DATE: 18 August 2018 at 10:03
TO: Current Members

Dear all,

Firstly, may I thank everyone who took the time and trouble to wish me a happy sixtieth birthday earlier this month. After so many years, Helen still manages to surprise me – this time with a trip to Hawaii, where we swam with dolphins and watched the sun set over Pearl Harbor. It was certainly a birthday to remember. We hope you too enjoyed your summer break from rehearsals.

Well, it is time to turn our thoughts to The Fairway Players' November production. After much consideration, we have decided to reflect the long, menacing nights of winter with Emlyn Williams' classic thriller *Night Must Fall*. I will direct and James will assist. This dark, nail-biting play has the benefit of a large cast with a variety of roles, so whatever your age or level of experience, do pop down on the audition nights: Sunday 9 and Monday 10 September. As ever, I ask that parents keep very young children at home. We can't expect little ones to sit still and quiet for two hours. If you need to alternate your audition nights – mum one night, dad the next . . . – it can be arranged.

If you have any friends or family interested in joining our friendly, welcoming group, do bring them along. Helen will organise very special *après*-audition drinks and nibbles, more about which later . . .

Regarding our last production, *All My Sons*. Well, it wasn't an easy journey, but we finally reached our destination. As you know from the newspaper review, it was a resounding critical success and, with a full house all three nights, it proved a commercial winner, too. Including the profits from ticket sales, we raised just under £4,000 for Poppy's appeal, all thanks to Sarah-Jane MacDonald and her dedicated fundraising team.

That brings me to the news that, only a couple of months ago, we thought we would never have the chance to deliver. Helen and I are bursting with joy to tell you: our darling Poppy is cured! She received the 'all clear' only this week from her new doctor at Mount More. Dr Saeed Mazhar ran a series of blood and bone-marrow tests, as well as a thorough set of brain scans earlier this month. He found no trace of her tumour and no tumour markers in her blood. It is infinitely better news than we ever dared hope for.

I naturally credit the scientists who developed such effective chemotherapy. I recognise, too, the skill and dedication of the doctors who diagnose and administer such treatments on our doorsteps, free of charge, day in, day out. Others may cite the power of prayer. We know so many of our friends have held Poppy in their prayers since she was diagnosed in the spring. I thank you all. But I know Helen and Paige have a further explanation for Poppy's miraculous recovery.

At the Yogathon last June, Poppy was given a very special present: a Healing Doll from Africa. This extraordinary wood-and-rag figurine is used on that continent to counter negative energy and thus promote physical and psychological health. While Poppy was in the midst of her chemotherapy we gave little thought to the doll, we simply placed it on the shelf above her bed to watch over her at night.

It was only recently, when Dr Mazhar expressed his surprise that her cancer showed such speedy and complete remission, that we looked around for possible explanations . . . Of course it may be pure coincidence. Whatever you are prepared to believe, Poppy is back to the noisy, vibrant little girl she was this time last year, and we couldn't be prouder of, or more thankful to, our circle of family and friends whose good wishes, help, support and positivity carried us through these challenging few months. From the bottom of our hearts, Helen and I thank you all.

There remains A Cure for Poppy, and the funds we raised for experimental drugs that she thankfully no longer requires. We have taken the decision, as a family, to donate the money to a variety of childhood cancer charities and comparable good causes, in order that other children, less fortunate than our own, may benefit. These donations have been made and the appeal closed.

We look forward to turning the page and starting anew. So, join us in a celebration of life, love and the future, in the River Room at The Grange after auditions on Sunday night, and together we will look forward to a happy, healthy and stress-free end to a challenging year.

Regards,
Martin Hayward

FROM: Dr Tish Bhatoa
SUBJECT: Can you help?
DATE: 18 August 2019 at 10:03
TO: Sonja Ajanlekoko

Dear Ms Ajanlekoko,
I am a doctor based at an independent medical centre near Mongoumba in the Central African Republic. Jonathan Ngongo gave me your contact details. He says you were a close friend of Samantha Greenwood, who volunteered with your organisation for many years, and that if anyone can answer my question, it is you. In short, I was led to believe Ms Greenwood died last year, in tragic circumstances at her home in England. Yet only two weeks ago I saw her here.

It was very early in the morning. A cloud of mist hung over the Ubangi River, but I'm sure I was not mistaken. I had just unlocked the waiting-room doors prior to morning clinic and suddenly sensed someone walk right up behind me. Yet when I turned, there was no one quite so close. It was only as I adjusted my eyes to focus further afield that I noticed her, standing quite still on the opposite bank. Her face had no particular expression, but she seemed to watch me. It was as if an ice-cold veil settled over me from head to toe. I looked aside, then looked back to confirm it had been a trick of the landscape. But no, she was still there. My eyes met hers for a long moment, until I finally had to turn away. When I glanced back again, she had gone.

At the time I was happy to explain this as a mirage, perhaps a side-effect of my malaria medication – that is, until I treated a lady here yesterday. She arrived in very poor health, having walked all the way from Boyabo, and knew nothing of anyone here. While I treated her at the roadside, she fixed her eyes on a spot over my shoulder and asked, 'Who is the white lady?' I glanced behind me. Nothing. 'She's still there,' said the woman. I smiled and reassured her that someone was clearly looking over her. That's when the woman gave me a very unnerving look and said: No, the white woman is watching *you*. Then she whispered '*sara hanga*' several times. *Sara hanga. Sara hanga.* It means 'Be careful'.

Ms Ajanlekoko, there are no white aid workers in this region at the moment. What's more, the lady described Ms Greenwood exactly as I had seen her that day by the river. Was I misinformed of her death? If so, then there is something I must say to her, and I wonder if you could tell me where she is based, or at least pass on the message that I would like to speak with her?

My kindest regards,
Dr Tish Bhatoa

FROM: Sonja Ajanlekoko
SUBJECT: Re: Can you help?
DATE: 19 August 2019 at 16:17
TO: Dr Tish Bhatoa

Dear Ms Bhatoa,
I am afraid you are too late. Samantha Greenwood indeed passed away over a year ago. A delegation from our UK office attended her funeral and reported on how sad the occasion was. From my correspondence with her, I know she intended to return to her work in the Central African Republic. It is a comfort to know she has arrived.

You have my assurance that if you wish to speak with her, you may, because whatever you do and wherever you are, please be certain of one thing: she watches you.

Sara hanga,

Dr Sonja Ajanlekoko, MBBS (Nigeria) 2008, DRCOG
Project Coordinator, Médecins Sans Frontières

Item published in the *Lockwood Gazette* online 14 January and in print 17 January 2020:

CHARITY FRAUD GRANDAD SENTENCED

Martin Hayward, 61, of Upper Lockwood, who netted more than £200,000 in a bogus charity appeal, was jailed today (14 January) for six years.

In 2018 Mr Hayward told friends and family that his granddaughter Poppy, four, had a brain tumour and could only be cured by treatment costing £1m.

The local community donated their hard-earned cash and held fundraising events over a period of five months, all the time encouraged by Mr Hayward and his family.

In fact, the child was in good health.

As money rolled in, Mr Hayward used it to pay off debts and build a swimming pool, telling increasingly desperate lies to maintain public interest in the appeal. He even conned local medical professionals into verifying his granddaughter's illness.

'The community is devastated,' said local mother Sarah-Jane MacDonald, who claims she was duped into organising a number of events. 'We were even led to believe the little girl had gone blind, but it was all a cruel trick.'

Local band leader Tony Zucchero contacted the *Gazette* to speak of his 'devastation' at last week's guilty verdict.

'My band and I, alongside members of the local community, gave up time and money to help a child in need. How anyone could tell lies like this is beyond belief.'

Initially, other members of Mr Hayward's family were implicated in the fraud, including his son James, 37, wife Helen, 63, and daughter Paige, 34, but those charges were dropped as Mr Hayward maintained he alone had planned the deception, and had lied to his family too.

A not-guilty plea was entered, on the grounds he was depressed and in the grip of a gambling addiction at the time of the offence.

At last week's trial, the jury did not agree.

In sentencing, Mrs Justice Limbert is quoted as saying, 'You cynically lied to those closest to you. You preyed on their kindness and pulled on their heart strings to gain as much money as possible for yourself.'

The case is linked to the death of nurse Samantha Greenwood, who fell from her apartment balcony in 2018. Isabel Beck, who worked with Ms Greenwood at St Ann's Hospital in Lockwood, pleaded guilty to murder and was sentenced to life imprisonment in January 2019. However, doubts about the safety of her conviction have been raised by her counsel, who claim to have found new evidence in correspondence not submitted at the original trial. The case is due to be heard in the court of appeal next week.

Item published in the *Lockwood Gazette* online 22 January 2020:

NURSE MURDER: MAN ARRESTED

A man aged 37 has been arrested on suspicion of murder following the 2018 death of nurse Samantha Greenwood.

Ms Greenwood, who fell to her death from Lower Lockwood Heights on 5 July 2018, was a nurse at St Ann's Hospital but had been due to travel abroad as a volunteer medic when she died. In a trial last year, her colleague Isabel Beck pleaded guilty to murder and was sentenced to life but following her release yesterday by the court of appeal, police arrested the man in Upper Lockwood.

FROM: Isabel Beck
SUBJECT: Hiya!
DATE: 23 January 2020 at 12:27
TO: Femi Hassan

Hiya Femi,

Sorry to bother you. I hope you don't mind me emailing. We didn't get a chance to speak after the hearing, but Mr Tanner pointed you out in the gallery, along with his other trainee (Charlotte?). I can't remember what he called you, but it was an 'articled' something. Anyway, it sounded very grand. I just want to say thank you for all the hard work you've done on my case. You are so clever to have worked out where everything went wrong, just from a few letters and emails. I can't imagine being that intelligent. Still, it must have been boring to read so many words – thank you again!

I hope James doesn't go to prison. He had no idea I was going to take the blame. We said everyone would assume she'd jumped. But the more I looked ahead, the more I knew it was something we couldn't leave to chance. The police are so clever now. I thought the whole thing would blow over quickly if I said I'd done it by accident. Sam and I were similar sizes, we had a disagreement – it could happen to anyone. When they started saying it was murder, not an accident, it became even more important to protect James.

He really and truly didn't mean to do it. With the twins still so young, Helen in hospital and Martin in so much trouble, James is needed at home like never before. The whole family, The Fairway Players – they all rely on him now. I didn't lie, as such. It could so easily have been me on the balcony with Sam that night. She was a very trying and provocative person and, if you ask me, that safety rail was far too low for such a height. I understand that soon afterwards they replaced the rails with Perspex sheeting on all the new flats.

I feel a bit embarrassed I've put so many people to so much trouble. I don't know how to repay you all, especially as I haven't got a job yet and still need to find permanent accommodation. Mr Tanner mentioned that developers have permission to build flats where The Grange was. Can you imagine the views! Apparently, even the Haywards' house has been repossessed and will likely be made into apartments. I'd love to live in one of them, but my social worker thinks it's best I move to a completely different area.

If I can't find a Band 4 post in a hospital, then a care home will be fine. I'm not fussy at the moment, but ideally I'd like to move where there's an active drama group. It's such a good way to meet new people and find friends. As hobbies go, the hours are long, and when you're putting on a show it can be stressful, but on the whole you meet interesting characters you wouldn't normally cross paths with. I could say the same about Colney Marsh Women's Prison, but as far as that episode is concerned, I've already put the past behind me and am concerned only with the future.

Between you and me, Femi, I'm seriously considering a complete change of career. These past few months have opened my eyes to the legal system. It seems so lofty and posh, but I met several quite normal people who made me think, 'Could I do that?' I don't mean I want to be a judge or anyone in a gown, but an assistant or a PA. I'm very organised and like helping people, so I'm sure I'd be an asset. It struck me many times during my spot of trouble that a courtroom is very like a theatre. It has a stage, an audience and actors – it's just the barristers know their lines, while the witnesses improvise. As soon as I'm settled somewhere I'll enrol on a course to get a legal secretary's certificate. Wow! Something amazing has just occurred to me. I've thought of a way I can repay you for your help with my case!

Mr Tanner said you are a 'bright, intelligent independent thinker' with a great career ahead of you. Well, I would love to gain some work experience as a legal secretary in the very near future. I could type letters for you, file things, take messages . . . I'd pay you back for all you've done for me, while I gain valuable experience for my future career. There's no need to confirm just yet, but let's keep in touch by email and, once I've started my course, I'll let you know. I'm really looking forward to meeting you finally. There's nothing as exciting as a fresh new start when the page is blank and the future is all for the making!

Lots of love
Issy xxx

Acknowledgements

For over a year my agents Lucy Fawcett and Gaia Banks at Sheil Land Associates were the only people who knew I was writing a book. I could not have done so without their wisdom, honesty and unflagging support and simply can't thank them enough.

It was a delight to work with my editor Miranda Jewess and her team at Viper, who brought *The Appeal* to life on the page. They include Graeme Hall, Mandy Greenfield, Art Director Steve Panton, Mark Swan at Kid Ethic and Lucie Ewin at Crow Books.

Thanks also to Cameron Roach, Head of Drama at Sky TV. Without his suggestion that I write a novel, you would not be reading one now; and to Fraser & Minnie Ayres at Triforce Creative Network, who convinced him to be my mentor in 2017.

Anyone who was ever a member of the Raglan Players in Northolt, between 1972 and 2013, played a huge role in my life, career and, ultimately, this book, whether you realised it or not. I hope *The Appeal* is as fitting a tribute to the joy of community drama as I intend it to be.

Without my dear friend and first writing partner Sharon Exelby I would not have written the play that set me on the path that led to this project. Meanwhile, I am in awe of her daughter Rochelle Griffin, along with Stuart, Ava, Faith and especially Betsy, whose fundraising campaign lit the spark of inspiration for this story.

Speaking of inspiration for *The Appeal*, I must mention the many thousands of medical volunteers around the world who give their time, expertise and sometimes their lives to help people in crisis. To those who shared their experiences, I am eternally grateful.

I won't assume I'll ever have another acknowledgements page to fill, so I'll seize this opportunity to thank the writers and creative professionals I've worked or studied with over the years. They include Sue Clayton, Heather

Wallis, Amanda Smith, Ross Olivey, Adam Rolston, Carl Tibbetts, Kate Brockett, Rosie Snell, Bernice Wolfenden, Mariama Ives-Moiba, Tsonko Bumbalov and Paula B. Stanic.

A big thank you to my friends, who are not only generous and understanding, but downright stoic in their support. These people have journeyed afar in freezing cold and sweltering heat, squinted at experimental fringe drama from rickety bench seats above pubs or in warehouses, and at the end told me what a great time they had. They include my oldest friends Alison Horn and Samantha Thomson, fellow witches Carol Livingstone and Wendy Mulhall, my almost-sister Ann Saffery and long-time Raglans Keith Baker, Felicity Cox and Terry and Rose Russell, who have all been great friends onstage and off.

Finally, I am forever indebted to my soulmate Gary Stringer, who loves, supports and encourages me, without ever suggesting I get a proper job.

About the Author

Janice Hallett studied English at UCL, and spent several years as a magazine editor, winning two awards for journalism. She then worked in government communications for the Cabinet Office, Home Office and Department for International Development. After gaining an MA in Screenwriting at Royal Holloway, she co-wrote the feature film *Retreat* and went on to write the Shakespearean stage comedy *NetherBard*, as well as a number of other plays for London's new-writing theatres. *The Appeal* is inspired by her lifelong interest in amateur dramatics. Her second novel, *The Twyford Code*, will be published by Viper in 2022. When not indulging her passion for global adventure travel, she is based in West London.

Find her on Twitter @JaniceHallett.